ROSE O'BRIEN

Air of Darkness

*To my mother, Pat, for always being my cheerleader.
To my husband, Erik, for the gift of time.*

1

Chapter 1

This must be what hell feels like.

Agent Alex Martinez tried not to cringe as a drop of sweat slid down his spine beneath his black T-shirt. The humid press of scantily clad bodies on the nightclub's packed dance floor had outpaced the air conditioning about an hour ago. The air was like a locker room, thick, hot, and pungent. Taking off his black leather jacket would have helped, but that would mean flashing the 9mm holstered under his arm. Not an option for an FBI agent who'd gone rogue and was tracking a case that was very far outside his jurisdiction.

A throbbing headache had taken up residence behind his left eye. The sleep deprivation had started dragging on him, too.

In short, he was miserable, pissed off, and kicking himself for being stupid enough to come here. But grief could make a man do stupid things. Reckless things.

Grinding his teeth in frustration, he scanned the undulating crowd for what felt like the hundredth time that night, searching for one face. Nick Salvadin was a low-level flunky who worked the clubs up and down Sixth Street. On paper, he didn't seem like much, but he was probably the only person who could shed any light on who'd killed Blanca.

Overhead, lights pulsed in a dazzling array of colors that danced over the fake stonework and stained glass that made the club, Revelations, look vaguely reminiscent of a Gothic church. There were even gargoyles leering from the corners. Weaving through the edges of the crowd, he worked his way closer to the bar. He tried to relax his notoriously military-straight posture into a more casual stance and let his features drop into something other than the ridged mask he'd been wearing since his friend had been murdered. Just blend in. That was difficult, considering his clothes included zero chains or PVC and his jet-black hair was free of dye. Revelations was a club that catered to the extreme. The music was extremely loud. The patrons were covered in an extreme amount of tattoos and piercings, and hair color tended to extreme hues not found in nature.

It was definitely not his scene. Up until she'd turned up dead, he would have said this wasn't Blanca's scene either, but this was the last place she'd been seen alive. Blanca Rodriguez had been like a sister to him, and he thought he knew what she was into. Clearly he'd been wrong. In the two weeks since she'd died he'd been tearing himself up about that.

They'd been through a war together. She'd saved his life more than a few times and in more than a few ways. He hadn't been able to return the favor this time, and it was ripping him apart. Blanca had survived two tours in Afghanistan only to come home and die at the hands of some psychopath, butchered and left under a bridge. An objective part of Alex's brain knew he was grieving and this probably wasn't the best time to undertake an off-the-books investigation while simultaneously bent on vengeance, but focusing on this was the only thing keeping him sane right now.

When there had been no movement on the case, Alex had started digging, calling in every favor he was owed and tapping every connection to get his hands on the case files. Austin Police had interviewed Salvadin because he'd been working that night and his vehicle had shown up on security footage leaving the club. The cops had written him off as a person of interest, but something didn't sit right in Alex's gut. His gut had saved him more than a few times in that war zone. It had served him well as an agent. He trusted it.

His gut said Salvadin knew more than he was saying and Alex was going to find out, even if he had to break a few fingers.

He pushed his way through the crowd again, angling for the stairs so he could do another pass through the upper balcony that wrapped around the second story of the building. Shoulders, arms, and boobs pressed against him, and he tried not to cringe again. A woman stepped on his foot and splashed her drink on his jeans.

Everything felt raw. Too loud. Too bright. What he wanted was to hide in a dark hole and get his head under control. But he wanted to find the people who had hurt Blanca more. The need for vengeance was a dark, clawed thing that huddled in his chest, scratching to get out.

As he made it to the stairs and took the first couple of steps, movement caught his eye. Greasy dark hair, worn shaggy and long. Too-pale skin from nothing but nightshifts. Dark eyes that darted around, landing on nothing, but seeing everything at once. The man slunk through the crowd with furtive movements that reminded Alex of a rat. The pointed chin and nose added to the impression.

Nick Salvadin had put in an appearance. Alex tracked him

from the corner of his eye as the man moved through the crowd. The weasel slipped into one of the booths along the back wall, sitting opposite a woman. She had alabaster skin, black hair cut in a bob and worn pin straight. Harsh red lipstick was a like a bloody slash across her face. Those lips were turned down in a severe frown as Nick started talking animatedly, his hands moving frantically and his eyes wide. The woman pointed an accusing finger at him and locked narrow eyes on the man. Someone was in trouble.

Alex glanced away, trying to keep from staring. He didn't want to get clocked as an agent. Nick needed to be oblivious if Alex was going to take him singlehandedly. He had a lot of questions for Nick. And if Nick didn't want to answer, he had an extensive knowledge of human anatomy and pain thresholds to draw on.

As his eyes drifted from the table, a flash of red in the crowd drew his attention.

She was tall, maybe six feet, with long platinum hair cascading down her shoulders and back. Black leather pants tucked into knee high black boots hugged impressive curves. The red silk of her top fluttered as she moved. Her back and neck were arched as her hips gyrated in time with the beat.

The air stopped moving in his lungs as he watched her, riveted in a moment of blistering arousal.

Her arms lifted over her head as she moved with the music, not dancing with anyone but herself. The lights caught in her hair, sparking in a dozen different colors. As she danced, she slipped through the crowd, seemingly unnoticed by the other dancers.

He was staring, and he couldn't help it, didn't even care. Even when she met his eyes and gave him a caught-you-looking half smile, his gaze stayed on her. His heart kicked hard against his ribs as something electric passed between them in that moment.

Dropping her gaze, she kept dancing, moving through a couple of turns and throwing a little shimmy in her hips. Had that been for him?

It just figured that the first woman to catch his attention in years would have to show up in the middle of a rogue op. It wasn't like he could walk up and give her his number. Besides, she was a distraction from…

Shit. Alex's head snapped around, but Salvadin was gone. He scanned the booths and didn't spot the little weasel. He quickly scanned the rest of the club, trying to keep the frantic look off his face and hoping that his movements looked smooth and not hurried and jerky.

Salvadin wasn't in the club, not that he could see. Damn it all to hell!

Turning his attention back to the dance floor, he ran a nervous hand through his hair. Think!

That's when he noticed that the wet-dream blonde had disappeared too. He resumed scanning just in time to see the door of the emergency exit into the alley slide shut.

Darting through the crowd, Alex made his way to the door without drawing too much attention to himself. He slammed the bar release on the door and stumbled into the alley and into something straight out of a nightmare.

Salvadin had his back to Alex and had Blondie pushed up against the brick wall of the alley, his hands locked around her throat while she clawed at his fingers. Alex rushed forward to help as Salvadin took one hand off her neck and cocked his fist back to swing at her face. She managed to leverage her arm against the hand at her throat and threw her head to the side.

Salvadin's fist turned the first few inches of brick to powder.

Alex stopped short, his brain stuttering as it tried to process what he was seeing.

While Salvadin was thrown off balance by the missed punch, the blonde brought her free hand up in a devastating uppercut that snapped Salvadin's teeth together and sent him reeling, releasing her.

"That was rude, Nicky," the blonde said, rubbing her throat and drawing herself to her full height. Up close, Alex could see that she wasn't just a curvy girl, she was built like a fighter.

"I told you I just wanted to talk," she continued. "And you decide to be a dick about it."

Salvadin growled at her, a low, hungry sound. Alex shrank back into the shadows by the door, drew his gun, and waited for Salvadin to make the next move.

The two circled each other, he with quick furtive movements, in a low stance, she with cat-like grace in a slow and easy pace. She bent and slid a slender black rod from her boot, never taking her eyes off the circling Salvadin.

Salvadin made his move, coming in low and impossibly fast, going for her knees. He realized his mistake too late, as the blonde caught the back of his head and slammed her knee into his face. Before he could bring his hands up to block, she brought the black rod across his face, drawing a trickle of blood from his mouth.

She grabbed a handful of his greasy hair and knocked Salvadin to his knees.

"You can make this so much easier on yourself if you just tell me what I want to know, Nicky," the blonde cooed as she leaned over the bleeding man.

He spit bloody mucus in her face and said, "Suck my dick,

bitch."

She didn't make a move to wipe the disgusting stuff of her face, but flicked her thumb along the black rod. A wicked blade emerged from a ball-shaped cap at the end, quick as a switchblade, gleaming in the dim yellow glow of the street lights filtering into the alley.

Bringing the tip of her blade to the man's throat, she said, "Nicky, I'm tired of finding dead people in my city, and I need you to tell me everything you know about that."

That got Alex's attention. She certainly didn't look like an investigator or a cop. She wasn't FBI. APD had already questioned Salvadin. Who the hell was she? She moved like a well-trained fighter, she talked like she was looking for answers, and she was faster and stronger than anything he'd seen. Come to think of it, so was Salvadin. Something was really off here, and Alex's solution to that problem was usually the same.

He raised his 9mm in a smooth motion and shouted, "FBI, freeze! Both of you!"

The distraction was all Salvadin needed. He swept the blade aside and brought an elbow strike against the inside of her knee, knocking her leg out from under her and forcing her to release his hair.

Salvadin scrambled to his feet and made a move towards the mouth of the alley. Alex moved quickly to block his way, his gun held in a shooter's stance in front of him. As Salvadin came closer, details started to register in Alex's brain.

He was moving too fast. His eyes were too red, like vessels had burst in his eyes, flooding the whites with crimson. His pupils were large black orbs in a sea of gleaming crimson. Blood trickled down his pale chin.

Right next to the long fangs that protruded over Salvadin's

lower lip.

Something twisted low and deep in Alex's stomach, a primal fear that told him to throw his gun down and run screaming for his life, but his gun hand remained steady as Salvadin continued to advance.

"I told you to freeze or I will put a bullet in you," Alex said in voice that was surprisingly strong, given the fact that his heart was making a mad attempt to claw its way out of his chest and up through his mouth.

At his words, Salvadin slowed to a cocky stroll and laughed, a grin on his face, and spread his arms wide in invitation. He kept coming.

Alex pulled the trigger, putting one in the guy's gut and one in his shoulder. Against his better judgment, he avoided the headshot because that would bring an avalanche of paperwork, and he needed the asshole alive to question. He might know something about what happened to Blanca.

Salvadin barely flinched as the bullets ripped into his flesh, his long strides never faltering. Blood trickled, but didn't pour from the wounds. Nothing was going right tonight.

Salvadin cocked his fist near his hip and brought it up in a flying cross to the side of Alex's head. He felt himself spinning before he slammed into a wall and slid down. Lights danced in front of his eyes and a sickening pain spread outward from where his skull had hit the wall. For just a moment, the old familiar panic gripped him.

Not here. Not now. He could not lose it in the middle of a fight. The panic had cost him everything once. It would not cost him his life. With a deep breath, he tried to wrestle his injured, panicking body under control.

Salvadin kept moving toward the mouth of the alley and the

sounds and neon lights of Sixth Street. College kids and club goers were streaming by, completely unaware of the battle taking place a few dozen feet away.

As Salvadin moved past Alex, a black sinuous length wrapped itself around his throat, yanking him back.

The blonde had the other end of what Alex realized was a whip, which appeared to have emerged from the end of the rod she'd been holding earlier.

Alex's vision blurred and spun suddenly. The former combat medic in him ran the triage. Severe concussion, possible skull fracture. Fighting for consciousness. Miracle he hadn't passed out yet. If he did, he might not survive. Without treatment, a subdural hematoma was probably going to end him.

The blonde dragged Salvadin backward as he struggled, gasping as the whip choked him. With a sweep of her leg, she knocked his feet out from under him. With some slack in the whip, he began to fight again, throwing punches and kicks as she leaned over him.

Her lips began to move quickly, forming whispered words that Alex couldn't make out from where he lay. After several seconds and one punch to her jaw, a bolt of crackling electricity flew from her right hand and went skittering over Salvadin's flesh. The fanged—man? creature?—slumped unconscious.

This was some straight up science-fiction bullshit.

The woman stood over the—God, could that really be a vampire?—and spoke into a mic at her sleeve. Alex struggled to move, to sit up, but he couldn't seem to make his limbs work. He could only lift his head to watch as two figures moved into the light from the dead-end part of the alley.

The two were dressed in black, one a dark-skinned man and the other an olive-skinned woman with brown hair. He recognized tactical gear hanging from their belts and from the man's pack. Professionals then.

The man moved to speak to the ass-kicking blonde.

"Do you always have to beat them bloody, Commander?" He asked her.

"No, just when they decide to be assholes," she shot back. "At least we know he probably knows something. Otherwise, why would he run?"

"Because you're one scary bitch," the other woman chimed in.

The blonde nodded at the unconscious form on the pavement.

"Lay down a glamour and load that piece of shit up. I want him in the interrogation room before the sun is up."

The man nodded at Alex. "What about him?"

"No worries. I got this. Give Ellie and Burdock the all clear. Rendezvous at HQ."

The man nodded, spoke into a mic clipped on his ear, and he and the brunette started dragging Salvadin toward the mouth of the alley. Just before they reached it, they shimmered and disappeared.

Shit. This was not happening. It was the concussion. That's it; the head injury was causing him to see all this crazy stuff. Either that, or he'd finally gone completely off the deep end.

The blonde walked slowly over to him, her boots clicking on the pavement, and squatted down in front of him. Even with a concussion, he still admired her impressive cleavage.

"Well, cowboy, it looks like you've seen six impossible things before breakfast," she said.

He opened his mouth to answer her, but his tongue wouldn't form words.

She reached inside his jacket pocket and pulled out his ID. His hands moved to stop her, but flopped uselessly. Her eyes moved over the badge and ID card, her fingers running over the badge.

"Agent Alex Martinez, FBI. I should have guessed. Had you pegged as local PD inside the club. Should have aimed a little higher it seems," she said.

Her hand moved over his forehead, brushing his hair back. A few whispered words moved past her lips. Her eyes closed for a moment before snapping back open, drilling him with her dark blue gaze.

"That's a nasty head injury you've got there. Let's see what we can do about that," she said, her soft voice moving over him, lulling him.

She continued to whisper in a language he didn't understand, her hand moving back over his skull to the area where he'd hit the wall. Warmth suffused the spot and spread down his neck. It felt like warm honey running over his scalp, and the pain began to ease.

She stayed like that for several minutes, a frown creasing her beautiful face at times.

"All better," she said softly, opening her eyes. Her hand, slender and smooth, moved to cup his jaw, and his hand rose to cover it. Her touch was so full of warmth, and he wanted to feel it just a little longer, to stare into those eyes and lose himself. Her other hand moved to cover his forehead again.

"I'm sorry, cowboy. I can't let you remember what happened tonight, but you probably don't want the memories anyway. Just try to relax."

Those words had the opposite effect on him. He tried to sit up, but he was still so weak. The whispering started again and he could feel her, like an alien presence in his mind, moving and sifting through his thoughts. It wasn't painful. It felt like a soft, silken hand lightly brushing his skin, lips moving in butterfly kisses. He resisted, mentally moving to block her every advance.

His body writhed; his head thrashed, trying to move away from her, all the while, her whispers filled his ears and his mind.

Her lips brushed his and he stilled, his body instantly flaring to life, and she deepened the kiss, sliding her tongue between his lips. That distraction was all she needed to move past all of his defenses. He could feel his memories of the night being snatched away. Like grains of sand, the more tightly he tried to hold on to them, the more easily they slipped through his fingers.

As she ended the kiss and pulled back, Alex let the darkness claim him. The last image he saw was her indigo eyes, staring into his.

2

Chapter 2

Alayna Blackwell pulled her rumbling Suzuki Hayabusa motorcycle into the garage entrance of the warehouse off 51st Street and killed the engine. One side of the cavernous space was taken up with several of the team's vehicles, while the other side was dominated by gym equipment and racks of various weapons the team used for combat training. With the push of a button, the garage door was rolling back into place, just another nondescript, quiet warehouse in a sea of other warehouses, seemingly deserted on a Saturday morning. The Council of Magickal Creatures maintained the building as the Austin headquarters for their primary strike team.

Alayna let her eyes adjust to the darkness. The garage had no windows and for good reason. Couldn't risk anyone getting a peek at what went on in here.

Her boots made hardly a sound as she moved across the concrete floor to the stairs and took them two at a time to the offices and interrogation rooms on the second floor.

Having heard the office door slam, Dumeril poked his head out of one of the three interrogation/conference rooms. Her second-in-command was tall and lithe, with the grace and silent movement common to the elven races. His skin was midnight black and almost seemed to absorb the light around him. Long white hair was pulled back from his face in a tight braid at his nape and he gave a flashing white smile that reached his deep, violet eyes.

"You changed clothes," he said, nodding at the black T-shirt and fatigue pants she'd traded for her club wear from last night.

"I managed to make it home for a minute. The red top was a loss, unfortunately. I really liked that one, too." She sighed.

"You are hard on clothes, girl," Dumeril said, shaking his head. "Did you get any sleep?"

"Nope."

"Did you remember to eat?"

Crossing her arms, she tapped her chin thoughtfully.

"I have a vague memory of a bagel at some point in the last few hours."

Nodding, Dumeril said, "Salvadin is all set up for you, Commander. He's been toasting for about two hours, and he's getting pretty uncomfortable."

Alayna steeled herself and put on her not-fucking-around face before pushing open the door to the conference room. Nick was in the corner, tied to a solid steel chair that was bolted to the floor. Bright morning sunlight streamed in through floor-to-ceiling windows on either side of him. His skin was lobster red, blistering and peeling in a few delicate places like the tips of his ears, the bridge of his nose.

When he saw her walk in the room, his fangs slid from his gums, nestling tightly behind his human-looking teeth. The whites of his eyes started to bleed to red, pupils dilating, heading to full vamp in a matter of seconds. The veins in his arms stood out against his skin as he strained against his bonds, feet pushing at the floor and his head thrashing from side to side. Just as he was ramping up, he seemed to deflate and shrink in on himself. Exhausted then. Good. Probably starving. Even better.

Alayna walked slowly around the conference table and pulled out one of the rolling chairs, placing it a few feet back from where Nick was bound. The red was starting to bleed back out of his eyes, his head was slumped forward slightly and his breath was coming a little too fast.

"You're not looking so hot, Nicky," Alayna observed.

"Fuck you, bitch," Nick spat.

"Now, is that any way to talk to the gal that's gonna save your ass?" she asked sweetly as she spun the chair and straddled it, placing her arms across the back, casual as could be. Her blue eyes met his, and she registered the fear he was trying so hard to hide. It was there, just below the tough guy, go-fuck-yourself attitude.

"I'll tell you a few things that I know, Nicky," she said softly. "I know that you didn't kill Blanca Rodriguez or any of the other people we've found."

She let those words hang in the air between them for a moment before continuing.

"I also know that you didn't dump her body."

What she didn't tell him was that Lu, the team's recon expert and a shape shifter had gone into wolf-mode last night and run her powerful nose over Nick's car. The slight scent of blood but not death. That truck hadn't been used to transport a body, and blood wasn't all that unusual in a vampire's vehicle, anymore than fast food wrappers would be unusual in the average person's car.

"What I need to know, Nick, is what went down at Revelations that night."

He strained again at the bonds, frustration evident in every inch of his skinny form, as greasy hair fell over his face. As his eyes met hers again, hate blazed across the distance between them, but there was something else, something that looked like a plea. But a plea for what?

"Who are you protecting?" she asked, her voice barely above a whisper.

Nick's exhausted body sagged again and she knew that was the right direction.

"Who was in the SUV with you that night?"

His eyes went wide and he tensed, but a second later he covered the fear. Bingo.

She rose from her chair and walked slowly to him, dragging her fingers lightly across his scalp as she crossed behind him. His hiss of pain filled her ears.

Real vampires, unlike those of legend, could withstand a certain amount of sunlight, especially if they wore sunscreen and particularly if they had recently fed. Most could pass for a normal human, albeit a particularly pale one, if they fed regularly and slathered on plenty of SPF 100. Still, most preferred to avoid sunlight whenever possible. It ate up a lot of energy to heal and that meant feeding more often.

Nick had been snared last night, so he didn't have any chemical help to protect him from the sun and she knew from his reaction when she walked in and his growing exhaustion that he hadn't eaten in over twenty-four hours.

"Dumeril, your knife," she said to the dark elf who had been leaning in the doorway during their conversation. His brilliantly white smile flashed in his inky dark skin and with a movement too quick for most eyes to follow, he pulled a wicked curved dagger from his belt and tossed it to her. Nick's eyes widened as the leather wrapped hilt hit her palm.

Alayna let a bit of a demented gleam creep into her gaze as she fingered the very sharp tip of the blade. Her mouth turned up as an answering fear coursed through the vampire, and he swallowed hard.

"You won't use that," Nick said. It was almost a question. If she started cutting, even that small amount of blood loss would compound his pain and exhaustion exponentially. "You don't operate that way, Blackwell. We both know you're not going to throw away your fair and just reputation now. Not on a little fish like me, anyway."

She kept the half smile in place and raised an eyebrow.

The tough guy routine always started to falter when the blades came out. Even the most badass vamps would crack eventually. The fear of Alayna, the Council, and of whomever Nick was protecting had him close to spilling everything. He just needed one last push.

With slow, deliberate movements, Alayna brought the razor sharp edge of the blade to the soft skin of her forearm. The bite of the fairy-steel barely registered as it opened a neat slice on the underside of her arm. Thank goodness Dumeril could be trusted to keep his blades in peak condition. She held her wrist up and let the blood run until it dripped down her elbow to the floor.

Nick stared, eyes transfixed on the blood. The red was back in his eyes, his fangs still extended. He was right. She wasn't about to start cutting up little fish like Nick. Besides, she had learned a long time ago that you caught more flies with honey than with vinegar. And the stuff running down her arm wasn't so much honey to Nick as it was crack cocaine.

His eyes met hers, disbelief warring with hope as his red

tongue darted out and ran over his fangs.

"You really offering me a taste of mage blood?" he asked, eyes narrowing. "It's forbidden. The penalty is death."

No one really knew what effect mage blood had on vampires and other magical creatures. Mages carried an unfathomable amount of energy around; it was what allowed them to control their element and weave their spells.

Legends and whispered horror stories told of vampires that gained god-like strength and the power to wield the elements as mages did. Others described crazed monsters tearing through whole villages single-handedly after ingesting just a mouthful.

"Just tell me what happened that night, Nicky," she whispered softly, holding her arm just out of reach of his questing tongue. Inwardly, she cringed, trying to keep the disgust off her face.

He was slipping. She could see it. Leaning closer, she placed the arch of her boot on the edge of the chair's seat, the toe hovering just over his balls. If he made a move, she'd make him regret it.

His eyes left the blood and returned to her face.

Here we go.

"See, what happened is Ricky, the head of security at Revelations, he texted me that night," Nick said, his voice high, his words coming fast. "I was working down the street at Maggie's. I took off sick and pulled my truck up at the loading dock at Rev. Then Jimmy Medina, the Culebra himself, gets in."

Jimmy Medina owned half a dozen successful bars in town, including the infamous Hellraisers, along with more real estate than anyone could accurately calculate and the most successful shipping company in the state. If you needed the hookup, particularly in the magickal world, Jimmy was the guy.

"So, I'm scared shitless and he's ducking down in the backseat and telling me to drive." Nick was really spilling his guts now. It was all coming out in a stream of consciousness, his red eyes darting back and forth between her face and the blood on her arm.

Alayna turned to Dumeril and he nodded, understanding her silent question. Yes, they were recording this.

"He told me to just drive. I headed south, across the river. Drove around SoCo for a while. Headed north and swung around the campus. Then he tells me to drop him off at Hellraisers. So I did. That's it. That's all I know."

"Bullshit," Alayna scoffed, rolling her eyes.

"I swear it!" he shouted, his voice high. He was desperate for her to believe him, but there was something else to it.

Hands on hips, she fixed him with a narrow-eyed glare. "If all you did was give one of the richest vamps around a ride home, then why did you try to kick my ass when I asked you about that night? You're awful fired up for it to be that simple."

Nick whispered something. It was so soft Alayna couldn't hear it. He was slumped forward, mumbling under his breath, almost jabbering, and rocking slightly. She was going lose him if they kept it up much longer.

Taking a risk, she leaned in to hear him.

"Covered in blood, covered in blood, covered in blood." He was saying it in a breathy voice over and over again.

"COVERED IN BLOOD!" Nick screamed and lunged at her throat, coming up short at the chains around his chest. He was fully vamped out, fangs extended, eyes crimson. Alayna managed to cover her flinch by turning away as she processed that info.

She needed to talk to Jimmy Medina in the worst way, but the guy was slicker than greased owl shit and was no doubt on a "buying trip" in South America right now, lying low to avoid the heat.

What had happened to Blanca was a major fuckup. The girl was not supposed to die. But why would a smooth operator like the Culebra, with nearly two centuries under his belt, screw up and kill a veteran turned college student? The guy had to have willing donors stashed all over town, and from what she'd heard, he'd gone all respectable and was drinking bagged blood these days. Something wasn't adding up.

She turned to Dumeril, "Get me a couple units for him."

He returned with two bags of blood, handing one to Alayna. She held the bag to Nick's mouth and pushed it against his fangs until they punctured the plastic with a little pop. With one hand she pushed his head back and he gulped greedily as the dark fluid flowed into his mouth.

When he had drained the first unit, she repeated the process with the second. Nick finished quickly and, with his fangs back in, regarded her with a steady gaze. His burns had healed, new skin forming before her eyes. The two bullets that FBI agent had put in Nick slid out of his shoulder and belly, clattering against the tile as they fell. The gaze that met hers was once again sane. Or mostly sane, anyway.

"You have no idea what you're getting in the middle of here, Blackwell," he said, his voice low. "I don't know exactly what's going on, but it's big, bigger than you and me."

"Thanks for the warning, Nick," she responded cheerily.

She wasn't scared of wading into the middle of anything. There was already an early grave with her name on it, courtesy of her rather unique powers. Whoever or whatever was behind these murders could just get in line if they wanted to be the one to punch her ticket.

"What else can you tell me?"

He sighed and paused, working up the nerve.

"There's a lot of trucks moving around, more than usual," he said, in a conspiratorial tone. "A lot more movers and shakers, in and out of the vampire-owned bars like Rev and Hellraisers. A lot of visitors from out of town and a lot of extra security around," he said. His voice was even now, matter of fact. "That is literally the last bit of info I know. I'm done."

A look of sadness crossed his face. His body was slumped again, not in exhaustion, just defeat.

"They're gonna know I told you," he said, bitterness in his voice. "They're gonna tear me apart. You might as well take my head right now, Blackwell. It'll at least be quicker than what they're going to do to me."

"You know I'm not gonna do you like that, Nicky. The Mage Corps takes care of those who help us." A small smile touched her lips. "I'm going to make you disappear."

Hope flickered in his gaze as he met her eyes. She patted his hand, still bound to the arm of the chair.

His fingers moved, quick as a snake, snapping at the limits of his bonds, straining, and clamped around her wrist. Adrenaline slammed into her and she cocked her fist back to deliver a punch, but hesitated when she saw desperation and not anger on his face.

Nick spoke again, his voice a little shaky, "Blackwell, watch your back. They know you're coming."

"Dumeril, get Theron on the phone and tell him to get his ass up here," she said, pulling her hand free and heading to the door. San Antonio was only an hour and a half away. Her brother could make the drive.

"No," he snapped, clearly miffed. He grabbed her bleeding

arm and pressed his fingers over the cut as they both stepped into the hall. Warmth flowed up her arm, and she could feel the sting as her skin knit back together. "I'm not talking to that dickhead, especially this early on a Saturday morning. You know what a raging asshole he is before noon."

"He's been mostly nocturnal lately, and you know how fire mages get when they don't get enough time in the sun," Alayna said, trying to ignore the tickling tingle in her arm as Dumeril's magick worked. "And Theron's the only one I trust to get Nick out of sight and to someplace safe."

"Then you talk to him. He's your brother. I'm not the goddamn Blackwell family answering service—"

"He doesn't answer my calls," she said, exasperated.

While Dumeril was technically her second-in-command, she wasn't exactly a stickler for military discipline. Her crew worked well together, they followed orders when they needed to and the grumbling was all good-natured and mostly playful. A sense of humor was the only way they got through the stuff they had to deal with every day.

Dumeril was right, though, she needed to talk with her older brother. The big fire mage was notoriously hard to get a hold of. He was the closest to her age among her three siblings, and while she loved him dearly, he always kept her at arm's length. Her whole family did.

She was twenty-seven years old, the commander of a strike team for an entire city, and even managed to behave like an adult on a fairly regular basis, but in many ways she was still treated like a child, shut out, cut off and left wondering.

Locking eyes with Dumeril, she gave the order. "Give him the assignment and set up a pickup time. Tell him that I don't care where he takes him, just make sure it is secret and safe. He needs to keep it off the Council and Corps radar until we know what we're dealing with. And, not that I need to tell him," she looked back to Nick tied to the chair, "but he needs to watch his back."

Dumeril muttered about mages needing to learn to send a damned text message, but she ignored him, taking her arm back and running her fingers over the now smooth skin.

"I knew there was a reason I hired you. You're the best damn healer this side of the Fae Realms, D," Alayna said, wistful.

He nodded like this was a known constant of the universe and said, "So, the head bouncer at Revelations texts Nick, faithful gopher and lackey, and tells him to get his ass and his SUV to the loading dock. Jimmy Medina, covered in fresh blood, loads up and hides in the back seat. Nick drives all over town, no doubt to shake any tails, and drops old Culebra at Hellraisers. Blanca Rodriquez's body is dumped a few hours later under the Congress Street Bridge and discovered the next day. It doesn't fit with the other cases. Things aren't lining up."

Alayna nodded in agreement. "Medina is a slick one. He's over two hundred, so it's not like he's some baby vamp who doesn't know how to keep his food alive."

Dumeril turned and started pacing, the fingers of one hand tracing the braids at his temple. One of his nervous habits.

"He's also shady as fuck," he noted.

Alayna's eyebrows shot up at that. "Yeah? I thought he was in imports or something like that. Latin America stuff."

"Oh, he is," Dumeril nodded. "He also runs drugs. Illicit substances and pharmaceuticals. Has his hands all over the black market."

"Drugs aren't my jurisdiction. I have my hands full trying to keep the more unusual citizens of Austin from eating each other."

"True that," Dumeril laughed.

"We need to talk to Medina. He's the first, best lead we've had in these cases. But how are we going to find him?"

Dumeril smiled, showing the slightly elongated canines that gave his people such a predatory appearance.

"Who do you always talk to when you need to know what's going on with the vampires?" Dumeril asked.

Alayna's smile matched his. "Dominic."

A short time later, they had moved Nick from the sunny conference room to a light-tight cell at the other end of the warehouse. Dominic was mostly nocturnal and wouldn't be available for several hours, so Alayna had some time to kill. She went to her desk, prepared to write her reports and perform he usual check-ins. Her mind raced around what Nick had told her, whirling and unable to come to a stop. There were still so many questions and so many pieces of a puzzle that didn't fit together. She'd looked at this from every angle, but it just wouldn't come into focus.

A headache was forming behind her eyes. Only one cure for that.

Screw the reports. Pulling her gloves from her desk drawer, she headed down to the gym to work the bag for awhile.

As her fists hit the big canvas bag in a rapid staccato, her mind began to clear and her thoughts started to still, quickly landing on that agent from last night. Alex Martinez, his ID had said.

The dude had some serious balls to try to take on a vamp with nothing more than a standard issue handgun. Most sapiens passed out from the fear the first time they saw a vampire show its predator face. The guy had stood his ground and had even gotten two shots off. A rare man. Her lip quirked up at one corner at the thought.

Punch, punch, jab. She danced on the balls of her feet, moving around the bag, her muscles warming and her heart rate increasing.

He'd been a total hottie, too. Gorgeous dark hair, spiky short. Beautiful dark eyes, so dark brown they had looked black in the dim light of the alley. Tan skin and a swimmer's physique. Nice muscles without being muscle-bound. And those lips. They'd been surprisingly soft and she could almost feel them as she let the memory pull her back several hours.

Hook-punch, ridge hand. The bag was taking the brunt of her frustration.

Idiot. Alayna wasn't sure what had possessed her to kiss him. She tried to tell herself that it was the best way to slip past his mental defenses, a necessary distraction. But the feel of that strong mouth under hers and the way he'd responded to her, an answer to her wordless question. She'd never forget it.

Nor would she ever be able to shake the glimpses she'd gained from his memories. Something had been off. During a memory wipe, it was unusual to be able to see and remember the subject's memories, beyond the recent ones she'd been trying to erase.

With Alex, she'd seen hours of dedicated work, mostly trying to track down criminals, she thought, probably his work for the FBI. Years spent training and studying, honing his skills. Flashing images of battle, terrified screams echoing in a desert landscape. Gunshots and blood, so much blood. She'd seen him pressing his hands over streaming wounds, handling needles and tying tourniquets. A healer of some kind? Maybe a medic, like Dumeril.

She froze, her arms dropping to her sides. Come to think of it, it had taken a lot more energy than usual to heal that head wound. Granted, it had been a nasty one that might have killed him if left untreated. She'd never been a particularly gifted healer, but usually it wasn't that hard for her. The encounter with Alex had been off all the way around.

She shook off the unease with an upper cut, then an elbow strike. Her techniques were landing with more force, rocking the heavy bag.

Alayna's thoughts spun back to that kiss. She'd stolen it from him, but he hadn't seemed to mind. He had tasted so damn good, like smoky scotch and hard, hot male. For those few seconds she'd felt more alive than she had in years, heart pounding, skin tingling, mind spinning. Knife hand.

Too bad that was all she'd ever get. Back fist. She'd probably—hopefully—never see him again.

Spear hand, round kick. Muscles screaming, she gave the bag everything she had, anger, frustration and regret pouring out with each punch.

3

Chapter 3

lex opened his eyes very slowly.

He immediately regretted it as sunlight dug its claws right past his eyeballs and into his aching brain. Shit. It felt like a swarm of fire ants had taken up residence in there and were trying to chew their way out. Angry fire ants.

And his mattress was suddenly as hard as a rock…and stank like urine and vomit. Wait, what? Deciding to chance it, Alex opened his eyes again, even more slowly and looked around. Instead of his bed, rough asphalt was under him, and instead of his bedroom, he found an alley stacked with garbage bags. A disorienting chill went through him. What. The. Fuck?

On reflex, he sat up quickly. Mistake. Big mistake.

Stomach rolling violently, head throbbing, he doubled over as wave after wave of pain and nausea pounded him. Was he having an aneurysm? That might explain what was going on.

The last thing he remembered he had been at work, at the FBI field office, clearing extradition forms on a bank robbery suspect. He had been about to go somewhere, but he couldn't remember exactly where.

According to his watch, it was 10:30 a.m. Saturday. His last memory was about 8 p.m. Friday. More than fourteen hours unaccounted for.

Alex checked himself for injuries and, finding none, stood up. Slowly. God, he hurt. Every muscle was stiff and sore, his bones feeling like they'd been pulverized and put back together with duct tape. Had he been hit by a truck or something? His ID was still in his pocket. His gun was…lying a few feet away. Picking it up, he checked the clip, found two bullets missing and holstered it. His wallet was in his jeans pocket, all the cash still in it. So, not a robbery, then, but why had he fired his gun?

Fishing his keys out of his pocket, he stumbled to the mouth of the alley and looked around. Sixth and, he checked the signs, Trinity. Just outside of Revelations. What the hell? He hated bars like that and wouldn't be caught dead there, given a choice.

A memory floated up through the headache. Stonework. Gargoyles. Dancers. Loud music.

He knew what the inside of the bar looked like, but he'd never been in there. That was weird.

It occurred to him that he had bigger problems than being seen at an overly trendy bar. He had no idea where his truck was. If he started walking the nearby streets he'd find it eventually.

Not knowing what else to do, Alex headed out down a deserted Sixth Street, kicking beer bottles and plastic cups out of his way, trying not to think about how bad he smelled.

* * *

After a shower and a few hours sleep, Alex loaded up in his truck and decided to head back to Revelations to get some answers.

When he'd arrived home earlier, he'd checked his case files and found his notes about Revelations and Nick Salvadin. That must have been why he was on Sixth Street last night, but he had no idea if he'd found Salvadin, how he'd ended up in that alley, or if he was any closer to finding Blanca's killer. He'd been on a rogue op and he'd fired his gun.

Bureau rules stated he needed to report the discharge of his firearm, but he had no memory of what happened or even if he'd been the one to fire it. It was a huge risk not filing a report, but it was a bigger one to let anyone know he was suffering from memory loss.

He needed answers about last night and he needed them fast.

Sixth Street was deserted in the early afternoon, and parking was not a problem. As Alex walked past the alley he'd woken up in earlier that morning, he scratched his head. He was really hoping he hadn't killed or injured anyone last night. There had been nothing in the news reports about a shooting.

Someone at the club had to be able to help him fill in the blanks. Pushing open the matte black front door of the club, he stepped inside, the smell of disinfectant slapping him in the face. Night clubs always looked terrible in the harsh light of day and this place was no exception. This was maybe the example that proved the rule.

The overhead fluorescents were on, and the red and black décor looked overly harsh, the fake stonework looked worse than cheesy. This place was not meant to be seen in daylight. He wondered what it looked like when the club was really swinging.

With that thought, he had an odd sense of déjà vu, something like a memory floating up. He could picture the dance floor and the bar packed with bodies. He shook it off. Maybe it was just his imagination.

"Can I help you?"

He turned at the sound of the husky voice behind him. A tall woman with pin straight black hair cut off at the chin and harsh red lips stood in a hallway that was carefully hidden past the bouncer's station.

"I hope so. My name is Alex. I was hoping to speak to the owner, if he's around."

The woman, dressed sharply in tailored slacks, a white blouse and a pinstripe vest, gave him an up-and-down look. Measuring, weighing and checking him out.

"Do you have an appointment?" Her face was a ridged mask, her too-red lips turned down in disdain.

He flashed his badge. "No, but this won't take long. I just have a few questions."

Her dark eyes narrowed for a moment before a slow, wolfish smile spread across her lips. A shiver of unease traveled up his spine, but he shook it off.

"I'm Camille Carerre, general manager for Revelations." She extended her hand. Her skin was as cold and pale as marble. "Mr. Spino is in a meeting currently, but perhaps he can take a moment."

A strange tingling crept up his hand where she held it and he pulled back. She took a slow step toward him, holding his gaze with hers. Her eyes were so dark they were nearly black and he could feel himself falling into them.

"Why are you here?" Her voice was low and a little sultry.

A spicy scent wrapped around him as she stepped closer, something like chilies and orchids. An instinctual step back and his shoulder blades hit the wall. She was on him now, those black eyes holding him more effectively than chains. Those cold hands were on his chest now, her fingers tracing patterns.

"I need answers to questions." His mouth was moving on its own. What was happening to him? Fear tried to bubble up, but it dissipated like smoke in a strong wind.

"Questions about what?"

"Last night." His voice sounded far away.

"What happened last night?"

"That's what I don't know. I was supposed to come here to find someone. Woke up in the alley out back this morning with missing memories."

Camille leaned into him, her breath brushing his neck, sending a shudder through him.

"So you're the one on the security tapes last night. The little air witch snared you with her memory spell. And you remember nothing?"

The things she said didn't make sense and his thoughts ground together like misaligned gears as he tried to process it.

"Tiny pieces coming back. Images. Sounds." His mouth was moving on it's own again, even as the pounding in his head became louder.

"That witch isn't as good as she thinks she is."

She threw her head back and laughed, a sharp sound that made him want to recoil.

Turning on a stiletto, she took his arm like they were old friends and led him down the hallway toward a set of double doors at the end. He tried to shrug off her grip. At least his arm was obeying his commands, even if the rest of him wasn't, but she was strong.

As she knocked softly and pushed the door open, Alex had a brief impression of a tall, muscular, dark-haired man rising from behind an overly large desk – compensating for something? – and a blonde woman sitting across from him, her back mostly to the door. As she turned, surprise evident on her face, his eyes met hers in a moment that seemed to stretch into hours. Indigo eyes.

His vision instantly went white, a blinding pain searing along his neural pathways, skittering over his nerves. A roaring sound filled his ears, like all the air was being sucked out of the room.

When his vision had cleared and he could hear again, he realized he was lying on his back staring up at an angry-looking guy with distinctly Italian features and the blonde woman. Her eyes were wide as she shouted.

"Damn it, Camille! What possessed you to drag a sapien FBI agent in here?" the blonde woman snapped.

The pain in his head was not receding and seemed to be getting worse. It was like the worst migraine he'd ever had times a gunshot wound. Maybe this was what dying felt like?

"I didn't know your fucked up magick was going to give him a seizure," Camille snapped back.

The blonde was stroking his forehead now, whispered words spilling from a set of truly gorgeous lips. Lips he remembered kissing last night.

Holy crap. It was coming back. Images from the night before bombarded him, the club, the fight in the alley, the way she'd fixed what must have been a serious head injury with some whispered words and a touch.

He remembered her kiss and he felt his blood heat up a degree or two. That had been one hell of a kiss.

And he remembered her words.

I'm sorry, cowboy. I can't let you remember what happened tonight, but you probably don't want the memories anyway. Just try to relax.

She'd drugged him or hypnotized him or something. He fought to sit up, desperate to reach the door. His legs refused his commands and everything south of his neck was numb.

"What the fuck did you do to me, lady?" he shouted at her.

"What the fuck are you and what the fuck is going on?"

"You're saying fuck a lot," she replied, her voice steady, a hand extended toward him, like he was a dangerous dog.

Nice agent, good agent. Don't mind the tranquilizer darts.

She turned to the Italian guy. He guessed this was the mysterious Mr. Spino.

"Dominic, we'll finish this later. I need to get him out of here."

Memories of the fight in the alley assailed him, and suddenly he wanted to be very far from the blonde woman. He remembered the way she'd fought, how she'd taken down that…thing. His heart suddenly pounded at the thought of that thing's face, those eyes and those fangs.

The things she did, the way she moved shouldn't be possible. They weren't possible in the world on the other side of the door; he just needed to get there.

Alex thought about going for his gun, holstered under his shoulder, under his jacket. It might as well have been a million miles away. The way Blondie moved, he'd never get to it before she beat him senseless or did that electricity thing she'd pulled the night before. That hadn't been a Taser.

Camille made a move toward him as he neared the door, but Blondie cut her off, earning a sharp glare and a sneer from the dark haired woman.

"Back off, Camille. I'll take care of it," she said, her hands sliding under his arms and lifting him to his feet. He weighed two hundred pounds, and she lifted him like he was a sack of feathers. As he rose, she steadied him, her hands spreading over his ribs on either side. He could feel their warmth through the thin cotton of his dress shirt. That kiss sprang to mind as he met her eyes.

Whoever or whatever she was, his body kept responding to

her touch with the hormonal version of a "hell, yeah." The mere thought of that kiss caused his breath to catch in his throat.

Leaning close, she whispered in his ear, "If you trust me for just a few minutes, I can get you out of here. Then, I'll explain everything."

Alex opened his mouth to tell her to go to hell, but he stopped himself. Everything that had happened so far indicated that he shouldn't trust her, but he needed answers in a bad way. He was so far off the map here that he was willing to at least listen to what she had to say.

"When we get out of here you have ten minutes," he replied, his voice low and harsh. He let her see the anger in his face. He didn't tell her what would happen after ten minutes because he didn't know himself. Her body relaxed a little and she turned to Dominic.

"We'll talk later."

"Of course, Commander," he replied, a slow smile spreading across his face.

She motioned for Alex to proceed out of the room and he replied, "Ladies first."

He wasn't about to put that woman at his back. He wasn't that stupid.

She just opened the other side of the double doors and they walked out, side by side. Alex opened his mouth to start firing questions at her, but she motioned for him to be quiet, glancing over her shoulder at the watchful Camille.

They reached the front door of the club and walked into the afternoon sunlight.

"T minus ten, Blondie. Better start talking," he said, letting a note of command snap in his voice.

She pursed her lips, studying his face, trying to read him,

trying to decide something.

"Clock's ticking," he reminded her.

She nodded, having come to a decision. "Follow me."

For the first time, he noticed what she was wearing. Leather boots, probably custom, clicked against the pavement. Stylish and girlie, but with practical heels. Tactical cargo pants hugged her hips, and a black T-shirt was stretched over the curve of her waist and breasts. No visible weapons.

They rounded a corner, onto one of the side streets off Sixth and she motioned to a cherry red classic Mustang convertible parked at the curb.

An appreciative whistle passed his lips.

"Yours?"

She nodded, a nervous smile tugging one corner of her mouth.

"Nice."

Just because she was mixed up with storybook monsters and had possibly inflicted some serious brain damage on him didn't mean he couldn't appreciate a fine piece of machinery.

Alex got in on the passenger side and admired the well-tended black leather interior. Anyone that owned—and obviously cared for—a car like this couldn't be all bad. Even so, his right hand rested on the gun holstered under his jacket.

The black rag top and the windows were up. They wouldn't be overheard.

As she slid into the driver's seat, her scent wrapped around him, smelling of cold mountain air and snow. Silence stretched between them. The tension was making his head hurt—even more than it already was.

"Just spill it," he said, irritation creeping into his voice. His voice sounded too loud in the close confines of the car.

The blonde gripped the wheel, rubbing her palms against the

leather wrappings. She let out a slow breath and closed her eyes.

"I don't know where to start," she whispered.

This was not the ass-kicking Amazon from last night. Her posture was slightly hunched, there were lines of exhaustion showing around her eyes and dark circles under them, the marks showing like bruises. She looked young, too young to be mixed up in…whatever this was.

And she'd let her guard down. His hand itched to pull the gun from its holster. She would answer his questions and quick if he did. But his gut said a softer approach was called for here.

"Why don't you start with your name?" He suggested in a soft tone that worked wonders in interrogations. I'm the one that can help you, it said.

"Alayna," she said. "Alayna Blackwell."

"What are you, Alayna Blackwell?"

She gave him a steady look that had his heart skipping a beat.

"That's a bit harder to answer."

4

Chapter 4

Oh shit.

Those were the only two words that were capable of forming in Alayna's brain at the moment. She eyed the tall, well-muscled man who was taking up most of the space—and all of the air—in her car. The same dark-eyed hottie with the delectable lips she'd been trying to forget just that morning by going ten rounds with the punching bag.

Thoughts swirled through her head like a storm. Why had the memory spell failed? How did she tell someone that everything they believed about the world was wrong? That all of things that hid under the bed, in the closet, in the shadows were real and were walking around like regular people, were regular people, for the most part? How did she sideline a determined and experienced investigator who was one short trigger pull from putting a bullet through her?

"I'm a mage," she said trying to slow her heart rate.

He gave her a look that must have been really effective on petty criminals—part scowl, part steady glare—and tilted his head slightly to the side.

"A magick user. We've been called witches, wizards, sorcerers, you name it."

"So that's how you did all that stuff last night, the electricity, fixing my head injury? Fucking magic?"

She nodded, eying where his hand rested on his weapon. Would he really shoot her?

"Do I look like stupid enough buy that explanation? It's more likely that you drugged me last night, something that made me hallucinate. Must have affected my memory. Maybe it's just now wearing off."

"I actually think you're very intelligent and that you're capable of looking at the evidence you've seen in a rational way. Why would I go to all that trouble when I could have just shot you with your own gun last night if I wanted you out of the way? Or left you die from that head injury?"

"Magick isn't real."

She held out her hand.

"Give me something of yours. Something you know I haven't messed with."

Slowly dropping his gaze, like he was reluctant to take his eyes off her, he pulled a small notebook from a pocket and held it out.

Taking it, she began to whisper, the sound like snowflakes falling on water, weaving her spell with her voice. It was a simple one. Within seconds, ice crystals formed over the surface and the paper stiffened. She fed the ice with her own energy, stacking the crystals on top of each other. Before long, the notebook was covered in a thin sheet of ice, and Alex had gone very pale beneath his tan. His mouth hung open slightly.

Swallowing hard, he took the notebook from her and turned it in his hands. Bending it, the ice cracked and fell away.

"Huh. Magick is real." He was silent for a long moment before he spoke up again. "What is your interest in Nick Salvadin?"

"Homicide investigation. I thought Nick might know something."

"And did he?"

It was her turn to be silent for a moment as she thought about how much to tell him. "He gave me a new lead, that's about it. What's your interest in him?"

"Blanca Rodriguez was a good friend. I'm looking for her killer. What kind of lead did he give you? I need to know."

So it was personal. Alex had the look of a man on a mission. There was also a punchy edge to him. Dark stubble covered his jaw, and he looked like he hadn't slept well the last few days.

"I'm not sure yet. I need to do some checking on that, but I'll tell you what I can, when I can." She paused for a moment. "And I'm sorry about your friend."

"Who were those people with you in the alley last night?" he asked, ignoring her attempt at sympathy and plowing on with his questions.

So focused. Alayna chuckled at the sudden change of subject. Nothing slowed this guy down.

"My team. We're in charge of policing and protecting the more unconventional citizens here in Austin," she said. "We keep the supernatural community safe from the scrutiny of the sapiens, who outnumber us ninety-nine to one, and do our best to avoid a torches and pitchforks situation."

She was going to be in so much trouble. Revealing the supernatural world to a sapien was strictly forbidden. The brass was going to strip her of command and throw her in a cell. She shuddered at the thought. Not how she wanted to spend what little remaining time on earth she had. And they were going to kill Alex, no doubt about that.

The Council would do anything to keep to the existence of the magickal races a secret from the sapiens. There was a vehement belief among the Council members that if sapiens ever discovered the creatures living in their midst, they would turn on the magickal races and exterminate them. And who could blame them for that thinking, given how sapiens treated members of their own subspecies just because they had differing skin colors?

"Sapiens? What does that mean?"

Clearly, he wasn't going to let this go. Trying another memory spell might fry his brain, and there was no way to know it wouldn't fail again. The only way to shake this guy was to turn him into a drooling vegetable or put him in the ground under a nice piece of granite. Or tell him the truth.

The guy had serious cojones. He'd stood up to a vamp in full predator mode and had just relived the traumatic experience when his memories came flooding back. He wasn't even breathing hard, and he hadn't shot her, so she knew he could keep his shit together when things went to hell.

The thought of turning someone so brave and beautiful over to a death squad made something in her chest hurt.

What if she could turn him into an asset? An investigator inside sapien law enforcement would be a valuable thing, maybe valuable enough to keep him alive should the situation ever come to light with the brass.

She didn't know if she could trust him, but it was the best option among the truly horrible options that were in front of her.

"You can take your hand off the gun. I'll answer your questions."

He laughed, a derisive bark. "What are sapiens?"

"Sapiens are you people, the mainstream," she said, frustration bubbling in her chest.

"No, we're humans, and you're…whatever it is you are," he said, sounding defensive.

"Let's get one thing straight: I'm as human as you are. And so was that vampire last night and so are the shifters," she said.

"Wait…there are shifters now?" he asked. "Like shape shifters?"

"Got it in one," she said.

"What do you mean you're all human?" he asked, a note of anger creeping into his voice.

"I mean," she said in a voice meant to calm him, "that there are more branches of human evolution than Darwin ever dreamed of. You are homo sapiens sapiens, plain old, white bread, vanilla human. Then there's me, homo sapiens mageus, a slightly different subspecies. All the same parts with a few energy efficient upgrades."

He was scowling now, like she was trying to tell him the sky wasn't blue or that the American Dream was a myth.

"Then there's old Nick from last night, homo sapiens vampirus, an apex predator that depends on the blood of sapiens for survival. They're not dead or undead, but they are fast and incredibly strong."

She realized she was sounding like a nature show host and it was freaking out Agent Martinez.

"Your eyes just got really big. Take deep breaths and put your head between your knees if you think you're going to pass out," she said.

He glared at her again.

"Don't worry, they don't usually kill their food—"

Just then, his stomach gave an impossibly loud gurgle. Alayna stifled a snicker and raised an eyebrow.

"Speaking of food, have you ever had a Mighty Cone?"

"A mighty what?"

"Mighty Cone. It's a food truck a few blocks from here. It's basically a vertical taco, but they have these fried avocados that are quite possibly the best thing you will ever put in your mouth," she explained.

The guy had a really puzzled look on his face now and was staring at her like she was crazy.

"I thought you might be hungry," she said, indicating his rumbling mid-section. "My treat, seeing as I left you in a frigid alley last night."

"I feel like I just pushed through the back of the wardrobe into Narnia and you're waxing poetic about fried avocados." Slowly, his hand lifted off his weapon and he mumbled under his breath, "This day cannot get any weirder."

Twisting the key in the ignition, she brought the roaring engine to life and pulled away from the curb.

"Challenge accepted." She flashed him a smile and said, "There's no reason you should face the crumbling of the foundations of your reality on an empty stomach, is there?"

5

Chapter 5

A few minutes later, Alex was holding a paper cone lined with a tortilla and filled with fried chicken and avocado. Alayna handed him a sweating glass bottle of beer and when he gave her a questioning look she said, "It'll help. Trust me."

They wandered back to where Alayna had parked the Mustang, well away from the group of food trailers, milling families, street musicians and scattered booths selling crafts. They sat on the hood eating and sipping their beers in silence.

Finally, he asked, "What did you do to me last night?"

Alayna had just started to relax a bit and instantly her posture tensed again. She crumpled her plastic fork in the paper cone and set it aside before wiping her hands on a paper napkin.

"First, I healed a pretty serious skull fracture," she said. "Then, I kissed you, mostly so I could distract you, and then I wiped your memory."

Turning, he met her eyes. That gaze was magnetic, pulling him in.

"Mostly to distract me, huh? It sure as hell worked."

A blush bloomed pink across her cheeks and throat. She

43

shifted nervously, and her thigh brushed his, spiking his heart rate. The truth was, her mouth could have distracted him from a mortar strike. It was continuing to distract him now.

"Why didn't the memory wipe stick?" he asked, trying to cover the fact that he was staring at her.

"I'm not sure. I've never had a spell fail like that," she said, rubbing her hands on her knees. "But I've heard stories of sapiens that are immune to magick, or at least resistant to it. They're called lìthseach—it means slippery in Gaelic—and they're kind of Teflon coated against magick. A spell might work for a while, but it eventually fails. But they're so rare, I thought they were just a myth."

Well, that was just impossible. He wasn't special. No one in his family was special. He'd never stood out at anything in his life. He was strictly middle of the pack, average.

"Maybe when you saw me, it triggered the spell to fail completely. You said you'd already started to remember a few details," she said. "What I can't figure out is why Camille sent you in there."

He told her about the strange encounter in the hallway with Camille, how his mouth had seemed to move on its own.

"Vampire pheromones. They can give sapiens brain fog and leave you open to compulsion or suggestion. She must have figured out what happened with the memory wipe from what you told her," Alayna said.

"And she sent me in there thinking that if I got close to you, my memories might come back?"

"Exactly," Alayna said. "And she knew the hot water I'd land in, too. That bitch has always had it out for me."

She was silent a moment as she absently played with a lock of her hair.

"Hot water?"

His protective instincts bubbled up. If she was in some kind of trouble because of him, he wanted to help. The memory of that fight in the alley floated up. The idea of her needing his protection was laughable.

She shook her head and waved off his question.

"If you really are a lithseach, you're in even more danger than I thought. Now that you know what's out there, you're probably going to start seeing through the glamours that elves and fey use to hide their appearance. Heck, you'll probably be able to spot vampires and shifters pretty soon, too."

She looked at him and concern was etched in her features. It had been a long time since anyone besides his mother had been concerned for him and the knowledge that maybe she cared sent something tingling across his abs and chest. He had the strangest urge to reach out and touch her face, to smooth that frown from between her brows.

She'd begun speaking again, and he focused on her words.

"I can't risk another memory wipe without causing serious brain damage. And unless you are the world's best actor, you're going to give yourself away the first time you see a fey on the street. There are a lot of people who would love to get their hands on a lithseach, for a lot of reasons, none of them good."

Anxiety twisted through his gut.

"So I've got a target on my back?"

She nodded, her eyes searching his face, for what, he didn't know.

"And if the Council or the rest of the Mage Corps finds out that I revealed us to an FBI agent, you could end up six feet under, and I could end up in a cell," she said, the stress evident in her voice.

Protectiveness surged again. He'd put her in danger.

"Wait, you've lost me. Again. Who are the Council and the Mage Corps?" Alex asked.

She paused. "The more I tell you, the more danger you're in."

"You pulled me down this rabbit hole, Alice. If I'm in danger, I need to know as much as possible."

She grimaced and nodded.

"Fine. The Council of Magickal Creatures is the governing body for everything that goes bump in the night. One member for each of the races: mages, vampires, shifters, elves and fey. They're elected by their people."

A derisive laugh slipped from him. "So, the monsters have discovered democracy. How progressive."

"It works. Well, most of the time, anyway," she said, shrugging. "Mages can pass most easily in normal sapien society, so we're the buffers between sapiens and the other races. So we have the Mage Corps."

"My head hurts," Alex said, rubbing the spot between his eyes.

"That's what the beer is for," she said.

He took a long pull from the bottle and sighed.

"So, you and this team, you were after Salvadin last night, too. And he gave you a new lead. What's next?" Alex asked.

Alayna stared at him, a puzzled look on her face.

"So, you believe me? About all of this?" Incredulity permeated Alayna's voice.

"After what I saw last night and experienced today, it's really not that hard to believe," he said.

After living in Austin a few years, it kind of made sense to him. The city's motto was "Keep Austin Weird" and there were plenty of weirdos in this town. And how much did anyone know about the people around them? He didn't even know the names of the neighbors he shared walls with.

"Salvadin's one of the first leads we've had in this case in months."

"How did you end up on his trail?"

"Salvadin is a known gofer and bouncer for several clubs," she said.

He gave her a look that said he wasn't buying that story.

"Our hacker cracked the APD system and got the footage from the night Blanca Rodriguez disappeared and found the interview notes from when the cops questioned him. I'm pretty sure he used his vampire compulsion to walk out of that interview without giving the cops anything of value."

"And what did he give you?"

"My turn," Alayna said. "What's the FBI's interest in this when APD is still investigating, albeit half-heartedly?"

Silence hung between them for a moment as he turned to stare at the tourists and shoppers on the street. He was going to have to trust her. He turned back and said, "I was checking into things off the books. I told you, Blanca Rodriguez was a friend."

"Wait, so this isn't on the Bureau's radar yet? That's the first good news I've had all day," she said.

"No, APD is still handling it. I tried to get the Bureau to pick it up, but one murder doesn't warrant FBI attention," he said, disdain creeping into his voice.

"It wasn't just one murder," Alayna said.

That snapped his head around.

"There've been six, so far. APD got to Blanca's body before my team could get to the scene."

He cursed under his breath. Six people. Sweet Jesus.

"So far, they've all been Hispanic, all undocumented, all recently crossed the border. Until Blanca. She's the aberration.

She was a war hero and a college student. Someone slipped up bad, and she's the key to catching them," she said, anger coming through her voice.

For the first time since Blanca died, he felt like someone cared.

Alayna hopped off the hood of the car, leaned her hip against the grill, and turned to him. Her dark blue eyes locked on his and she spoke softly. He could fall right into those eyes if he wasn't careful.

"So, the way I see it, we've got two options," she said. "I can try that memory wipe again, but it might cause some serious brain damage."

Alex stiffened, moving backwards out of reflex.

"Or we can work on this case together," she said in the same soft voice. "You've got good instincts, and I could use a resource inside sapien law enforcement to let me know their next move."

"I really want to skip the part where you scramble my brains," he said, his voice surprisingly steady. "But I just want to find the bastard who killed Blanca and put a bullet through him. And then I want to go back to my life."

He'd worked hard to put his life back together, picking through the pieces of his shattered dreams to do it. If he was what she said, he might have to run. Starting over was the last thing he wanted to do.

Alayna was silent for a moment, her head down as she mulled his words.

Her eyes met his. "Help me with this case and I'll do everything I can to give you a shot at the killer. And I'll teach you what you need to know to hide yourself. It's no guarantee, but it might give both of us a fighting chance at making it through this intact."

He needed intel if he was going to get this target off his back.

She was the one that had it. If he was ever going to get back to his life, she was the key.

Alex looked back at the busy street, but he was really seeing Blanca's autopsy photos. There was a nasty thing—or things—out there killing people. From what he'd seen, this woman and her team might be the only people that could stop the next murder and help him figure out what had happened to Blanca.

"I'm in."

* * *

Alex looked down at the card Alayna had given him before they'd parted ways at the food truck park.

A.Blackwell

512-555-7649

On the back, she had written an address on Red River Street and 11 p.m.

Here he sat on a deserted Red River Street. The clock on his dashboard said 10:45.

He'd spent the intervening hours since he'd spoken with Alayna processing how much his world had just changed.

His Army training had taught him to identify threats and formulate strategies to eliminate those threats and he was falling back heavily on his training now.

If what Alayna said was true, there were thousands of creatures in this city that would probably be able to spot him in a crowd, mostly because he'd likely betray himself by staring. Or cringing, gibbering, or screaming.

He didn't know exactly what this lithseach thing was, but he understood that it made him a target and he was going to do everything he could to minimize his profile.

Maybe with his help, they could catch Blanca's killer. Maybe with her help, he could learn enough to keep himself alive. And when this case was over, he could go back to his real life, the one he'd scraped together from the ashes. Nothing was certain, but he had to try.

With that decision, he checked one of his most pressing concerns off of his mental checklist. Mental checklists were his comforting old friends. As an Army medic in Afghanistan, his checklists had served him well, allowing him to clear his mind, think quickly, and act to save wounded soldiers and civilians when bullets and mortars were flying around him.

Assess the situation for safety concerns, visually and verbally triage patients, establish treatment options in the field, stabilize, and evacuate.

The checklists were so clean, emotionless and dispassionate. Just like he needed to be if he was going to survive more than five minutes in a world where movie monsters walked around like regular people.

His next concern was Alayna's request that he pass on information from the sapien law enforcement investigations—damn it, he was already starting to think in the terms she'd used—into the murder they knew about. But her team had slipped easily into the APD network, so he wasn't providing them with any information they didn't already have. And the FBI had yet to take an interest in the cases, so he wasn't jeopardizing federal intel and putting his job in danger.

He'd just be using his skills—and maybe some of the records, resources and search capabilities of the Bureau—to help an independent investigator locate a threat to public safety. The fact that the independent investigator in question could shoot lightning from her fingertips and heal a skull fracture with a few words was not relevant. Alayna and her team were probably the only ones that could handle this threat. His conscience was clear about helping them.

He didn't really know why, but he trusted Alayna. Maybe it was because she had probably saved his life. He didn't even really hold the memory tampering against her. He sensed that she had just been trying to protect him. Maybe it was because she wanted to find Blanca's killer as badly as he did.

Bottom line, if he walked into this meeting tonight, he was all in. He opened the door and climbed out of his truck.

Red River was one block off the freeway and ran north and south along the edge of the entertainment district. A few blocks north, Sixth Street was in full swing on a Saturday night. The glow of neon and the frantic motion of a spotlight spilled over the tops of the old buildings, bleeding into the night sky.

But down on this end, it was dark and quiet.

As he shut the door of the truck, the sound echoed down the empty street. Chilly moisture hung in the February air, shimmering as it condensed on the windshields of the empty cars that lined the street. Alex opted to keep his leather jacket on over his black T-shirt and heavy-cloth khakis. The leather offered some protection in a fight and hid a few surprises.

He walked past shuttered shops, protected by metal roll-down doors and restaurants that were closing up for the night.

When he arrived at the address he'd been given, he checked the map on his phone again. This couldn't be right.

The building looked like it had seen better days before it was abandoned and left to rot. It was an old brick two-story and had probably once been a cotton or grain warehouse, like many of the buildings north of the river in the oldest part of the city. A long wooden porch, bowed in the middle with age, ran along the front of the building, and the steps on either end had holes big enough to break an ankle in each of the treads. The windows in the front of the building were spray painted black from the inside. There were no street numbers on the outside of the building, but the numbers on the buildings to either side confirmed this must be the place.

Alex spotted a small brass plaque beside a black metal door. It was crusted over with green corrosion, so he hopped up on the porch to get a better look. A little rubbing revealed the words engraved in the metal.

The Dusty Trail.

He stepped back from the plaque and looked up and down the porch. This was the address, and this was the right place, but where was Alayna?

Had he been set up?

His hand went for the gun holstered under his arm, and that's when he heard it, strains of music floating through the cool night air. It was like the chirp of a cricket, hard to pinpoint the direction of the music's origin. It faded and then returned louder, like a failing speaker. He shook his head, trying to figure out if his ears were playing tricks on him.

Alex looked back up at the building and his vision slid in and out focus, like a camera lens that couldn't quite find the sweet spot. His stomach rolled as a wave of nausea hit him and he closed his eyes, breathing deeply, desperate to find his center. His equilibrium shifted violently, and he felt like he was falling and spinning at the same time. He was about to toss his lunch all over the porch when he became aware of lights penetrating his closed eyelids. The music was getting louder.

He opened his eyes slowly, and the first thing he saw was

a strand of Christmas lights. They were the older style with the over-sized glass bulbs and they were wrapped around the posts of the porch and bordered the door. The black door remained, but he could see figures moving through the windows, which were no longer painted black. The building didn't look abandoned anymore, the old stonework and brick looking as fresh as the day they were installed about a hundred fifty years ago.

A brightly painted wooden sign—that sure as hell hadn't been there before—hung above the porch.

The Dusty Trail.

Weird.

Alex wasn't sure why he was suddenly seeing a very different building from the one he had been standing in front of just a few seconds ago, but he was learning to save his questions until the end of the presentation.

The door was locked. He knocked twice and wasn't surprised when a hulking bouncer opened the door.

The dude was easily over six and half feet tall and as wide as the door. His face looked like it had been slammed in a car door a few times, and his dark hair looked like it had been cut by a weed whacker.

The human wall glared at him and Alex tipped his head back in order to meet his eyes.

"Name?" the giant asked in a voice so gravely it sounded like two slabs of concrete grinding together.

"Alex Martinez."

The Hulk lumbered to the side and Alex stepped inside the Dusty Trail.

The place looked for all the world like an old-time saloon. A large wooden bar occupied the entirety of the right-hand wall, and a huge mirror behind it made the space look larger than it was. Unlabeled bottles of various sizes, shapes, and colors sat on shelves behind the bar. Twenty or so stools lined the bar and about twenty round wooden tables filled the room. The place was packed and growing warm from all the bodies, the chatter a mid-level din.

As he searched for Alayna's face in the crowd, he started to notice some details that quickly had his skin crawling and his breath coming fast. A group of men and women sitting near the door had delicately pointed ears. A woman at the bar had shimmering scales on her neck and the backs of her hands and hair as green as seaweed. A man in the corner had intense blue eyes that looked like they were—no, they couldn't be—glowing.

A black-gloved hand landed on his shoulder. With his nerves pulled as taut as a piano wire, Alex reacted on instinct and nearly had the man in an arm lock before the other man stepped away.

"Whoa there," said the dark-skinned man. Alex recognized him from the alley the night before. "You look like you've seen a ghost."

"There are ghosts now?"

The newcomer laughed.

"She said you were smart, but even she's wrong occasionally."

A high-pitched voice spoke up from the vicinity of Alex's waist.

"Stop being such a catty bitch, Dumeril."

A girl, who looked about six years old, pushed past him from the entrance and headed to the bar. A dark blue cloak covered her slender shoulders, but the hood had fallen back to reveal long brown hair woven in braids along the side of her face.

"Why is there a kid in a bar?" Alex asked.

The one she'd called Dumeril burst out laughing again.

"I like him. He's funny. Let me buy you a drink, funny man," he said.

The little girl had managed to scramble up on a bar stool and ordered a margarita from the bartender. In her tiny hands, it looked like a fishbowl. Dumeril soon had a dark, frothy draught in his hand and was pressing a glass of whiskey into Alex's.

"I think you're going to need this," he said.

Oh, awesome, it was a double. Alex downed it and set the glass on the bar, wiping his mouth with the back of his hand.

That's when his vision started to do that focus in and out thing again. The face of the little girl changed, blurred and slid back into focus. She smiled and showed two rows of pointed, shark-like teeth, both top and bottom. Her nose was much longer, larger, and hooked like a beak. Her eyes became bigger, the overly large irises and pupils ringed with a white starburst set in deep lapis blue.

Alex felt his stomach drop as he stared at something out of the Grimm Brothers' nightmares. Wrestling every fight or flight instinct he had, he turned away, trying to control his breathing.

The girl wasn't the only one whose appearance had changed. Dumeril had looked like a regular Black dude just a few seconds before. Now he was staring at a man with pointed ears peeking beneath white hair, violet eyes, and skin as dark as printers ink. He smiled, showing unnaturally long canines. Alex fought a wave of dizziness and gripped the edge of the bar to keep from falling on his ass.

Dumeril moved up beside him. "It gets easier." When Alex gave him a puzzled look, he added, "The glamour's slipping, I mean. By the look on your face, I'm guessing they're slipping right and left."

Alex nodded, signaling the bartender that another drink was

desperately needed.

"Pretty soon, you won't see them to begin with."

The bartender set another double whiskey down in front of Alex. He took it carefully and downed half of it.

"I don't understand how any of this works. Glamours, vampires, witches, you, her." He indicated the sharp-toothed creature that up until a minute ago had looked like a cute little girl. "One minute, this building looks abandoned, the next, it looks like a bar."

"Glamours are blankets of illusion. They let people see what they want to see. They work on the sapiens, and the more oblivious vampires and shifters. But if you look right at a glamour, and you know what to look for, it dissolves."

Alex nodded, finishing the rest of his drink.

"Look, I don't mean to be rude," Alex said, keeping his voice low, "but what the hell is she?" He indicated the girl-creature who was pretending to be very interested in her drink.

"Ellie," he said, stressing her name, "is a gnome."

This thing sure didn't look like the cute little ceramic statue in his mother's garden.

In a softer voice Dumeril said, "She's small but fierce, so don't piss her off."

Ellie eyed him from her seat further down the bar and lifted her chin sharply.

"'Sup, dawg?"

Alex closed his eyes and started rubbing the spot between his eyebrows with the knuckle of his index finger, a nervous gesture he'd picked up somewhere between Kabul and Baghdad. All of this was just un-fucking-real.

"Over here," Dumeril said in a raised voice, holding up his hand in the increasingly crowded bar.

Alex glanced toward the entrance. The olive-skinned woman he had seen the night before was moving through the crowd, her bobbed black hair brushing her shoulders. There was no sickening blurring or sliding, and her appearance remained the same. Alex breathed a sigh of relief.

"Hey, it's the *pendejo* from last night," said the woman as they approached the bar. "How's your head?"

Alex didn't appreciate being called a dumbass as a greeting.

"Muy bien, gracias." He was fine, thanks. He shot her a smile. That let her know he'd understood what she'd called him and that he could drop it.

"Just kidding, dude," she said, slapping him on the back. A distinctive Laredo accent touched her words. He could hear the street in her tone and would bet his last dollar there was a switchblade in her boot. "We're glad to have you on the team. I hope the fuckwads," she indicated Dumeril and Ellie, "haven't been giving you too hard a time."

Ellie flipped her off and went back to her drink.

"I'm Guadalupe Herrera, but everyone calls me Lu," she said extending her hand. He shook it, noting the barely-leashed strength in her hands and arms. She wore a black tank top that showed off well-muscled shoulders. The way she held her body marked her as a fighter, but her hands and face carried none of the tell-tale scars.

As he turned back toward the crowd, he was pretty sure there wasn't a glamour left in the place that he wasn't seeing right through. There were beings of every size in the crowded bar, from tiny flitting things that must have been fairies to the bouncer, who now looked something like a storybook troll, with green and black splotchy skin and small tusks jutting from beneath his lower lip.

Alex took a deep breath and let his thoughts settle, found his center, like he'd done hundreds of times when the bullets were flying and a buddy's blood was leaking through his fingers. It was all just training. And he could train himself not to freak every time he saw a freak.

From the corner of his eye, he saw the front door of the place swing open and the pale flash of platinum hair.

Alayna breezed in and offered the troll/bouncer a kiss on the cheek, saying something that made the bruiser laugh. From the gravel in the creature's rumbling chuckle, it didn't do that very often.

As she moved into the bar, the crowd parted for her, keeping their distance. Their stances said it was out of respect, not fear.

When she made it to their group, Alex noticed a little bounce in her step, a contained excitement, and she turned a dazzling smile on her assembled team members. And him. That smile made his thoughts grind to a halt and his guts twist in a knot for a second.

After a brief moment of silence, she gestured to Alex and said, "Well, what do you think?"

Dumeril laughed.

"I think only you could get excited about finding the one sapien that could get us all a Council death sentence," Dumeril said dryly. "But if you're excited, I'm excited." He ended with a higher, sing-song voice, flashing some jazz hands.

"So, is this the sape?"

The question had come from a guy who had stepped up behind Alayna, his voice pitched low so it didn't carry to the other bar patrons around them He was tall, taller than Alex, marking him at well over six feet. His skin was a mix of olive, copper, and mocha and his features could have let him pass easily for

Hispanic, Indian, Native American, or Middle Eastern. He had military training written in his posture, stance and attitude.

Alayna whirled on him and her voice cut like a knife.

"What have I told you about that word, Sergeant?"

That put some steel in his spine. The newcomer snapped to attention and fixed his gaze on the wall behind her. Whew, Alex had been there a time or two and knew a dressing down when he saw one.

There was a subtle sharpness in her voice that all good leaders seemed to be born with. It was quiet, but carried the understanding that they could tear your head off and shit down your neck if you stepped a toe out of line.

She got right up in big guy's grill, her face inches from his chin thanks to her high-heeled boots, and in a voice as smooth as silk said, "Say it again and I'll give you a new definition of misery, Burdock. Agent Martinez is kindly considering lending us his expertise, and if you fuck this up I will take it out of your hide, mage."

A sharp, "Yes, ma'am" was his only response.

Alayna turned back to Alex, flashing the barest hint of a secret smile. "I think you've met everyone except Sergeant Attitude Problem, also known as Burdock."

The guy gave Alex a look that could blister paint and he decided to offer him a nod instead of a handshake. Alex wished Alayna hadn't stepped in like that. Keeping the rank and file in line was part of a commander's job, but respect and teamwork between two people couldn't be forced, especially right away. If he decided to work with the team, the confrontation with Burdock would have to come later.

Walking onto an established team was something that Alex had plenty of experience with. He'd had to do it a few times. The new medic was always a welcome sight, but he'd still developed a few tricks along the way for assimilating.

Alayna grabbed a Mexican martini at the bar and waved the group to a table tucked into an alcove at the back.

As they settled in around the table, she took a seat next to Alex and he appreciated her closeness. His element was about two galaxies back and he felt extremely out of place. At the same time, her closeness made his pulse speed up. She smelled like the air after a thunderstorm, and that scent was making his thoughts jumble.

Alayna sketched a bare outline of his background for the group and explained quickly what had happened that afternoon and her decision to bring him on board with the investigation.

"Between us and sapien law enforcement working separately, we've come up with very little on these murders," Alayna said. "I figured it was time to work together."

She added, a note of excitement creeping into her voice, "Plus, he's a lithseach, and you just don't see one of them every day."

"I'm sure the Council would like to get their hands on him," Burdock said. "We're taking a big risk in not reporting him."

Alayna shot him a look that screamed *shut the fuck up, you're scaring the new guy.*

"He's more useful where he is," she said. "I'll choose the right time to broach the subject with the brass, and that's the last I want to hear on the subject."

Alayna gestured to Ellie, her midnight blue cloak hiding much of her figure and making her appear tiny in a chair made for much larger creatures. He sensed it would be extremely impolite to offer her a booster seat.

"Alex Martinez, meet Ellyjobell Ningle," Alayna said. "Ellie is our sniper, as well as our security and technology expert.

Anything with a circuit board, she can hack it, and she's never met a lock she couldn't pick. She's also the deadliest knife fighter this side of the Fae Realms. Piss her off and she'll carve your kidney out and hand it to you before you can blink."

The little gnome extended her hand, "Call me anything but Ellie and you'll piss me off."

"10-4, ma'am," Alex said, his hand dwarfing hers as they shook.

Lu sat next to Ellie.

"Lu is our recon and surveillance expert," Alayna said. "And she's the most talented shape shifter I've ever seen. Avian, feline, canine shapes, nothing slows this girl down. You need anybody tailed, talk to her. She's also in charge of all the cameras and equipment."

Alex nodded.

"Dumeril DiNialo," Alayna said, gesturing to the smirking creature in the chair next to Lu. "He's our team medic and the biggest smart-ass you're ever likely to meet, but he's also a hell of a fighter, so we let him hang around."

Alex nodded. "I'm not exactly sure how to ask this, but, uh…what are you?"

Dumeril rolled his eyes. "Looks like you picked a real smart one there, Commander."

"Reeeer," Ellie said, mimicking an angry cat.

Alayna held up a hand to signal that was enough.

Dumeril sighed. "I'm a Svarturan. Sapiens don't have a lot of legends about us because we're not a bunch of attention whores like vampires, fairies, and elves."

Alayna chimed in. "The few legends there are come from Scandinavia and they mistakenly refer to Dumeril's people as dark elves."

"That is a term Svarturans consider to be derogatory as we

are nothing—I repeat, nothing—like those humorless sticks-up-their-asses elves," Dumeril snapped.

Alex nodded. He could respect that and made a mental note to do whatever it took to get on Dumeril's good side. In his experience, it paid to be friends with the medic, especially when people started bleeding.

Last up, Alayna turned to the man seated to her right.

"Burdock is a fire mage and our demolitions and weapons expert. You need anything that goes boom, you talk to him," Alayna said.

Alex extended his hand. Burdock just looked at it and pointedly met his eyes. They clearly said Alex wasn't welcome here. Burdock turned to Alayna.

"I want to formally register my reservations about bringing a sapien in on this investigation," he said, drawing out the syllables of the word sapien.

"Yeah, yeah, yeah, reservations noted," Alayna said, waving her hand like she was shooing a fly. "We need to get to work on this case. Lu and I will hold down the fort tonight. Everyone else, get some rest. I want each of you to spend some time with your copy of the case files and bring some new ideas to a meeting at HQ first thing tomorrow evening. I'll take tonight and bring Agent Martinez up to speed. Clear?"

Everyone nodded.

"Then I'll see you all tomorrow."

As the rest of the team rose and left the table Alayna turned those startling indigo eyes on him.

"You're coming with me, cowboy."

* * *

Alex flopped into his bed just before 4 a.m., barely bothering to pull sheets and blankets over himself, and letting exhaustion take him.

It felt like he'd been running non-stop for forty-eight hours. In a way, he had, his bout of unconsciousness in the alley notwithstanding. While he could pull that kind of crap when he was twenty-one, his thirty-year-old self was used to keeping more regular hours these days.

Maybe three years with the Bureau had made him soft. God, he hoped not. He was going to need everything he had keep up with the crazy crew he'd met tonight, not to mention add something to this murder investigation and keep his own hide intact in light of all the creatures that might want a piece of it.

Alayna had given him the grand tour of what he had dubbed the Bat Cave. The warehouse had a well-stocked motor pool, training facility, crew quarters and offices. The armory was a little heavy on the medieval weaponry and featured few firearms.

"What's with the museum replicas?" he'd asked Alayna.

Most members of the Mage Corps, it turned out, preferred traditional bladed or blunt weapons. Shifters and vampires could move faster than almost anything in existence and only high-caliber firearms had any chance against their healing abilities.

As for mages, they were usually able to shield themselves from bullets using their powers. Elves and fey could manipulate dimensional rifts and move out of the path of a bullet in the blink of an eye.

Guns were largely impractical and had been deemed by many to be too much of liability in a close fight.

That's not to say there weren't a handful of Desert Eagle

.50 cals, several shotguns and a few high-powered automatic rifles tucked in a case. An assortment of very well cared for sniper rifles, complete with military-grade scopes, were the sole property of Ellie, she told him.

Sleep was calling his name, but thoughts continued to rattle around in his head, distracting him.

It was clear that Alayna had a good setup and a good team. They just weren't ready for a murder investigation on this scale.

"Most of the time, it's one body that turns up and every other vamp or shifter or whatever is more than willing to point fingers at exactly who did it. Everyone knows that we can't afford any scrutiny from sapiens, and they sure as hell don't want the Corps to come knocking," Alayna had said over a dangerously strong cup of coffee in her office.

Most of the time it was easy to track a rogue element, he'd learned. They were typically insane or sloppy, usually both. It was more akin to tracking a rabid animal.

Occasionally, there was a nest of shifters or vamps that let their natures run away with them, or a group of mages that went megalomaniacal and decided to end/take over the world. That's when the doors got kicked in, blades were drawn, and blood was spilled.

But sometimes, perhaps once in a generation, a smart supernatural killer came along.

Everyone on the team had been trained in basic investigative skills, but so far, even with experts in tracking and hacking, they had come up with few usable leads.

With the case files spread out in front of him, Alayna had outlined what they knew and the conclusions she and the team had come to. Unfortunately for all of them, he agreed with the assessment.

1. They were dealing with a smart killer or killers.

2. There was something more to this case than random killings.

3. And someone was playing with them.

When they were discussing those case files he'd seen something in her face, some small moment of vulnerability. For all their training, for all their expertise, for all their general badassery, this team was up against something new, different and just a little bit scary.

Alex had been there a time or two. So many times in Afghanistan, they never knew what they would find around the next bend in the road, behind the next door, down the next alley. He could only pack his med bag, load his weapon and hope that training, guts, and brains would be enough to get through the mission.

But for Alayna, it was different. She had obviously taken the weight of this on herself. That was a hazard of leadership and he'd seen it before. She was blaming herself for lack of progress. Each new death was like a hammer blow and she couldn't let the team see what it was doing to her.

For some reason, though, she let him see, just for a moment. She was tired, sad, and sick to death of people turning up dead in her town. And she felt like she couldn't talk to anyone about it.

He wanted her to talk to him about it.

Ever since that night in the alley, he'd felt an odd connection to this beautiful and enigmatic woman. She was such an odd mix of pragmatic seriousness and toughness, blended with a wicked sense of humor and bursts of enthusiasm and optimism. And that tantalizing glimpse of something softer, something almost wounded, made him want to know everything about her.

What made her tick?

And what would it be like to touch her, to let his fingers play over that pale skin? Would she blush? What would it feel like to run his hands through that silken hair? Wrap it around his fist?

Whoa, dude. Back up.

It had been a long time since he'd let his thoughts drift in that direction, particularly about someone he was working with. Not since Kelly.

No! He wouldn't go there. He'd promised himself that he would keep his night-time hours free from thoughts of those who hadn't made it back. It was vital for his sanity. He could think about them when the sun was up and suffer few consequences, but in the wee hours, if he allowed those ghosts into his thoughts he might not sleep for days.

His thoughts settled on Alayna again and he relaxed, remembering the way her hand felt on his face that night in the alley, cool and soft, and how her lips had felt against his, warm and luscious. A pleasant warmth took up residence in his chest at the thought.

The tension was leaving his body, and he felt himself sinking into the mattress. As his scattered, spinning thoughts turned to dreams, he was hit with an image of a little girl with long pale blonde hair, almost silver.

She was sitting on the side of a mountain, green spring grass waving in the wind. A basket with sandwiches and plastic cups sat beside her. She was having tea with a dragon.

* * *

Early the next morning, Alex was just hitting his stride on the treadmill when his phone rang.

It was his boss. It was so unusual to get a call from Agent Sam Allen, especially on a Sunday, that Alex immediately killed the treadmill and hopped off.

"Martinez," he answered.

"I just got an urgent memo from on high that you've been reassigned. Did you know anything about this?" Sam asked.

Sam was a relatively low-level agent, assigned to manage the handful of agents in the Austin field office. When Alex had first gone to work for him, he'd thought he was nothing but a pencil pusher who had been passed over for better assignments. Fiftyish and balding, with a mustache and a bit of a paunch, Sam wasn't going to win many fights. As he'd gotten to know him, though, Alex came to understand that Sam was actually a hell of an investigator, with a near-legendary attention to detail. Give Sam a pile of documents seized from some shady operator, and he could put together a case in one afternoon that would make federal prosecutors weep with joy.

"I haven't heard a word about it," Alex said, a deep frown creasing his brow. This was going to throw a hell of a wrench in his chances of finding out who killed Blanca. And how was Alayna going to teach him to hide his lìthseach nature? An odd sense of disappointment hit him at the thought of not seeing Alayna again. "Where have I been posted this time?"

"Right here in town," Sam said. "Some special task force."

Sam was quiet for a moment and Alex knew he was compulsively rubbing the corner of his mustache, a move he'd seen him do a thousand times when Sam was mulling something over.

"This is really weird, Alex. I know everything that goes on in this town, and I haven't heard word one about a special task force. The memo doesn't even list an address for your new assignment, just a phone number for you to call to get instructions."

Sam rattled off a number, and Alex saved it in his phone.

"Watch your back, Alex. This is some kind of clandestine shit. Holler if it hits the fan."

Alex thanked him and signed off with assurances that he would check in with Sam later if he could.

Curious, Alex punched in the number. On the third ring he heard the tell-tale click that indicated a forwarding program had kicked in. A few seconds later, Alayna's voice came over the line.

"Did you get my memo?" She was smiling; he could hear it in her voice.

"So, you're the special task force I've been assigned to? How did you make that happen? I thought you weren't connected to the government."

"Technically, we're not," she replied, her serious tone kicking in. "But we have plenty of people placed at all levels. It helps to keep all channels open."

Alex was silent for a moment, trying once again to process just how much his life had changed in a single weekend.

"Alex, you cool with this?"

Not entirely, he wasn't. What was this going to do to his FBI career? He'd worked so hard to get here, to put this life together. He'd fought hard for it. For an agent with high ambitions, every assignment was critical. How would it look if his file had time unaccounted for on a clandestine operation that certainly wouldn't have any case notes or performance reviews attached?

At the same time, Alayna was his best chance at finding Blanca's killer and clearing his conscience. That was more important than a temporary blip in his career. If he didn't have to split his time between his white collar crimes case load, he could devote a hundred percent to this case. And as soon as this case was wrapped up, his career could pick up where he left off.

"Please tell me my personnel file says I've been reassigned to the X-Files."

"I can't confirm or deny that." The smile had returned to her voice. "See you tonight, Agent."

6

Chapter 6

Alex pulled his truck into the garage at HQ and killed the engine. Alayna had texted him and told him that he'd be meeting with Lu, the team's recon and equipment specialist.

He moved across the open garage space to the training area. HQ appeared deserted. He guessed the rest of the team hadn't made it in yet.

Alex found Lu sweeping around the edge of a training mat, her broom moving in quick, precise strokes. Her hair was pulled up, and she wore a faded Clash T-shirt and jeans.

"Hey Alex," she said without looking up. "I'm just finishing a little cleaning. We'll get started in a minute."

"That's cool," he said, trying to relax the tension in his shoulders. "Is there are chore wheel I need to sign up for, or something?"

She laughed. "Nah. Alayna hired a local shifter mom to come in and do the cleaning around here. It used to be my job, though, and it kind of relaxes me. Especially when I'm having a hard day."

Lu finally looked up as she trudged to a closet and tucked the

70

broom inside. Her shoulders were a little slumped and she had dark circles under her eyes.

"Hard day?"

"Well, worse than some, but not as bad as others," she said cryptically, a small smile tugging at one corner of her mouth.

She visibly shook herself, almost like a dog, and her expression brightened a little.

"Alayna asked me to put you through some skills assessments, see what you bring to the table besides your investigative skills, a complete disregard for personal safety, and your good looks."

Alex tensed. He was so far out of his element that he wasn't sure how he was supposed to react to the "good looks" comment.

"Uh…" was all he could manage.

"Chill, dude. I'm not coming on to you. I don't poach."

One of his eyebrows went up quizzically. He wasn't seeing anyone, but decided to let the comment slide. Integrating with new teams could be so awkward.

Lu moved around him and headed down a hall.

"Gun range is up first," she said over her shoulder as he followed.

She keyed in a code on a numerical keypad and they stepped into a room. The lights came up as they entered, controlled by motion sensors. An impressive array of firearms and weapons filled the walls.

"Welcome to the armory. Pick a handgun and an assault rifle and we'll get started."

He pulled back his jacked to reveal the 1911 holstered under his arm. Lu nodded and tossed him a box of .45 hollow points and some extra mags. Setting them aside, he headed straight for the M-16 and pulled it off the rack. It was like shaking hands with an old friend. He collected more extra mags and ammunition and sat on a stool to start loading. Lu joined him, snapping cartridges into a magazine with practiced efficiency.

Before the silence could stretch, Alex dove in with a question. Lu was a talker, and he hoped he could find out more information about this team he'd be working with.

"How did you end of working for Alayna? You said you started as a cleaner?"

Lu breathed out a laugh and said, "That crazy puta saved my life."

Alex kept his eyes on loading up the mags.

"She scraped me off the floor of a meth house on the east side, strung out and bleeding from the beating my drug dealer boyfriend had just given me."

Lu launched into the story. Max had been a shifter and Lu's boyfriend/dealer/pimp. Alayna's team had come busting into that meth house like dark angels. Seems Max had killed a street level pusher and Alayna got wind of it. As the team came tearing through the house, Lu had actually taken a swing at Alayna, who'd put the shifter on the floor as easily as breathing.

"She was such a fucking badass. Max ran a pretty ruthless crew of shifters, and Alayna and the team put every one of them in handcuffs or a body bag that night."

Max had ended up under the Mountain, the maximum security prison the Council maintained for magical creatures. Lu had been offered a choice: jail or rehab.

"I picked rehab. Alayna drove all night to this center way out in West Texas that caters to magical creatures. I thought that would be the last time I saw her, but she wrote to me, came to visit. I walked out of that place with a plastic grocery sack with some clothes and a toothbrush and not a dollar to my name. I had no idea where I was going to go," she said, pausing to slap her thigh. "And there was Alayna, waiting at the curb, leaning on that fucking Mustang of hers."

She'd offered Lu a job cleaning the HQ and one of the dorm-like crash rooms to live in. It turned out that cleaning really relaxed Lu. It was sort of like zen meditation, she said. As she focused on her recovery, Alayna had showed her how to get her GED online, take college classes.

"Alayna always encouraged me. It was like there was nothing she thought I couldn't do."

Pretty soon she was ordering and maintaining equipment for the team. She and Alayna also started working on Lu's shifting ability. Lu had been raised by wolf shifter parents, but as they started working, she discovered she could do birds, cats, small mammals, just about anything. That kind of ability was unheard of in the shifter world.

"When our last recon guy quit the team, Alayna offered me the job when he was barely out the door."

"She sounds like an amazing boss."

"You don't know the half of it. It's actually really unusual to have non-mages on a Mage Corps team. All of us have pasts that are, shall we say, problematic. Except for Burdock. He's a Boy Scout," Lu said. "But it was a big career risk for Alayna to hire us, and she did it anyway."

That info made Alex's ears perk up.

"Does she usually take a lot of risks?" He asked, careful to keep is voice neutral.

"Only with herself," Lu replied. "Nature of the beast I guess."

When his eyes snapped up to meet hers, Lu looked ever so slightly panicked, like she'd said too much.

"Air mages," she said with a shrug. "Never look before they leap. Because they can kind of fly."

Alex was pretty sure there was more to it than that, but decided to wait for more info.

Snapping one last cartridge into a magazine, Lu rose from the bench.

"Come on, *bato*. Let's see what you got."

* * *

Alex ran into Alayna as he emerged from the range, his button-down shirt splattered with fake blood.

"Cut it a little close?" She pointed to the simulated gore.

"Close enough," he said. "Lu is a tricky range master. One of her little contraptions snuck up behind me and almost took me out at the knees before I could tag it."

The contraptions had been made from ballistic gel and red corn syrup. Targets of various sizes were rigged on tracks along the floor, walls and ceiling. They were designed to come whistling out of the darkness and scare the crap out of anyone on the range floor.

"He did really well, Commander," Lu called from behind him. "He's as good as Burdock," she continued, dropping her voice to a whisper, "and maybe a little better. His scores put him as the top marksman for the team."

Alayna whistled, clearly impressed.

"I thought you were a medic. Why does a medic need to shoot well?"

He laughed. "My personal brand of preventative medicine was rounds downrange. Fewer bad guys means fewer ways my people could get hurt."

"Change into something comfortable and meet me on the training mat. You're handy with a gun—let's see how you are with hand-to-hand."

That had Alex smiling. Hand-to-hand had always come easily to him throughout his Army and FBI training. Alayna might be in for a bit of a surprise.

After changing into a pair of sweatpants and T-shirt, he found Alayna already on the mat, still wearing the black cargo pants and matching T-shirt that he was beginning to think of as her uniform.

"Shoes on or off?" he asked.

"How many street fights have you gotten into in your bare feet?"

Leaving his running shoes on, he stepped on to the blue training mat, which was inset into the concrete floor of the warehouse. Alayna waited in the center, her stance relaxed.

A palm-heel strike was flying at his face before he could blink. It looked like his new boss wasn't wasting any time in trying to take his head off. He dropped his head and torso to the right to avoid the strike, his right hand coming across his body to deflect the blow.

He allowed his momentum to carry him further right, stepping close to try for an elbow to the side of her head. She dodged beneath it and aimed a punch for his kidney, but he was fast enough to twist and move his opposite forearm to block.

It continued like that for several minutes, each landing a rare kick here or a punch there. Suddenly, Alayna dropped low and swept her leg across the back of his ankles, catching him off guard and landing him flat on his back. The breath left his lungs in a rush and he struggled to roll to his side.

Alayna was on him in an instant, completing the roll for him, slamming his face into the mat. Without rising from her crouched position, she snaked an arm beneath his neck and around his windpipe, cutting off his air. One knee pressed into the small of his back, bending him backwards and her right leg wrapped around his hip.

He struggled for a second before realizing that he was truly stuck. He tapped her arm three times as he started to see spots.

She released the hold, but her hands lingered on him, heating his skin through his T-shirt. Her breath fanned the back of his neck, and he almost shivered.

"You have to be faster," she said sharply, disengaging so fast she nearly pushed away from him.

"I was holding my own," he replied as he caught his breath and wiped sweat from his face.

"I was warming up," she said.

They continued like that for nearly an hour. Alex could hold his own in a stand-up fight, but Alayna had a bag of dirty tricks that would make Navy SEALs envious. She was able to throw him into two joint locks and pinned him twice more.

As they stood once again, she said, "Last shot. Give me everything you've got, cowboy."

He moved in next to her, deflecting a strike at his head, and twisted her into a wrist lock that she shouldn't have been able to get out of. She flicked her fingers in his eyes in a loose strike that had him dodging and she was able to slip the hold. A backhand strike landed squarely in his throat and he staggered back, gasping as his trachea nearly collapsed.

He found himself on his back again, not knowing how he got there. Alayna was straddling his waist, pinning his wrists to the mat. He couldn't breathe, and not just because of the throat punch. He could feel the heat of her against his stomach through the pants she wore.

His pulse pounded, and if he was honest with himself, it

wasn't just from the exertion of the fight. Her clean scent, like mountain air in winter, wrapped around him. Strands of her platinum hair had escaped from her ponytail and fell over her shoulder to tickle his face.

Those eyes locked with his and heat bloomed across his skin, pooling in his limbs, making them heavy.

"We're done," Alayna said, springing to her feet.

She picked up a towel from the edge of the mat and dabbed her face, though she didn't appear to be sweating.

She turned, tossed him a towel and said, "I think you've got a good shot at not getting your throat ripped out on the first day, but those hand-to-hand skills need some work. The whole point of bringing you on was to keep you from getting killed. Four days a week, I want to see you for an hour on the mat, understood?"

"Yes, ma'am," he responded, a small smile touching his lips.

As bruised as he was, he would be glad to let her toss him around. She could pin him anytime she wanted. But it was as close as they could ever get. As soon as this case was over, he was going back to his real life, he reminded himself. This was not his world, and he did not belong here. This training session had proved that.

Alayna hooked the towel around her neck and headed for the locker room.

"Don't feel too bad," Dumeril's voice said from the garage area.

Alex turned to see his tall, dark-skinned form roll out from under one of the cars on a mechanic's board. He stood with languorous grace and sauntered over to where Alex was massaging a sore shoulder that Alayna had nearly yanked out its socket.

"She happens to be one of the most accomplished hand-to-hand fighters in the Mage Corps. She's trained with masters in Karate, Kung-Fu, Krav Maga and more styles that I can't pronounce," he said. "She's had to."

"I don't understand. If she can do magick, why does she need this stuff?"

"The same reason the Army trains in hand-to-hand when they have guns: sometimes it's all you have," Dumeril replied. "And besides, Alayna's a Whisperer. Her magick is not exactly a combat asset."

"I don't know what a Whisperer is, but I watched her take that vampire apart the other night by shooting lightning from her hands," Alex said.

"And if Nick hadn't just had the ass kicking of a lifetime, if he'd been just a little faster, Alayna might have had her throat torn out," he responded. "The Whisperers are, at the same time, the weakest and strongest members of the Mage Corps."

"Why is that?"

"Whisperers are labeled air mages, but they're really not. Other mages can control one element with nothing but a thought. Whisperers can control all the elements, and then some, but they have to use their voice. It takes longer. That's a liability in combat."

He paused briefly, meeting Alex's eyes with a steady look, like he was considering his next words.

"But given enough time, they can weave spells of terrifying power," Dumeril said. "Hence, the weakest and the strongest."

"So, why does she need to know how to fight so well when she could rain down holy hell on the bad guys?"

Dumeril turned and started to head back to the garage.

"Why drop a nuclear bomb when a knife in the dark will do?" he said quietly.

7

Chapter 7

Alayna stuck her head under the hot, pounding spray of the locker room shower and let it wash through her long hair and over her shoulders, taking the scent of Alex with it.

She'd been short with him at the end of the workout, but being that close to him had put her on edge. Everything about him, his dark dancing eyes, his easy smile, the feel of his hard muscles under her hands, had reminded her that it had been weeks since she'd gotten laid.

There just hadn't been time lately to go out to the bars. Because she was a Whisperer, male mages wouldn't touch her. Why get involved with someone who almost certainly wouldn't live to see their thirtieth birthday?

So she picked up sapien men in bars. She'd pick out the best looking, shallowest guy in the place, have a few drinks with him, and strongly suggest they go back to his place. It wasn't like they could go to hers. They never got her real name, but they always had a lot of fun. Come morning, she'd ghost before the guy woke up and promptly forget all about him.

But Alex was different. He was charming and funny, and she liked being around him. Too much. It was becoming hard to forget what his mouth felt like against hers. While it was tempting to act on her attraction, she wouldn't. First off, she didn't sleep with people she worked with. That was a hard and fast rule. Second, the guy had kind of put his life in her hands, and it would feel like taking advantage. Third, she was destined for an early grave, and it wasn't fair to get involved with anyone.

And they would get involved, if she made a move on him. Alex was not the kind of guy she could just fuck and forget. He was the kind of guy she could care about. That would tie her to this world and that was a complication she could not afford.

He'd actually done surprisingly well today, given that he didn't have the reflexes, strength, or speed of any of the magickal races, but she couldn't let him know that. She'd lost good personnel because they got cocky, complacent or arrogant. That wasn't going to happen to Alex. He would become the deadliest fighter she could mold him into, even if their workouts left her tied in frustrated knots.

Shutting off the water, Alayna quickly toweled off, used a few whispered words to draw the moisture from her hair and threw on a clean T-shirt and cargo pants. She found the rest of the team already gathered in the conference room. A freshly showered Alex was with them, his dark hair wet and glistening, some of it falling over his brow. Her fingers itched to brush it back.

"I'd like to review where we are so far with these murder cases," Alayna said, mentally shaking herself and stepping over to a wall that served as a white board.

Pictures of the six victims were posted in a row across the top, their names, when available, were written beneath in different colored marker. Photos of the scenes were taped below them. Colored lines that corresponded to the different victims connected documents, photos and names written and posted on the board.

"I'll do the victim rundown, since I handled the exams on the ones we found and reviewed the reports for the ones APD found," Dumeril said.

Six dead bodies. All the victims were under thirty. Five women and one man. The first three victims had been found in very remote locations and Alayna and her team had gotten to them first. The last three had all been left around Lady Bird Lake, right in the heart of downtown. By some miracle, the team had gotten to them first. They hadn't been so lucky with Blanca. All of the victims were Latina or Latino. All had signs of severe neck wounds. All had been in the country without documentation, except for Blanca.

Blanca Rodriquez was the aberration, as Alex had noted earlier. She was a fresh kill, hours old, dumped out in the open for any sapien wandering by to see. The other bodies had been moderately to severely decomposed when they'd been found.

Looking over the photos and scenes, it was clear their killer had a type.

"These body dumps have gotten progressively more brazen. That's not a good sign." Alex said, his gaze lingering on Blanca's photo. "What else have we got?"

Ellie spoke up.

"Based on what the commander got out of Salvadin, I've been doing some checking—and by checking I mean completely illegal hacking—into some of Jimmy Medina's businesses and accounts. Medina Trucking is a gigantic operation, so it's going to take some time to go through everything, but my gut says not all of those trucks are going where they're supposed to," she said. "As for the bars and some of his other side businesses, those look mostly legit. All of his properties check out. But it just doesn't feel right. I'll keep digging, but unless we have a few years to wait around for the results, I'm going to need more to go on."

"Thanks, Ellie," Alayna said.

Lu chimed in that she was organizing remote video surveillance for some of Medina's businesses. Burdock remained silent.

"So," Alex said. "We're lacking witnesses to these murders and any substantial physical evidence. All we've got to go on is the word of a low-life lackey that one of the richest guys in the city left Revelations covered in blood the night Blanca died. Do I have that about right?"

Alayna nodded.

Alex got up and crossed to the taped up pictures. His fingers absently touched the photo of a smiling Blanca.

"How much do we know about the victims?" he asked, looking over the photos of decomposed bodies.

Next to nothing, it turned out.

"Follow the victims," Alex said. "When you know more about them, you'll know more about who killed them. If you can trace their steps, you might find out what happened to them."

He turned back to the board.

"This might sound stupid, but is there anything in the hocus pocus department that might help us out here? Can you conjure up a vision, talk to a ghost or something?" Alex asked.

Dumeril snorted and Ellie laughed out loud.

Alayna shot them a look and said matter-of-factly, "Visions don't work like that. They're uncontrollable and unreliable even on the best of days and no one here is practiced at scrying. As for ghosts, a spirit with enough of a consciousness left to answer questions is rarer than a two-headed rattlesnake."

Most "ghosts" were just emotional echoes of an event, like a piece of recording stuck on a loop.

"Even if you could find a ghost, you'd need a Seer to see and communicate with the spirit. The Mage Corps lost its last Seer about a hundred years ago."

Seers were sapiens that were born with or developed the ability to see and speak with the dead. They were about as rare as a lithseach and were highly sought after.

"Ellie, stay on hacking Medina's network. See if you can get into his cell phone. Lu, stay on the video surveillance. Dumeril and Burdock, you're researching our victims. Track down contacts for next of kin, friends, enemies. We'll arrange for interviews later. Start establishing timelines for each of them," Alayna said. "Alex, you're with me. I've thought of a possible witness we need to talk with."

* * *

Alayna pulled her jacket collar tighter against the chilly February air as she and Alex left the Mustang in a parking lot near the hike and bike trail that ran along the shore of Lady Bird Lake. At this time of night, the dirt trail was deserted, with only faint blue emergency lights at foot level illuminating the trail.

Though it was right in the heart of downtown, with the glittering skyscrapers towering over them, it was heavily wooded and secluded.

They made their way down the trail for about a quarter of a mile until they came to a low spot near the bank where the water lapped, inky black in the darkness.

"What are we doing exactly?" Alex whispered.

"Questioning a possible witness," Alayna said. "Who just happens to be a river spirit."

"Oh, good. Something easy, at least," he said, the sarcasm clear in his voice.

"Actually, yeah," Alayna said, tossing a smile over her shoulder as she moved to the water's edge.

She bent down and scooped her hand through the water, sending an arc splashing across the surface.

"Llorona! Alayna Blackwell, Mage of the Council, summons you," she shouted across the still water. "Now, get your soggy ass out here. I need to ask you some questions."

The ring of her voice died in the air, and silence descended around them again. A minute ticked by with only the sound of frogs and crickets in the distance. Llorona loved to keep people waiting.

Suddenly, several large air bubbles broke the surface of the dark water. Slowly, a shape appeared about ten feet from shore, a black dome gently rising above the surface of the water.

Gradually, the apparition rose, revealing a creature with long, waterlogged black hair hanging over fish-belly white skin. Her hands dripped black river mud as did the toes that protruded beneath a ruined and tattered off-white dress—toes that hovered several inches above the lake's surface.

She felt Alex tense beside her and suck in a breath. His eyes had widened slightly, but that was the only outward sign of his fear.

The creature's face was mostly hidden by its dripping hair, but Alayna could see black empty eye sockets in a bloated face covered in dark veins. Her mouth was a dark hole with blue, swollen lips pulled back over green teeth.

The Weeping Woman, or La Llorona as the Spanish and Mexican settlers of the area had named her, had answered her summons.

Legends about Llorona were everywhere. Some said she was the spirit of a woman who had drowned her children. The reason for the drowning was always different depending on who was telling it, from revenge on a cheating husband to just plain madness.

Others said she was a witch who had been drowned in the river by angry townspeople. Parents used the story of La Llorona to keep children away from rivers and lakes by telling them that the weeping woman would snatch them and drown them if they got too close to the water's edge.

The legends, it turned out, were right on that point and wrong on most of the others. The spirit of the rivers of Texas was much older than the legends about her. She was as old as the rivers themselves, possibly older.

The ancient spirit could appear in many forms, like a beautiful woman, an elderly man, but her favorite was the terrifying river corpse look.

"What do you want, airwalker?" Llorona's voice was little more than a hiss.

"A few weeks ago, someone dumped a dead body, a young woman, under the bridge north of here. Did you see anything?" Alayna asked.

The creature's voice hissed, "I see everything that touches my water."

Alayna paused for a moment. One had to weigh their words carefully when dealing with ancient spirits.

"Can you tell me anything about the people who left that body there?"

"I can do better than that," the creature hissed. Before she could blink, the creature had closed the distance between them and hovered inches from her. Her fetid breath stirred the tendrils of hair around Alayna's face.

"I can show you. For a price."

"What's it going to be this time?"

"Blood," the creature hissed. "Just a few drops."

"You know I can't do that," Alayna answered.

"Tears, then. Yours always taste so sweet."

"Deal."

Alayna knelt by the edge of the water and pulled a small glass vial from her pocket and thought of the saddest thing she could.

Slowly, tears welled at the corners of her eyes and she caught each of them in the vial. As she took a deep breath, there was a shuddering in her throat as she tried to suppress a sob. She thought she'd covered it until Alex put his hand on her shoulder. Shock coursed through her for a moment, a strange heat following in its wake. Comforting gestures were a foreign concept to her, and she had no idea what to do. But it felt good, so she left his hand there.

Llorona's icy flesh slid along Alayna's cheek, cupping her chin in a putrescent hand, a hiss of pleasure on her dark lips.

Alex's hand tightened on her shoulder as he prepared to pull her away. His protectiveness was just as foreign as his comfort. Only her team had ever protected her because of who she was to them. Everyone else tried to protect her because of what she was.

She reached up with her free hand and wrapped her fingers around his to reassure him that she was fine. The slight roughness of the calluses on his hand grounded her enough.

The vial was soon full. She capped it and handed it to Llorona.

"A treat for later," Llorona said as the vial disappeared into the folds of her sodden dress.

She touched Alayna's face again, in a disgusting parody of a caress and said, "Do you still think of your father when I ask for tears? Does it still cause you so much pain?"

Alayna jerked her face away and growled, "Show me what you promised."

"Very well."

Llorona floated back and images began flickering in the surface of the water, like reflections, rippling with the slight movements of the water. In the images Congress Street Bridge towered overhead. The headlights of a car were reflected off the pillars of the bridge as a vehicle was parking in a lot a few yards from the water. She could make out part of a license plate.

Two men appeared near the bank of the lake, moving in from the direction of the headlights. Both had muscular builds. One had short dark hair, the other a sandy brown and shaggy cut. Dark Hair had a sheet wrapped bundle thrown over his shoulder. He carried it as if it weighed no more than a feather pillow. Vampires.

Dark Hair swung the bundle off his shoulder and let it hit the ground. Sandy grabbed the edge of the sheet, and Blanca Rodriguez's bloody corpse tumbled out of the unrolling sheet, splashing one grey-fleshed hand into the water.

Alex's jaw clenched hard, and his lips pulled back in a snarl as he tensed beside her. A slight tremor went through him, but it wasn't fear. It was rage. His friend had been tossed out like garbage. Vengeance was written in those dark eyes.

"Looks good to me," Dark Hair told Sandy. The images apparently came with sound.

The two quickly turned and left, the images fading quickly in the black water.

"Satisfied, airwalker?" Llorona hissed.

"Yes," Alayna answered, her voice quiet.

She picked herself up from the gravel shore and dusted the knees of her cargo pants.

"Until next time, Llorona."

"I'll be here," the spirit said, a lightness touching her voice that made Alayna think she might have been making a joke. A bubbling hiss followed them up the bank as they returned to the trail. It sounded almost like laughter.

* * *

Alex seethed with anger as they walked in silence back to the Mustang. Watching what had happened to Blanca had set rage burning through his chest. She'd been tossed out like yesterday's trash, that neck wound a red scream against her flesh.

Adding to the impotent rage was the image of that creature touching Alayna. He'd had to fight every instinct not to rip her away from the thing, until his body had nearly trembled with the effort.

Alayna's tears had dried, leaving her face a little puffy and splotchy. Alex thought it made her look adorable—and a touch vulnerable. He was pretty sure that she didn't cry very often, and definitely not in front of other people.

They got in the Mustang and she sat for a long, silent moment, hands on the wheel, not making a move to start the car.

"Why does it make you sad to think about your father?" he asked.

She gave him a shocked look. He couldn't believe he'd just

said that out loud.

"Because he's dead," she said simply.

The silence descended between them, and not the companionable silence he was beginning to enjoy with her. This was strained, but he had to know, was desperate to know more about what made this woman tick. He pressed on because he couldn't leave the tension hanging between them.

"How did he die?"

She shot him a look that said she was thinking about biting his head off and eating his guts for dinner.

He wisely kept his mouth shut and waited. With a sigh, she sank back into the leather driver's seat. The long day and night had carved dark circles under her eyes.

"Violently," she answered. "Like most mages, he died violently, far from home. I was eight."

She still hadn't started the car. Her posture was hunched and her fingers drummed against the steering wheel as she thought. He kept his mouth shut, giving her the mental space to decide.

"He was a fire mage, a ranger, one of the best. He went on missions all over the world, fighting the enemies of the Council. He and some other rangers were sent to eliminate a group of rogue mages. They were trying to raise something," she said. "Something from another realm. No one was very clear about what exactly."

Her eyes were fixed on something distant, maybe something twenty years distant.

"Everyone at the Academy had parents serving in the Corps. It wasn't unusual for someone to be pulled out of class to learn one of their parents wasn't coming home. We all lived with that fear. It didn't make it any easier when my brother Xander showed up with the news. One look at his face and I knew.

"He told me our father had died bravely. I've been living with the ghost of that ever since. We all have."

"My dad was a cop in San Antonio," Alex said. "He was shot to death on a routine traffic stop."

Her face softened and she said, "I'm sorry."

"I've lived most of my life as the son of a dead hero," Alex said. "So I get it."

"It's like living in a shadow you can never escape."

"And everyone is watching to see if you'll live up to what he did."

He'd been six. Old enough to remember his father and old enough to feel the weight of everyone's expectations. He now had to live the life his father had never had the chance to experience and he had to live up to his heroic sacrifice. An impossible order, but one he'd done his best to fill. There were a lot of days when he felt like he had failed miserably.

"Jeez, enough of this sad stuff," she said, starting the Mustang and throwing it in drive. "Let's get a drink."

* * *

Alayna sipped her venti Italian dark roast coffee in its cheerful green and white cup, letting the heat soak into her hands.

She'd given Ellie the partial license plate she'd seen in Llorona's vision. While Ellie ran the plate and tried to find a match for the vehicle that had been used to dump Blanca's body, she and Alex sat on a darkened street south of the river.

They could have gone back to headquarters to wait, but the truth was she liked being alone with Alex, and she wasn't ready for the night to end.

An occasional car passed, bathing them in slowly sliding white or yellow light.

The silence was companionable, punctuated only by the sound of their breathing and the usual sounds of the city in the early morning hours: crickets, sirens, a car alarm, and the drone of a tree frog in a nearby greenbelt.

Alayna's mind was not so peaceful. Internally, she cursed Llorona for dredging up the ghost of her father. His death had ripped her world apart and that was when her family had begun to fracture. Her mother had lost herself in her work as a healer, trying to save others as she had not been able to save her mate. Alayna's brothers and sister had retreated into their own pain, shutting each other out.

And she was going to die, just like her father, probably sooner rather than later. It was why she would never have children. Why she would never have a real relationship. She wouldn't cause someone else the kind of pain she'd endured. Especially someone like Alex. He deserved happiness.

"So…this Academy you mentioned, where you learned to use magick," Alex said, his deep voice breaking her out of her maudlin thoughts. "Did it have moving staircases?"

"Ha ha, very funny," Alayna said, taking a sip of her coffee. She'd dumped an insane amount of sugar in it, making her teeth ache slightly. Using magick burned calories like a furnace. "It wasn't anywhere close to Hogwarts. The Academy was patterned after the Spartan agogi. Later, they added a program similar to Navy SEAL training, just for funsies."

Just like the military schools of ancient Sparta, the Academy took mage children from their families at age seven to begin training. Attendance at the boarding school, which was located high in the Rocky Mountains in Colorado, was mandatory.

Early years focused on the basic education most school kids

received: history, mathematics, writing. There were intense martial arts classes for several hours a day. When a student came of age and developed their powers, much of the school day was devoted to practicing techniques to control their abilities. They studied strategy, military tactics and learned about the non-sapien races, the ones they would potentially face in combat as full members of the Mage Corps.

While every student learned how to fight, many would never have the talent to serve on the front lines. They learned to become healers, logicians, ritual mages who could funnel limited power into divination spells and the like. Some would go on to live very normal lives by sapien standards, infiltrating key agencies around the globe to protect the interests of the Council. They would watch, observe and manipulate in small ways, like Alex's convenient reassignment to a special task force.

"That still makes me very nervous," Alex told her.

"It shouldn't," she said, glad for the distraction of his conversation. "The primary objective of those mages is not to blow their cover. They watch, they report, they act in very small ways. And believe me when I say that they do everything they can to avoid conflict. They're not like sleeper agents. In fact, they've managed to stop a few wars."

"Really?"

"Wars cause a lot of problems, you know, besides the death and destruction," she said. "Wars bring all the bad things out of the woodwork. All that chaos makes it too easy for them to prey on battered, wounded and defenseless sapiens. At the same time, it makes it hard for mages and members of the Corps to move around safely and undetected."

She paused for a moment, considering how much she should tell him.

"And wars can cause…openings," she said quietly.

Alex gave her a look that was becoming quite common between them, the one that said she was going to have to elaborate for the newbie.

"The strife, the pain, the destruction of war, it can leave scars on a place," she said. "You're a soldier, I know you've seen it."

He nodded. "I've seen places like that. I always thought it was me projecting my own feelings on the place."

"You weren't imagining it. Those scarred places, sometimes bad things, angry spirits mostly, can collect there. Predators that feed off pain and death are drawn to those places. Peace is always our primary objective. It just makes our jobs so much easier."

"A worthy goal, but I know firsthand how badly things can go for peacekeepers," Alex said, sipping his coffee.

"I told you about my school, why don't you tell me about yours?" she said, changing the subject.

"Not much to tell really," he said, looking out the window as if he was seeing something else. In profile, he was striking, with a strong jaw and brow. "I grew up in a working class neighborhood in San Antonio. After dad died, mom went back to work as a teacher. I have a little sister. We didn't have a whole lot growing up, but we had each other."

Alayna envied him that.

"I wanted to go to medical school and become a doctor." A note of derision crept into his voice, like it had been a foolish idea. "The Army offered me the money to do it."

And it had offered him the opportunity to live up to his father's heroic legacy, she thought.

"It didn't exactly work out the way I planned," he said.

Just then, Alayna's phone pinged softly. It was Ellie. Alayna took the call, inwardly cursing. She wanted to find out more about why he wasn't saving lives in a hospital right now instead of chasing a killer with her.

"What's up?" She tried to keep the irritation out of her voice.

"Ran that partial plate. Got a few possible matches. One is likely, but…I'm running into a tangle of shell companies here. I don't think I'm going to have anything for you to check out tonight, Commander. You should come on back to HQ."

"Roger that, we're heading back in."

She was reluctant to let Alex go and leave the quiet, dark space where it was safe to say things she'd never said out loud to anyone else. But she'd just lost her excuse.

8

Chapter 8

Two nights later, Alex found himself riding shotgun in Alayna's Mustang, shielding his eyes from the setting sun. He had been working nearly nonstop, only leaving HQ to sleep. They'd been driving for several minutes when he realized that they weren't headed to the warehouse. Alayna had pulled the 'stang on to northbound Interstate 35 and had long since missed the turnoff for HQ.

"What's up? Where are we going?"

"I have someone I want you to meet," she answered.

When she didn't elaborate, he decided not to press. Alayna usually told him when he needed to know something. Besides, she was relaxed, having bled off the nervous energy she normally carried in her shoulders and hands. A smile lit her features, and the evening air was blowing through her hair as she opened up the engine. The setting sun turned her pale skin gold and he was very aware of how close she was, his blood heating despite the chill in the air.

Progress on the case had been frustratingly slow and tensions were high. It suddenly didn't seem important to press her about where they were going.

He trusted her, he realized.

After about forty minutes, Alayna signaled and took an exit just north of Round Rock. They were in the odd empty space between Round Rock, Austin's largest suburb, and the southern edge of Georgetown, an old historic ranching town about an hour north of the city.

They were surrounded by open fields with a smattering of red and white Hereford cows quietly grazing. She maneuvered the car through the freeway underpass and drove by the entrance to the Inner Space Caverns.

The Caverns had been discovered decades before when crews were blasting to build the interstate highway. They had stumbled on a series of caves with beautiful formations of stalactites and stalagmites formed by the dripping of mineral-rich water over several thousand years.

After the discovery of the Caverns, they had been turned into a cheesy roadside attraction where visitors could tour the caverns, pan for gold and buy overpriced rocks that had been put through a polisher.

Alayna drove past the entrance and pulled off near the gate to a private dirt road.

"The combination is 5678," she told him.

He got the hint and hopped out to open the padlock and the gate. She drove through; he locked it behind them and got back in the Mustang, thoroughly intrigued about where they were going.

They bumped slowly along the dirt road for several minutes. Alex heard Alayna whisper for a few moments and saw the look of concentration come over her face that meant she was weaving a spell. The dust kicked up by the tires settled slowly behind them, leaving the air clear and hiding their presence from any passersby in the growing darkness.

Alayna parked the Mustang on the road, her smile growing and the fading sunlight dancing in her eyes and catching sparks in her hair. God, she was beautiful. And she was excited about something.

Alex couldn't guess who they were there to see. The field that spread out from beside the dirt road went as far as he could see and there were no houses, trailers or other cars.

Alayna grabbed a black duffel bag from the trunk and headed toward a small grove of trees about a hundred yards away down a slight slope.

"Come on," she said, excitement in her voice and a spring in her step.

Alex followed a few steps behind through the knee-high grass, watching her platinum curls bounce against the back of the black T-shirt she wore. This was the most carefree he'd seen her in the many days since they'd met. Sure, he'd seen glimpses of silly moments in the office, when she was teasing Burdock about being too serious or getting in a movie quote battle with Ellie. Alayna had a wicked sense of humor, and it was obvious to him that she made a conscious effort to crack a few jokes around the team to keep spirits up. But those moments were rare beams of sunlight through dark clouds.

Most of the time, her duties pressed her shoulders down and left her frowning at her laptop screen. She'd lift her hair and rub her neck and shoulders in the most sensual way. It drove Alex crazy. He wanted his hands to be the ones rubbing the tension from her shoulders, his fingers running through her hair.

Other times, she'd take her anger and frustration down to the gym and practice with the heavy bags. He'd already seen her tear one old canvas bag that had been repeatedly patched with duct tape wide open, its sand spilling onto the floor. Alayna had unhooked the chains near the top of the bag, tossed it aside and hung a fresh one.

But now, she seemed…lighter. Between her brisk steps toward the grove, Alex could almost swear he saw her skip. Maybe. Just once.

As they neared the trees, Alex could see that it was a small grove of pecan trees that circled a rough ring of stone. Not just stones, it was a cave.

It was nearly impossible to see from the surface, with only a small lip to indicate its presence. The mouth of the cave was huge and plunged straight down into the darkness. Alayna pulled a length of climbing rope from the duffel, looping it around the closest of the pecan trees. She stepped into a harness, pulling it up around her thighs and waist. She eyed Alex and tossed him a larger version. She quickly hooked up carabiners and descenders while Alex got his own harness situated.

"You know how to do a sky drop, right?" she asked.

"Yup, the Army taught me well," Alex said. He didn't say that tying off to a pecan tree would be a lot easier than the helicopter drops that he'd had to do. And this time, no one was shooting at him.

Alayna looped her arms through the duffel and wore it like a backpack. She cracked two glow sticks and dropped them down the mouth of the cavern.

"It's only about forty feet down, and it's a bare, even floor," she said before kicking off the edge and disappearing into the dark, the only sound that accompanied her was the whir of the descender.

Alex clipped in and followed her, well and truly intrigued

about why she suddenly had the urge to go spelunking. He could see Alayna's silhouette against the green glow of the sticks on the floor.

As she reached the bottom, she called, "Hey, Z, it's me. I brought a friend. Don't eat him."

Alex's eyes went a little wide at that. Who could she be talking to, down here in the dark?

A deep rumbling sound, almost past the edge of his hearing, answered from the darkness to his right. A shiver went up Alex's spine. When his boots hit the ground, he unclipped and slipped into a defensive crouch, his hand instantly going to his firearm. Alayna touched his hand in the darkness, and he could see the green glow of the sticks glimmer in her hair as she shook her head.

"He's friendly," she whispered.

She moved away from him, leaving only the ghost of her body heat in the chill of the cave. He heard her rummaging in the duffel bag, and suddenly a lantern flared to life.

The cave was a large dome, with an inky blackness off to the right that looked like an underground lake. The mouth of the cave was a gray circle above them, where the last rays of daylight shone through.

Alex's eyes were beginning to adjust to the darkness. In the lantern light, he could see a shimmer to his right. It could have easily been a deposit of quartz or mica that was glistening in the darkness, but there was a void. Something darker than the cave walls. And the glimmer had a…wet quality to it.

"It's been too long, Little Sparrow."

The voice that came from the darkness sounded like a combination of breaking rocks and wind whistling through cracks.

The glimmer in the corner seemed to detach itself from the cave wall and move closer to them. Alex could hear crunching footsteps moving over the limestone gravel of the cave floor. As it moved into the lantern light, Alex saw the shadow of a massive reptilian head. It was covered in black overlapping scales. Its yellow eyes had a diamond-shaped iris, like a goat's. A set of horns protruded up and back from the top of its head and thin spines and whiskers covered its face. Long, sharp teeth were visible behind its scaly lips.

The creature's muzzle was a couple of feet across and its narrow head was maybe six feet long. The thing brought its nostrils, which sat on top of its muzzle like an alligator's, close to Alex and drew a deep breath. Alex could feel the force of the sniff tug at his clothes a bit.

"Sorry I haven't been by much, Z. I've been busy, trying to solve some murders and all," Alayna answered. "This is Alex. He's working with me."

The mass of black scales moved closer and Alex could see a long, thickly scaled neck. Its two front feet had four padded toes, like a dog or a big cat, and massive black claws that looked like they had been carved from obsidian. It leaned its head closer and sniffed again.

"He is a sapien," the thing rumbled. "But there is something different about him, something I have never smelled before."

Those yellow eyes studied Alex, the diamond iris scanning back and forth.

Alayna moved next to Alex and he could feel the heat of her body beside him.

"Alex, this is Z."

She turned up the intensity of the lantern and it cast its light much farther, much higher.

The thing before him was fully revealed. It had four legs, all with padded feet and wicked claws. The back legs were reverse articulated, like a dog's or a horse. Massive wings were folded along its back, an almost translucent gray, shot through with veins and long structural spines, like a bat. Standing on all four legs, its body was about the size of a short school bus. There was a tail coiled around its back feet, a scary spike with four bladed fins capping the tail. Its whole body was covered in tiny overlapping scales about the size of size of the nail on Alex's pinkie finger. The scales were faceted, like tiny jewels and they glittered in the light.

"Is…is that a.." Alex couldn't bring himself to say it.

"Dragon?" Alayna said. "Yes."

"That's impossible," Alex said. "They don't exist."

"Just like vampires, shape shifters, elves and gnomes?" Alayna said. "Don't believe me? Touch him. He likes to be scratched behind the horns."

Z obligingly laid his head down on the cave floor. The top of his head came up to Alex's chest. He took a deep breath and reached up to scratch the dragon. As he ran his fingernails over the leathery skin at the base of his horns, where there were no scales, the dragon began to growl in the back of his throat. Alex almost jerked his hand back before he realized the dragon was purring.

After a few seconds, the dragon lifted his head slightly and looked at Alex, then to Alayna.

"This one has no magick," he said, a note of incredulity, if that was possible, touching his gravelly voice. "He is a void. The magick slides around him."

"Yes," Alayna said, "He's a lithseach."

"I thought they were a myth," the dragon rumbled.

"A dragon just called me a myth," Alex said in disbelief. He pinched the bridge of his nose, fighting a headache.

Z brought his face close to Alex again. Alex stiffened and held still as the dragon brushed his whiskers and leathery spines over his bare hands and arms. They tickled, and he tried not to shudder.

"There is more," the dragon growled. "There is a well within him. Great and empty. Open it and it will fill."

"What the hell does that mean?" Alex said.

"I do not know. I can only tell you what I sense within you."

Alex turned to Alayna. In the light of the lantern, her face had turned grave. When she caught him looking, she pasted a smile on and moved to the duffel bag.

"Enough of the spooky talk, Z," she said. "It's time for your treats."

She pulled out several plastic grocery sacks and opened one. With a whispered word and a slap to the bottom of the bag, she sent several sandwiches flying into the air. The dragon arched his long neck and snapped them out of the air one by one.

Alex sniffed.

"Peanut butter and jelly?"

"They're his favorite. When I was little, I used to sneak them out of the kitchens at the Academy and take them to him in the middle of the night," Alayna said, a bright smile touching her lips at the memory.

"How did the two of you meet?" God, that question sounded so weird when applied to a witch and a dragon.

"It was about a year after Dad died. My mom and siblings weren't any help and I didn't have any friends. I was kind of doing the reckless self-destructive thing. So, I used to sneak out of the Academy at night. The wind on the mountain peaks was the only thing that seemed to make me feel better."

Z spoke up, "One night, a sudden spring snow storm blew in and brought this tiny creature to my cave."

"We didn't speak each other's languages, at first. But I've always had this crazy ability to pick up other tongues. I was able to pick up Draconic in a few hours and I taught him English."

Alayna looked at him over the top of Z's head, her nails scratching behind his other horn.

"He was a runt and got left behind when the other dragons left this dimension. His tribe had been gone about hundred years when we ran into each other. He was starved for company, which is probably why he didn't eat me on sight. And, honestly, I was pretty eager for a friend myself."

She got that far away look as she remembered.

"We went on midnight flights all over the Rockies, hunting deer and moose. Eventually we didn't even need to speak; we could communicate telepathically."

Alex watched as she grew quiet for a moment.

"He's my familiar," she said. "We didn't know it was happening then, but we were bonding."

"Wait, what's a familiar?"

"Most mages have them. They're usually an animal, a magickal creature, sometimes a spirit that corresponds to their element. They let you store extra energy for spells, talk to them telepathically and some mages can even see through their familiar's eyes."

"I'm guessing it's pretty unusual to have a dragon as a familiar," Alex said.

"I've never heard of it happening before," she said. "The mages hunted the dragons almost to extinction for their scales and bones, which are harder than any material on Earth. Hostility ensued."

Z's rumbling voice interjected again, "I was left behind when I was very young and had not learned to fear mages."

"Wait…" Alex said. He was remembering something, a dream, yeah. A little girl sitting on a green and windswept hillside, having tea with a dragon.

"I had a dream. I think it was about the two of you. The dragon looked just like Z," Alex said. "You were having tea."

A frown creased Alayna's face.

"How could you know that?" Alayna asked, worry creeping into her voice.

She stood from where they had been sitting on the cold gravel, tossing sandwiches to the delighted dragon while they talked.

"I used to have tea parties for Z," she said softly. "When we were still learning each other's languages."

Alex stood, and she whirled on him.

"You picked up some of my memories somehow," she said, a note of accusation in her voice. "It must have been during the memory wipe. That shouldn't be possible!"

"Don't freak out," Alex said. Moving to her, he touched her upper arms, keeping his touch gentle.

"I'm not," she said, not moving away from him. "It's just that…I think I got some of yours too."

He looked into her eyes and took a deep breath. His hands moved to her shoulder blades, bringing her slightly closer.

"What did you see?"

"Blood," she said, her gaze becoming distant. "Sand. Pain. Death. There was shouting. You had needles and tubes, bandages and vials. I think you were healing someone."

Alex felt tightness in his chest. He wished she hadn't seen that. Most of the time, he wished he hadn't seen that either. He took a shuddering breath. The dragon's voice interrupted them.

"The hour grows late," he rumbled, rising to his full height. "I wish to stretch my wings. Does the Little Sparrow wish to stretch hers?"

He craned his long neck around over his shoulder, his eerie yellow eyes glowing in the darkness.

Alayna's distraction was instantly gone, her face coming alive.

"I'll get the gear," she said excitedly.

She pulled some leather rigging from the duffel and set about buckling a harness around Z's broad chest and over his scaly back. The dragon lowered himself to the ground and Alayna leapt atop his back, clipping her climbing harness into the leather rigging. She motioned for Alex to follow.

She leaned down to give him a hand and he placed a foot on Z's elbow to hoist himself up behind her. He knew what was probably going to happen next as Alayna clipped his harness into the back of hers.

"Put your arms around me and hold on tight," she said excitedly.

"Wait a second, are we actually—"

Alex's arms shot around her as he felt Z's weight shift and the massive gossamer wings unfold behind him. He had just a second to think that they were much bigger than he thought they would be before Z gave a massive beat of his wings and undulated his powerful body launching himself into the air.

Alex's stomach dropped as the dragon gave a few more beats of his wings, rising toward the cavern's ceiling, which was dotted with stalactites that threatened to impale them. They moved in a slow circle about the cavern before Z turned for the opening.

It's way too small! Alex thought before Z folded his wings and shot through.

The Mustang was a quickly dwindling red speck in the darkness as they climbed fast, headed for the low ceiling of spring clouds above them. Water droplets collected on his skin as they passed through the clouds and Z leveled out.

Alex could see lights in the distance, peeking in patches through the clouds as they passed overhead. He could see the larger patch of lights just behind them that must be Round Rock. As Z banked softly to the left and turned north, he could make out the lights of Georgetown. Here and there, he could see the lonely green mercury vapor lights that some of the ranch houses kept on.

Soon they'd left it all behind, with only an occasional lonely set of headlights visible on a nearly deserted country road, speeding off in the darkness and completely unaware of the creature that glided silently through the night.

* * *

Alayna was taking too much pleasure in the feel of Alex's strong arms around her waist and the feel of his muscled chest against her back. The heat sinking into her from his body fought off the chill wind that whipped past them.

She'd flown with Z thousands of times over the years and it had never been quite as exhilarating as this. Then again, she'd never taken anyone along on a ride with her before. As underground dwellers, Ellie and Dumeril were suspicious of flying. Burdock was distrustful of dragons—along with almost everything else. Lu could transform into any number of birds or bats and didn't need a dragon to fly her around, thank you very much.

It felt like she couldn't draw enough air into her lungs. It might have been the altitude, but she didn't think so.

There was something about Alex that made her heart race when he was around, especially when he touched her. She'd never been a touchy person. Her parents were so busy with their duties when she was living at home, and then at the Academy she'd been kept largely separate from her siblings. She'd always suspected that her being a Whisperer had made her untouchable to the people around her, whether it was conscious or unconscious.

An odd thought occurred to her. Alex had touched her more in the past few days than almost anyone else in her life.

Her thoughts drifted back to what he'd said in the cave about his dream. She'd never had a spell fail like the memory wipe had with Alex. Sometimes mages ended up with impressions of memories as they sifted through them during a wipe. These had been more vivid than any she had experienced in the handful of memory wipes she'd had to do on sapien bystanders over the years. Instead of being like movie clips, Alex's memories had been a full sensory experience. She could smell the blood. She could feel what he had felt: the pulse-pounding adrenaline rush and nearly overwhelming fear, the determination to save his comrades, and sadness as a life slipped away under his hands.

But he'd ended up with some of her memories in exchange. They were in unexplored territory with Alex and his abilities as a lithseach. Z's words had worried her. *Open the well and it will fill.*

Maybe Alex wasn't just magickal Teflon. Maybe he was more like a magick vacuum, or a black hole. Maybe he could draw it into himself.

If that was true, he was in even more danger than she'd thought.

She shook her head. She could worry about Alex and his mysterious abilities later. For now, she would enjoy the feel of the wind as it rushed around her. And she would enjoy the feel of Alex's body against hers.

But this was as close as they could ever get. A momentary flare of pain bloomed in her chest at the thought. When they found Blanca's killer, he was going back to his nice, normal life. He'd made that clear enough. And she couldn't have any real ties to this world. Not if she was going to do her duty when the time came. And she could see herself getting very attached to Alex.

Z suddenly stiffened beneath her, his head turning to his left and his neck extending straight out. He'd spotted prey. She was about to shout to him to forget it because they had a newbie on board, but she felt him begin a turn to the left. Once he was zeroed in, there was no stopping him.

"Hang on!" she shouted to Alex. His grip tightened around her. She had just a moment to revel in the feel before Z folded his wings in a dive. It was like the first drop at the top of a roller coaster times a thousand. Alayna wrapped the leather rigging around her forearms and gripped tight with her knees. She felt Alex inhale sharply behind her.

Alayna spotted the unsuspecting deer that Z had in his sights just a moment before he extended his claws.

Alex's face was near hers as he gripped her tightly, just over her shoulder. She expected him to scream as the world rushed up to meet them, but instead he let out a loud, "Yee-haw!"

I might have to keep him, she thought, a smile tugging at her lips.

The deer perked up at the last second because of Alex's shout and tried to make a break for it. The dragon changed direction with a slight shift in his wings and wrapped the deer in his front claws. With a quick bite to the back of the neck, the deer went slack.

Z climbed a bit, circled, and landed near a greenbelt of trees growing beside a creek that meandered through pasture land. Alayna and Alex bailed off. She poked the dragon in the neck.

"Next time, a little warning, kamikaze," she said, but there was no anger in her voice. If it was possible for a dragon to shrug, Z did before beginning to cook his prize with gouts of flame from his mouth.

Alex backed off quickly.

"He breathes fire too?"

Alayna nodded. There were two glands inside his neck, just at the back of his throat, she explained. When the two chemicals were mixed and exposed to air, they caught fire, a little like napalm.

"I could have used one of him in Afghanistan. Would have made moving through the mountains a lot easier, and a mobile flamethrower the size of a school bus would have come in handy." Alex said. Then he stopped. "How is it that no one has noticed a dragon living just a few miles outside of a major U.S. city?"

Alayna laughed. "He keeps a low profile for someone that weighs a couple tons."

The dragon was nearly impossible to spot from the ground once he was in the air, an adaptation that had kept dragons shrouded in myth long enough for them to escape to a less crowded dimension. The dragon didn't go after anyone's livestock, which kept him from drawing the attention of the few locals in the area. He preferred wild game, like the deer that Z was currently reducing to charred bones, anyway and said that cows were fat and stupid and offered no sport.

"How many dragons are left?"

"Just him as far as I can tell," Alayna said. "There could be a few hiding in the high places of the world, the Himalayas, the Alps, the Rockies. And I've always suspected that a few of them had taken to the deep places of the ocean, but there have never been any conclusive sightings. No, Z is probably the last of his kind in this world, and I've done everything I can to protect him."

"So, what is he doing in Texas?"

"He came with me when I graduated from the Academy. I'm just lucky I wasn't assigned to some place like New York City; I would have had a hell of a time stashing him then," she said, laughing. "I never told anyone at the Academy about him, but I always suspected that they knew. I wonder sometimes if Z's bond with me didn't play a role in my assignment here."

"Anyway, we lucked out and found these caverns, and I was able to buy the land they sit under. There are more deer and wild boar than a stunted dragon like Z can eat, and it's sparsely populated enough that he's never been spotted. A pretty sweet deal all around."

Alex looked stunned for a moment. "Stunted?"

"Yeah," she said. "Most dragons are three or four times his size when they're fully grown."

"He's an amazing animal."

"Those whiskers around his face can sense electromagnetic fields and magickal energy," she continued. "And legend has it dragons can open portals to other dimensions, like the elven races and the fey can. I believe it. All the dragons went somewhere, trying to escape the humans…and mages like me that were after their scales and bones to turn into armor and weapons."

Alex pointed to the handle of her whip that was sticking out of the top of her boot.

"Like that one?"

The weapon shimmered as she pulled it out of her boot and placed it in his hands.

"It's made of living dragon scales," she said. "That's the mistake that the mages made. They killed the dragons and were only left with dead scales. When a dragon dies, the magick leaves them, but the scales they shed naturally are still alive."

While the dead scales the mages had used for centuries were harder than diamonds, but flexible as plastic, they were static, difficult to forge and required extremely high heat and expensive, strong metals to connect to them.

Living scales, she explained, responded to magick. By combining her abilities to control the elements, Alayna could coax the scales into any shape she wanted, connect them to each other, bind them. And the living scales still reacted to magic. She could release the silver knife from the tail end of the rod and she could deploy a retractable whip that could extend dozens of feet.

Alayna took the rod from his hands and watched his face as she released the sinuous black length of the whip to coil on the ground. With a flick of her wrist it retracted instantly and silently.

Alex was smiling when he met her gaze. Those dark eyes of his made something flutter in her stomach.

"That is so cool," he said, a note of awe in his voice.

While he wanted to return to his world when this case was over, he certainly liked learning about hers. Worried that he'd see her thoughts, she tore her gaze from his and slipped the whip back in her boot.

"I have no idea if the scales respond to me because I'm a Whisperer or because Z is my familiar," she said, trying to fill the silence. "I like to think sometimes that if the mages had taken the time to learn the dragon tongue and establish a relationship with them, that they might have been able to make weapons like this. Then, maybe there wouldn't be so few of either of us left."

Alex was silent for a moment, a frown causing a line to appear between his brows. She had the urge to touch it, caress it away, replace that frown with an entirely different expression.

"Maybe it's better that mages didn't have access to those kinds of weapons. You said the reason the magickal races keep a low profile is because you're all outnumbered. Well, if the mages had allied with the dragons, and if you all had weapons like that, maybe it would be my kind that would be outnumbered."

She opened her mouth to argue, but said instead, "Never thought about it like that."

He was silent for a moment before continuing, "I've been to war. I've seen power corrupt people. And if powerful weapons are on hand, they're eventually used to hurt somebody."

With his words, a shadow had descended over his features, like a cloud blocking out the moonlight.

Alayna didn't know what to say to that and the sound of Z crunching through the last of the deer bones saved her from having to answer.

"I wish to be gone from here, Little Sparrow," Z said, rising to all four feet. "The sky calls me."

"Saddle up!" Alayna said as she rose and headed toward her dragon.

* * *

As they neared the cave mouth, Alex felt his stomach drop through his knees as Z dove for the opening. He shot straight down and opened his wings like a parachute the instant he was through. They came to a jarring landing beside the underground lake, gravel and small stones flying into the air as Z slid to a stop.

Alayna quickly gathered her duffel, the lantern and other supplies, threw Z one last PB&J that she'd hidden, and kissed the dragon goodbye on his scaly snout.

Alex was hooking up the ascenders when Z padded over to him.

"I am pleased to know you, Alex," the dragon said. "Remember, if you open the well, it will fill."

Alex didn't particularly want to think about what the dragon had said about his lìthseach-ness, but he nodded to let him know he heard.

The dragon moved off down a stone passageway set in a wall that Alex had not seen before.

Using the ascenders, they made good time to the cave mouth. It was a little after 2 a.m. when they made it back to the Mustang and Alayna pointed the headlights toward Austin and let all four hundred fifty horses under the hood run.

9

Chapter 9

Alayna felt like she was carrying twenty-pound weights on her shoulders as she dragged herself into the office the next morning. While everyone else was already there, they were all looking as rough as she felt. They'd all been putting in more than a few extra hours on this case.

Ellie was nursing a cup of coffee that was nearly as big as she was. She had stopped bothering to throw her glamour when Alex was in the warehouse, and her overlarge eyes looked bloodshot.

Lu was yawning in a way reminiscent of a big cat, her lips pulling back to expose canines that were just a shade too long by most standards. Sometimes she forgot to pull them all the way back in when she shifted back to her default human form. Alayna made eye contact and tapped her own canine to subtly let her know. Lu sat up and touched a tooth with the pad of her thumb, nodded and smiled at Alayna to show that she had fixed it.

Burdock was quietly tapping away on a laptop and occasionally making small *hmm* noises to himself. She wasn't sure if he'd left the office at all. Since he wore the same self-imposed uniform of black fatigue pants and tight black T-shirt everyday, it was hard to tell.

Her eyes landed on Alex. He was wearing an old set of desert camo fatigue pants and tan T-shirt that showed off the thick muscles in his arms. His black hair was tousled, like he hadn't bothered to comb it, and stubble was coming in along his jaw, like he'd skipped shaving that morning. A little of that FBI polish had rubbed off, and he looked absolutely delectable. Her hands itched to feel that stubble rasping under her fingertips.

She'd kept him out late the night before visiting Z, but he made tired look amazing. She, on the other hand, was looking decidedly the worse for wear. After she'd dropped Alex at his condo earlier in the morning, she'd been unable to sleep. She wasn't sure if it was that exhilarating flight or her increasing sexual frustration that had her tossing and turning. After abandoning any hope of sleep, she'd spent several hours poring over the case files, but hadn't gotten very far.

She knew she looked a bit of a mess, her long, blonde hair piled in a knot on top of her head, stray curls spilling out to touch her shoulders. The dark circles had been just a little darker when she'd looked in the mirror this morning, but there was nothing she could do about that.

Crossing to her desk, Alayna dumped an armful of file folders on the already cluttered surface. She tossed the keys to the Mustang on the desk and they disappeared into the snowstorm of paperwork.

Across the room, Alex casually poured himself a cup of coffee from the communal pot by the wall, already blending with her team.

"Be careful with that stuff," she told him, nodding at his coffee cup. "Ellie's brew can peel paint."

"Just the way I like it," Ellie chimed in. "Strong enough to keep the badgers away from the den."

She had to stifle a laugh when Alex took a sip and almost choked. The coffee was dark, strong, and thick, and Alayna could smell Ellie's proprietary blend of spices in it, which may or may not have included a shot of chili powder.

"I like it strong," he said, his voice sounding like he'd just taken a shot of whiskey.

Alayna pulled two sheets of paper from one of the file folders. They were ragged at the top where she'd torn them out of her sketch pad.

"I'm not the greatest sketch artist in the world, but are these close to what we saw in Llorona's vision?"

"Pretty close," Alex said, taking the papers from Alayna. "May I?"

She nodded and he sat down at his desk, pulling out a pencil. He changed the jaw on one sketch and adjusted the nose a little. On the other, he changed the spacing of the eyes just a hair and made the lips a little thinner.

"That look right?"

She cocked her head to one side and examined the sketches.

"Yeah. That looks closer. How did you do that?"

"I'm a man of many talents," he said, a smile turning up one corner of his mouth. "And I've always had a knack with faces."

She flashed him a smile without thinking and met his eyes. That twisty, fluttery feeling in her stomach started up again and spread to her chest, sending tingles all the way to her shoulders. Why could one look from him could do that? Part of her wanted it to stop, but part of her wanted to see if he could make her tingle anywhere else. She shook that thought away, afraid he'd see it in her eyes, but he'd already turned to hand Ellie the sketches.

"Scan those and see if they turn up any hits in your database," Alayna told her. "Facial recognition on a sketch is a long shot, but I'll try anything."

"This could take awhile, Commander."

Alayna needed something to get her blood flowing, or she was going to fall over. Hell, it looked like they all did.

"We should probably hit the gym," she said to Alex. "If that search comes back with any hits, we might be hitting the streets tonight. I need to know you can hold your own."

She signaled to Dumeril, Lu, and Burdock, and they all headed downstairs to the training area, which was covered in exercise mats and weapons racks.

Reaching in one of the cabinets that lined the wall, she tossed Alex two eight-round Airsoft paintball pistols. He pulled a tactical rig off the wall and buckled it around his waist, holstering the two pistols. A sheathed Ka-bar knife was added to the belt and he tied a retractable riot club to his left hip.

Smart, she thought. He's covering all his bases.

Dumeril pulled two dull machetes used for training off one of the racks. Dull was a relative term, though. While the blades wouldn't be able to take Alex's arm completely off, they'd deal some pretty deep flesh wounds if he let the Svarturan get too close.

A tiny shiver of fear for Alex tried to crawl up her spine, but she pushed it down. He was a big boy; he could take care of himself. Scratch that, he was a man. A grown-ass, well-trained man who had lived through a war. He didn't need her protection. She had to take the net out from under him sometime.

Across the mat, Lu let out a soft groan. She'd removed her T-shirt and stood in a black sports bra and a pair of stretchy yoga pants. Her shoulders hunched, and she bent at the waist. Alex looked over, his eyes going wide, his expression becoming concerned.

There were rippling movements beneath her skin that signaled the change. Muscles that hadn't been there a second ago bulged. Her arms grew longer, the fingers stretching until they ended in lethal looking claws. Her jaw dropped open a little and longer teeth began to protrude from her gums, leaving bloody streaks against the ivory color.

Snapping, popping sounds filled the air and one after the other, her legs bent backwards at the knee, creating reverse articulated joints.

Lu's breath was coming heavy, tiny whimpers and cries escaping as her body morphed into something out of a horror movie. Alex looked like he was about to be sick. He was frozen in place, his arm extended slightly toward Lu as if to help, but unsure how to do that. He needed to see this.

"It's hurting her," Alex whispered to Alayna.

"Change always hurts," she replied. "She's moving a lot of bone, muscle, tendon and ligament to create that shape. Shifters learn to deal with the pain, but it's always there."

Lu moved to a bench along the wall and wrapped overly long fingers around a bottle of orange sludge that she emptied into her fanged jaws.

"Liquid energy," Dumeril said, pointing to the bottle. "When shifters change, they're still subject to physics, including conservation of mass and energy. When she gets big, she burns a lot of energy and needs to refuel. When she gets small and sheds mass, she gives off a wave of heat when the excess energy is dispersed."

Alex looked at Lu's new, monstrous form and said, "That is so cool!"

He moved closer to her. She stood over seven feet tall now, heavy muscle bulging in her arms and legs. The bristling dark hair that covered her skin gave her some protection, but also made her a shoo-in for a blockbuster horror movie. The eyes that moved in her elongated face were still Lu's; that hadn't changed.

Alex moved toward her slowly, like he was approaching a wild animal.

"I'm still me, Alex," she said, her voice about five octaves deeper. "I won't bite."

"Yes you will," Alayna said. "This might be a training session, but I don't want you to hold back with him. We need to know if he can handle himself in the field. I mean, don't rip his throat out or anything, 'cause that's just messy, but don't pull your punches."

Lu nodded and took up a position at one end of the mat. Dumeril moved opposite her and spun the handle of the machete in his right hand. Burdock stood back, popping his knuckles. Alayna took up a position on the edge of the mat between Dumeril and Lu, drawing her whip from her boot.

From her belt, she drew a small, thin object about a foot long, with a glossy black finish. She grasped an edge with her left hand and flicked her wrist, opening a vicious bladed fan.

Most mages chose weapons that corresponded to their element. Fire mages seemed to be the only ones who liked firearms. Earth mages loved their swords and staffs. Even though as a Whisperer she could control all of the elements with her voice, she was still an air mage at heart and preferred her fans and her whip. They were true weapons of the air and it took less effort to channel and direct her powers through them.

With a whispered word, a sinuous black length about the width of her thumb emerged from the whip and coiled on the edge of the mat. She gestured to Alex with the handle, indicating that he should stand in the middle of the mat.

Something bad was coming, and it was time to see if Alex could handle himself in the field. She gave the signal to Dumeril to begin.

* * *

A nutcracker. That's what they'd called it back in hand-to-hand class during his Army basic training. One guy surrounded by three or four opponents who attack first one at a time and then all together.

Dumeril moved first, swiping the machete in his right hand upwards at Alex's chest. Alex snatched up the riot club with his left hand and blocked the swing, drawing the K-bar in a smooth motion with his right hand and bringing it in a back handed slash, the dull edge of the knife laid back against his forearm. He aimed the blade for Dumeril's ribs, but the Svarturan was too fast, dancing backward easily.

They moved like that for several minutes, dancing, dodging, spinning, diving, and deflecting. Dumeril landed a couple of lucky swipes across Alex's bare forearms, drawing thin ribbons of blood that made his grip on the riot club slippery.

Dumeril aimed a cross swipe at his head and Alex threw himself backward, turning the move into a backward roll. As he rolled, he dropped the K-bar and the riot club. He drew the Airsoft and came out of the roll on one knee, both hands on the paintball gun.

Dumeril managed to deflect one of the pellets with the flat

of the machete, splattering it on the floor a few feet away. Two others landed solidly in the center of Dumeril's chest, orange paint speckling the ink-black skin of his face.

"Nice," Dumeril said, moving off the mat and setting the machetes on the floor.

"My turn."

Burdock's voice was right behind him. As Alex spun, he barely dodged the punch that went flying by his left ear.

The mage caught him under the ribs with a solid uppercut. Alex's breath whooshed out of his lungs and he back peddled as quickly he could to get some space to catch his breath. But Burdock was on him before he could blink, landing a punch to his temple that had him seeing stars. He stumbled and went down on one knee.

Alex had known the confrontation with Burdock was coming, he just hadn't expected it this soon. The guy didn't like him and had made that pretty damn clear. This was a dominance game. He'd seen it play out hundreds of times.

The mage pressed his advantage, grabbing him by the front of his shirt and hauling him up. As his fist drew back to land a punishing blow to Alex's face, flames erupted up his arm. Burdock had not come to play, and if that blow landed, it was lights out for Alex, maybe even permanently.

For a split second, he caught sight of Alayna. Her eyes were wide with fear. For him? She looked like she wanted to jump in the middle of this, but he sent a silent thank you that she hadn't. This had to play out.

Fortunately for him, Burdock had underestimated him. If Burdock was going to bring a flamethrower to a fist fight, he was going to pull out his own bag of dirty tricks. Alex felt his opponent's weight shift to deliver the blow and he made his move, delivering a punch of his own. To the inside of Burdock's knee.

The leg buckled as the mage grunted in pain. Alex didn't give him any opportunity to counter, delivering a series of body blows to that knocked Burdock on his back. Alex moved to pin him and they came face to face on the mat, each struggling for a better position.

"You don't belong here, sape," Burdock ground out between gritted teeth.

"Not gonna argue with that."

Alex landed a punch to his ribs and earned a strangled grunt.

"We solve this case and I'm gone. Until then, just ignore me, like you do everything that isn't work."

Burdock didn't reply, just bared his teeth. The spot where the mage gripped Alex's arm suddenly flared with white hot pain. Out of reflex, he launched himself backwards. Burdock raised a hand that danced with blue flames. Alex looked down to see the skin of his arm was red and blistered.

When he looked up, Burdock was already on his feet and winding up a fireball. On his knees, there was no way Alex could get out of the way in time. This was going to hurt. He closed his eyes and turned his face from the impact.

Only there was no impact. When he looked up, he saw Burdock's eyes were wide and his jaw was hanging slightly open. So was everyone else's.

Alayna's voice split the silence, "Break it up!"

When she shoved Burdock off the mat, he didn't resist.

"What happened?" Alex asked as he climbed to his feet.

"That fireball just…dissipated. I've never seen anything like that." Her voice was quiet.

She fell silent and turned away, her hand covering her mouth, which meant she was thinking. When her gaze landed on Burdock, her eyes narrowed in a look that said he'd done fucked up.

Dumeril chimed in, "Do you think this has to do with him being a lithseach?"

"I'd say that's a damn good bet," she said.

Alayna turned, that bladed black fan shimmering in her grasp. With a flick of her fan and handful of whispered words, Alex felt a pressure change headed his way. A gentle breeze brushed his face and ruffled the hem of his T-shirt, but behind him, a rack of weapons went flying, and a bench overturned from what looked like a gale-force gust.

Alex looked back to Alayna to see her jaw hanging open slightly. He stood still as she flicked her fan again, repeating the whispered words. She must have been using the fan to direct her magick.

This time, he heard a howling wind that threatened to tear him off his feet, but just as before it seemed to go around him only to toss equipment around behind him like leaves in a storm.

"You should have been tossed head over heels from those gusts, but they went around you..."

Over the next few minutes, Alayna threw gusts of wind, pulled water from a nearby barrel and launched it at him like a water cannon, blasted tongues of flame in his direction. All of them failed to reach him. They seemed to flow around him like he was a rock in a stream.

None of them had ever seen anything like it.

"I've seen mages and elves and fey that can throw up magickal shields to protect themselves, but they're usually visible, and they require a lot of effort to maintain. You're not doing that."

She continued forward until her hand rested against his chest.

"And I would be able to feel it if it were a shield."

"It's passive, Commander," Dumeril added.

Alayna stilled for a moment, thinking.

"Experiment," she said, keeping her hand on Alex's chest. She flicked her fan again, but this time, the gust of wind was weak, barely stirring the dust on the floor. She moved her hand to his forearm, her delicate fingers warm against his skin. When she flicked her fan, the gust was barely perceptible, no more than a whisper of air.

She stepped away and aimed a full-force blast across the warehouse, bouncing a weapons rack off the wall and causing one of the heavy punching bags to sway on its chains.

"My magick doesn't affect you and contact, particularly skin-to-skin, affects my ability to weave a spell," she said. "Remarkable."

She moved away from him, appearing to be lost in thought. Without looking back, she flicked the whip out, hooking it around his ankle and pulling him onto his back with a thud. The sound of Lu's laughter filled his ears and he could feel his face turning red.

"Don't let your guard down, ever," she said. "You might have some resistance to magick, but it's spotty. Burdock managed to burn you. And weapons can still hurt you."

"That round goes to you then," Alex said, climbing to his feet and moving a little slower than he liked.

The small injuries he'd picked up so far were starting to add up. The burn on his arm was really starting to hurt, but he wasn't done yet. He turned to Lu and raised his hand, palm up, flicking his fingers in a "bring it on" gesture. The hulking shifter obliged and charged across the mat toward him. He lowered his stance, crouching down to distribute the force of her charge.

As she closed, he grasped her forearms, shifted his weight back, and placed his foot squarely in the middle of her chest. Alex let himself fall backwards and used Lu's momentum to carry her up and over him. He extended his leg at just the right moment and sent Lu thudding to the mat behind him.

"Commander?" Lu's voice sounded odd. Alex pulled himself into a crouch.

Both of Lu's arms had quickly shrunk to their default, human-looking size.

"I don't believe it," Alayna said, rushing to Lu's side. "You made her shift back."

Alayna's eyes were wide as she turned to look at him. Lu stared at him, and he saw something he never thought he'd see in the eyes of a woman that could change into any number of nightmares: fear.

"Does it hurt?" Alayna asked Lu.

"No. It just kinda tingles," she said, hugging her arms to herself and rubbing her hands over her upper arms.

"Can you stand for him to touch you again? I'd like to see what we can learn about this," Alayna said.

Lu nodded and Alex moved toward her. He gently touched her face and almost recoiled as he felt the muscle and bone shift under his fingers. The teeth retracted back into her gums and, soon, it was the same old Lu sitting in front of him, her monstrous body melting back into its original shape.

He felt a wave of warmth wash over him as her extra mass was converted to energy and dispelled.

"Goodness gracious," Alayna said, to no one in particular. She turned and looked at Alex. "What am I going to do with you?"

* * *

Alex emerged from the shower and moved slowly to his locker, aching muscles screaming. Alayna had continued to put him through a grueling hand-to-hand workout, with Dumeril as backup. She'd sent an uneasy Lu to help Burdock prep the weapons and equipment. Alayna was betting that Ellie's search would turn something up by sundown, and they were going hunting.

They'd tried a few more magickal assaults, but she'd quickly called a halt when even Dumeril's most complex illusion had failed to confuse him. She was concerned about the magickal energy that was being thrown his way. They had no idea if he was dispelling it or—and this was a horrifying thought—soaking it up.

As he was pulling on a pair of his old desert camo pants, he noticed bruises beginning to form on his legs. How much longer could he keep up with these people? Magick might slide off him, but Alayna's kicks and Burdock's punches hadn't.

The fire mage probably still didn't like him, but from looks that had passed between them after that sparing session, there was at least a grudging respect there. They could work together. For as long as it took to solve the case, anyway.

He heard a knock at the door and Alayna's voice call, "You decent?"

"I haven't been decent for years," he answered, "but I have clothes on."

She came around the small bank of lockers and paused when she saw he didn't have a shirt on, her eyes going to the floor. He thought he might have detected the slightest hint of a blush on her pale cheeks.

"That was a rough workout," she said to the floor tiles. "I just came to check on you."

"I've got some pretty impressive bruises, but I'll live," he said, slipping a sock on his left foot.

"You should see Dumeril," she said. "You got several good swipes in with that Ka-bar. He's knitting his skin back together as we speak."

"Think he could do mine next?" Alex held up the cuts that had barely scabbed over.

She moved to the end of the bank of lockers behind him and leaned her shoulder against it, looking uncomfortable.

"Those are some nasty scratches on your back," she said.

"Yeah, Lu tagged me with those claws just before she shifted back. They're not deep, though."

"That was a really cool move, by the way," she said. "I mean, the circle throw, not the whole making her change back thing—"

He shifted on the bench suddenly, turning to look back at her.

"You're nervous. Why are you nervous?" he asked, staring at her face until she met his eyes.

"I've never dealt with anything like this before," she said finally.

Was she talking about his abilities…or him?

"And you think I have?" he said, his voice rising slightly. "You've pulled me down the damned rabbit hole, Alayna. You're telling me I'm some sort of magickal anomaly and we're hunting what looks like a vampire serial killer. I almost got flame punched by a dude straight out of a comic book, and you introduced me to a dragon last night. And you're the one that's freaked out?"

"I didn't mean it like that," she said, moving to sit next to him on the bench, facing in the opposite direction.

She touched the scratches on his bare back, and he hissed in pain.

"I wonder if I could heal those…"

He didn't say anything but took a deep breath and closed his eyes as she placed her palm flat against the wounds, her fingers curling slightly over the top of his shoulder. He tried to focus on how good it felt for her to touch him. She was close now and her scent filled his nose, honeysuckle and mint from her shampoo, and under that was the scent of the air just after a thunderstorm.

Her whispered words were soft, each syllable connected to the next until they sounded like a gently flowing stream. The room fell away around him, her words filled him, his muscles relaxed, and there was only the two of them.

The softness of her hair brushed his skin as she laid her head against his bicep and her arm went around his bare waist. She was a warm counterpoint to the cold, soothing feeling where her hand touched his wounded shoulder. His left arm went around her back and settled on her waist. He buried his face in her soft curls, breathing deeply. Alex wasn't sure the last time he'd felt this relaxed with someone, this close. It was almost intimate. There was just their breathing and their heartbeats. He had the urge to pull her into his lap and kiss her senseless, but he was afraid to break this tenuous, floating moment between them.

She pressed closer, her breath brushing his throat. Her hands moved over him, skimming gently. The sensation of cold water flowed over the burn on his arm, his cuts. His breath was coming faster now and his eyes slid shut as relief shivered through him.

He had no idea how long they stayed entwined like that, but eventually Alayna stirred and he let her go, reluctantly.

They each opened their eyes, like waking up from a dream, and she met his gaze for a long, breathless moment. It would be so easy to reach for her, slip his fingers into her hair and kiss her, first her mouth, then her pale throat. He swallowed hard and looked away, air finally entering his lungs again.

He looked down at his shoulder. The scratches were gone.

"You did it," he said, a smile tugging one corner of his mouth. "I thought you said magick didn't work on me anymore."

"It seems to change, depending on your mood," she said softly. "When your adrenaline is up, nothing can touch you. But when you're relaxed or distracted, it seems like I can slip past your defenses. With little spells at least. Even so, that took ten times the energy and concentration it usually does."

"It seems you're good at that," he said, keeping his voice low. "Slipping past my defenses."

He looked down at her hand resting on his thigh.

Her eyes widened and she snatched her hand back. A small chuckle escaped him. Maybe she wasn't the only one who could slip past defenses.

She stood abruptly and straightened her shirt. It was suddenly cold without the heat of her pressed against him, like ice water splashed in his face.

"I'll see you upstairs," she said over her shoulder, her voice tight, as she headed for the locker room door.

Alex wasn't sure what had just passed between them. His first instinct was to stop her from leaving, but he held himself back. It was dangerous to get involved with women he worked with. Particularly when they faced a potential combat situation. It was Kelly all over again.

Fiery fingers of panic tried to claw through his chest at the thought of her and for a moment, he couldn't breathe. Images, memories, assailed him, flowing like a raging river before his eyes. Red hair. His hands slick with blood. Blue eyes staring sightlessly.

His heart pounding hard enough to bruise his ribs, he forced his eyes open. His breath sawed loudly in the silent room. He focused on the lockers in front of him. He was here now. He was not there. That was the past. This was the present.

Swallowing hard, he pulled air into his lungs.

In. Out.

In. Out.

It was over. He was safe.

In. Out.

Gradually, his heart slowed and he could breathe normally again. Unfortunately, he would never be normal again.

10

Chapter 10

"What have you got for me, Ellie?" Alayna said as she entered the office, trying desperately to shake off the nervous energy in her blood. Touching Alex like that was a bad idea.

"Good news, Commander. My facial recognition software turned up a hit off one of your sketches," the gnome said. She swiveled her flat screen monitor around to show Alayna the scan of her sketch alongside the photo of a man.

"That's him," Alayna said, recognizing the sandy haired vampire from the vision La Llorona had shown her. "Who is he?"

"I got this from a Homeland Security file. Border Patrol flagged his ID and started a file on him. Name is James Davis. Nothing but a couple of speeding tickets in counties near the border, but he makes a lot of trips across the river. File says he works for Samuels Trucking, which, by the way, is one of Medina Trucking's subsidiaries, but he doesn't have a commercial license." Ellie scanned down the file she was compiling on their mysterious vampire and continued, "He's never been tagged by any of Corps agents. I could send this to a representative for the Families."

Alayna shook her head. The Families were the closest thing the vampires had to a government. They were representatives from the strongest family lines. They maintained the birth and death records for their kind. Every vampire, natural born or turned, could trace their lineage back to one of the seven original families.

When a vampire sought to turn a sapien, they had to get permission from the Families to do it, and they rarely gave permission.

While the Families might have information on their mystery vamp, without knowing which family he belonged to, inquiries were more likely to tip someone off than they were to produce usable information. The political situation among the magickal races could be described as delicate on the best of days. Right now it approached the consistency of spun sugar. Best to go through her own channels.

Alayna had to walk this line every day, and it made her job so much harder. Busting bad guys would be so much easier if she didn't have to put up with the political bullshit.

Ellie turned the monitor back around and began pulling up pages.

"Do we have an address on him?" Alayna asked.

"It's an empty lot in East Austin," Ellie said.

"I'm guessing James Davis isn't his real name either," Alayna said.

"Looks like a ghost in the system to me."

"I think we're looking at one of Jimmy Medina's fixers," she said. "Any luck tracking Medina, hacking his phone, anything?"

"He's been silent, Commander," she said. "It's only been a few weeks since Blanca Rodriquez's body turned up. He's gone completely to ground, and we probably won't see him for a while."

"Well, we've got a photo at least. Even if it is a fake name and a fake address. And we've got a connection to Medina."

"What's our next move?" Ellie asked.

"We've got to track this guy down. He's our best bet to find out where Medina is and who is behind all of these murders," Alayna said.

"How do you want to do that? He's obviously no slouch when it comes to fake IDs if he can fool Homeland Security."

"I need to go see the one vampire in town who's still talking to us," she said.

* * *

Alayna tried to push her nervousness away as she pulled up outside of Revelations, taking a deep breath as she shut off the Mustang's rumbling engine.

The late afternoon sun was starting to warm what had been a chilly day, at least by Austin standards, and Sixth Street was nearly deserted, with just a few people wandering between Ropollo's Pizza and the scattering of tourist shops.

She punched the button on her alarm system as she hit the front door, fully aware that anyone watching the building would know exactly who she was here to talk to. At this point she didn't care. There had been so little movement on this case; she was ready for someone to make a move. It would be so much better if they just came at her.

As she pulled open the black lacquered doors, Camille was already waiting in the bouncers' area, a fake smile plastered on her face.

"Camille," Alayna said simply, as she turned and headed down the hall to Dominic's office.

"Commander Blackwell," she returned in a grating saccharine voice that followed Alayna down the hallway. "He's expecting you."

Another deep breath and she pushed open the door to Dominic's tastefully old world-style office. The darkly handsome vampire looked up from his computer monitor, his midnight eyes met hers, and a warm smile lit his features. Her old friend rose with his usual casual grace and came around the desk to greet her.

He looked thinner than when she'd seen him a few days before and she wondered if he was getting enough to eat. His carefully tailored three-piece suit hid it well, but she could see it in his face. As he pulled her into a hug and brushed her cheek with a feather-soft kiss, she felt some tension uncoil within her. She'd been nervous about how he'd react to her visit.

"I've been worried about you, Lane," he said in a low voice. "We never did get to finish that conversation about those unfortunate events."

She stepped back and took one of the two seats opposite his desk.

"It's been a little busy around the office," she said.

He laughed. "Isn't it always?"

Rather than going back behind his desk, as she'd expected, he took the seat next to her, putting him within easy arms reach. Before she could find the voice to tell him why she was here, he spoke up.

"I've been dying to know what's up with that FBI agent from the other day?"

"Oh, that's a long story," she said, trying to deflect.

"For you, I have all day." He sat back and laced his fingers on one knee. She filled him in with as few details as possible. Failed memory wipe, lithseach, yada yada, working together until the case is solved.

That caused one of his dark brows to rise in surprise.

"A sapien law enforcement agent in the middle of a Council investigation. The brass must be in fits."

"The brass doesn't know," she said, shaking her head. "And they aren't going to find out. I've managed to keep it mostly to the lower levels."

She hadn't filed any formal reports on Alex's involvement in the investigation. His transfer had been done through her own channels, and she'd marked it strictly need-to-know. She silently thanked the gods again that she had the level of autonomy that she did as a team commander.

Dominic laughed and said, "Well, they certainly won't find out from me. I'm not exactly in regular communication these days."

And that was partially her fault.

Dominic hadn't always been a nightclub owner. When she'd joined the Austin team out of the Academy, he'd been the team's reconnaissance expert. A vampire as a member of the Mage Corps had been pretty unusual at the time, but not unheard of.

Dominic had never marched to anyone else's beat, and as the young scion of a powerful family, he was allowed a certain amount of latitude. It was normal for young, natural-born vamps to live a mainstream life in their first century.

Still, Dominic's decision to join the Mage Corps had been met with a lot of resistance from the Spino family, Alayna knew. He'd been essentially disowned for the ten years he'd served. Even after his rather abrupt exit two years ago, his relationship with his family was still strained.

Even when he was in the Corps, he'd never had much use for Council politics, even though his father had done rotations as the vampire representative on the Council.

Dominic was a rebel, through and through.

It was one of the reasons they'd gotten along so well when he'd been a part of the team. He'd welcomed her, dismissing the other mages' concerns that her being a Whisperer would be a liability in combat.

They'd been joined at the hip for years, always cracking each other up with jokes. Dominic had been the first man in her life who hadn't kept her at arm's length because of her abilities, and they'd been close.

A little too close, it turned out.

She shook that thought away and pushed the rising guilt back down in her gut.

His voice brought her back to the present. "You're taking some big risks for this sapien."

There was curiosity in his narrowed eyes and a small smile tugged at the corner of his mouth.

"I know," she said, looking down at her hands. "I just have a feeling about this one."

He was silent a moment before his eyes suddenly went wide. "You like him!" Surprise and a note of teasing threaded through his voice.

"Shut up," she said defensively. "No, I don't."

Dominic's rich laughter filled the room.

"I can smell it when you lie," he said. The teasing tone was still there, but there was dark note just under the surface.

"This is beyond awkward."

"Come on," he said, waving a hand dismissively. "That stuff

between us is ancient history. We're friends again."

He was right. They'd worked hard to get back to this point after their falling out, and she didn't want to lose one of her oldest friends again.

"It doesn't matter if I like him, nothing can happen. We work together."

"Still sticking to that rule, huh?" He turned the assessing gaze on her that had made him a formidable battle tactician once upon a time.

"Listen," she said, desperate to change the subject. "I need your help, Dom."

"Anything," he said, letting the line of questioning drop.

"Let's start with that night at Revelations," she said. "When Blanca Rodriguez died."

"I wish I had more for you, Lane," Dominic said, again calling her by the nickname he'd picked for her. "Like I told you before, the cameras aren't much use. We've been over the video footage from the night she disappeared. The footage from the dance floor is too hard to make out. The camera over the front door doesn't pick her up coming in, but there are other entrances that aren't covered. And we don't have cameras in the VIP rooms."

He paused and gave her a steady look.

"So far, the only connection to Blanca Rodriguez that anyone can turn up is that she had a napkin from the club in her pocket. That doesn't mean she was here that night."

Alayna took a deep breath.

"Was Jimmy Medina here that night?"

"The Snake?" Dominic looked slightly worried at that, his dark brows drawing together. "I don't know, but let me pull up the VIP reservations for that night."

He moved around the desk and bent over his monitor, not

bothering to sit down.

"It looks like he was on the guest list for one of the VIP rooms that night, but that doesn't mean he showed up," Dominic said.

"I have it on good authority that he did," Alayna said, watching his reaction carefully.

He looked up from the screen as if waiting for her to say more. She met his gaze and stayed silent.

"Does Medina have some connection to the murder?" he asked, his expression grave.

"I'm not sure. Right now I just need to find him, but he's gone to ground," she said. She pulled out her phone and brought up the image of the mysterious James Davis and showed it to Dominic.

"You familiar with this vampire?" she asked him.

Dominic took the phone from her and studied the picture.

"He looks familiar, but I couldn't tell you his name," he said, handing the phone back.

"James Davis is the name on file with the feds, but we both know that's a fake," she said.

Vampires never gave their real names to the sapien government. They might have a few dozen names and identities over the course of a lifetime, but they never put their real one on paper.

"You think he's one of Medina's boys," Dominic said and didn't wait for Alayna to confirm it. "If I were you, I'd ask around Hellraisers. That's where that crowd hangs out."

Alayna tossed her head back and laughed.

"I like my skin where it is, thanks," she said.

"I'm serious," Dominic said. "That's your best bet to find some answers."

"Fair enough," she said. "Can you check your tapes again and see if Jimmy Medina shows up?"

"I'll go one further and put out my feelers, see if I can turn up his whereabouts," he said, flashing her a smile.

"I'd appreciate it," she said as he came back around the desk and assumed his seat beside her. There was a tension in his movements she'd missed before. That, coupled with his weight loss, made her ask, "You look different. Is something wrong?"

He looked down, a small wistful smile curving his lips. "I'm seeing someone."

Relief flooded through her and she smiled.

"Anyone I know?"

"It's Camille. It's been going on a few months."

His general manager and bodyguard? She didn't really seem like his type, but people changed. If he was happy, she was happy.

"That's great. Mazel tov," she said, touching his arm.

"Thanks," he said, meeting her eyes.

She saw warmth there. As happy as she was for him, she needed to get back to the office.

"Hey, listen. Thanks for everything you're doing to help with the investigation."

"Like I said, anything for you, Lane," he said, leaning forward and tucking a strand of hair behind her ear. "Just be careful. Medina is young, rich and dangerous. Thinks he owns this town and that the rules don't apply to him."

He paused as he leaned back in his chair.

"I could come with you to Hellraisers. I'm not so out of shape that I can't suit up and kick some ass for old times sake."

That made her smile. As she rose to her feet, she said, "I have no doubt that you could, but I think we can handle this."

As she turned to go, his voice stopped her. "Are you taking

the lìthseach?"

She turned to look back at him. His expression was neutral, but something hard glittered in his eyes and his mouth had tightened to thin line.

"Yeah," she said, her shoulders going tense. "I think so."

His easy smile returned.

"Just stay safe out there. I don't know what I'd do if something happened to you."

***

As Alayna climbed the steps to the office, nervous energy was crawling under her skin. That conversation with Dominic had left her so discombobulated that she would be better off going ten rounds with a punching bag. But she and the team would be heading to Hellraisers. Possibly tonight.

As she strode through the door and headed for her desk, Alex caught her attention. His dark eyes narrowed as he focused on her and his head came up. That powerful body uncoiled, and he was around his desk, concern bringing out the little crease between his brows.

"Can we talk?" He eyed the conference room and she nodded.

He closed the door behind them, shutting out curious stares from Ellie and Lu, but he didn't sit down.

"You're so jittery, you look like you've had six shots of espresso. What gives?" he asked.

"None of your business," she snapped, the words reflexively flying from her mouth before she could stop them.

He held his hands up, defensively.

"If it has to do with the investigation into my best friend's murder, I'd kinda like to think it is my business," he said slowly, choosing his words carefully. "Who did you talk to? What's got you shook?"

She made the mistake of looking up at him. If she had found anger in his eyes, she could have matched it, raged at him. Instead, she found compassion. Damn it. Some of the tension uncoiled within her and she was suddenly reminded of that embrace they'd shared in the locker room earlier. It had started out as healing, but it had shifted to something else. The way they'd held each other had been far too intimate, had felt far too good.

He put his hands down slowly, but his gaze still held hers.

"I thought we were working on this together," he said, closing the distance between them. His hand caressed her shoulder and moved down the back of her arm. His touch was an anchor, pulling some of the anxiety from her. "Maybe I read the situation wrong, but this was starting to feel a little like a partnership."

Alayna was quiet for a moment before she answered. "I've never had a partner. I don't know how that works."

He was so close his chest was almost brushing her breasts.

"A good partnership is based on understanding each other's goals. I'm here to do two things: Find Blanca's killer and learn enough to protect and conceal myself from the things that live in your world. That's it." He paused for a moment and leaned into her. When he spoke, his warm breath brushed her neck. "What do you want, Alayna?"

She took a deep breath, struggling to control her hammering pulse. Her heart rate had nothing to do with his nearness, she told herself, closing her eyes to shut out the sight of his chiseled and deliciously stubbled jaw

"I want to find this killer," she said matter-of-factly. In a softer voice she said. "And I want to keep you safe."

His other hand rose to cradle the back of her other arm and she moved imperceptibly closer to him.

"The more information I have, the safer I am," he said.

She finally opened her eyes and met his gaze.

"It was better that you weren't there," she said. Her voice was husky, and she almost cursed herself. "My relationship with that source is…delicate. And your presence would have made an awkward situation worse."

He frowned at her, his eyes narrowing again as he assessed her. There was a startling intellect behind those eyes, and she'd do well to remember that. He might be devastatingly handsome, but unlike the sapien men she engaged in one-night stands with, Alex was not stupid.

"Why don't you fill me in?" he asked.

She stepped back, needing distance from his touch if she was going to discuss this, and it suddenly felt ten degrees colder. Turning, she took a seat at the conference table. Alex didn't join her, instead remaining on his feet, his arms crossed over his big chest.

"I went to see Dominic," she told him.

"The owner of Revelations? The one whose office I had a magickal seizure in?"

"That's the one."

"Why would that be awkward?"

She hesitated before she continued, and she could see Alex making a mental note of that. "We used to work together. He was the team's recon specialist before Lu."

"And the awkwardness has something to do with why he isn't on the team anymore, am I right?"

The guy was too good at interrogation. One question flowed

into the next, and he was good at reading her. Too good for comfort.

She fell silent and kept her eyes on his and off the muscular chest that stretched his T-shirt. That masculine spicy scent of his wrapped around her and went right to her head. He'd sensed a weak point and was moving to exploit it. A part of her wanted him to find it, wanted to talk about it with someone.

"What happened, Alayna?" His voice was low, inviting her to open up and spill her secrets.

She looked down, afraid he'd see the guilt and pain in her eyes, and sighed.

"Dominic and I were best friends, once," she began.

She and Dom were thick as thieves for years, but not long after she'd taken over command of the team, their relationship changed from easy going to something else. Dominic became aggressive with his attention. There had been inappropriate comments, some in front of the team.

"Then he came on to me."

Alex moved one of the chairs to sit across from her. His knee almost brushed hers as he leaned forward, his elbows on his knees, his expression neutral.

"Dominic and I were both working late in the warehouse one night," Alayna continued.

Alayna had been stretching her muscles after a long session at the computer and standing at the window looking out at the city. It had been dark in the office, only the glow of the computer monitors and the lights of the city illuminating them.

Dominic had come up behind her.

"He said that we needed to talk," she told Alex. "I knew it was coming. I'd seen the way he'd changed. What I wasn't expecting was for him to grab me and kiss me as soon as I turned around."

Alex tensed at that, the muscles around his jaw standing out and something feral sliding through his eyes. When he stayed silent, she continued.

She'd been horrified and pushed him away.

"I asked him what he was doing, and he said we both knew what had been going on for a while. I reminded him that I was the commander and that I couldn't have relationships with team members. It just creates too many problems. It can distract people in combat."

Dominic had stepped away from her, running his hand through his hair in that way he did when he was frustrated. She desperately didn't want to lose her friend, but this was uncharted territory for her. Dominic had been the first man in her life to treat her like she wasn't cursed. She'd never before been seen as attractive to anyone who'd actually known her. Or maybe she'd never let them get that close. Maybe it was a little of both.

"I still remember exactly what he said to me 'So you're going to keep fucking sapiens you pick up in bars like a dirty slut when you know it's me you're supposed to be with?'"

Alex grimaced at the coarse words.

"I told him that I wasn't going to defend my choices or live like a nun. If mage men don't want me, I'll get it somewhere else."

"Those men are idiots," Alex growled. "If they can't see past their hang-ups, they don't deserve you."

His voice was low and fierce. Something inside her lit up at his words, but she pushed it down, not daring to acknowledge what he'd said and continued like she hadn't heard him.

"Dominic tried to apologize, but what he'd said hurt."

Alayna made the best of the situation she'd been dealt. Because of her status as a Whisperer, other mages regarded her with a mix of fear, suspicion, but mostly pity. In mage society it was typical for mages to start hooking up when they were still in the Academy.

Their kind was fading, dying out, and pregnancies were so rare, but so important to the continuation of mage-kind—and to the balance between the shadow races. Most got started early.

If she hadn't been a Whisperer, Alayna would have been fending off offers from some of the most powerful mages out there. Her parents had managed to have four children, an extremely rare event. And each child was born under a different element. Something never heard of before.

In fact, before she'd hit puberty and her powers had manifested as the Whisperer's curse, many within the Council hierarchy thought that she and her siblings, each of them able to control a different element, were the fulfillment of a well-known prophecy. The Blackwell children were supposed to save the world, restore balance, close the door against the darkness, and bring peace to the Earthly realms.

Everything had changed when her curse had manifested. It had torn her family apart. It felt like other members of the Corps blamed her for being the one who ended their hope for peace. As a Whisperer, her days were numbered. It was why she chose casual hookups with sapiens she met in bars over wasting her time with relationships that could never work.

Besides, she had her work. That was all she needed until her time came.

"I told Dominic to get his feelings under control or he was off the team. He tried to argue with me that we should be together."

She never let the team see it, but she was angry, angry to her core. She was treated like an incompetent by her superiors, when she had more destructive power within her than any mage alive. Her family had been torn apart by what she was, her mother and siblings choosing to distance themselves from her and each other as a way to deal with her inevitable early death.

Her loneliness had cracked her foundations and let anger sink in deep. She covered it well, but Dominic and his fucking attitude had brought it all to the surface. Her team members had been her only friends, and Dominic had been the closest among them.

"I shouldn't have, but I screamed at him that he couldn't tell me what to think or feel. I was so angry at him. I lashed out. I called him a predator and said some bigoted things about vampires. I'm not proud of it."

The look of hurt that had crossed his face could still conjure horrible feelings of guilt within her. She could never claim to have broken anyone's heart, but she thought she might have come close that night with Dominic.

"He turned in his resignation the next day," she told Alex.

"And you're still friends?"

"We are now, but it's taken a lot of work and years to get back to this point," she said. "I think he understands now. And besides, he told me he's with Camille. He's over me."

Alex considered what she said for several moments before switching gears.

"What did he tell you when you went to see him?"

She filled him in on the conversation and told him about her plans to check out Hellraisers that night.

"So, it's a rough joint, huh?"

"The roughest," she told him.

"And you trust Dominic's intel?"

"Absolutely. He even offered to go with us, suit up for old time's sake. I told him no."

Alex nodded before rising to his feet. "Guess I better get my dancing shoes on. We going loaded for bear?"

Before she could answer, Dumeril burst through the door. "Hey, we caught a lead," he said.

Burdock was right on his heels. They'd been out trying to pin down their victims' time lines, as Alex had suggested. It had taken all day, they explained, but they had managed to track down some girls who knew two of the victims. The women had been turning tricks on the northeast side of town. Dumeril, had been able to tap some of his old contacts from the black market left over from his days as the underground doctor for Austin's non-sapien races. They'd spoken to folks that knew the two women.

"It looks like they didn't know each other," Dumeril said. "But they worked the same part of town."

The women had disappeared several months apart, and no one had thought they would turn up dead. In that crowd, girls left town, disappeared for months at a time, or set up in different parts of town. Neither victim had a pimp. Each had been an independent operator.

"Several of the girls we spoke with said that before they disappeared, the victims had been approached by someone named James," Burdock said. "When we showed them your sketch of our mystery vamp, they said it was the same guy."

"Why didn't APD pick up on this?" Alayna asked.

"Your guess is as good as mine, but in these situations I find it usually boils down to human laziness," Dumeril said. "These women were undocumented and working the streets. They weren't the kind of victims that catch a lot of attention, and the lack of physical evidence makes it hard to turn up any leads. These are the victims no one fights for and our killer was counting on that."

"So now we just need to find this James guy," Alex said.

Dumeril nodded.

"I may have a lead on that, too," he said. "I put out my feelers to the more shadowy side of the black market and word is that this vamp hangs at Hellraisers most nights. In fact, he's supposed to be there tonight for some backroom poker game."

Alayna groaned.

"That's the second time today that club has come up as our next stop," she said, frustration evident in her voice. "And it sounds like we need to go tonight."

"Hellraisers is a rough spot, no doubt," Dumeril said. "But if we're smart, I think we can snag this guy and get out with a minimum of mayhem. Here's how we do it."

11

Chapter 11

Hours later, Alex sat in the passenger seat of the Mustang, parked on a deserted street in South Austin. The area was mostly warehouses, garages, and machine shops. It was after midnight and the area was eerily empty and quiet, the wind whistling between the white-painted industrial buildings.

The team had spent the afternoon preparing for their trip to Hellraisers, examining maps of the area, blueprints of the building, checking weapons and talking tactics.

It was so similar to the prep work Alex had done for missions in Iraq that he found himself reaching for the reassuring weight of his medic's bag and running through mental checklists of drugs and instruments.

He'd almost asked Alayna if he should put together a kit, but thought better of it. He didn't particularly want to go there, not after what happened the last time he'd played paramedic. Fear gripped his belly at the thought of having to work on any of his new team members. Besides, Dumeril was the team medic, and from what Alayna had said, the Svarturan's skills were beyond anything Alex could do with pressure bandages and IV lines.

Hellraisers was down the street and around the corner from where they'd parked. To any casual observer (who couldn't see through glamours), the bar would appear the same as any other warehouse in the district. To anyone that could see through the illusions, the metal building looked like a combination of the scariest biker bar and some of the toughest gang hangouts he'd seen in San Antonio.

In the dirt parking lot, there was a mix of motorcycles, muscle cars, and luxury sedans that screamed drug dealer.

Alex looked through the back glass of the Mustang and saw the team's white panel van pull up a block and a half behind them, on the other side of the intersection.

Alayna's voice pulled him back around. "Remember, we're going in to nab this James person and bring him in for questioning. We're not going to get fancy. This is the roughest bar for a hundred miles. Keep your head down and head for the door if it gets crazy."

The black leather boots he'd seen her wearing that first night in the alley were back. The handle of her amazing expanding whip was in one boot and a wicked knife in the other. Tucked into the tops of the boots was a pair of supple black leather pants. They didn't move like any leather he'd ever seen before. This was fairy leather, made in the Fey realms, she'd said. It hadn't been cut off an animal; it had been grown and shaped. The material was expensive and hard to get, but it was almost impossible to cut, and any tears knit back together on their own. And it breathed like silk, she said.

Right then, Alex had to fight the image from his mind of what it would be like slide them off her gorgeous legs so that he could concentrate on what she was saying.

Don't. Go. There. She'd made it pretty clear with her tale of

Dominic's hasty exit from the team that office romances were not in the cards. Hearing how the guy had treated her had set something hot and ugly smoldering in his thoughts. The list of people he wanted to beat senseless wouldn't fill a Post-It, but Dominic was officially on that list.

It was getting harder to ignore his physical responses to her, but he needed to keep this attraction under control. It wasn't just her ban on office romances that was keeping him from reaching for her. He had a bad track record of getting attached to the women he fought beside. Blanca's death had set him on a perilous path of vengeance, and he'd never had so much as a lustful thought about her. Then there was Kelly. Her death had nearly torn him apart. It ruined his life.

Alex couldn't let that happen again. He'd worked so hard to put his life back together into something he could be proud of. As soon as this case was over, he was going back to that life. Gorgeous witches with moonbeam hair and dangerous jobs did not fit with that plan.

As Alayna ran through her radio checks with the team and Alex double checked his weapons, the memory of her pressed up against him as they'd flown on Z's back rose in his mind. There was no denying that there was a connection between them. It wasn't just that they had managed to swap some memories during that botched memory wipe. When he looked at her he could sense the smallest tendrils of feelings for her taking root.

She was such a mystery. One minute she was hard-hitting muscle and flashing weapons, kicking his ass on the mat. The next, she was touching him, melting against him, taking him on dragon rides. She seemed to love showing him new corners of her world and, if he was being totally honest, he loved going with her.

Ellie's voice crackled over his ear piece. "We're good to go on your signal, Commander."

"Let's go."

Alayna pressed a button, and the top of the Mustang began to retract. They got out of the car and she hit the button for her specialized alarm system as the rag-top finished tucking itself away.

"Expecting trouble?" Alex asked.

"You never know when you might need to make a quick getaway," she replied.

She drew her fingers over the hood, tracing a pattern and whispering a few words. There was a flash of red and the image of a Celtic knot blazed into existence for a moment before disappearing.

"What was that?"

"A ward. A little extra layer of magickal protection should anyone try to mess with the car."

The rest of the team was bailing out of the van. All except Burdock. Alayna had ordered him to stay with the van in case they needed a pick up or back up. He was the ace in the hole, but he was pissed as hell about being left as the rear guard.

Dumeril was dressed much the same as Alex, black fatigue pants, long sleeve shirt and combat boots, but Lu looked like she was heading to the gym. She had an oversized black racer-back tank top and stretchy knee-length exercise pants. It allowed free range of movement and could accommodate sudden growth.

Ellie was a silent shadow that moved in behind them as they approached the bar. Her cloak was an odd material that shifted color in the light, black to blue to gray. It covered her from head to toe and the hood completely hid her face. Combined with her height, it was pretty easy to miss her.

Alex didn't want to know what kind of weaponry bristled under that cloak.

Alayna was in the lead as the group hit the front door. Dumeril and Alex were right behind her. Lu and Ellie hung back a few steps.

As the windowless metal door opened, Alex saw a small, dark outer room with a couple of very mean looking bouncers. Their recognition was plain when they saw Alayna. Their already pale faces got a shade whiter. She didn't have to say a word, but gave them a look. The bigger of the two stepped aside to let them pass.

The first thing that struck Alex as they entered the main room of the bar was the speed at which silence descended. It was like a mute button had been pushed.

Rough didn't begin to describe this place. The floors were a splintering hardwood and a gigantic bar dominated the left-hand side of the long room. The walls were covered in yet more rough wood planking. The tables and chairs scattered around the room were battered and scarred. The primary decoration and source of illumination was neon.

There wasn't a metal surface to be found anywhere. Alex could see why Alayna had left Burdock in the van. The big fire mage would have been a dangerous addition to this environment.

Every eye in the place was locked on them. Some of the people at the bar had more than two. There were a couple of hulking trolls in the corner sipping from stone mugs that could have easily held five gallons. Many of the things at the bar hid beneath cloaks and hoods, but a few were pulled back to reveal green scales, slimy black skin or raw bony ridges. More than a few had frightening red eyes.

This place made the Dusty Trail look like Disneyland.

There was a group of bruisers in leather jackets huddled around a couple of tables, their jackets sporting the same patches declaring them "Los Lobos."

"Shifter biker gang," Dumeril whispered to him.

The vampires were easy enough to spot. Tall, slender, and all of them painfully beautiful. They grouped together like they were too good to mix with the rest of the riff raff. While they looked tough enough in their own right, they were significantly more polished than the other creatures around them, done up in leather and silk. Slumming it.

Alayna met the stares, glares, and gazes without saying a word. Slowly the gazes slid away and conversations began to resume, but more softly than before.

Alayna signaled the bartender, a big well-muscled vampire, and he met her at the end of the bar.

"I run a clean operation here, Commander," the bartender began. "No drugs. And all my licenses are in order."

His eyes flickered over her shoulder to where several customers sitting near the door were making their way outside.

"I'm not here to check up on you," she said, cutting him off. "I just need to talk to a vampire named James. Heard he's here tonight. Then I'll get out of your hair."

She leaned over the bar and shook the bartender's hand, slipping a small roll of hundred dollar bills into his palm.

"What's this for?" he whispered.

"Why don't you decide that when I leave?" she said, an enigmatic smile touching her lips.

"He's in the back room," the bartender said. "And he's not alone."

"Thanks," she said as she turned to rejoin the group.

There was a black door on swinging hinges on the far side of the big room. Alayna nodded toward it and the team fell into formation behind her.

She hit it with both hands and breezed into the back room like she was making an entrance to the VIP room at a nightclub. She was all smiles.

"Heya, fellas," she said to the seven men sitting in the room. "I need to talk to James."

Dumeril had caught the door as Alayna entered, letting the rest of the team through and releasing it to swing shut.

The five guys were clustered around a rough looking table, cards in hand. Alex instantly recognized them as vampires. He was learning pretty quickly how to spot them, mostly in the way they moved.

There was cash, a few gold chains, a watch and a couple of bags of blood on table. They'd clearly interrupted a poker game.

A couple of the guys had on expensive suits and flashy jewelry. Alex would bet dollars to donuts that the drug dealer cars in the lot belonged to them. Two others were dressed like bikers. One had a face full of piercings and a shaved head.

Alex quickly noted two guys seated on either side of the door, tight T-shirts stretched across bulging pecs and biceps. Shifters, if he had to guess. The muscle.

One of the leather-clad vamps stood. He looked young, maybe early twenties, with close cropped sandy hair. He had a lean face and his dark eyes had a dangerous look. He was a dead ringer for the vampire they'd seen in Llorona's vision. The rotting bastard who'd dumped Blanca's body like she was garbage.

Alex's vision went red around the edges, and he had to hold himself back from lunging across the room at the guy.

"Blackwell," the big vampire said, his voice deep, with a mocking tone. A secret smile was tugging at the corner of his mouth.

"James, I presume," she said.

His silence was his answer.

"Need to ask you a few questions," Alayna said. "We can do this here or back at the station."

"What if I say no?"

Alex wanted to wipe the stupid mocking grin off his face.

"It's really up to you how this goes down," Alayna said quietly, her hands raising nonchalantly from her hips.

"Is this the part where you tell me we can do this the easy way or the hard way?"

Alayna took several slow, swaying steps toward the tall vampire until she was close enough to touch him. In those boots, she didn't even have to look up to meet his eyes. Alex suppressed a laugh. This guy didn't know what he was in for.

"I honestly don't care what you do," she said quietly. "We both know there's no easy way here. I know a fucking set up when I smell one."

The other four guys at the table were on their feet in a split second, eyes bleeding to red. Alex heard a popping sound next to him and looked down to see that the hands of the shifter next to him were elongating and growing some very sharp looking claws.

Lu let out a warning growl, and Alex heard a rustling sound in her direction. Dumeril had his hands behind his back, ready to draw his blades. Alex's hand went to his .45 and he made eye contact with one of the suited vamps across the table. The ridiculously huge diamond rings on those big hands could take off half his face. Those weren't rings; they were carefully disguised knuckle dusters.

The tension in the room was stretched to the breaking point.

"Just tell me one thing, one professional to another," Alayna said. "Who hired you to kill me?"

"Who said anything about killing you, sweetheart?" He purred. "My client wants you alive."

With that, he lunged at her throat, fangs stretching past his taut lips.

Alayna dropped low, sweeping a boot out and knocking the legs out from under James. Her silver knife was in her hand in a flash and caught the punked-out vampire in the gut as he made a move toward her from behind.

Dumeril leapt into the fray, his two deadly kurkis emerging from the sheaths on his back, carefully hidden beneath his shirt. James was attempting to rise when Dumeril met him with a flurry of strikes from the curved knives, drawing bleeding lines across the vampire's eyes and face.

James screamed and fell to the floor as Dumeril stepped past him and delivered a kick to his chin that knocked him out cold.

As the big vampire fell, a shot rang out, the sound bouncing off the wood paneling in the small room and making Alex's ears ring. Blood was splattered across the rough wood floor and a chunk of James's skull was missing. One of the suited vamps was holding a smoking chrome-plated .40.

Guess whoever hired this crew didn't want James talking about his body dumping activities.

Alex didn't want to risk pulling his own gun with this many friendlies in the room. Instead, he drew the handle of his asp from his belt and snapped the retractable baton to its full length. With his right hand, he drew his Ka-bar, the black-bladed knife a promise of violence he intended to make good on.

The vampire with the gun had his back to Alex, and he took full advantage of the blind spot. The staggering blow from his baton landed before the sound of the shot had faded. The gun clattered to the floor as the asp connected with the guy's forearm, and Alex was pretty sure he'd heard at least one bone snap.

The vampire rounded on him, his ruby eyes gleaming with menace.

"The Council must be hard up if they're dragging sapiens to the fight now," the vampire said, adjusting those face-removing rings. He was favoring his right arm slightly.

This vamp had gone full predator, long fangs extending over his lip, and he looked thirsty.

Alex crouched low in a fighting stance. He knew this type. He dressed like a gangster and preferred to run his mouth before a fight. This type was thick on the ground where he'd grown up. The key was to draw them in, lull them into a false sense of security and let them overextend themselves.

Alex smiled.

"I'm not sure what a thapien is. It's a little hard to understand you with that lisp, dude."

The vamp charged, left fist swinging to connect with Alex's jaw. Classic.

Alex ducked under the wild swing and stepped in close, delivering a crushing blow to the left side of the vamp's skull with the asp. He heard the satisfying crunch of bone. He followed it up with a twisting jab to the ribs with the Ka-bar. Alex felt the knife slide in like butter and sliced across, earning a scream from the vamp and spray of blood.

Alex slammed the asp repeatedly against the back of the vamp's neck until he went limp.

He turned in time to see the big hairy thing wearing Lu's clothes tackle one of the shifters by the door. They went down in a tangle of hair, fangs and claws. A flash of movement to his right caught his eye.

Ellie was tangling with the other shifter. The tiny gnome looked like she was clearly outmatched, with the hulking shifter towering over her, long claws reaching for her, fangs dripping like he was just waiting for a taste of her blood. He was becoming more and more feline by the second, and Ellie looked like she was about to be a kitty treat.

Alex was going to wade in when the little gnome suddenly grabbed the edge of her cloak and flicked it in the direction of the bruiser's eyes. Blood sprayed from his face, and he clutched his eyes. She spun, and blood spurted from the arms protecting his face. He quickly lowered his arms, clutching the deep cuts on one with the hand of the other, blood dripping on the floor.

Ellie flew straight at the shifter and the top half of his body was lost in the flutter of her cloak.

Alex heard a gurgling scream. Ellie threw back the edge of her cloak to reveal that she was straddling the back of the shifter's neck. A dripping red dagger was in her hand and the shifter's neck was open from ear to ear, blood pouring down to soak his shirt.

That's when Alex noticed a glimmer along the bottom edge of her cloak. The entire edge was covered in a thin, flexible silver blade. A bladed cloak? Yikes.

As the dying shifter began to drop to the floor, Ellie jumped off his shoulders, landing silently with a gymnast worthy dismount, and disappearing into the shadows at the end of the room.

Alex turned back to see Alayna and Dumeril rising from the other two unconscious vampires. In the corner, Alex heard a loud snap and Lu rose above the other shifter, whose neck was at an odd angle, his eyes staring emptily.

"Crowd's getting restless," Ellie said from the doorway.

"Wall's too thick to punch through in the time we have, and it would draw too much attention," Dumeril said.

Alex heard Alayna curse. She touched two fingers to her earpiece and he heard her voice crackle over the channel, "Burdock, we're going to need a pick up at the front door."

Alex heard his affirmative come over the line.

"Form up and stay tight," she snapped.

Alayna had her knife and her whip in each hand, the whip coiled to keep it off the floor. Dumeril had his kukris, Ellie had a dagger in each hand and Lu had her blood-stained claws and teeth out. Alex drew his .45 and moved his K-Bar to his left hand, gripping it like a knife fighter, dull edge back along his forearm. The asp, he stowed on his belt.

The group formed a rough ring, with Alayna at the front, and pushed the door open slowly.

Alex had thought Hellraisers looked like a rough bar when they'd walked in, but he was learning the true meaning of rough now.

Almost everyone in the place was on their feet. The vamps had gone full predator, even the bartender, long fangs gleaming in the neon and red eyes glaring in the dim light. The shifters were looking predatory themselves, most having already shifted or heading there quickly. The Lobos were living up to their name and had shifted to wolves the size of small ponies. A few customers had their heads down and were trying to ignore what was happening.

"Commander Alayna Blackwell of the Mage Corps," she identified herself in a voice loud enough to be heard. "I'm on Council business. We walk out of here and everyone gets to keep their skins where they are."

The team moved as one, roughly back to back and scanning the room. The shifters and the vampires were dangerously still, hunter's eyes trained on the team.

It was a good bet the guys in the back room weren't the only ones who'd been paid to be here tonight. The shifters and vampires eyeing them now were the insurance policy to make sure Alayna was delivered.

Alex's grip tightened on his .45. Not happening. Not while he was still breathing.

Suddenly, one of the wolves lunged at Alayna, and she lashed out with the knife, earning a yelp from the shifter. That was all the signal the others needed. The vampires poured from the right and the wolves from the left. Alex got a couple of shots off, striking two of the vampires in the chest, but they kept coming.

Alayna spun, flicking the whip overhead. It grew in the space of a half second and slammed down on the floor, now easily as big around as Alex's thigh. It was like a thunderclap going off in the small space, and it left Alex's ears ringing. The old wood floor cracked along the path of the whip, sending planks and large splinters flying into their attackers, knocking most off their feet.

"Run!" Alayna shouted.

Didn't have to tell him twice. The group split to move around the rift Alayna had created in the floor, Alayna, Dumeril and Alex to the left, Lu on the right with a cursing Ellie in her fur-covered arms.

The panel van pulled to a screeching halt at the curb just as the team pushed past the front door, the two vampire bouncers more than happy to stay out of their way. The sliding panel was open and Lu tossed Ellie in first and followed her. Dumeril climbed into the front with amazing speed and grace.

Alayna headed for the back bumper and Alex followed, jumping aboard and grabbing onto the small ladder in back as he sheathed his knife. The .45 was in his right hand, the left wrapped around the ladder and Alayna pressed in next to him.

The wolves hit the front door as Burdock hit the gas. The creatures were faster than anything Alex had seen before, and he squeezed off several shots as they closed with the back of the van, chasing them down the street. Two of the wolves yelped and went down, but four more were still hot on their heels.

Alayna whispered several words, her right hand extended toward the wolves. Alex wished she'd hurry up because those things were getting closer and the bullets weren't doing as much damage as he'd hoped.

Lightning crackled from her fingertips, and one of the wolves went instantly unconscious, dropping limply to the pavement.

"Drop us at the Mustang, Burdock, and keep going. Draw them off," she said into the headset.

The van slowed, and Alex hit the pavement in a roll, popping to his feet, his weapon trained on where he'd seen the wolves last. Alayna hit the ground running, her descent slowed by a gust of wind that lifted her hair.

Two of the wolves continued after the van, but one peeled off and loped toward them.

She tossed the keys to the Mustang through the air toward Alex and said, "You're driving!"

With a shout and a wave of her hand, the ward she'd drawn earlier, flashed and disappeared. Hopefully it was disabled.

He caught the keys with his left hand and sprinted for the car, vaulting over the top of the driver's side door and sliding into the seat, thankful Alayna had left the top down.

Alayna did the same on the passenger side, already weaving

her next spell. He jammed the key in the ignition and threw it in gear.

"Punch it, Chewie! We gotta get outta here!" she shouted.

He laughed at the Star Wars reference. He hadn't felt this alive in years. A big grin was plastered on his face.

"Grrrrawr," he shouted in a reasonable approximation of a Wookiee growl.

Alayna tossed him a smile over her shoulder and released her spell, sending something that looked like a blue ball of goo over the back of the Mustang. It took the wolf full in the face, spreading icy crystals over its fur and freezing it to the pavement.

Alex headed for the interstate at high speed, looking for the panel van.

Burdock's voice crackled over the headset.

"We've lost them, Commander. Returning to base."

"Roger that," she said. "See you there."

Chapter 12

"Well, that was a shit show," Dumeril announced as they all filed into the office.

Alex wouldn't go that far in his assessment of the op. Upside: the team had come out relatively intact, aside from a few cuts and bruises. Downside: they hadn't gotten any new information about the case, and the one guy they'd been able to connect to Medina's operation was dead.

"Someone set us up," Lu said.

"And whoever it was wants you alive, Commander," Ellie added.

As the team took up positions around the office, Alex leaned on one of the desks, his arms crossed over his chest, the sole of one combat boot resting against the side. His casual stance did not match the adrenaline-fueled turmoil that was rolling like thunder through his chest.

He hated coming off a fight like this. Every nerve in his body was singing, alive, but the fading adrenaline was going to leave him with nausea and a headache. Never failed. Until then, though, he'd have to deal with jitters and poor judgment.

"Hellraisers came from two different sources: from Dominic

and from Dumeril's black market contacts," Alayna said.

"Could Dominic have set us up?" Lu asked.

"I don't doubt it for a second," Burdock said from where he leaned against the door to the rarely used conference room. "I never trusted that vamp as far as I could throw him."

Alayna paused where she was pacing near the window. She was fuming, nervous energy and anger bleeding off her in waves.

"It doesn't feel right," she said. "He mentioned it as one possible lead we should check out. And besides, Dominic knows our capabilities and that crew of jokers was nowhere near a match for us. We need to consider that Dominic was fed the info by one of his sources."

Alayna was brushing that encounter at Hellraisers off, but it had felt pretty dicey to Alex. There were a few moments where he hadn't been sure they were all going to make it out of that bar.

"Dumeril, what about your black market contacts?"

"Oh, they're shady as fuck. I dropped serious cash for the info about James, but it's possible Medina gave them more. He must know we're on his trail and he's trying to take us out."

They talked around the problem for a few more minutes before Alayna called a halt. They were all tired and could come back at the situation in the morning.

Before he knew it, he was alone with Alayna. The darkness of night pushed at the windows and the overhead lights and the glow of computer monitors did little to keep it at bay. He gripped the edge of the desk, trying to still some of the energy skittering just beneath his skin.

She moved up beside him, as silent as a specter, but he felt the heat of her as her electric scent wrapped itself around him. Could she sense the tension that was coiling in every one of his muscles? He didn't look at her, couldn't look at her.

"How are you doing?"

At the touch of her fingertips, he couldn't help but look down at where her small, pale hand rested on his darkly tanned bicep. He didn't want to tell her that he loved it when she touched him. He didn't want to tell her that the excess adrenaline in his system made him want to push her up against the wall and taste her mouth.

A tremor went through him as he fought the urge to put his hand over hers, trap her against his flesh. It would be so easy then, to turn and pull her against him, let her feel the erection that was straining against the heavy cloth of his fatigues.

It was always like this after a fight. He needed to fuck something. That was the biggest reason he had ended up in Kelly's bed back in Afghanistan. Coming off a firefight, she had been a convenient outlet for his adrenaline-fueled sexual needs. And he had done the same thing for her.

The thought of what happened to Kelly threw a bucket of ice water on the fire burning in his pants. He needed to remind himself what happened when he got involved with team members in the middle of a combat operation, because that is where Alayna and her team her team were headed.

All of the signs were telling them that bad things were ahead and tonight had cemented that.

He gently took her hand from his arm, letting his fingers brush hers for just a second.

"I'm fine," he said. "A little jittery. I just need some food and some sleep."

She nodded, but her eyes didn't leave his face and she still looked concerned.

"This isn't my first rodeo, Commander. I know how to handle

myself in a fight, and I know what to do with myself after a fight."

"I wasn't questioning that. You did really great tonight. I just needed to make sure…" she paused, searching for something. "Never mind. Get some sleep."

He stepped in close to her, resisting the urge to touch her. It was dangerous enough, being this close. He leaned down and spoke in her ear, his voice softer.

"If you want to know the truth, I haven't felt this alive in years," he said.

Straightening, he gathered all of his resolve, turned and walked out the door.

"Sweet dreams, Commander," he called as he headed down the stairs to the warehouse floor.

* * *

Half an hour later, Alex was tossing down his equipment bag as he locked the door to his condo behind him. His keys landed on the table beside the door and a stack of mail that had been piling up in his mailbox went beside them.

He just wasn't spending much time here these days. Even so, he didn't bother to turn on any lights as he headed straight to his bedroom. He'd grab a quick shower and then sleep for about twelve hours. The earlier adrenaline rush had abandoned him, leaving him shaky and exhausted.

He looked out the window. Still a couple hours until dawn.

As he moved through the bedroom to the master bathroom, he grabbed the hem of his T-shirt and began to pull it over his head, wincing slightly at some soreness in his right shoulder. He wasn't sure when that had happened, but it didn't much matter.

Before the black material could clear his face, something hit him in the back of the head. Hard.

Colored lights flashed in his vision, and he felt his knees hit the floor. Another blow hit at the base of his skull. He clung to consciousness, but he crumpled bonelessly to the floor, the T-shirt still over his head, and listened. The cool tile of the bathroom floor pressed against his face through the shirt.

There were two voices, speaking barely above a whisper.

"Boss wants him alive. Tie his hands and drink him 'til he's too weak to move."

Adrenaline hit Alex like a sledgehammer at those words, and fear twisted in his gut. Vampires. And he was completely outnumbered and on his own.

The first voice was about two feet behind him on his left. A second voice grunted in acknowledgment about three feet behind him and to his right. He could hear their heavy steps on the carpet just outside the bathroom.

Alex tried to remain as still as possible. He was lying on his left side, more or less, with his legs tucked up. His ankles were near the bathroom doorway.

As he felt fingers touch his leg, he lashed out with one combat boot-clad foot and connected with something solid. By the crunching sound and the grunt, he'd guess it was a jaw. That attacker fell back against the door frame, and Alex lashed out toward where he thought a throat might be. He was rewarded with a horrible crunch and gurgling noise.

Just as Alex managed to flip onto his back, the other attacker was on him, and he was incredibly strong. One hand clamped around Alex's neck and the other connected with his ribs once, twice.

The air left Alex's lungs in a rush. He struggled to pull the

T-shirt the rest of the way off his face, but the attacker's hand had trapped it against his throat. His airway wasn't cut off completely by the attacker's grip, but he knew it wouldn't be long before he lost consciousness from lack of oxygen, especially if he kept using it up fighting like this.

He managed to get a hand and an arm free from the T-shirt and reached for his attacker. His fingers touched a face. Alex made a fist, hauled back and connected with that face. He put his hand out again and pressed it flat against his attacker's jaw, pushing up and away, hoping to get some breathing room.

After struggling for a few seconds, Alex noticed that his attacker was getting weaker, the grip on his throat less vice-like.

Several blows landed on his stomach and chest, but they were less focused and carried far less force. Alex managed to maneuver his other hand free and push the material of his shirt back down enough to see.

As his eyes focused in the darkness, he saw a large, muscle-bound guy, shaved head, pale skin. Probably a vamp, but no fangs in evidence. Alex reached for the 1911 on his right hip, but it was gone. He'd stored it in his equipment bag for the walk up to the condo. It wasn't nice to freak out the neighbors by walking around in tactical gear with a gun on your hip. It might be Texas, but most people still weren't comfortable with guns out in the open.

He cursed that decision for a second, before remembering his back up. He reached down and pulled his Ka-bar from the sheath on his right calf. It took a second to get it clear of the hem of his pants. When he felt the grip solidly against his palm, he drove it across and up, right into the throat of his attacker.

His attacker's scream turned into a gargling hiss, and Alex felt the body fall backwards and off his knife. Finally, he managed to push the T-shirt off his face, leaving him shirtless. That was when a boot connected solidly with his right side. He was guessing the first attacker that he'd kicked had healed and was on his feet. It was dark in the bathroom, but he could see a shadowy outline to his right.

Alex flipped the knife in his right hand and stabbed downward into the attacker's thigh. He was rewarded with another scream. Fingers clamped around his hand, crushing his bones against the grip of the knife. That was fine with Alex. He put all his weight on the knife and used it to pull himself upright.

Alex felt the knife's blade slide through muscle and scrape along the femur. His attacker grunted with pain and hit Alex across the jaw. With only one of the attacker's hands on the knife, Alex was able to pull it free just as he levered himself into a crouch.

The knife wasn't silver, and vampires could heal quickly. They might be a little weaker from having come in contact with his skin, but it wouldn't last for long. He needed firepower.

He scrambled out of the bathroom and through the bedroom, catching the door frame in his left hand to spin him into the hallway without breaking a stride. He could hear both attackers getting to their feet in the bathroom.

He just had to get to his bag. Luckily, he hadn't zipped it shut. The knife was transferred to his left hand while his right dove into the bag. The grip of the 1911 slid into his palm, and he brought it to bear in one smooth motion. Time seemed to slow down.

His attacker—this one had dark hair and a face that looked like it had been hit by a truck—was just three steps behind him. His fangs were out, and his eyes were so red they nearly glowed.

Alex fired without hesitation, hitting the vamp square in the forehead. The .45 caliber silver-coated bullet didn't leave much behind. The vamp stumbled one step and crumpled, his body slamming heavily to the floor inches from where Alex crouched. The second vamp slowed and put his hands up. The vamp glanced behind him, and in a split second he disappeared back into the bedroom. Alex didn't have a chance to fire. He just crouched there breathing heavily.

After a moment, he rose to his feet to follow the vamp, his weapon out and at the ready. He put his back to the door frame, spun and scanned the room. His FBI academy teachers and drill instructors would be proud.

He noticed then that the door to his balcony, the one off his bedroom, was open. The vertical blinds drifted in a gentle breeze. He moved slowly to the small balcony, but no one was there. He looked over the edge to the street sixteen stories down. It was empty.

*** *** ***

The elevator was moving entirely too slow for Alayna. She bounced on the balls of her feet as it ascended to the sixteenth floor of Alex's condo building. She'd been getting ready for bed when Alex had called, and she stood in the elevator in over-washed yoga pants and a hoodie.

His voice had sounded eerily calm as he told about the attack and the dead vamp. She may have broken land speed records getting from her place to his condo downtown. She'd left her bike parked on the sidewalk in an effort to save time.

Nausea rolled through her stomach. They'd come after him. How on Earth had they found him? How did they know who he was, much less where he lived?

She'd told herself that she could protect him and she'd failed. Guilt tightened her throat and her eyes stung for a moment. If something had happened to him…

Couldn't let herself think that way. He was alive. They'd figure out where the leak occurred and then she'd hunt down everyone responsible. Her hands balled into fists at the thought.

After what seemed like half a century, the elevator chimed softly and the doors opened. She bolted down the hall, counting off numbers until she reached Alex's unit. She knocked impatiently and the door opened a few seconds later.

She froze for a beat. He was dressed in soft grey cotton pants and a black T-shirt stretched over the muscles in his chest and shoulders. His face was blank, but his eyes were wary and haunted, like a cornered predator. There was a tension in his body that he was trying hard not to show. Most of all, he just looked tired.

There were red splotches on his face and neck that showed under his tan skin. Those would be nasty bruises in the morning. Cuts and scrapes marked his hands, the scabs just starting to form.

Without thinking, she reached for him, her hands going to either side of his face. A slight stubble prickled against her palms. The warmth of his skin was a reassurance. He was alive. He was intact.

His eyes met hers as she moved her hands down his neck, over his shoulders and down his arms. Even beat to hell, he felt delicious under her hands, all wonderfully corded muscle and heat.

He hissed when she reached his wrist, and he grabbed her hands to stop her tactile inspection.

"Alayna, I'm fine," he said, his voice gentle.

"I just needed to make sure."

She slipped her arms under his and pulled him close, her face pressed to his shoulder. Every muscle in him tensed for a moment in surprise, his arms slightly raised for a second until he brought them around her.

"I'm so sorry, Alex. I never meant for you to get hurt."

"I'm a big boy, Alayna. I knew what I was signing up for. Thanks to you, I had a fighting chance against these guys."

She looked up at him.

"If I hadn't dragged you into this they never would have known about you."

"If I'd kept digging into this case on my own, they would have found me eventually. I wouldn't have stood a snowball's chance in hell then."

She nodded, her thoughts spinning with a thousand what ifs. He caught a knuckle under her chin and brought her gaze to his, causing her stomach to do a little flip and all the thoughts to come to a screeching halt.

"Whatever happens, I'm better off with you, Alayna. I'd rather go down fighting than living in the dark."

She turned to the corpse just a few feet from the front door. Alex had covered it with an old tan bed sheet. Dark blood had soaked through it and was pooled on the polished concrete floor of the hallway.

Alayna lifted the sheet and peered underneath.

"Nice shot," she said simply.

"Thanks."

"I'm really impressed. There's not many people that could fight off two vampires and live to tell about it, much less take one down."

"Anyone you recognize?"

She flipped the corpse on its back and started going through the pockets. No ID. A pair of plastic zip ties in the back pocket of the jeans. Nothing else.

"This guy was the muscle. I'm guessing the guy who split was your entry man."

She rose and examined the front door. No scratches around the lock, so it wasn't picked, and it hadn't been forced.

She nodded toward the bedroom. "May I?"

Alex nodded and followed her. It felt weird to be in his home. The place wasn't big, just a kitchen and living room combination to the right of the entrance and a hallway to the left that led to his bedroom. The place looked like a picture from a modern furniture catalog, all right angles, glass, chrome and earth tone fabrics.

The bed was neatly made and for a moment, she imagined him in it. Naked. She knew what the muscles under his shirt looked like and she'd bet the rest of him looked just as good.

"I haven't moved anything," he told her, breaking into her reverie.

She crossed to the still open balcony door. The balcony itself was tiny, maybe five feet by seven feet. It was just a blank square of concrete with bars and a railing in powder coated steel. He hadn't even bothered to put a plant out here.

She examined the door. No signs that it had been tampered with.

"None of the windows were open or broken?"

"They're sealed. They don't open."

He paused a moment and said, "I think they came through the sliding door."

"What makes you think that? The lock is intact."

"Because I don't usually lock that door," he said, a little sheepishly.

"Seriously?"

"I live on the sixteenth floor," he said defensively. "I had no idea vampires could fly. Besides, I never thought anyone would come after me. I still don't know how they found my address, much less identified me."

"First of all, they don't fly. But they can climb very well, and they can jump further than you'd think," she said. "In fact, I'm guessing your second attacker jumped from here to that building across the street."

She pointed out the building across from his high rise. It was about twelve stories, brick, with a flat roof.

"You think he could have made it that far?" Alex asked, incredulous.

"Without breaking a sweat," she answered.

"Do vampires sweat?" he asked.

Only Alex would wonder about that at a time like this.

"Not that I've noticed," she said. "And I've never thought to ask. As to how they found you, they have resources, hackers, informants. I should have anticipated this and put up some firewalls around you."

She had never dreamed that the creatures they were hunting would pay any attention to Alex. He wasn't a direct threat to them. It was her they should be worrying about. But she had more security than most, her home was untraceable, and no one with two brain cells to rub together would come after a mage commander on her home turf. Even if by some miracle a hit was successful, the Corps would come down on those responsible like avenging angels.

The non-sapiens that chose to do wrong never went on the

offensive with Corps personnel. It was an unspoken rule, a code among the thieves and cutthroats. They wouldn't hesitate to kill Council agents that moved against them on their own turf, but to target a member of a Corps strike team personally was unheard of.

"Someone is getting desperate," she said. "Or they saw you as a weak spot to get to me."

She glanced back at the sheet-covered corpse in the hallway.

"Fortunately, they vastly underestimated your skills," she said.

These were far from professionals. Street muscle most likely. No one she recognized. They'd run the ID on the dead guy and figure out where the leak was.

"In the meantime, I think you should get out of town," she said.

He scowled.

"Absolutely not," he said, crossing his arms.

"I need to know you're safe, Alex."

He moved to her, running his hand down the back of her arm and she had to fight to keep from trembling beneath that touch.

"I can handle myself," he said gently, glancing meaningfully in the direction of the corpse.

"You've proven that. Just do this for me, please."

"Why?"

She sighed with exasperation and broke the contact with him. She couldn't tell him the real reason. She couldn't tell him that she was falling for him. Heck, she wouldn't even admit that to herself.

"When you agreed to join the team, I promised to protect you—"

"You never promised me that," he said.

"I promised myself that."

Silence stretched between them for several moments as they both looked anywhere but at each other. Finally, their gazes caught. She let him see the guilt, the fear, and the edge of panic at the thought of losing him in her eyes.

"I don't run from a fight," he said, his voice as firm as stone. "And I'm not leaving you."

Something in her chest squeezed at his words.

"Well, then, pack a bag because you're moving in with me."

13

Chapter 13

Alex froze. Of all the things he'd thought she'd say, he hadn't expected Alayna to suggest he move in with her. "I can stay at HQ," he told her.

"I'd feel better if you were close by."

He opened his mouth to argue and then shut it. There was a note in her voice that was just short of a plea.

"I'll pack a bag," he said, finally, a smile tugging at his mouth. "Roomie."

She smiled and he felt that twisting feeling in his gut again. What was he thinking? He already had trouble getting thoughts of her out of his head, her scent out of his nose. Staying with her was going to be torture. Sweet, delicious torture.

He threw clothes, a toothbrush, deodorant and a spare pair of boots into an old leather travel bag that once belonged to his father. He grabbed the silver St. George's medal his mother had given him when he joined the army from his nightstand. He threw in his Kindle and added his phone charger. He was packed in less than two minutes.

Alayna looked surprised when he joined her in the living room so soon.

"I travel light," he told her.

"Good to know," she said. "Because we don't know how far we may end up going."

He carried the bag to the door and set it down beside his equipment bag. He made sure his weapons were all in order, and then he nodded to the body.

"What are we going to do about him?"

"We're taking him to the roof," she said, wrapping the sheet tightly around the body. She levered the body into a sitting position and hoisted the two hundred pound dead vampire over her shoulder like it was a sack of potatoes.

"Get the door and make sure the hallway is clear," she said, her voice carrying the slightest hint of strain.

Alex knew that she was strong, but he hadn't realized she was that strong.

As they walked out onto the roof 37 stories up, the skies were still dark and the stars were still out. Under different circumstances, it would have been a beautiful morning.

Alayna walked to the middle of the roof and flipped the body from her shoulder to the concrete.

Kneeling beside the body, she held her hands out over the form beneath the sheet, sensing the edges, finding the currents. The necessary words formulated themselves in her mind and she let them flow from her, channeling the element of fire.

Fire was, by far, the most difficult element for her to control. Her voice crackled like flames, rising and falling in pitch and tone, like a campfire. A controlled burn, like this one, was one of the most difficult elemental exercises she knew.

She concentrated the heat in the vampire's abdomen and let it slowly spread outward. She increased it where necessary and moved some heat away from areas that were burning quicker. Slowly, the body began to turn to ember and ash, falling apart like a log in a fire.

Just as the sheet caught fire, the form collapsed to nothing but gray ash. With more whispered words, a wind flowed over the roof and carried the ashes away, a swirling mist in the lightening morning. The whole process had taken maybe five minutes.

"Whoa," Alex said.

She turned and saw…something in his eyes. Was it fear? Amazement? Both? It was hard to tell, but that look put her on edge. Was he about to push her away like every other male she'd ever been interested in?

He extended a hand to help her up. As she stood, her head spun and she stumbled, landing heavily in his arms.

"Sorry," she said, a little embarrassed. "Fire weaving takes a lot out of me."

She looked up and met his eyes. His arms were tight around her and she was pressed against his chest. His face was hard and his eyes were now unreadable. She had a sudden powerful urge to caress his face. Would he let her? If she kissed him, would his lips taste as wonderful as they had that night in the alley?

Her heart leapt at the idea.

He broke their eye contact as he placed her left arm over his shoulders and hooked his right arm around her waist. She leaned on him until they reached the elevator, where she stepped away from him and leaned on the wall.

"That was…" he said into the silence. "Terrifying."

Alayna felt a momentary pang at that word. She'd known it would happen eventually. It always did. Anytime anyone got close, they pulled away. Her power, her curse, they doomed anything more than friendship. She'd entertained fleeting, secret thoughts that maybe Alex was different, but you couldn't be attracted to someone that terrified you. Anger snapped within her.

"Should we have called the Coroner to the come and pick up the body? How about the police?"

"Excuse the hell out of me. You just cremated someone in front of me. Forgive me if I'm a little creeped out right now."

"Does my power scare you, Alex?"

She wasn't sure what she wanted him to say, but part of her wanted him to see past what she was and see who she was.

He let a long breath out before answering, his gaze assessing. A dark intelligence was running calculations in his eyes.

"Sometimes," he said finally. "Mostly, I'm in awe of what you can do. I just keep wondering why you think you need me around."

She met his eyes, silently begging him to understand, to see. He was this fascinating new thing that had come storming into her life, a life that had started to go a little gray around the edges.

"You're good in a fight," she said.

He left his place on the opposite elevator wall and took a step toward her.

"You have people that can shape shift and throw fire. You don't need me."

"You're wrong," she said. "Ever since that night in the alley something has been screaming at me to keep you close. I don't know why or how yet, but you fit into this somehow. I've survived this long by listening to my instincts, and I'm not about to stop now."

He smiled.

"You sure it's your instincts that are telling you to keep me close?"

Turning a surprised look on him, she saw those dark eyes were teasing, but his mouth was set in a hard line. She longed to run her tongue over those lips.

The elevator dinged and saved either of them from having to say anything more.

As she stepped away from the wall, her head spun again. When it stopped spinning, she realized she was in Alex's arms, one behind her back, the other beneath her knees.

"I'm OK, put me down."

"I'll have to politely decline, Commander. You need water, food and rest in that order. That's my professional medic's opinion," he said, his back military straight, his demeanor all business. As he stepped off the elevator on his floor, he asked, "Can you do that thing you did with the fire to living people?"

"I could," she replied. "But they'd have to hold really still, and it requires more energy and concentration than it would be worth. If I want to kill someone, there's lots easier ways to do it."

He shot her a look.

"That came out wrong."

Alex was somehow able to unlock his door and open it without putting her down. He kicked it closed and gently set her on the couch. Overbalanced, he almost followed her down, but caught himself with a forearm on the back of the sofa.

He stayed like that for a second and brushed his hand over her forehead.

"You're cold," he said, pulling his hand away. He fetched a blanket from an armchair and spread it over her. She tried to sit up, but he pushed her back down again with a firm but gentle hand on her shoulder.

"I'm not to be fussed over, Agent," she said firmly, a slight snap in her voice. "I don't need to be coddled."

He shot her a look that said, "stay put" and headed for the kitchen.

"Weaving fire usually messes up my internal temperature for a little while. Mostly though, I need water," she said. "And sugar, carbs, anything with calories. I'm freaking starved."

He popped a bowl of instant oatmeal in the microwave and smothered it in honey and a mound of dried apricots.

She levered herself up to sit cross-legged on the couch, the blanket tucked around her legs. The effort didn't seem to cost her as much as when she first stood up on the roof. Perhaps she was regaining her strength.

She wolfed down the oatmeal in under a minute. He pulled out several bags of frozen fruit from his freezer and dumped them in the blender, adding protein powder, almond milk and more honey.

She gulped it down.

"That's it," he said. "You cleaned me out. I don't keep a lot of food here during the best of times, and let's face it, I've barely been here since I went to work for you."

She nodded and started to get to her feet. When he moved to help her, she waved him off.

"I'm fine," she said. "Really."

She walked slowly to the counter where he was rinsing the dishes.

"Thank you, Alex," she said.

Something in her voice made him look up and meet her eyes.

"You're welcome," he said.

"I'm not used to anyone trying to…take care of me," she said hesitantly.

"It's OK. I used to see it every day in the Army. COs don't

like to accept help, even from the medics. They don't want to appear weak. A part of my training was how to talk them into letting me do my job. If they weren't a hundred percent, the team wasn't a hundred percent."

He put the dishes away.

"But Dumeril must do this for you all the time," he said.

"Not really. Dumeril isn't the type to fuss. If I'm bleeding, he just grabs whatever part is dripping blood and heals it without asking me. If I push myself too far during training or a mission, he wouldn't notice until I pass out. Then, he'll slap me awake, shove an energy bar in my hand and glare at me until I eat it."

"You still hungry?" Alex asked.

"I'm good to drive home," she said.

They rode the elevator down together and put his bags in his truck. She went out to the sidewalk where she'd parked her bike, started it up, and met him at the entrance to his underground garage. He followed her west across the city, the first pink rays of dawn lighting the sky.

* * *

Alex followed the souped-up black motorcycle as Alayna drove through the city. She was gorgeous, her yoga pants clinging in all the right places as she leaned her body across the sleek black monster of a bike. Her blonde hair flowed in waves from under her black helmet and danced in the wind as she drove.

Not for the first time, he wondered what it would be like to touch that hair, run his hands through it, wrap it in his fist as he kissed her hard.

Before long, they were winding into the canyons west of downtown. The bike's engine revved as she took a series of steep winding turns faster than she probably should have. The houses in this area were large modern masterpieces that sat on huge treed lots.

Alayna signaled and pulled the bike into a driveway that wound up and to the right. Her home looked like a log cabin had made love to a Victorian mansion. It was two stories, but smaller than many of the homes in the area. There were screened porches that wrapped around both levels.

The outside was covered in cedar plank siding and the trim was a dark forest green. The lot was so heavily treed that he couldn't see the house fully until he was right next to it.

He followed Alayna around back to a large garage where she parked the bike next to her Mustang. He pulled his truck in next to it.

He whistled appreciatively.

"Nice place."

"Thanks," she replied, as the garage door slid closed. "I needed a place without a lot of neighbors and that didn't get a lot of traffic that could screw with my wards," she said.

She explained that she owned several acres on either side, what amounted to most of the ridge. The house was at the top of the ridge, with the land sloping sharply beyond her back garden into a heavily wooded ravine.

Her entire property was covered with magical protection wards. The ones around the property could be triggered by any being with a malevolent intent. There were even more wards on the house.

As they were about to step inside, she stopped him at the door. She hung a small clay pendant in the shape of a spiral on a black cord around his neck.

"I don't think you'll set my wards off, but just in case, this will let you through any of them without any trouble."

He held the charm in the palm of his hand as he examined it. He hated jewelry, but strangely, he liked this. He tucked it inside his shirt and he liked the way it felt next to his skin.

"Thanks," he said.

Her home was all dark woods, rich fabrics and granite surfaces. The furniture tended to antique. She pointed out a large kitchen that looked like it didn't get much use and a living room that looked untouched.

She pointed out a bedroom on the first floor, obviously a guest room.

"This is yours," she said. "Bathroom's through there."

He tossed his bags on the bed. The room was done in shades of blue, the walls a lighter color, the comforter on the bed a deep navy. The furniture was all dark woods, like the rest of the house.

He unpacked quickly and found Alayna in the kitchen. She was in the process of drizzling chocolate syrup on several scoops of ice cream.

She licked syrup off the palm of her hand and the breath caught in his throat. When she slid her index finger between her lips and sucked it with a little kissing noise, he almost passed out.

"Want some?"

He shook his head, keeping the counter between them.

"One of the few perks of the job," she said, nodding toward the ice cream bowl. "Weaving magick burns a hell of a lot of calories."

She lifted the bowl in one hand and spooned a bite between those perfect lips. Her shoes were off and as she padded around her home in her bare feet he realized that she was relaxed for the first time since he'd met her.

And she was absolutely gorgeous.

He longed to pull her against his body, let her feel exactly what she was doing to him. Her lips would taste like chocolate and her tongue would be cold when it brushed his. His hands would slide into her hair, and she would let out a breathy little moan. Then he'd—

"Alex?"

"Huh?"

She laughed.

"I said, would you like a tour of the rest of the place?"

He nodded and followed her up the stairs.

The upstairs featured the same floor to ceiling windows as the rest of the house. Most of the second floor was taken up with a huge empty expanse of smooth hardwood floor. There was a weapons rack in the corner and a stand with a speed bag. There was a heavy punching bag hanging from a chain bolted to the angled ceiling.

"This is a beautiful dojo," he told her.

She licked ice cream off her spoon.

"There's more," she said excitedly.

She touched a switch on the wall and the windows slid open on three sides, opening on to the wrap around porch. The view was amazing, and the air flowing in was crisp and clean.

"This is my favorite place in the house," she said. "I feel like I can breathe and move here."

She pointed out a changing room and bathroom on the fourth wall and told him to use the training area whenever he wanted.

He frowned.

"Where do you sleep?" he asked. "It seems like there's a bedroom missing."

She laughed and he followed her downstairs, then past his room and her library/office. She opened a door and stepped out onto a section of the screened-in wraparound porch. There was a large four-poster hung with a cream sheer canopy and curtains to the left of the door. There was a large armoire against the exterior wall of the house and a sitting area with a small sofa, chairs and a table done in white wicker with floral cushions.

It was light and delicate and feminine, and it fit Alayna so perfectly. He touched one of the sheer curtains on the bed and rubbed the material through his fingers. This was the real Alayna. The relaxed, laughing woman who slept in the ultra-feminine room, this was her.

"You sleep outside?"

"It's an air mage thing," she explained. "All the elements have their quirks, especially when it comes to sleeping arrangements. Earth mages like to sleep underground. Fire mages are super warm sleepers and they like to have a fire going, even in the summer. Water mages like to live near the ocean or lakes and rivers. I suspect that's why my brother, Xander, lives in New Orleans."

"And you need fresh air, I'm guessing?"

A smile lit her features as she nodded. "My parents used to find me asleep in trees when I was little. I've never been able to sleep well inside."

Alex looked back at the bed and he could picture with perfect clarity how she would look with her platinum hair spilling over those pillows. He closed his eyes and tried to get a grip.

"You look really tired," Alayna said. "Hit the sack. That's an order."

"You should probably do the same, Commander. Just a suggestion."

* * *

When she heard the door to Alex's room close, Alayna let out the breath that she hadn't realized she'd been holding.

It felt so odd having someone here, having him here. This was her space, and she was so used to being alone in it.

And she liked it that way, she told herself as she crawled into bed. Even though it was after dawn, she would still get some sleep. With all of the tall cedar trees and the deep porch roof, it was dim enough.

She didn't let people get this close, but here was Alex, just a few feet away, probably crawling into bed just like she was. Sure there was her team, but when she hung out with them, it was at a bar. They never came to her home. There were the guys she picked up in bars, but they didn't even know her real name, and she never bothered to remember theirs.

It had been about three weeks since she had gone out and hooked up. She'd picked up the last guy in a dive bar on East Sixth. He'd been tall and blond, a banker or something to do with finance. He'd been artfully scruffy. It was the kind of roughness that was carefully cultivated and totally artificial.

He'd been decent in bed, enough to release her tension and keep her from climbing the walls.

But compared to Alex, he was a pale shadow. Where the forgettable fling had a carefully cultivated scruffy look that was trying just a little too hard to cover up the blandness, Alex had the military polish and precision that was barely containing the roughneck underneath.

She had watched that government-issued rigidity rub off a little over the past week, and she longed to see it slip completely. What would he be like if he let that epic control slip for just a moment?

As she closed her eyes and tried to sleep, she let herself slip into the fantasy of what it would be like. He was strong, and his arms would feel so good around her. While his arms were powerful, his hands would be gentle, caressing her face, twining in her hair.

His lips would be firm at first, but would soften as their kiss went on. His tongue would sweep into her mouth, possessing it, possessing her.

She felt her skin flush and she shoved the fantasy away. No one could possess her, and she could never let anyone get close to that point. She wanted Alex, perhaps more than she had ever wanted anyone in her life. It scared her.

Alex was not hers. He could never be hers. She would never be the one to watch his control slip, the one that he pulled desperately into his arms and kissed like she was air and he was a drowning man.

What she would do was catch this killer. And she would protect Alex for as long as she had left so that he could go on and live his life. He deserved that chance at happiness, or at least, some kind of peace. With that resolved, she rolled on to her side and drifted off to sleep with Alex in her thoughts, wrapped around her like a warm blanket.

* * *

Alex pulled the comforter back and slid between the cool, dark blue sheets. He was so tired that his bones ached. His fatigue had settled deep in his gut and felt like it was eating him from the inside out.

He closed his eyes and fell almost instantly asleep, darkness and fatigue wrapping themselves around him and pulling him down.

Sometime later, he came awake, feeling something touching his chest. Delicately soft hands moved up over his ribs, tracing the line of his pectorals. Little nails lightly raked the skin around his nipples. He gasped, his eyes adjusted after a moment to find Alayna lying next to him.

It was dark outside the windows and the room was covered in dim shadows. That didn't seem quite right to Alex. Hadn't it been dawn just a minute ago? Had he slept all day? Hell, didn't matter, she was touching him, her hands chasing away the questions.

Alayna was a bright flame in the dark room, her hair the color of moonlight and skin shining like a pearl. Her hands were dancing lightly over his stomach and hips. He sucked in a breath.

"What are you doing?" he asked her, his voice hoarse with sleep and desire.

"What I've been wanting to do since that night in the alley." Her soft, warm breath brushed his throat as she whispered the words.

She leaned forward and brushed her lips against his, her slender fingers twining in his hair. Her skin sliding against his felt like silk and her mouth tasted like honey. That moonbeam hair fell around his face in a perfumed cloud as she pushed him back against the pillows.

His heart began to pound against his ribs, the muscles in his chest going tense as arousal flooded his veins like rushing wildfire.

He pulled her to him, feeling the satin of her nightgown sliding against his chest. His arms wrapped around her and he took control of the kiss, rolling her under him and pinning her to the bed. She felt so good underneath him, warm and soft in the right places.

Alex ran his hands along the curves of her waist and hips and reveled in them. Her body was strong, she was strong, and he loved that strength.

To be wanted by a powerful woman was a heady thing. He met her indigo eyes, almost black in the dark, and she gave him a witchy look through her lashes that said she couldn't wait to have him.

Her mouth against his was demanding, claiming. Her tongue slid along his bottom lip and he groaned against her mouth. She took that opportunity to slide her delicate tongue against his. It reminded him of that night in the alley, and his body responded with a fresh flood of heat along his nerves.

She broke the kiss and pulled back, her hand against his jaw. The tender touch nearly undid him. His breath coming fast, he closed his eyes and pressed his forehead to hers.

His hand touched the delicate, silken skin of her thigh and pushed the lacy hem of her nightgown up. When his hand brushed her hips, he realized she wasn't wearing any underwear, and he groaned softly against her neck. As he did that, he felt goosebumps chase down the skin of her throat and chest.

He captured her mouth with his again and reached to touch the slick heat between her thighs.

* * *

Alayna arched against Alex as he touched her. His fingers felt incredible as he stroked the sensitive flesh between her legs. When one finger gently rubbed her clit, she nearly came off the bed. He caught her breathy cry of ecstasy against his mouth and he laughed softly in his throat.

He pulled the top of her nightgown down and drew one nipple into his hot mouth, his teeth scraping ever so lightly over it. That, combined with what he was doing to her clit nearly overwhelmed her with sensation. She was enveloped in ecstasy and on the edge of a screaming orgasm.

It never happened this fast with the guys she hooked up with at the bars. They were usually drunk and she was lucky if she got any serious foreplay before they got down to business. That was okay sometimes. She was skilled enough to get herself off if she was on top, which most guys didn't mind at all.

She wasn't exactly sure how she had ended up in Alex's bed. The last thing she remembered was going to sleep in her own bed. Hadn't that been just after dawn? Why was it so dark outside? And she definitely didn't remember wearing this silky white nightgown to bed. She was pretty sure she'd gone to bed in a pink tank top and pajama bottoms with cupcakes on them.

Those thoughts flew from her mind when Alex's hand moved away from her, and he lifted his head. She almost whined in frustration when he moved to cover her body with his and she felt the tip of his cock touch her opening. Oh, goddess, she wanted him so badly. Her skin felt like it was on fire and everywhere he touched, she could swear it sizzled.

She was pure sensation. Her brain felt drowsy, and her head was spinning a bit. She felt him move against her, the delicious slide of his hard flesh against her soft—

Alayna awoke with a start to find her cell phone's alarm going off, telling her it was time to get up and get dressed. She turned it off and flopped back onto her bed, the bright light of the afternoon streaming onto the porch.

She'd been dreaming. Of Alex.

Her face felt hot and she ran her hands over her cheeks and forehead, which were dotted with perspiration.

It was just a dream. OK, maybe the best dream of her life, but just a dream. It had felt so real, though.

Why couldn't it be real?

She pushed the thought away, feeling embarrassed. How would Alex react knowing that she had been having the mother of all wet dreams about him?

Her body was screaming for release. She'd been so close in the dream. Couldn't the damn alarm have waited five more minutes?

She sighed and rolled out of bed, pulling a robe on over her cupcake pajamas and headed upstairs to the bathroom by the dojo. In the shower, she could take care of this tension herself and hopefully not give herself away by blushing when she saw Alex next.

As she passed by his room, his door was thankfully shut. She'd let him sleep a little while longer.

* * *

Alex awoke with a start and realized that he was alone in his bed. He was disoriented for a moment. He'd just been about to—

"Fuck," he groaned in frustration.

Holding Alayna in his arms had felt so real and for a few brief moments, he'd felt...whole. He'd felt relaxed and tense at the same time, happy and nervous, sure and scared.

Looking down, he saw that one part of him had not realized that it was a dream. Damn it. He threw the covers off and headed for the shower to take care of that.

14

Chapter 14

When Alex walked into the office at HQ a few hours later, he saw that Alayna had not taken advice regarding rack time. He'd managed to catch a couple of hours himself and had woken up to a text from her saying that she was headed to the office.

She was in fresh clothes and leaning over Ellie's desk, deep in conversation with the gnome. As he approached, he noticed the oversized coffee cup on the corner of Ellie's desk was empty. Sliding it off the desk while the ladies were discussing something on Ellie's huge three-monitor display, he refilled it with her special brew and put it a safe distance from Ellie's elbow.

"You are a prince among men, Martinez," she said between sips without taking her eyes off the screen. "Ah, sweet caffeine. Best thing in the Earthly Realms, by far. Most of the elvish races might turn their noses up at artificial stimulants, but those douche bags don't know what they're missing."

"What are y'all working on?" Alex asked, leaning a hip against Ellie's giant desk.

"I pulled the security footage from your apartment building

and I've been tracking the bad guys using traffic cameras and other security cams in the area. Looks like they entered the building across from yours, climbed to the roof, and they must have jumped over to your balcony."

A video clip was playing on a loop of the two vampires that attacked him climbing a stairwell superhumanly fast.

"I have some of my own facial recognition programs running. This runs everything from the DMV to Costco memberships. If these guys have ever had a photograph attached to their names, I'll find them."

The little gnome's fingers flew over her keyboard as manipulated several programs at once.

"This might be the break we need in this case," Alayna said, turning to Alex. "All because someone got sloppy coming after you."

She continued, "Let me know when that program comes back with something. I've got reports to file."

Alayna stepped away and Ellie sat back.

"All we can do now is wait," the gnome said.

Alex was curious about Ellie. As good with a computer as she was with a blade, the little hacker didn't say much unless it was lay the snark on someone.

"Where did you pick up the mad tech skills?" he asked her.

Ellie gave him side-eye beneath a raised eyebrow.

"Come on. Your program is going to be running for a while. I just want to know more. Are all gnomes good at tech?"

She snorted loudly.

"Back in the Fey Realms, we don't really have electronics. A few tinkerers like to work with steam power, but that's about it. Nah, those losers wouldn't know how to turn on a computer, much less how to use one," she said derisively.

"So how did you get into it?"

"Picked up working for a criminal syndicate on this side of the dimensional rift, if you must know."

"Say what?"

"Yup, I used to be total dark side. Until Alayna came along."

"Come on, you've got to tell me more now."

And she did. Ellie had grown up the child of gnomish artists, but she'd always been the "black badger" of the family. She'd paid a fey to open an illegal portal to the Earthly Realms and jumped without a visa. But it turned out she didn't have many skills. She'd turned to thieving to survive.

"Got in debt to some very bad supernatural characters. I was forced to go to work for them."

But she'd taken every opportunity to learn from the underworld types she was surrounded by.

"I'm guessing that's where you learned to use a blade," Alex said.

"From some of the best cutthroats in the world," she said. "Leaned how to be better with computer. Before long, I was stealing priceless works of art, billions of dollars in corporate files, you name it."

Until she'd fallen for a trap.

"Alayna set me up. Put an artifact in the open she knew my bosses would go after. I had to go in person. I ghosted past security, but she and her team were waiting for me."

Ellie had two choices after that: go to the Mountain, the Council's max prison, or go to work for Alayna.

"She and I worked together to take down the assholes I used to work for. We somehow lived through that, and here I am."

So, Alayna was the type of person who could overlook someone's past. The more he learned about her, the more liked and trusted her.

"Criminal to law enforcement. Must have been a massive shift," he said.

"Not really. Work's pretty much the same. Maybe a little more dangerous. But the difference is, I can trust the people at my back."

She gave him a pointed up and down look. She had better be able to trust him or she'd cut him to ribbons, that look said.

"You can trust me, Ellie. You're the gal that's going to help me figure out who killed Blanca. I've definitely got your back. But I don't think you need it."

She was silent for a moment before she continued. "I've gotten pretty good at taking care of myself, no doubt. But none of us ever knows when we're going to need backup."

"What I think you're trying to say is you're glad I'm on the team?" He turned a smile in her direction.

She was rolling her eyes when the computer chimed happily.

"Gotcha!" Ellie said excitedly as photos and information began pouring across the screen.

"That's him," Alex said. "The one who ran."

"This one's got a record with sapien law enforcement for assault and several other violent crimes. Looks like he's been flagged by Corps' operatives in Dallas for possible involvement with racketeering schemes against members of the supernatural community."

Her hands were flying again as she read.

"I'm starting to see some patterns to movements here," Ellie said. "Let's see how this matches up to financial records."

With that, she was silent as windows, and information flew across her screen like scattering birds.

* * *

Alayna knew she should be concentrating on what Ellie was saying as she outlined what she'd found, but her mind kept drifting back to that crazy dream she'd had about Alex. The team sat around the conference table as Ellie pulled up images on the large LCD screen at one end of the room. The photo of the dead vampire from Alex's apartment appeared on the screen and jerked Alayna back to the here and now.

"I'm not sure of his name exactly," Ellie said. "He's used a lot of aliases. So I have dubbed him Douchebag Dickweed."

With a couple of keystrokes on her wireless keyboard, she enlarged the image.

"From what I can tell, this guy is hired muscle, and not the expensive kind," she continued. "He comes with a record, and he's not discreet."

Next she brought up a series of what appeared to be bank statements.

"I was able to track his financials down and I noticed a payment from a shell company that had come up in connection with Jimmy Medina's operation."

She highlighted the payment on the screen. Apparently, for the low price of ten thousand bucks, you could have your very own FBI agent, delivered in whatever condition you wanted. Alayna shuddered to the think what might have happened if Alex had been a little slower on the draw. Word was, Medina was ruthless with those who crossed him.

Alayna spoke up. "So we have a connection between the bruiser and Medina. Great. But that doesn't get us any closer to finding Medina himself."

Ellie held up a finger and then started clicking away on her keyboard again. More documents appeared on her screen. And photos of three warehouses.

"I was able to connect that shell company with property tax records for these three warehouses," she said. "That's where he slipped up."

Alex rose from his seat and moved to the screen to study the photos.

"Where are these?"

"Different areas of the city," Ellie replied. "All of them are located close to the interstate and set up to load and unload eighteen-wheelers."

"How is all of this connected to our victims?" He asked, turning to look at Ellie.

"I've been looking at what financials I can find on Medina's companies, and I've got a bad feeling," Ellie said. "The figures don't add up, and you don't have the level of shell companies that I'm seeing if your operation is legit."

"What are you saying?" Dumeril asked.

"I'm saying that we likely have multiple layers of illegal enterprise here," she said. "This network gets bigger the more that I look at it. And he's moving a lot of trucks, particularly close to the border."

Alayna watched as Alex processed this. It was good to see him diving in, making himself a part of the team. He wasn't holding himself back like he had before.

"Are we talking drugs? Coyotes?" he asked, using the slang term for people that smuggled illegal immigrants across the border, usually for huge sums of money.

"I'm not sure what those trucks are moving, but I think it's a good bet that all of our victims, except for Blanca, got too close to whatever it is," Ellie said.

Alex straightened, his eyes brightening for a moment.

"Stakeouts," he said, looking to Alayna for confirmation. "We need to stake these warehouses out."

Alayna nodded.

Ellie cackled and began rubbing her hands together as she reached for a tablet computer.

Lu leaned over to look at the screen. "You said the magic word, dude. She's ordering new GPS trackers online."

While Ellie sang softly under her breath about new toys, Alex said, "Three warehouses—we're going to have split up."

"Lu is the recon expert," Alayna said. "She can coordinate."

"Dumeril and Burdock can work as a pair on the north side warehouse. Ellie and I can work the east side warehouse," Lu said.

She turned to Ellie. "You can do your computer stuff remotely, right chica?"

Ellie waved at her with one hand, her eyes focused on her tablet. Lu nodded.

"Alayna, you and Alex should take the south side warehouse," Lu said, a big smile on her face.

Alayna didn't particularly like that smile. Lu was up to something.

"It sounds like a good plan," Alayna said. "Lu, get your equipment sorted. We're going to need trackers, recording equipment, scopes, thermal imaging if you've got it, power sources, and secure communications.

Lu nodded and started making a list on her smartphone.

Alayna turned to Alex.

"Have you ever run across smuggling cases when you were with the FBI?"

"I worked as part of a team on a couple of drug and gun

running cases," he said. "It was always as part of a joint task force, though, so I was handling mostly low-level stuff."

She nodded, processing that.

"I'd like you to run over the files Ellie has come up with and see if you find any markers or indicators from your previous experience. Anything that stands out. I'd like to know what we're dealing with as soon as possible," Alayna said.

15

Chapter 15

Across town, Alayna popped another cold French fry in her mouth, trying to stave off low blood sugar. Alex sat beside her in the passenger seat of the SUV, sipping what was no doubt equally cold coffee.

They had already placed wireless cameras on the roofs of nearby buildings and now they were logging license plates, makes and models of the trucks that came through. She should have been bored, but Alex was good at making conversation, telling her funny stories from his childhood.

"And that's how I learned that snipe hunting is not a real thing," he said. "Never quite forgave my cousins for leaving for leaving me in an empty field in the middle of the night with a bag and a flashlight."

"How long did it take you to figure out that it was a trick?"

"About three hours." At her stunned look he said, "Oh, come on. I was eight."

At eight, she'd already been a year into her Academy training, learning how to swing a sword and fight hand-to-hand. She was once again reminded of how very different their worlds were. It was possible Alex didn't belong in this one, no matter how much she wanted him to.

"Don't suppose you have a spell for X-ray vision. Would make this a whole lot faster and easier if you could see what was in those trucks," Alex said.

"I wish I had that kind of juice, but a spell like that would drain me in minutes."

"Drain you?"

"Yeah. Mages carry around a lot of energy, but it's finite. If I weave a spell that requires more energy than I have, it can knock me out, even stop my heart. Luckily, we can recharge, given enough time, but if we ever hit zero, it's game over."

"Yeesh. Forget I asked," he said. "I guess there's something to be said for doing it the old fashioned way. There's been more than a few times when watching things carefully gave me insights I never would have gotten with a short cut."

Alayna wished more mages understood that, but they had to discover the hard way that magick was rarely the best solution to any problem. For mages that weren't limited by the Whisperer's curse, magick was extremely effective in combat. Unless, the opponent you were up against had stronger mojo.

Some water mages could channel their element into rituals to divine the future. While those visions could be extremely useful, allowing the council's forces to plot battle strategy and make key financial investments that kept the Corp extremely well-funded, the visions could also be tricky and obscure. More than one team had been lost because a cloudy vision had been misinterpreted by the diviner.

No, more often than not, it came down to careful planning, meticulous training and solid intel collected with blood and sweat to make sure an operation went smoothly.

The conversation flowed easily in the dark, close confines

of the SUV. They talked investigations and battle strategy. His mind was so sharp and processed things so quickly. It was one of the things she loved about him. Her brain ground to a halt for a moment at that thought.

That was dangerous territory, and she needed to put the brakes on that kind of thinking. Now. Glancing over, his face was mostly in shadow, the screen on his laptop having gone dark from disuse. She took that stray thought back out and examined it closely.

Alayna had known that she was attracted to Alex the moment she saw him. If it had been just that, she would have compartmentalized. All her life, she'd been attracted to men she couldn't have. But this wasn't just physical. Not anymore.

They'd spent too many hours, just like this, crammed in close quarters, talking, training. Alex was smart and funny and, under that rigid military discipline and government polish, he was kind of sweet.

She mentally poked that stray thought again. Yup, she was developing feelings for him. Heck, already had. This was bad. It could compromise her as a leader. Would she make the right call if it came down to Alex's safety versus her duty?

Her gut twisted at the thought of him being hurt. But her duty came first, had to. Right?

She'd worked incredibly hard and sacrificed so much to get where she was. Every Whisperer before her had been kept secreted away in the highest security locations. They were like nuclear weapons kept in silos.

She'd had to fight for combat training. She'd fought for the chance to join a team. She'd fought to be considered for command, even though she'd been the most qualified by far. She'd had to fight to include non-mages on her team. The higher ups in the Mage Corps were sticklers for tradition, and they held on to their role as the police of the magickal races jealously.

Non-mages in the Corps were rare, and they were usually lone operatives. She had a reformed thief turned hacker, a recovering drug addict, and an exiled Svarturan prince working alongside one of the most accomplished fire mages of his generation.

Her command, her team, they were everything to her.

And then there was Alex, a sapien, a lìthseach the rarest creature of all. And his skills were only just beginning to reveal themselves.

She felt a connection with Alex that she had never felt with another person in her life. Even with the stress of this case, all the questions, the danger hanging over them, she felt the need to keep him close, just for a little while.

For the duration of this operation, she would enjoy him, and then she would find a safe way for him to get on with his life. And she would get on with hers, what was left of it, and take his memory with her when she went.

When her number was up, it was up. She couldn't control when her curse would claim her, but she refused to dwell on it.

She was going to save as many people as she could before it was time to check out. And if she could save Alex, make sure he could live his life in peace; that would be her greatest accomplishment.

"What's with the sourpuss?" Alex asked, his voice intruding on her dark thoughts. "You look like someone kicked your puppy."

Alayna turned and tried to paste on a smile.

"Just can't stop turning this case around and around in my head," she lied.

"Ruminating doesn't help, believe me," he said. "Let's talk about something else."

Mentally fishing around for a topic, she landed on, "Tell me about your family." She almost winced at how lame that sounded.

"Not a lot tell, really. Mom's a teacher in San Antonio, even though she should have retired years ago. We're pretty close. She, along with Blanca, they encouraged me to apply to the FBI after I got out of the Army and my career plans kind of imploded." He went silent for a moment, swallowing hard. Before she could press him on that comment, he continued. "All in all, pretty boring, right?"

"Actually that sounds really nice, to have people that care about you like that."

"It is nice, most of the time," he said, taking a sip of his coffee. "When my mom isn't bugging me to find a girlfriend, get married and have babies."

Alayna smiled at that. "So what's stopping you?"

"The same thing as you. My job, the horrible hours, the constant threat of danger." He smiled, poking her gently in the shoulder. "And my boss is real hardass."

She smiled back and bumped his shoulder with hers. Silence stretched for a moment. Before there was any more awkward talk of marriage and babies, she grabbed two GPS units and reached for the door handle, whispering a shadow cloak spell. Within moments, ribbons of inky shadow surrounded her.

Alex whistled appreciatively.

"My brother Xander taught me this trick," she said from within the miasmic, twisting cloud. "He can use water vapor to bend light."

"Be careful," Alex said as she slid out of the SUV and moved low and fast over the pavement.

Alayna was able to slip the devices, one onto a trailer, the other on to a truck, and was back at the SUV in less than two minutes.

She climbed back in beside Alex and let the ribbons of shadow fall away. Her breath came a little quick, and her heart was racing. Controlling water was one of the most difficult things for her. Water and air were diametrically opposed to each other on the elemental compass. Air was east, ruled by the four winds. Water was west, ruled by the moon.

Simple water spells came to her, and she was a fair healer in a pinch, but she'd never be anywhere near Xander's ability with the element. He could do absolutely terrifying things with his power.

"You mentioned your brother taught you that. I've noticed you don't talk about your family much," he said.

"Not much to tell really," she said. "Dad died on a mission when I was eight. Mom threw herself into her work. She's one of the chief healers and an advisor to the council. I have an older sister and two older brothers."

"Are they like you?"

"They're mages, if that's what you mean. But they're not cursed." His eyes darkened at that. Alex didn't seem to like it when she applied that word to herself. How little he understood. "Theron's the closest in age to me. He's a fire mage and a Ranger, meaning he works solo and gets sent all over the place."

"You mentioned a Xander?"

"He's the next oldest. He's a water mage, also a solo operator." She very carefully didn't elaborate on the type of work he did. When your big brother was the deadliest assassin in the world, it was kind of hard to explain that in casual conversation.

"Kayla's the oldest," she continued. "She's an earth mage. She ran away from the Academy during her last year. It was right after I found out that I was a Whisperer. No one in the family has heard from her since."

She tried hard to talk around the lump in her throat, but her words still came out sounding wet. Why did she have to bring up Kayla? It was a subject that never failed to make her tearful.

"She disappeared?" Alex asked.

"She left," Alayna said sharply. "There's a difference."

After a moment her mouth surprisingly kept moving. Why did she feel so comfortable telling him all this?

"When dad died and then we found out I was a Whisperer," she said, "it changed everything. It was a one-two punch that tore my family apart. There was just too much pain for any of us to be around each other anymore."

Alex shook his head.

"I don't understand the problem people seem to have with you being a Whisperer. I've seen the things you can do. They're amazing," he said. Softly, he added, "You're amazing."

His deep brown gaze, framed with lashes that belonged in a Maybelline commercial, met hers and held it. Alayna's breath caught for a moment. Here in the shadows, wrapped in the silence of the nondescript black Explorer, it seemed like they were the only two people on Earth. She felt comfortable with him in a way she never really had with anyone else before. Like she could spill all of her secrets to Alex. And for a moment, looking into those gorgeous eyes, she thought that he might accept them.

Shaking her head, she broke eye contact. "People are frightened of power. Particularly a power they don't understand."

It was also a power that would eventually claim her life, but she couldn't bring herself to tell him that. Alex was the only man she'd ever known that didn't look at her with pity in his eyes.

She took a deep breath and continued. "A Whisperer's life is a lonely one by design and by necessity. We're able to control all four elements and weave spells that no other mage can. Traditionally, attachments are discouraged. Wouldn't want one of us going all revenge spree because a lover was killed in battle or something."

Really, it was so that going to her death would be easier when the time came.

"That doesn't sound fair," Alex said, a note of indignation in his voice. "You can't help the way you're born."

"No one ever said life was fair, Alex," she said. "In my experience, life is short, brutal, and full of pain. You take the happy moments where you can and you do as much good as you can before you go."

"God, you sound like me when I was in the Army," he said, a wry smile tugging at his mouth. "After I lost a few friends, I started to keep everyone at arm's length. It doesn't work, you know. It took me a long time to figure out that attachments are the only thing we have in this world, the only thing that keeps us here."

She met his gaze again, and this time she felt a twisting feeling deep within her. He was too intense, and this space was too small. She was too far off balance. Her thoughts spun back to what he'd said earlier. The words fell from her mouth, and she almost immediately wished she could take them back.

"Why did you leave the Army, Alex?"

He took a deep sharp breath. Why, why, why had she asked something that invasive? Clearly it was a sore subject for him.

"I was tired of the blood and death," he said. "And it was time to chase other dreams."

"The FBI?"

"No," he said. "There was another dream first, but it didn't work out."

"What was it?"

He locked gazes with her for a moment, studying her. Wrapped in the shadows, it felt safe to say things.

"I wanted to be a doctor," he said.

"What happened?"

He silent for a long moment, staring at his lap, looking like he was picking through words to find the right ones.

"There was this girl…" he began.

* * *

Alex took a deep breath and told Alayna about Kelly. The vivacious redhead had been transferred to the unit he was assigned to during his third tour. They were on convoy protection duty running between the base in Ramadi and other nearby outposts.

It was dangerous work. They hit IEDs, got ambushed, and ran into trouble on a near weekly basis. Kelly had quickly become the life of the unit. She was funny and could hold her own against all of the teasing that came with being in a mostly male unit.

She was one of the guys and gave as good as she got. Alex had mostly kept to himself, but Kelly drew everyone in. Before long, they were friends. And not long after that, they were friends with benefits.

Kelly knew what she wanted and she went after it. And she had wanted Alex. While fraternization was against the rules within units, it wasn't exactly like the brass could do anything about it. As the medic, he usually had a tent or a barracks room to himself. Kelly spent more than a few nights there.

Alex didn't delude himself into thinking he was the only one she slept with, or that she loved him. He had accepted her advances because she was a beautiful woman, and it was convenient. He hadn't loved her exactly, but he had cared about her.

They were screwing around for about four months when the ambush happened.

It was a typical convoy run. The reports of insurgent activity had been relatively slow, and the unit was a little more relaxed than they had been in months. The first IED hit the second truck in the six-truck convoy. The second bomb took out the fourth and fifth truck. Alex had been in the sixth.

As he'd dismounted, scrambling to get his gear looped on his shoulders, he'd found bodies all around him. The shooting started, bullets flying, hitting the ground around him with little puffs of sand.

He dove for cover behind the remains of the fifth truck, checking fallen teammates and doing a mental triage.

He cataloged the ones that were dead, the ones he could stabilize and save, and the ones who had no hope.

Then he'd found Kelly.

The blast had torn open her abdomen, and she was bleeding out fast. She was deathly pale and as the sand around her turned red with her blood, Alex desperately packed her wounds. In the back of his mind, he knew there was no hope, and that there were other soldiers that needed his help.

His arms were covered in her blood up to the elbows and his hands slid over the slick surfaces of her organs, intestines, stomach, liver, passing beneath his hands.

Her green eyes had locked on his and she grabbed his hand, holding on with desperate strength.

"Alex, I'm scared."

He'd never forget the sound of her weak, thready voice. It was like Death himself had reached out and grabbed him by the throat.

"Just hang on," he'd said. "I'll have you fixed up in a minute."

He'd turned his attention to packing her abdomen. When he'd looked back up, her green eyes were open and staring at the impossibly blue desert sky. She wasn't breathing.

"I'm so sorry, Alex," Alayna said quietly as he finished.

In the weeks following Kelly's death, he'd been closed off and shut down. He'd lost plenty of people. There had been nothing he could do. So why did her death tear him up when the others' hadn't? All he could think was that it must have been the straw that broke the camel's back. Kelly had been the one to break him. It was Blanca that had held him together.

So, he went through the motions with robotic precision until it was time to go home. He collected his discharge, qualified as a paramedic and started applying to medical school. He'd been hell bent on making his dream of becoming a doctor a reality.

But then the panic attacks had hit him.

"We picked up a gunshot victim on my third day on rotation. He was bleeding bad, screaming. I lost it, froze, blacked out. I ended up huddled in a corner of the ambulance. My partner was able to stabilize the guy, but just barely. That man could have died because I couldn't keep my shit together."

"I just couldn't handle bleeding patients," Alex said. "So, I gave up my dream of being a doctor and decided to be an agent instead. Turns out I can handle dead people just fine. It was actually Blanca that suggested it. She heard the Bureau was looking to hire more veterans and she kept shoving the application at me until I turned it in."

"FBI agent is a good dream, too," Alayna said quietly.

"Most of the time it's really boring, if you want to know the truth. But it has its moments," he said, looking at her intently. "And now you know the whole embarrassing truth."

"It's not embarrassing," Alayna said. "I'm sorry for the pain you've been through, but I'm not sorry it brought you to me."

She reached out and grasped his hand. Shock coursed through him for a moment before he closed his fingers around hers, savoring the feel of her skin against his.

He could feel her pulse against his palm and he fought an almost overwhelming urge to kiss her. Was she reaching out as his friend, his partner, his guide to her crazy world? Was there pity in that touch? Or was she reaching out because she craved his touch as much as he craved hers?

It was so hard to read her expression in the darkness. His mind flashed over what she had said about Dominic's departure and her rule about not dating team members.

Alex couldn't stand the thought of losing her. Alayna had been like a firework going off in his shadow of a life. She was warmth and light and excitement. One wrong move and she might push him away. He didn't know how to tell her that he longed to pull her into his arms, kiss her, make love to her.

He couldn't tell her that he fantasized about the way her lips would feel against his. She would be like fire in his arms, he knew. But if she could reject a friend she had known for years, what would she do with someone she'd known a couple of weeks?

He covered her hand with his other one and closed his eyes, committing the feel of her, the scent of her to memory. Maybe there was a way to make this work between them. Maybe he could go back to the life he'd worked so hard for and find some way to keep her in it.

16

Chapter 16

More than a week went by, with the team tagging trucks, combing surveillance videos from the warehouses, and tracking the movements of Medina's trucks and men.

It hadn't exactly been an easy few days, Alayna mused as she pulled her bike into the garage at HQ. She and Alex could have ridden together, but she preferred that he have his own vehicle, just in case, and she liked to have a few minutes to herself on the drive in.

Having Alex sleeping just a few feet away every day was not exactly conducive to sleep. He was invading her dreams more and more. Sometimes, she dreamed of blood and sand, pain and death. Other nights she dreamed of Alex, holding her, kissing her, just sitting and talking with her. In her favorite dream, they flew off together on Z's back, soaring among the stars and never looking down.

As she entered the office, Ellie called her over.

"Hey, boss, I think I got something you want to see," she called out.

Alayna joined her at the desk and peered at her screens over her shoulder.

"Just a question," said Alayna. "Do you ever go home, Ellie?"

"Home doesn't have this kind of data connection or server capacity," Ellie said.

She pointed at the middle of her three screens, which was displaying a map with red lines marked all over it.

"What am I looking at?" Alayna asked.

"A compilation of our GPS tracking data and surveillance records," Ellie explained, pointing to a dot in the center of the map where several of the red lines appeared to converge. "I think this might be another warehouse that wasn't on our list."

"Give Lu the address and the satellite photos so that she can get surveillance set up on that place. Alex and I will stake it out tonight."

"I ran the records on the property. It's owned by another shell company, and it's not connected to any other properties or companies. I swear, Medina's got more shells than the beach."

"It's how he's been so successful at avoiding notice until now," Alayna said. "Tell me about his runs to the border."

"All his pickups are in Nuevo Laredo and Matamoros. Their next stop is this new warehouse I discovered. From there, those trucks end up any number of places," Ellie said.

"Is there any way to tell what he's hauling?" Alayna asked.

"Not without opening the trucks or getting someone with enough juice for X-ray vision up next to the trucks," Ellie replied. "I suppose we could try infrared cameras on the trucks going and coming, but it's unreliable if the trucks have been on the road for awhile."

Ellie clicked around on her screens and typed a few things.

"Boss, I think we need to start considering some internal recon on some of these buildings. Lu and I could get us what we need in just a couple of days."

"I don't like it, but it doesn't look like we have any better options," Alayna said.

"Don't worry, boss, this ain't our first rodeo. They'll never even know we were there."

"I believe you," she replied. "Pull the blueprints for the buildings and pull the team in. We'll plan tonight and do the recon tomorrow night."

Ellie nodded and got to work.

* * *

Alex closed his eyes, blocking out his teammates and the inside of the Sprinter van and tried to center himself for the thirtieth time. His blood was too hot and he gave up and started compulsively checking the velcro pockets on his tac vest to make sure he'd have everything he needed quick to hand.

There was a good chance they'd be kicking in some doors tonight. Part of him was excited by the prospect, but another part was absolutely terrified. The last time he'd done something like this he'd been wearing sergeants' bars and a medic's patch.

True to their word, Ellie and Lu were able to make quick work of the first three warehouses they had been staking out. Lu was able to slip into one in the form of a little brown field mouse, using her keen sense of smell to locate what she was sure was a shipment of drugs, everything from cocaine to methamphetamines to heroin, hidden among a legitimate shipment of car parts.

Ellie had slipped into another warehouse and uncovered a shipment of guns hidden in crates of fruit and tequila. The third warehouse had come up clean.

If Medina would risk running drugs and guns, chances were he had completed the trifecta and was in the flesh game, too. Could be prostitution or a coyote operation or both. Based on everything they'd collected from the GPS trackers, this warehouse might hold evidence of that.

But they needed to play this one smart.

The whole team, minus Lu, was sitting in the panel van geared up and ready to go.

Dumeril's quiet voice reached them from the front seat, "I think I've got a visual on Lu. Either that or this mouse is very curious about our van."

Alayna opened the back door and scooped the little brown mouse in her hand. The creature skittered behind a rack of computer equipment near the back of the van and they could all hear grunts, popping sounds and the unsettling tearing noises that were associated with Lu's transformations. After a few minutes, she emerged, slipping a black T-shirt over her head and grabbing a gallon jug of thick orange sludge that she used to refuel after her changes and began to chug it.

"I didn't notice anything suspicious in the shipments that were stored in the front part of the warehouse," Lu said between gulps of the gritty sludge.

Alayna sighed, disappointment pushing her shoulders down.

"But there is a sealed room in the back I couldn't get into. No windows either," Lu said.

Alayna perked up like Lu had just told her the warehouse was full of cupcakes.

"How many people?"

"Six warehouse workers, looks like a mix of shifters and sapiens, plus four vamp guards," Lu said. "But I don't know what's in that room, and that makes me nervous."

Alayna nodded and had Ellie pull up the blueprints of the building. This mysterious room wasn't on the plans. Lu pointed out their two best entry points and where the room was.

"I think we should split up. Alex, Dumeril, and I will take the front entrance. Burdock, Lu, and Ellie, you'll take the side entrance. Try to minimize the casualties for the workers and guards because I'd like to question them when we're done. Move through the main warehouse as quickly as possible and secure the entrance to that room. Any questions?"

The team shook their heads silently, checking their weapons and securing their gear. They grouped outside the van into their entry teams and Alex pushed down another bubble of nervousness that tried to claw its way out of his chest.

He had on a tac vest, his twin 1911s were on his hips, and a tactical shotgun loaded with silver rested in his hands. A small med kit was in his backpack. He'd debated whether or not to bring it. He wasn't a medic anymore, and the team had Dumeril. They didn't need him. Ultimately, it just made him feel better to have it.

Alayna gave a double click on her radio mic that signaled it was time to move out. As the other group moved away, Alex lost sight of them. His group turned the corner and headed for the front entrance of the warehouse.

It was a dark night, with clouds obscuring the moon and stars. Unsurprisingly, there were no exterior lights on the warehouse. Vamps and shifters could see in the dark and they probably had cameras on the exterior. Hopefully, the glamour would hold up enough to fool them until they could get inside.

As they reached the person-sized access door located beside a large closed rolling door, Alex heard three clicks over the radio that signaled the other team was in place, and Alayna's answering three clicks.

She started softly whispering, while Dumeril counted down from ten on his fingers. As he curled his last finger, Alayna hit the door with a blast of air and fire that knocked it off its hinges, leaving it in a twisted molten heap by the opening.

As they entered the building, Alex heard an answering boom off to the side where the second team would be entering. Alayna moved through the opening first, taking the handle of her whip from her boot, but not extending it.

She was whispering again, her left hand extended palm up, a ball of crackling energy floating above it. Dumeril was next, drawing his kukris from the sheath on his back near his waist. The blades were silent as they slid free.

Alex stepped through the door, covering the rear, his shotgun at his shoulder and pointed at the floor.

Chances were, everyone in the building had heard the twin booms of the doors exploding. The warehouse was dimly lit, but Alex was still able to pick up movement to their right.

"On your two o'clock," he whispered to Alayna.

"Roger."

She moved silently in that direction. A moment later, he heard a single whispered word. Light flared, there was a sharp crack and the air suddenly smelled of ozone. Two bodies dropped to the floor, unconscious.

Two other figures emerged from between shipping crates, Dumeril hit them with some sort of spell that immobilized them.

So far, everyone they'd seen wore jumpsuits—probably warehouse workers.

They heard a shout from the back of the warehouse and the sound of something hitting the floor. The second team moved into view.

"Two warehouse workers are unconscious and tied up in the back," Ellie said, her voice barely above a whisper, but clear enough through the mic.

"Any sign of our guards?" Alayna asked.

Lu shook her head and pointed at a wall not far away that had a solid metal door set in it. Must be the room she had mentioned and it was a good bet their guards had retreated there.

Burdock tried the door, and when he found it was locked, held the handle until it started to glow orange. He wrenched it, lock and all, out of the door and tossed the molten metal lump on the floor. Alex noted that the flesh of his hand was unburned. Being a fire mage had its perks, apparently.

Burdock gave the door a solid kick with his booted foot, and it swung open so hard it bounced off the opposite wall. Burdock moved through the room like a predator, scanning back and forth with his assault rifle.

He gave the hand signal for "all clear" and the rest of the team began moving through the door in formation, Alayna and Dumeril, followed by Alex and Ellie, with Lu bringing up the rear.

The room was dark, with no windows and no lights. The first thing Alex noticed was the smell. It was like a hundred port-a-potties had been left in the hot sun for a week, the overwhelming smell of human waste mixed with the tang of chemical disinfectant. Under that was the stench of human body odor.

Alex heard a click to his right, and the room was flooded with light from overhead. Ellie stood a few feet away, one hand on a metal switch and the other covering her nose and mouth. Her large eyes narrowed, but not from the glare.

Alex followed her gaze back into the room. It was full of welded wire cages, about five feet tall. They lined both walls of the long room, with an aisle between them.

Crouched figures were cowering in the corners of the cages, covering their faces against the light. A sickening feeling grabbed Alex in the gut as he realized they were people. Each of the fifteen or so cages had one or two people in them. Most had dark matted hair. What was left of their clothing was torn and filthy.

Most of the cages were too small for them to stand or stretch out. In each cage was an orange bucket. Some of them were overflowing with waste.

One woman started to cry. On the other side, a man scrambled to the front of a cage and stuck his fingers through toward Alex. In a painfully hoarse voice he begged Alex in Spanish to take him out of this place before the devils came back.

Alex made eye contact and squeezed the man's fingers gently, placing a finger against his lips to signal for silence. He looked to Alayna, to see what their next move would be.

She was standing still, as if rooted to the spot in shock. When he looked closer, Alex could see that her body was shaking with anger, her jaw clenched, and her hands were fisted at her sides.

A high-pitched cry went up from a cage at the far end of the row. The breath caught in Alex's throat. The sound had come from a child.

Alayna's head snapped around at the cry, and she was in front of the cage in a few quick, determined strides, Alex not far behind her.

Four small children, ranging in age from maybe five to eight years old, were huddled in the back of the cage. Hard to tell if they were boys or girls. Shaggy, dark hair hung in all their faces.

Their eyes were wide and bright against the filth that covered their skin. They were a tangle of too-skinny arms and legs as they clung to each other.

One child pointed frantically behind Alayna, her eyes wide and stark white against her dark hair. She and Alex turned to look in the same moment and saw the four vamp guards moving toward them, guns drawn.

Alayna's body tensed, her fingers curling into claws as her eyes fixed on the vamps. She stepped forward, putting herself between the children and the approaching menace. A low growl emerged from her throat. It was an unearthly sound that raised the hair on the back of Alex's neck. He could feel the air around her start to crackle with energy.

The vamps froze where they were, but Alex wasn't sure if it was from a spell or because Alayna had scared them that badly.

Alayna's growl rose several octaves as it climbed toward a screech. Her eyes had gone red rimmed, and her mouth was pulled back in a snarl, exposing her teeth. Alex glanced back down the aisle to see Dumeril, eyes wide with a fear Alex didn't know the deadly Svarturan could feel. His arms were out, and he had pushed Ellie and Lu behind him. Burdock was beside him, down one knee with his rifle trained on the vamps.

Alayna's screech had risen to a keening wail that pierced Alex's ears and he looked back at her. What he saw made his blood run cold.

She seemed to glow from within. Electricity crackled along her arms. The air was stirring around her and smelled of a thunderstorm. The skin around her eyes was a burning angry red. Her long hair floated around her head, dancing and writhing with a combination of rising wind and static electricity.

Her feet rose slowly off the ground, and her clawed hands

extended toward the vamps. Suddenly, like an invisible chain had been snapped, she flew forward, the toes of her boots dragging on the stained concrete. Her voice rose in a piercing, horrible song. Alex's only thought was that this much be what a Banshee sounded like.

She reached the first vamp with terrifying speed, and her hand disappeared into the flesh of his throat and emerged a split second later with a section of the vampire's spine clutched in her slender white fingers. Alayna's head tilted to the side slightly as she looked at the column of blood and bone, as if trying to figure out what it was.

Black blood poured from the vamp's mouth and throat and he fell to the ground, already dead. The vampire to his left rose in the air as if an invisible hand were clutching his throat. He clawed at his own neck, digging deep bloody furrows in the flesh.

Alayna hovered, her toes brushing the concrete, her arms extended, that screeching song pouring from her mouth.

Another vamp's chest poured fresh, red blood as if he had been opened by a scalpel from throat to groin. His intestines fell to the floor, but still he stood rooted to the spot, his mouth open in a silent scream. The vampire's ribs suddenly snapped outward in a spray of red. A twisted lump of red flesh flew from the vamp's chest and landed at Alayna's feet. Alex recognized what had been a heart.

The one hovering in the air started to scream as the flesh around his neck began to split and bleed. A second later, the scream was silenced as vamp's head was torn from his shoulders.

In a flash, Alayna had glided over in front of the fourth and final guard. The cutting screech had died by a few decibels.

"We need one alive, Commander," Dumeril's shout came from

behind Alex.

Alex had moved a few paces closer to Dumeril and away from the blood bath he was witnessing. The three vamps had died in the space of a few seconds, and Alex had never seen anything more terrifying. He had seen soldiers overcome with anger do some terrible things, but nothing like this.

It was like Alayna had been possessed. This was otherworldly and terrifying magick. It made the rooftop cremation days earlier look like a tea party in comparison.

At Dumeril's words, Alayna's head snapped around with a frightening, almost alien quickness. The fourth vamp disappeared in a shower of blood.

They could hear meaty thumps of what used to be the vampire hitting the concrete. None of the lumps of flesh were identifiable as anything that used to be a body part.

That horrible song seemed to fade for a moment as she floated toward them. Alex nearly reached for her, desperate to soothe the anger that had taken her over. Suddenly, the keening song ratcheted up again as her face twisted in a feral snarl. She began to fly up the aisle toward the team, toes dragging the concrete, arms extended and eyes burning.

"Shit!" Dumeril shouted. "It's mage rage! Run!"

As one, the others turned to run for the door and Alex was right behind them, moving faster than he had in years. He wasn't sure what was happening, but he knew he wanted to be as far away as possible.

He was barely through the door when Burdock slammed it behind them. He ran his hand along the seam and a glowing bead of molten metal appeared.

"That'll hold her for a few seconds," Burdock said. "Take cover!"

Alex rolled across a shipping crate and came down in a crouch beside Dumeril.

"What the fuck is happening to her?" Alex shouted.

"Mage rage. Happens sometimes when mages lose control of their powers. They'll kill anything they see as a threat. The only way to stop her is kill her, knock her out or wait until one of her spells drains her enough to stop her heart."

There was a banging noise at the door and then the screech of twisting metal. All of the team members had managed to scramble behind shipping crates. Alex peeked over the one he and Dumeril were hiding behind to see Alayna floating through the door.

He made a split second decision. He wasn't going to let Alayna die and he wasn't going to let anyone else get hurt. He vaulted on top of the crate and leapt with everything he had in her direction.

He threw his arms wide and caught her around the shoulders, dragging her to the ground in a spinning tackle. Her scream cut off abruptly and they hit the concrete hard. Her nails scrabbled against his tac vest, tearing at the nylon.

Somehow, Alex managed to land on top, straddling her waist. He was able to pin her wrists beside her head, but he could feel that she would overpower him easily in just a few seconds.

Without thinking, he leaned forward and pressed his lips to hers.

Time seemed to stop. Her mouth softened from a snarl and the growl died in her throat. Her lips moved against his, answering his kiss with one of her own. A soft, breathy sigh escaped her. Alex felt her muscles relax and she stopped fighting his grip.

Desire twisted in his chest as he felt her mouth move against his, felt her body arch beneath him.

Power slammed into him, pulsing along every nerve ending. It felt like he had grabbed a live wire and couldn't let go. He realized that magical energy was flowing from Alayna and into him, his lithseach abilities going to work.

She went slack as she fell unconscious and he pulled back to see her eyes, which were no longer rimmed in red, were closed and she was breathing easily. She looked like she had just drifted off to sleep.

Alex looked up to Dumeril, Lu and Ellie standing over them, staring in disbelief. Burdock was nearby, scanning all directions, his rifle at the ready.

Dumeril offered Alex a hand up and he gently released Alayna, already missing the contact.

"You are the craziest son of a bitch I've ever met," Dumeril said matter of factly, turning to speak into his cell phone.

Alayna's unconsciousness wasn't the result of a physical injury. Treatment called for fluids and she'd probably need some glucose. Under normal circumstances, her powers burned a lot of calories. What had just happened was not normal.

As he scooped Alayna into his arms, he overheard Dumeril calling for containment, cleanup, and memory wipes. The Svarturan gave the person on the other end a brief rundown of their situation and the number of hostages, omitting Alayna's brief stint as a demon-possessed hell bitch.

She was heavier than she looked. Her frame was slender and athletic—he couldn't help but notice—but was densely built. She carried almost no equipment and wasn't even wearing a vest. He'd have to talk to her about that. Despite her ability to block bullets in mid-air, it didn't hurt to have an extra layer of protection.

He lifted her unconscious body into the back of the van and

laid her gently on one of the benches. It was cold without the heat of her pressed against him.

Alex got to work cleaning the blood from her face and hands with alcohol wipes from his kit. Luckily, her black tactical gear didn't show the considerable bloodstains.

She had several oozing cuts on her right hand, probably from where she had crushed that vampire's spine. He cleaned them and sealed them with liquid bandage.

He found a vein in the inside of her left elbow and started a bag of saline. He injected a healthy dose of glucose into a port in the bottom of the bag. With nothing else to do, he knelt beside her, pressing his forehead to her temple. The copper scent of blood was in her hair, but underneath that was her usual electric scent. He took a deep breath and held that scent in his lungs.

He'd almost lost her, and it scared the shit out of him.

When had this stunning, funny, terrifying, impossibly stubborn, achingly vulnerable woman become that important to him?

His face flushed hot at the thought of what he'd just done. At the time, he had been half sure that was going to be the last move he ever made. What had he been thinking? The move had been a lot like jumping on a live grenade. His thoughts had been for Alayna, the team, those poor captives, and last of all for himself.

He looked down into her relaxed, serene face and wondered where the thought had come from to kiss her. He wasn't sure if he was trying to distract her, like she had done to him in the alley that night they met. Picking the thought up in his mind and examining it, he set it aside as a possibility.

Maybe he had been trying to appeal to some part of her that felt affection for him? It was possible, but he wasn't sure what

Alayna felt for him. There were times when he met her eyes that something passed between them, like a circuit being connected. But almost as soon as he noticed it, one of them, usually Alayna, would look away and the moment would pass like it had never happened.

A thought struck him. Did he know, maybe on some subconscious level, that his abilities as a lìthseach would drain the magick fueling her rage? That had to have been what caused her to stop, to lose consciousness. It made sense based on what he had experienced so far with his new abilities.

On the bench, Alayna began to stir, pulling him from his thoughts. He pressed his hand to her face, gently brushing his thumb across her cheek. If she was still in the grip of the rage, the skin-to-skin would power her down again, he told himself. In reality, it just felt so damn good to touch her.

Slowly, her indigo eyes opened and they met his. She looked confused for a moment, but relaxed again. Her hand covered his, pressing his palm against her cheek. Her eyes drifted closed and she sighed, "Alex."

His name on her lips, said in that voice, had his cock instantly hard. She'd just been through something horrible. He needed to get a grip.

Suddenly, she tensed, her eyes snapping open and the pale flesh of her face and neck blushed the most adorable shade of pink. Consciousness had returned fully.

He had to fight to keep from laughing.

"What the fuck happened?" she said loudly, struggling to sit up.

She didn't have the strength and toppled into his arms. He helped her to a sitting position on the bench and knelt in front of her, her hands in his.

"Easy now," he told her in a soft voice, tucking platinum strands behind her ear. His fingers lingered for a moment on the flesh of her neck, just below her ear. There was a stillness and a tension between them, a kind of spell that seemed to hold them both frozen.

Alayna broke the spell as she shook her head as if trying to clear it.

"Tell me what happened."

"You mean, you don't remember?"

She paused, shaking her head again.

"Not much," she said, her eyes narrowing in concentration. "I saw those people…I was more angry than I've ever been in my life."

She was silent for a moment, rubbing her eyes.

"There was blood…then I woke up here."

"You don't remember anything else?" Alex asked.

A part of him was disappointed that she didn't remember his heroic move, their kiss. He knew he would hold on to that particular memory for the rest of his life.

"I don't think so," she said, her voice soft and uncertain at the look on his face.

She was silent for a moment before she asked very softly, "What happened?"

"You saw some children locked in a cage like animals and you killed the monsters who were keeping them there," Alex said. He relaxed slightly when he realized that he was clutching her hands tightly in his own, his muscles bunching with tension.

She nodded. "Then what?"

"You turned on the team and chased us down. Dumeril called it mage rage," Alex said. At the horrified look on her face, he continued quickly. "No one got hurt. I tackled you and…got you to stop."

"I've seen someone in the grip of mage rage before," she said, her voice incredulous. "How the hell did you get me to stop?"

He winced, hesitating. She'd burned down a friendship with Dominic because he'd admitted to having feelings for her, and she'd known him for years. She'd known Alex for weeks. Kissing her was decidedly a violation of the no dating team members policy. And he'd done it without her permission. How fast was she going to ditch him?

"I kissed you," he said simply.

She froze, her eyes going wide, her mouth falling open in shock. Slowly, her hand lifted to his face, her eyes never leaving his. The touch was soft, reverent.

"You crazy man," she said softly. "You could have been killed. What were you thinking?"

His eyes closed and he swallowed hard past a throat that felt thick with unspoken things.

"I couldn't lose you," he said finally, his voice barely a whisper.

When he opened his eyes again, she was closer, and then her mouth was on his. The kiss was soft, but without a hint of tentativeness. It was thank you, it was relief, it was awe—it was all the things she couldn't say with her voice. But it also tasted like regret.

Fuck that.

His arms came around her and he pulled her hard against his chest. His fingers tangled in her hair and his mouth claimed hers, his tongue sliding between her lips. She tasted like sunlight. A breathy moan escaped her lips, and he almost came undone at the sound. Her hands were in his hair, holding him to her.

Before he could think, he'd lifted her off the bench and took her place, pulling her on to his lap until she straddled him. He let her feel how hard he was for her, let her feel how much he'd wanted her.

Her hands cradled his face as her mouth moved against his. His hand found her breast, too hard against her soft flesh. She moaned against his mouth again.

Suddenly, there was a noise from outside the van. She stilled against him, every muscle tense. Slowly, she pulled away, eyes wide, her lips swollen from his kiss.

Without warning, she scrambled off him, jerking up short when the IV line in her arm went taut.

"I'm so sorry," she said, her hand covering her mouth in mortification.

"Don't be. Do you hear me complaining?" He leaned back on the bench and spread his legs slightly. Let her see what she was doing to him.

She'd felt his hard on, she'd been practically grinding against it.

"I shouldn't have done that," she said, her eyes going to floor. "We shouldn't have done that."

"Why not?"

"That can't happen again, Alex." Her voice had gone up and octave and taken a sharp edge.

"I ask again, why not?" His voice was low and even, his gaze on her steady. "We're two consenting adults."

"I can't get involved with team members. This is my command, my team, my duty. I can't be an effective leader if I'm worried about you. There're a lot of things going on here that you don't know. I may not...I can't make the right decision if I need to."

There was so much fear and agitation flowing through her, she was practically vibrating. She'd just been through a hell of an ordeal and here he was, half an inch from fucking her on the floor of the van. He'd let adrenaline and relief at having survived take over his brain. What had he been thinking? He'd been down this road once before, with Kelly, and it had ended in disaster. Was he so eager to repeat that mistake?

"I'm sorry. You're right," he said, holding up both hands. "We just lost our heads for a minute. Adrenaline high. Survivor's rush."

The words felt hollow, like a lie. A part of him wanted them to be true.

"Exactly," she said, relief flooding through her frame. "So we can just put this whole thing behind us and pretend it never happened."

* * *

The cleanup process had taken a couple hours, and it was nearly midnight. An eight person team had arrived from Houston so quickly that Alex was sure they had used a teleporter to get here. Heck, for all he knew, maybe they had.

Alex and Lu had conducted the interviews with the children and adults in the warehouse, while Dumeril worked in tandem to check them out medically.

Most of them were basically all right physically. The folks that had been held the longest had been there about three weeks, as near as they could tell. They were all malnourished and very dirty, but there were no injuries or serious conditions among them.

Mentally, that was another story. Hopefully, the memory wipes worked and these people would forget the horrible things they had seen and would go on to live normal lives never knowing about the dark things that lived in the shadows.

Alex talked with a young man who appeared to be about twenty-one as he cleaned out a cut that had gotten infected.

His story was similar to most of the others he'd heard already. The young man, Miguel, had lived in a small town in Chihuahua. He'd heard about jobs in Texas and found a coyote. The price he was asking was much lower than what most of his friends and family who had crossed the border had paid. Even though he was suspicious, he couldn't afford to pass up the deal.

Miguel had been loaded in a van with five or six others. They'd driven to a truck stop near the border and had loaded up in an eighteen-wheeler with false compartments in the walls. Boxes had been loaded in the truck to make it look fully loaded and they'd set out. When they'd arrived in Austin, they were taken off the truck, beaten, and thrown in the cages.

Every week, a group of adults and children would be moved out. Ages of people ranged from five to about thirty-five. Miguel had never seen anyone older or younger than that. He wasn't sure what happened to the people who were taken from the warehouse, but he never saw them again.

Miguel grabbed Alex's arm as he was bandaging the newly cleaned cut and begged him not to send him back to the monsters and not to send him back to Mexico.

"Everything is going to be fine," Alex told him in Spanish, using his best medic voice.

Miguel had calmed a bit and Alex handed him off to a large man with Asian features who was wearing a zip up clean suit like the kind crime scene techs wore. The last of the captives were moving toward a series of vehicles parked inside the warehouse.

The leader of the cleanup team said that their memories after crossing the border would be wiped. They'd be given residential documents and IDs and set up in cities scattered around the southwest. It sounded to Alex like the best possible outcome for those involved.

He looked over at Dumeril as he cleaned his hands with alcohol gel.

"That was a hell of a move you pulled today," Dumeril said, moving next to Alex where he leaned against a metal table they had been using to do examinations. Alex didn't have to ask which move he was talking about.

"Yup," Alex said simply.

Dumeril gave him a rueful look.

"Seriously? What were you thinking?"

"To be honest, I wasn't," Alex said. He was silent for a moment before he continued. "I just reacted with gut instinct. I was trying to protect the team, the captives and Alayna."

"You sure as hell weren't concerned for yourself. You got lucky. Real lucky. If those freaky-ass powers of yours hadn't kicked in, she probably would have torn you into little bitty confetti-sized pieces, before moving on to the rest of us."

Silence stretched between them.

"When you said that it could kill her, I stopped thinking. My gut's saved me more than once, so I trusted it."

Dumeril laughed and slapped him on the back.

"I'm glad your gut is smarter than your head," Dumeril said. "I just wanted to say thanks."

Alex nodded and moved to start packing up his med bag.

Dumeril's voice sounded loud in the now empty warehouse when he spoke.

"You should tell her how you feel," Dumeril said.

Alex shot him a look.

"And how do you know how I feel about her?"

Dumeril laughed. "Your move today was pretty obvious there,

hot shot," he said. "But besides that, it's written all over you. It's in the way you look at her, the way you tense up when she's around."

"You know why I can't tell her," Alex said. "It's a non-starter."

"Is this about what happened with Dominic?" Dumeril asked. "Her whole, 'I can't date a team member' policy?"

When Alex nodded, Dumeril made a noise in his throat that told him exactly what he thought of that.

"Dominic was an asshole about the whole thing, and it was his choice to leave. He thinks he's freaking God's gift to the universe, and he just couldn't stomach that Alayna didn't want him in that way. Furthermore, she makes the rules, she can break the rules. Girl's just wound a little too tight, if you ask me. Too afraid to let go."

Alex was silent as he took this new information in.

"I kind of also thought that maybe you and Alayna had something going on," Alex said hesitantly.

A surprised laugh burst from Dumeril's throat, stretching into a long belly laugh. Wiping his eyes he said, "Oh, honey. First off, I only date men."

At Alex's startled look Dumeril laughed again and gave him a look that said "you wouldn't be on my list in a million years."

"Secondly, I don't date humans. You're all fucking crazy."

That drew a laugh from Alex and he felt the tension leave his body.

"Yeah, that's pretty accurate," he agreed.

Dumeril moved next to him again.

"Look, Alayna's been dealt a shit hand in this life and she deserves to have a little happiness. And you do too."

Alex didn't look at him as he finished packing his bag.

"I'll think about it, man."

"Don't think too long. You never know when a mission will be your last," Dumeril said, slinging his own bag over his shoulder and heading for door.

When they reached the van, Ellie, Lu, and Alayna were already there.

"Well, we all survived, so that's something," Ellie said. "There's just one thing we have left to do."

Alex mentally prepared himself. Would they need to debrief? Unpack the van? What?

"We all need to get good and drunk," she finished.

"I second that," Lu said.

"Probably not the best idea guys…" Alayna tried to chime in.

"This is about unit cohesion, Commander. We all saw some shit tonight. You know how we deal with that in a healthy way?"

"Therapy?" Alex asked.

"Yeah. My therapist's name is Patron and he's seeing patients on Sixth Street right now."

17

Chapter 17

Alayna threw back yet another shot and slammed the glass down on the bar, wiping her mouth with the back of her hand, and laughed at something the guy next to her had said.

The music was raging in the after hours club they were in, and she hadn't really heard him. She was pretty sure his name was Jonathan. He was tall, well built in the way that guys who spent all their free time in gym were. He had spiky blonde hair and nice eyes. She was pretty sure he said he worked in finance.

Not that it mattered.

He was just her type. A little shallow, only interested in sex and clearly not interested in asking too many questions.

She'd get a couple more drinks in him, hail a cab and get him back to his place for a little fun before the sun came up.

Then it was back to work on this case. There was nothing she could do for the next few hours while she waited for reports from the cleanup team on what they learned from the hostages. And she'd let the surviving warehouse workers stew for a few hours before she came at them with more questions. Chances were they didn't know much. Unfortunately, she'd turned the only ones who'd likely known anything in vampire confetti.

No, for the next few hours she was determined to scratch a few itches.

She had this game down to a science by now. She knew the right kind of guys to pick and she always talked them into going to their place by making up some excuse about her sister being in town.

She knew just what to wear, too. Gone was her combat gear, replaced by a stretchy, tight tube dress in attention grabbing hot pink. It showed off her chest and legs and always attracted just the kind of men she preferred.

As she looked around the club, she noticed that Dumeril was chatting up some guy at the end of the bar. Ellie had run into someone she knew and had disappeared into a corner somewhere. Lu had lost herself in the crowd.

Alex was at the other end of the bar, nursing a whiskey and lost in his thoughts. Drunk women kept throwing themselves at him, and he kept waving them off. Alayna refused to think about how sexy he looked leaning up against the bar in those jeans and that tight black T-shirt.

The memory of that kiss in the van flashed in her mind and even just the thought of it made her blush slightly. She didn't know what had possessed her to put her mouth on him. Stupid, stupid move. It didn't matter that it had been the single hottest kiss of her life. Just kissing him had been hotter than all of the sex she'd ever had.

When she realized she was staring at him, she pulled her gaze away. This couldn't happen. Attachments were out of the question. It didn't matter how good he looked right this minute or how much she wanted him.

She felt a hand on her shoulder and Lu's voice was by her ear.

"I know that look."

Alayna spun on her best friend. "What look?"

"The look of someone longing for the thing they won't let themselves have. I'm an addict, I'm intimately familiar with that look."

"I don't know what you're talking about," she said, ducking her head to avoid Lu's gaze.

"You know I can smell it when you lie."

"I'm not. I jus—"

Lu held up her hand and pinned Alayna with a look.

"That boy's got it bad for you. That move he pulled today. I'm sure he spared a thought for the team and the hostages, but that hero move, it was about saving you. When Dumeril told him the rage could kill you, he was up and over that crate before we could blink."

Something twisted in her chest at those words.

"That's just it, he risked his life for mine. I can't let this go any further with him than it has. You know why."

Lu sighed deeply enough that she heard it over the music. "Why are you so bad at letting yourself be happy?"

A flare of anger surged in her chest, but she pushed it down. "I'm not bad at that. It's that I can't lose control, because we all saw tonight what happens when I do."

With that, she turned her back on Lu and began moving through the crowd. She found Jonathan—or was it Brent?—and as she did, the crowd parted, and she caught sight of Alex. A girl with long dark hair and a barely-there top had her hand on his chest, giggling. He was smiling back, his body language open, his face close to hers.

Something painful howled inside her, but she shook it off and took a sip of the drink that the guy she was now pretty sure was named Brent had ordered for her. It was something fruity and far too sweet, but she drank it anyway as she pulled him back on the dance floor.

As Alayna let the beat settle over her, JonaBrent mostly stood there while she ground up against him in time with the music. He began to move with her, and she liked the feel of his gym rat muscles under her hands. The flex of his arms and chest and abs through his thin shirt felt like heaven, and his cologne smelled delicious. She couldn't wait to strip him, and if the half erection she could feel through his jeans was any indication of things to come, it was going to be a really fun night.

And she deserved a little fun, didn't she?

It'd been weeks since she'd picked up a guy, and she was aching for it. She'd been working hard on this case. Alex had been a distraction to be sure. She knew there were some in the Corps hierarchy that would frown on this behavior if they knew about it, but what they didn't know wouldn't hurt anyone.

She gave everything to the job, and one day soon she'd give her life without a second thought. But before she went, she was going to dance and get drunk (well, tipsy at least), and she was going to get laid.

She'd never have love or a real family, but she could have this.

Suddenly, a memory of working out with Alex popped into her head, the way he'd felt pinning her to the mat. The way his hands had felt on her sweaty skin, the way his body had felt pressed against her. He'd always been all business, but there had been moments when she'd caught him looking at her, and there had been something in his eyes that she could almost believe was heat. There had been moments when he'd touched her that she thought something had passed between them. He'd said the kiss was a mistake. Had he meant that or had he been lying? And what hope did they have for anything other than heartbreak? He wanted so badly to return to his old life when this case was over, resume the FBI career he'd worked so hard for. He deserved that, and he deserved love and happiness. That certainly wasn't something he'd find with her.

Damn it. She tried to push the memories away, but they kept flooding back. She wanted Alex, but she couldn't risk it. Her time was limited; she'd always known that, and she wasn't going to break anyone's heart when she left.

She turned and flung her arms around JonaBrent's neck and kissed him, slipping her tongue past his lips. He responded by pulling her close and grinding his erection against her.

She opened her eyes and looked past him as his fingers tangled in her hair. Alex locked eyes with her. His face was expressionless, even though the dark haired girl was laughing at something he'd said. The moment stretched between them. The music seemed to fade until it felt like they were the only two people in the club.

Alayna broke eye contact first and grabbed JonaBrent by the hand, dragging him toward the exit. She didn't dare look back at Alex or she would lose her nerve.

* * *

Alex tossed and turned in Alayna's guest bed. He'd lain down a few minutes before, and every time he closed his eyes, he saw that look Alayna had given him in the club before she left with that blond douchebag.

It had been a message. She'd been clear almost from the beginning. No dating team members and she considered him one. Every interaction with her played through his head. That first night in the alley, that mesmerizing embrace in the locker room, all those work outs where something would pass between them with a touch or a look. That crazy sex dream he'd had about her. And, God, that kiss in the van. He'd thought his skin was going to catch fire.

In his head, it all added up to one thing: she wanted him. Maybe as much as he wanted her. So why the message tonight?

If she was trying to say that she didn't want to have anything to do with him by dragging some random guy off to fuck him, he'd received that message loud and clear. As he tossed restlessly, the sheets tangling around him, he decided something. She was pushing him away. For what reason he didn't know, but he was going to let her. They had no business getting involved. He'd wait until dawn, when she was sure to be asleep, pack his stuff and move into one of the rooms at headquarters.

The two of them needed some distance. And they needed to wrap up this case as quickly as possible. The sooner he got back to his old life, his real life, the better.

He heard Alayna's front door open and close and the sound of her soft bare footsteps moving through the house. She'd taken off her boots to avoid waking him. Was it sad that he could identify the sound of her footsteps?

He glanced at his phone. It had only been forty-five minutes since he'd left her at the club. Must have been one hell of a fast quickie. He did some mental math. With the time it took to get a cab at this time of night and the distance out to her place on the west side, she must have gone home almost straight from the club. She wouldn't have had time to go home with that guy.

The sound of the door to her bedroom/porch closing reached Alex's ears and he sat up in bed. He could hear her getting ready for bed, and after a few minutes he could hear her tossing and turning, too.

One question kept echoing in his head: why hadn't she gone home with that guy?

The insidious thought kept coming back to him. What was she doing? What were they doing?

He tried for several minutes to calm his mind, using his tricks from his Army days to shut out the noise in his head. Instead of trying to cancel out bomb blasts, he was trying to quiet the nagging voice that was telling him to go to her right now.

He threw the covers back and slid from the bed. If neither of them were sleeping, he'd tell her about his plan to move out in the morning. Maybe then he could get a sense of what was going on here.

He moved toward her bedroom, raising his hand to knock on the screen door, when he saw that she wasn't in her bed. He looked up and his breath left his lungs in rush.

She wore a white satin nightgown that clung to her curves. Her feet were bare as they moved across the grass of her backyard. She moved through a complicated series of movements. It was a martial arts form, but she made it look like the most delicate dance. Her eyes were closed and the dew collecting on the grass clung to her feet as they whispered across the ground.

He stood frozen, spellbound for a moment, before his feet started moving as if pulled by some magnetic force.

As he drew closer, he could feel and see air currents around her, dancing in little swirling eddies and vortices. Bits of grass, tiny spring wildflowers and pieces of dried leaves danced on the air around her. It was, quite simply, the most beautiful thing he had ever seen.

Several sets of golden eyes glowed from the darkness, and Alex realized the trees were full of owls and night birds that were silently watching her. Off to his right, a little heron stirred near the pond. They were all as transfixed by her as he was.

Creatures of the air were drawn to her magick, her beauty, her power. And she didn't even realize the hold she had on all of them. On him.

Without realizing it, his hand lifted toward her and her name left his lips on a whisper. "Alayna."

She spun and dropped into an elegant fighter's crouch at the sound. One leg, tucked beneath her, the other extended to the side. One hand came down to rest on the grass, the other was extended to her side, ready to strike.

A couple of the birds startled and took flight, and the plant bits fell around her, the spell broken along with her concentration.

Embarrassed, he stepped forward quickly. "I'm sorry! I didn't mean to startle you."

She rose gracefully when she realized it was him. Her arms came across her chest and she rubbed her biceps, not meeting his eyes. She seemed a little embarrassed too, having been caught in a private moment.

"It's okay," she said quickly. "I couldn't sleep," she added, trying to explain.

"Me either," he said.

Silence descended between them and they locked gazes for a moment across the empty expanse of grass.

Just as she took a step toward him, he said, "I'm going to move my stuff to headquarters tomorrow."

Her face registered shock and then something like disappointment. That surprised him.

"Oh," she said, her voice quiet. "Okay."

In the space of a moment, she seemed to gather herself, and a small smile appeared on her face. It was one that he was coming to recognize as a mask she sometimes wore because it never reached her eyes.

"And I was just getting used to having you around," she said. "Is it because I snore really loud?"

She was trying to joke her way out of this and that pissed him off.

"Look, we both know it's getting weird. Between us. I just want to get rid of the tension. Keep it professional, like you want."

A look of hurt crossed her features for just a moment before she nodded. He turned his back to her and ran his hand through his hair, trying to ease the regret that look stirred in him.

This was the best move. It had to be.

He took a step toward the porch so that he could go back inside and pack, but he stopped.

He wasn't sure what possessed him, but he heard his voice say, "I have a question."

She was silent. It was now or never.

"Why didn't you go home with that guy tonight?"

Silence fell between them. He started to wonder if she had slipped away when he felt the heat of her against his skin. Her fingertips brushed his bare shoulder blade, and he almost shivered beneath her touch.

Her breath was warm against his skin when she whispered near his ear.

"Because he wasn't you."

Awareness hit him like a sledgehammer to the chest.

He spun and pulled her against him, his fingers cradling the back of her neck. He had a split-second to register her blazing indigo eyes and then his mouth was on hers. All he could think was that this must be what the eye of a hurricane was like, simultaneously quiet and electric, still and stormy.

Her lips were soft and sweet against his mouth and her scent, like the air during a thunderstorm, swept over him. She was impossibly warm against the bare skin of his chest. Electricity danced across the skin of his back and shoulders where her fingers dug into his flesh, pulling him closer.

The satin of her nightgown slid against his skin, warmed by her body. When her soft little tongue brushed his lower lip, he almost lost his mind. He groaned against her mouth and pulled her closer to him.

She was strong. He knew that from their workouts together. But just now, she felt almost delicate in his arms. He loosened his grip.

She broke their kiss and touched his cheek, his stubble rasping against her palm. Her breath was coming fast and her lips were gorgeously swollen from his kiss.

"You don't have to hold back. You won't hurt me, Alex," she whispered.

His own breath was coming fast and his heart pounded. She was right on so many levels. Could she see it in his eyes? Did she know that he would follow her through hell and back and would die before he let anything touch her?

Her eyes met his, and he was lost. He could almost feel it happen. The last scales that had protected his heart fell away under that indigo gaze. The last part of himself that he had kept away from her slipped away and joined the rest of him in loving her.

He gently caressed her face and kissed her again. Softer, this time.

He was determined to do this right. He would not go too fast and lose her. He would not be the same as all the others she had slept with. If she took him to her bed, it would not be the casual, drunken sex he knew she used to keep her frustration at bay.

Her lips moved to his neck and his hands clenched in her hair, trying to maintain something like control.

"I need you, Alayna."

The words slipped out before he could choke them back. He was losing himself and he almost didn't care.

"I need you, too," she said against his throat, her warm breath and the vibrations of her voice sending ripples of sensation across his skin. "From the moment I saw you."

Her words caused something to tighten in his chest to the point of pain. He brought her gaze to his.

"Isn't this moving a little fast?" he said.

"We could all die tomorrow," she answered, a little smirk curving her lips.

He laughed.

"That's a cheesy line. It's not going to work on me. I have standards," he said jokingly, his voice soft and just a little rough.

Her face grew serious and she ran her fingers through his hair, casually exploring him.

"I've held myself back from you for weeks because I didn't want our feelings for each other to cloud our judgment, but that's already happening, and we really could both be dead tomorrow, and I don't want to go another night without you."

The simple truth in her voice made his heart squeeze. He swallowed hard. She had him. He was hers.

In a swift movement he swept her into his arms, one arm around her shoulders, the other behind her knees, and lifted her against his chest. She let out a little gasp and a nervous giggle, steadying herself with her hands on his shoulders.

"I don't know," he said softly, his lips brushing hers. "Sleeping with the boss is not a great idea."

"I think it's the best idea you've had."

"But will you still respect me in the morning?" he asked her.

She threw back her head and laughed as he carried her to her bed.

* * *

Alayna slid to the floor as Alex stepped inside her bedroom, and she delighted in the drag of her skin against his. Afraid that all the talking had cooled the heat that had exploded between them just moments before, she wrapped her arms around his neck and kissed him with everything she had.

His arms came around her like iron bands, pulling her against that chest that was as hard as stone and as warm as a gentle fire. She lightly scraped her nails along his scalp, and he groaned against her mouth again.

She was pulling out all the tricks that she had picked up over years of nothing but one night stands. She knew how to get a guy frantic and panting in a matter of minutes and how to communicate exactly what she wanted with nothing but her body.

Stepping back from him, she slipped the nightgown from her shoulders and let it pool at her feet. His eyes went wide with shock for an instant before they narrowed again, a dangerous level of arousal burning in those dark depths. She moved to drop to her knees in front of him, grasping the hem of his silk pajama pants.

"Not so fast," he said, his voice taking on a rough edge. "I'm not some quick fuck you picked up in a bar."

Her eyes flashed as she met his gaze, but she decided not to resist as he reached down and pulled her to her feet, fitting her against him again. Completely naked, she knew she should be cold, but all she could feel was heat when he was near her.

His hand gently caressed her shoulder where it met her neck and his gaze followed his fingertips as they traveled down her arm and, with soft feather touches, stroked her breast.

He was acting like they had all the time in the world, and she felt like her skin was about to catch fire.

His touch sent ripples of electricity dancing along her skin. A desperate need was clawing at her belly. She wanted him inside her with a dangerous intensity. Her hands on his skin became urgent, her nails lightly raking his flesh.

He stilled her hands with his before moving his fingers playfully across the curve of her hip and pulling her close.

He breathed deeply, like he was taking in the scent of her and memorizing it. His lips pressed lightly to her temple. "Relax, slow down. We've got all night."

She stilled in his arms for a moment, just enjoying the feel of him against her, taking his uniquely male scent into her nose. He was spice and musk.

He captured her mouth with his. His kiss was slow and sensual, almost leisurely. Alayna lost herself in his skilled embrace, letting him work his own kind of magick with his mouth on her lips and neck.

She didn't spend a lot of time kissing the men she took to bed. Make-out sessions were not high on their lists of priorities, but she found herself savoring every nip, the slide of his tongue and the feel of his arms around her.

When she broke the kiss, they were both breathing hard. When she met Alex's gaze, she could see his inner walls coming down. There was raw heat and naked desire in his eyes. She realized that she had seen tiny glimmers of those feelings when she had caught him looking at her the last few weeks, but seeing the full intensity of those emotions now caused a delicious clenching within her.

Stepping back, she brushed the fingertips of one hand over the top of her breasts and sat back on the bed. Crooking one finger, she parted her mouth and gave him her best come hither look. They'd see just how slow he wanted to take it once she got him in bed.

Color rose in his cheeks beneath his tan, and his substantial erection strained at the seams of his pajama pants.

"Take them off," she whispered.

"Not just yet," he said.

She gave him a little pout, and he laughed. Gods, he was gorgeous. How on earth had she kept her hands off him this long?

When his dark eyes, which too often held glimpses of sadness and regret, were dancing with laughter like they were now, it made her heart race. And those Maybelline lashes that framed them added just enough of a soft touch to the otherwise rugged planes of his face.

He stepped toward her and her gaze came to rest on his mouth. His lips were slightly parted as his chest rose and fell.

She remembered the feel of those lips on hers and wondered what they would feel like on other parts of her. Her nipples? Her heart beat faster just thinking of it. Her pussy? Her breath almost caught in her throat at the thought. Without realizing it, her thighs parted slightly and her hand moved to touch her clit.

Alex closed his eyes and growled softly through gritted teeth at the sight. She was determined to shatter that rigid control of his.

She wanted him wild when he took her.

She rose to her knees on the bed, her hand still on her soft folds, which were becoming slick from wanting him.

With her other hand, she touched his chest. She had dreamed of what he looked like beneath those tight black shirts he favored. He wasn't muscle bound by any means. He was built more like a swimmer, lean and hard, with perfectly defined muscles in his arms, torso and thighs. The plains of his chest looked like they were cut from stone and contrasted perfectly with the slightly rounded swells of his shoulders.

And those abs. She wondered what they tasted like and she bent at the waist, running her tongue over those ridges of flesh.

He groaned again and took a shaky breath. She could feel the pulse of his abdominal artery against her lips as she kissed and nipped his stomach. As she worked her way back to his mouth, her world suddenly spun, and she found herself on her back, one leg hooked over his shoulder and his mouth poised above her pussy.

She gasped as she met his gaze. So much for control, she thought, as his mouth came down on her. She let out a groan of her own as his tongue found her opening and slid inside. Her body arched off the bed and his hands found her waist, securing her right where he wanted her.

She moaned again as his tongue moved to circle her swollen, throbbing clit. It was a breathy sound, full of ecstasy, and unlike any sound she had ever made before. Commanders of the Mage Corps did not make porn star sounds, she chided herself.

All thought flew from her head and she cried out as he drew the sensitive flesh into his mouth, sucking lightly and flicking it with his tongue. The vibrations of his soft laughter pulled the tension within her even tighter.

She arched again, gripping the bed sheets on either side of her and felt the blissful waves of climax crash into her.

It could have been minutes, it could have been hours later when she came back to her body. Almost involuntarily, she covered her face with her hands and peeked at him over her fingertips, a flush creeping into her cheeks.

"Don't tell me you're getting shy now," he teased, discreetly wiping his face with the edge of the sheet before he took her in his arms again and placed his mouth on her neck.

"I don't think I've ever made sounds like that before," she said, laughing.

She'd had orgasms with her one night stands, sure. But it had never been anything like that.

"It's different when you're with someone who cares about you," he whispered against her throat, just below her ear. "You know that, right?"

The last had been said so quietly she almost didn't hear him.

She was silent so long that he lifted his head and looked into her eyes. She knew that he could see a lot of emotions there, and she was suddenly terrified. He was stripping away all of the carefully laid defenses around her, and what really scared her was that she didn't care.

"I didn't know that until now," she said quietly.

Alex pulled her fiercely against him and buried his face in her hair, just holding her for a long, still moment.

She reached between them, her hand sliding past the waistband of those damned pajama pants. She made a note to burn those as soon as she got them off him.

Her fingers brushed his erection, and he hissed. When her hand came around the base of his shaft and began to stroke him, he groaned through his teeth.

She moved down his body slowly, kissing his chest and stomach, while increasing the pace of her strokes, adding a little twist at the top. When she reached the waistband of his pants, she pulled them down and off, taking the head of his cock into her mouth. He was big and thick and tasted faintly of salt. She ran her tongue over the length of him and sucked as much as she could into her mouth, which was barely half. She stroked the base with one hand and ran her nails over his abs with the other.

He moaned again and sat up abruptly, his hands on her shoulders.

"Wait," he said, a note of pleading in his voice. "Please. I want to be inside you when I come."

She looked up and nodded.

In one swift move, she was under him. He rose above her, hard muscles rippling and she felt the tip of his cock at her opening. She dug her fingers into his hips, but he resisted her and entered her slowly. It was pure, delightful torture.

She felt every inch of him slide into her slick heat. Her head thrown back, she moaned at the incredible feel of him stretching her, filling her.

Her breath caught on an ecstatic gasp as he moved within her. That delicious tension began to build again. He lifted her shoulders off the bed and his mouth found her nipple. Electricity zinged between her breast and her pussy and she cried out, burying her hands in his thick black hair, holding his mouth against her.

The new angle was rubbing her already swollen clit just the right way, and the strokes of his cock sent waves of pleasure through her body with each movement. His hard, muscular arms supported her, wrapping around her as he held against his chest. The guy clearly knew what he was doing.

The graceful, hard strength of him was overwhelming as he took complete control of her body. She had never surrendered control during sex before. It was terrifying and amazing and somehow freeing all at the same time. And it was all too much for her. She threw her head back and nearly screamed as her orgasm tore through her.

Alex fisted his hand in her hair, holding her there, as she heard him groan and felt him spasm within her.

His voice filled her ears in that moment.

"I love you, Alayna," he said through gritted teeth.

She felt his release in every tight muscle of his body and in the soft warmth that filled her pussy.

Breathing hard, he gently laid her back down and withdrew from her body, wrapping his arms around her as he pulled her sheets over them.

A little shaken by what she thought she'd heard, she buried her face against his chest and began to drift toward sleep, vowing to herself to deal with it in the morning. For now, though, she would enjoy every moment of this.

For the first time in her life, Alayna slept beside a man. Her last thought as exhaustion and sleep claimed her was that she had never felt anything better in her life.

* * *

It took Alex a few moments to figure out where he was as he struggled toward consciousness. Faint morning sunlight warmed his face and the skin of his chest, shadows dancing as it filtered through trees. A light breeze blew across his body, bringing the scent of a woman. Not just any woman. Alayna.

He reached out sleepily, wishing for the warm, soft feel of her. She wasn't beside him, but this was her bed.

It came back to him in a rush. He'd made love to her. And then he remembered what he'd said right as he came inside her. He'd told he loved her.

Damn it.

He groaned and rolled over, beating his head against the pillow a couple of times. Embarrassment heated his cheeks, and he wished he had a freaking time machine so he could go back and tell last-night Alex to not be such an idiot.

Alayna had fought so hard against any emotional entanglements between them. And he'd gone and said the one word that was guaranteed to send her running. So what if it was true? Should have kept that to himself until she was ready to hear it.

He took a deep breath and sat up. He'd have to face her sooner or later. He grabbed his pants off the floor and pulled them on and headed to his room. His phone was blinking, indicating that he had a text. It was from Alayna. Taking a deep breath, he opened it.

"Heading to the office. See you later," it read.

The time stamp was marked about an hour before.

A sick feeling settled in his stomach. Had he ruined everything with that stupid admission last night?

Chapter 18

"I think we all know what we're looking at here," Alayna told the team.

She stood at the head of the conference table that the team was seated around. Alex had rolled in a few minutes ago, and she'd been able to avoid meeting his eyes so far. When she looked, would she find anger there?

"Based on the interviews that Alex and Lu did with the captives and our tracking data, I think it's safe to say that Medina and his goons are using vehicles we haven't seen or tagged to move the captives out of that warehouse and on to wherever it is they send them."

The captives that had been able to talk told them that other people that had been held with them were moved out every few days, maybe once a week. It was hard to tell because the room they were kept in hadn't had windows.

They did know that they were moved in large fleet vans because they'd pulled them into the warehouse to load them. None of the people loaded in those vans ever came back, they said.

Alayna had a sick suspicion what happened to those people.

Dead bodies with signs of vampire predation, plus people being held and moved like cattle, well, that added up to one thing.

"Someone is running a blood buffet," she said.

Unfortunately, they didn't know where the meals were being served. And the bodies being dumped the way they were made absolutely no sense to anyone at the table.

"Could it be a delivery service?" Budock asked.

"We don't know yet, but it's certainly on the list of possibilities," Alayna said. "It might explain the body dumps, if they're serving inexperienced vamps that don't know how to dispose of a body discreetly."

"They may have thought it was discreet. Sapien law enforcement probably never would have put it all together," Dumeril said. "Blanca's murder was the aberration. We think she died at Revelation or one of the other nearby clubs. Maybe Medina ordered a late dinner and got sloppy?"

"I think Blanca was a message," Budock said.

"What makes you say that?" Alayna said.

"They couldn't have dumped her in a more public place," Burdock said. "There was no hiding the bite marks. They may as well have dumped her on our doorstep."

"He's right," Alex chimed in. "In every case study I've seen, when a body dump gets that public, someone is trying to get attention."

"But if someone is running a blood buffet, why would they want attention? It doesn't make any sense," Alayna said. "We can circle back to that. What I'm really concerned about is whether they still have captives somewhere. I want all of you to put your ears to the ground, knock on the door of every informant, snitch and insider in this town. We're going to flush these bastards out."

"They'll know we're coming," Alex said.

"That's the point," she replied. "They've had no problems coming straight at us. I say we do the same to them."

As the team rose one by one and left the room, Alex lingered, finally catching her eye and holding it.

It wasn't anger that she saw in his gaze. There was a fire snapping in those dark eyes, a low, slow burn that made something in her stomach flutter.

Alayna came around the table and headed and for the door, her shoulders squared, her body tense, and her eyes locked on his. In a move that was entirely too smooth, he rose, shut the door and blocked it with his body. Those big arms were crossed over his chest, his head was slightly tilted to one side and one eyebrow was raised.

Silence stretched to a painful, quivering tension as she met his eyes. Enough. She couldn't stand it anymore.

"We have work to do," she said making a move around him. Mistake. He shifted and she came right up against that chest. She should have stepped back, but her treacherous body refused to do it.

"Not until we talk about what happened last night." His voice was low, the same voice he'd used in bed last night. Her cheeks instantly heated at the thought of the things he'd said when he'd held her against him, moving inside her body.

Then he'd said those words. *I love you, Alayna.*

Last night shouldn't have happened. That's what she wanted to tell him, but her mouth was too dry to form words. Not that she could string words together right now, not with the way he was looking down at her.

Sleeping with him was a terrible idea. In her head, she was trying to chalk it up to hormones and her lack of sexual activity over the past few weeks. But she was lying to herself. This thing with Alex was beyond physical, was beyond chemistry. Those words he'd said proved that.

And it couldn't happen.

His hand brushed her waist, and she stepped closer without thinking, that hand coming to rest at the small of her back. Her breath was coming faster and now and she was having a hard time controlling it.

She was about to open her mouth, to tell him what, she didn't know, but he spoke first.

"About what I said last night. That wasn't when I meant to say it or how I meant to say it," he said. "But I did mean it. I do mean it."

Shit. She was really hoping he was going to take it back, blame it on the moment. Plenty of guys said stupid things when they were about to come. Nope, not her Alex. Apparently, he made life-changing declarations.

"You don't even know me," she said.

"I know enough."

He knew nothing. If he did, he'd run from her. When he found out, he would run from her.

"I have so many secrets," she whispered.

"You'll tell me when you're ready."

"And when I do, they'll tear the heart right out of you."

He was silent for a moment before he leaned down and said in her ear, "I don't expect you say it back."

Good thing, too, because she could never say those words. Even if they were true. Which they weren't, she told herself firmly.

She pushed past him and it took every ounce of her considerable willpower not to look back at him.

* * *

A few hours later, a large basket of tequila bottles clanked against Alayna's hip as she slammed the Mustang's door and started to climb the grassy hill, Alex a few steps behind her.

The moon was hidden behind heavy clouds, and the darkness wrapped around them as they walked. They didn't talk as they moved through the wooded area. The beings they would be speaking with could already hear their approach and chatter might seem impolite.

She was grateful for the silence. The conversation with Alex hadn't gone well this morning, and the tension that had formed between them was making her itchy. She longed for the easy-going camaraderie they'd had before.

They moved through an oak grove and emerged into a clearing at the top of the hill. Alayna set the basket down, opened a bottle, and took a long pull, wiping her mouth with the back of her hand before returning the bottle to the basket.

They waited several minutes, the night sounds of insects, birds and furry things in the bushes settling around the two humans like a cloak. Alayna felt more than heard the sound of wings on the air. It was the pressure change that gave it away. A fire or earth mage would have missed it, but you couldn't sneak up on a air mage from above.

Alex jumped back as the bird landed with a huge *WHOOMP* in front of them, its brown and black feathers fluttering and its golden eyes flashing in the dark. The body was about five feet tall, with huge clawed feet that had dug furrows into the ground on landing. Its wings must have been about fifteen feet across as it settled them around its feathered body. Its head was somewhere between an owl and an eagle.

It was decidedly a raptor, with a sharply curving beak that looked like it was made to tear flesh. Its yellow eyes were huge and round, with large black pupils that seemed to drink in the dark. Its feathers were a mottled brown and grey that blended perfectly with the trees in the dark. It stared at them from under sharply protruding brows that reminded Alayna of a bald eagle or a great horned owl.

The creature's stare was deeply unnerving, and Alayna knew exactly how a rabbit must feel when it heard those wings rushing toward it. That feathered head tilted to the side, and fixed on Alayna and the basket.

This was one of the Lechuzas, the bird witches of Texas and Mexican legend. The legends had it they were witches that could transform into giant birds. Some said they hunted the unwary or the sinful who walked on dirt roads at night.

The legends had it all wrong.

Alayna screeched several times, different lengths and different tones, in the formal greeting. The creature replied with a series of hoots and whistles, the traditional answer to the formal greeting.

The Lechuza shook itself, ruffling its feathers and settling its wings more tightly around its body. A screech filled the air along with the familiar sounds of a shifter in transition. Bones snapped and tendons popped. In the space of a few seconds, a man with deeply tanned skin and long dark hair stood in front of them. He would have passed for human easily if it weren't for the luminescent yellow owl eyes that stared out of his face.

"Tequila? Really?" The former bird said, a Laredo accent coloring his words. "That's kind of racist, you know."

The Lechuzas weren't humans that transformed into birds; they were birds that could transform into humans. These were rare creatures indeed in the supernatural world, with maybe a hundred or so scattered around Texas and northern Mexico. They hunted in small groups of six or seven, usually family groups.

They took game, small animals, sometimes livestock. Never humans. Alayna had put them on notice years ago that if they took humans, even the drunk and unwary humans they favored as prey, she'd take them all out.

His voice didn't sound quite human. The tone fluctuated, and it trailed to a low squawk at the end of his sentences.

"It's Texas. Everyone likes tequila."

The birdman let out a squawking, hissing laugh.

"I'm just messing with you, Dragonrider. What can I do for you?"

So, he'd seen her and he knew about Z. It made sense that he would know about another arial hunter in the area. She wondered what he'd do with that information.

He bent down and picked up one of the bottles.

"El Diamante de Cielo? This is the good stuff, chica," he said. He whistled in appreciation, but it sounded more like an owl's hoot.

"Only the best for my friends," Alayna said. "I need to know if you and the other Lechuzas have seen anything weird happening in or around your territory."

"Chica, we're just outside of Austin. Weird is a relative term. I need specifics, you know."

"Vampires. Making meals out of humans. You seen anything like that?"

The birdman moved within inches of Alayna, walking with a slow, sensual grace that wasn't even in the neighborhood of human. He could pick a handsome form, she mused. He was young, well-muscled. He was also naked.

He touched one of the locks that had come loose from her ponytail and ran it between his thumb and forefinger.

"That's just nature, mi bonita. Predators and prey."

His nakedness didn't unnerve her, though she was sure he meant it to. She'd been around plenty of handsome naked men in her life. All of them had been strangers like this guy. Except the one that was glaring at them across the clearing. Alex was the furthest thing from a stranger she'd ever known.

"These guys are messy eaters. The sapien authorities are starting to get itchy. Nobody wants that," she said.

He moved around behind her, trailing his fingers across the back of her neck. Under different circumstances, she might take him up on his not-so-subtle invitation.

Her eyes moved to Alex standing nearby. He was practically vibrating with the effort he was putting into keeping still. Was he jealous?

She felt warm breath on her neck, and the Lechuza whispered in her ear.

"They're organizing hunts. About thirty miles northeast of here. The vampires bring the humans in, turn them loose in the woods, give them a head start. They never last more than a couple of hours. They drain 'em dry and load the bodies up when they're finished."

Whoa.

Her eyes went wide, and she turned, the chief of the Lechuzas catching her around the waist and pulling her against his body. She could practically hear Alex growling from where she stood. She shot him a look that said she could handle this and he'd better not move a muscle.

"Judging by your reaction, I'm guessing that was big information," he said, putting his mouth inches from hers. "Is tequila the only thank you I'm going to get for that?"

She pushed him back with a hand on his bare chest.

"Are they hunting in your territory?" she asked.

"Yeah, the edge of it. But they come in force, usually about ten of them. We've only got five in the group right now."

"And you're not strong enough to take them on," she finished.

Anger flashed in those hunter's eyes.

"Everything in me wants to rip their flesh with my talons, but we can't risk it."

"If I brought in six heavy hitters, together we'd probably outnumber them. If you provide the arial support, I'll provide the ground crew. How do your hunters like the taste of vampire flesh?"

"I like the way you think, airwalker. And you have good taste in hooch." He trailed off and looked away, considering what she had said.

"What the hell? No one lives forever, right? Meet me here tomorrow night. Midnight. Me and mine will fly your crew in so the vamps don't hear you coming. You can fly in on your own, right?"

She nodded.

"It's a deal then," she said.

"Not so fast, chica. When all of this is over with, let me take you out and then we'll call it a deal, yeah?"

Alayna smiled.

"You've got some balls," she said.

"Yeah, they're right here on display. You like what you see?" His smile was brilliant, and his voice was teasing.

Her eyes never left his face, and her smile never left hers.

"You're a shameless flirt, Feathers. Let's see if we live through this run first, shall we?" she said.

"It's Rolando, sweetheart. And I have a really good reason to live, now."

She gave him a penetrating look from beneath her lashes as she turned and headed back down the hill. Alex followed, silent and brooding.

* * *

Alex was half asleep in his room at Alayna's when he heard the front door open and close. Alayna had sent him home a couple hours before when his eyes had started to blur from exhaustion. The team had been working nonstop to compile the intel they'd gathered and prep for the raid with the Lechuzas.

Footsteps were moving down the hallway. She'd kept her distance today. He'd freaked her out with his admission the night before, so he'd resolved to give her some space. Even so, it had been all he could do to keep from growling at Rolando earlier. He wasn't territorial or possessive when it came to women. But Alayna stirred up all kinds of new things.

The footsteps reached his door. Before he could call out to her that he was awake, his door opened a crack.

He stayed silent and still, wondering what she was going to do.

In the darkness, he couldn't really see her, but he knew it was her through some combination of her scent, the sound of her breathing, and the way the figure in the door held herself. She was already so much a part of him that he was sure he could find her even in the darkest of places.

The figure slipped into the room like a silent shadow and moved to the side of the bed. Should he let her know that he was awake? Did she already know? She seemed to have super senses most of the time. He tried to keep is breathing even and his eyes closed.

There was the rustle of clothing and the thump of boots hitting the hardwood. The scent of her skin reached him, and her delicate fingers ghosted over his hair before gently caressing his cheek. He suppressed a shudder of pure pleasure at her touch and he was instantly hard.

His eyes snapped open and met hers for a second before he wrapped his arms around her and pulled her under the blanket with him. The satin of her skin slid against his, carrying the chill of dawn with it. She was naked.

She gasped as he rolled half on top of her, the gasp turning to a moan as his erection settled heavy between her thighs.

"You're warm," she murmured as her hands moved over his back and she buried her face where his neck met his shoulder. Her body was sagging with exhaustion, but she was practically vibrating with a likely combination of caffeine and determination.

"How did it go?" he asked softly.

"I think we've done all we can. Either we live through tomorrow or we don't," she said. "Called the brass, but reinforcements are currently unavailable. We're on our own unless I can call in a favor."

Her voice cut off as Alex's mouth moved over hers in a slow kiss.

"You are not calling anyone," he said, his voice low and husky. "You need rack time. I need rack time and your team needs rack time. We can get back to it in a few hours."

She started to protest until he lowered his head and drew one of her taut nipples into his mouth. A groan escaped him as she responded to him, wrapping her arms around his shoulders, digging her nails into his flesh.

The night before had been explosively hot between them. Now, he wanted slow. He wanted sensual. He wanted to taste every inch of her skin and feel her come apart in his arms multiple times until she passed out beside him from exhaustion.

As he moved his tongue over her sensitive skin, she murmured, "Is this what you meant by rack time?"

He laughed against her, using his tongue and teeth until she was arching and breathless beneath him.

The night before had been all heat, raking nails, desperate hands, flashing teeth and urgent tension. It had been a gale-force thunderstorm.

This was gentle touches, languid kisses and caresses. The tension was still there, but it had reached an odd kind of comfort. This was more like a slow and gentle rain on a summer night.

Alex was aware that this was the first time Alayna had ever been with someone for the second time, and he was determined to show her how amazing that could be. He brought his hands to either side of her face, holding that deep blue gaze for a moment before he took her mouth again.

She reached between them, pulling his boxers off his hips. Her fingers found his erection, teasing him, urging him. He bit his lip in an effort to maintain control. Slow. Gentle. He kept repeating the words in his head like a mantra.

Her hands were becoming urgent where she touched him, and he growled against her mouth. She arched against him in invitation, and he could feel her slick heat slide against his cock. A shudder went through his body as he tried to hold himself back.

He touched her face again and brought his mouth to her ear.

"What about protection? I know we didn't use it last time. I'm clean, but—"

She stilled his words with two fingers on his lips.

"I can't catch anything from sapiens, and you can't get me pregnant."

She ran the fingers she had used to shush him against his lower lip and he sucked them into his mouth, scraping lightly with his teeth and flicking his tongue over the tips.

A moan slipped from her luscious lips and she rose up, wrapping her arms around him again, hands clenching in his hair.

He positioned himself at her opening and slid in slowly, catching the ecstatic noises she made with his mouth. She arched, taking him deeper, and dug her nails into the muscles in his back.

A slow and sensual rhythm began between them. Her soft noises of pleasure urged him on, but he held himself back. She was trembling, and her soft cries grew more desperate as he increased his pace.

He caressed her face again and he brought her gaze to his, holding it.

She was so unbelievably beautiful in that moment. Platinum curls spread out over his pillows, her pale skin glowed in the moonlight spilling through the window and her eyes were deep pools in the darkness, somewhere between blue and black.

He still couldn't quite believe that this stunning creature with her incredible strength and power had taken him into her arms, into her body. But he was beginning to suspect something. For all her strength, for all her power and despite the image she tried to project of being above it all, he knew the truth.

Alayna Blackwell was lonely, and she longed for love, just like everyone else.

He would give her that love without asking for anything in return. Like an offering of food left for some elusive wild creature, he would put his heart out there. If she took it, he would revel in the taking. He wasn't ready to hope that she would offer him anything in return, but he couldn't deny that he had imagined a future together on the other side of this case. Fear of something was holding her back from him. He didn't know what was causing it, but he would stay by her side until that fear disappeared.

Her trembling increased and he let his body off the leash, giving her what she wordlessly asked for.

"Alex." His name on her lips was a plea, a prayer, a question, and a cheer all at once. His heart squeezed at the sound of it.

Her inner muscles spasmed around him, and he came with her, pouring his release into her.

After a moment, he started to move off of her, afraid of crushing her with his weight. She pulled him back, wrapping her arms around his back and stroking his hair with one hand.

Alex relaxed into her, relishing the feel of her in his arms and loving the feeling of being cradled in hers. As his heartbeat slowed completely, he withdrew from her body and rolled to his side, pulling her against him, desperate not to lose the connection between them.

He felt wetness on his chest and saw her try to surreptitiously dash something from her cheek.

"Are you OK?" he asked. "Did I hurt you?"

He heard the note of panic in his voice and felt a little sick to his stomach suddenly.

"Don't be silly," she said, snuggling against his side, trying to pass it off like nothing had happened.

He lifted her chin until he could see her eyes, shimmering in the moonlight. Holding her gaze, he remained silent, giving her the space to tell him if she wanted.

After a moment, she cracked.

"I've never done this. I've never felt this," she began, hesitating. "And there is something bad coming. I can feel it. It's something horrible and it could rip us all apart. And I can't do anything to stop it."

When she was silent for a moment, he reached out and stroked her hair.

"We're soldiers, so we know that feeling better than most, but everyone goes through that at one point or another," Alex told her.

"I've lost people," she said quietly. "More than I like to think about, but…this is different."

"I know," he said, stroking her hair slowly, rhythmically. "You just take it one day at a time, you stay honest with yourself and the other person, and you tell people how you feel about them, because there may come a day when you won't get another chance."

She was silent for a long time and Alex wondered if she had drifted off to sleep. Finally, she said, "You speak from experience."

"You know I do," he said.

Alayna looked at him.

"I'm sorry," she said.

"Don't be. The last thing I want between us is regret or apologies," he said, staring into the darkness.

Her silence was her answer as she snuggled against his side and slowly relaxed into sleep.

Chapter 19

Alex checked the magazine on the M-16 strapped to his chest. It was an old habit before a fight. He checked and rechecked his equipment multiple times before a mission. In addition to the rifle, he carried twin 1911s on his hips, a couple of flash bangs, his Ka-Bar knife, and a full medic's loadout in a backpack.

He checked the extra mags for the 1911s that he had stashed in pouches on his tac-vest. They were loaded with spelled ammo that Burdock had given him. The fire mage stood next to him, moving through much the same pre-fight ritual he was. They were all loaded for bear and out for blood.

Burdock pulled something from his pocket and stared at it for a long moment. It was small and fit in the palm of his hand. A photo maybe? When he caught Alex looking, he glared at him and stuffed the thing back in his pocket.

"Time to saddle up," Burdock growled, his eyes on the sky.

At the sound of rustling feathers and flapping wings, Alex looked up to see the flock of Lechuzas descending toward the clearing where he and the rest of the team waited. He watched as Ellie stood and strapped on a pack full of electronic gear. If there was any kind of security system at this hunting ground, she'd stroll right by it. Burdock was leading their smaller team and Alex was assigned to watch Ellie's back while she worked her hacker magic.

Lu carried no weapons. They'd agreed that she'd shift when they arrived, after they'd all had a chance to get a handle on the situation.

He watched as Dumeril checked the grips of his kukris in their holster at the small of his back and Alayna checked that her throwing knives, whip and battle fans were attached at her belt.

Alayna had put him with Burdock and Ellie, explaining that if they found hostages, she needed a Spanish speaker and someone with medical training. As long as no one was critically injured, he would be fine. Even so, nervousness clawed at his gut and adrenaline poured into his bloodstream like an addictive drug.

His thoughts were interrupted as five of the large birds landed and folded their gigantic wings around them. One did a kind of hop-walk on clawed feet toward Alex. It nodded its head once, its large yellow eyes fixed on his. The creature unfurled its wings, and with four mighty pumps of its massive flight muscles, it was about six feet off the ground.

Alex turned quickly and noticed that the other five Lechuzas were doing the same thing. The creature's taloned feet wrapped around each of his shoulders and upper arms. Air swirled around him, ruffling his short dark hair, as the creature flapped its wings and lifted them into the air.

The claws wrapped all the way around his arm, but the angle at which he hung was a little uncomfortable. Alex ignored it. They didn't have far to go.

The treed landscape slid by beneath his combat boots. It was just after midnight on a cloudy, moonless night. They were unlikely to be seen by sapien eyes, even flying just a couple hundred feet off the ground.

Alex caught a glimpse of Alayna flying alongside him. Her platinum hair streamed behind her in an undulating mass of silver and gold. She was dressed head to toe in fairy leather, jacket, pants and boots in inky black.

She looked like a witch out of a fairytale. The only thing missing was a broom. She was otherworldly, ethereal, powerful. And he was completely under her spell.

Glancing down, Alex saw a set of outbuildings, painted black, slide by beneath his feet. His brow furrowed. Texans never painted anything black. Anything inside would roast in summer. This must be the place.

As if reading his mind, the Lechuza carrying him squeezed his right shoulder to signal that the drop was coming up. He relaxed his muscles and when the birdman released him about fifteen feet off the ground, he hit the ground and rolled.

As he came up, his M-16 was in his hands, and he was scanning for targets. Alayna came to a landing a short distance from him, dropping gracefully to a crouch. The rest of the team were dropped from varying heights, rolling in near silence to their feet before joining them.

Alayna motioned for silence. They had their assignments. Everyone re-checked their equipment and formed up. They split into two teams. Alayna, Dumeril, and Lu were together and were assigned to eliminate any vamp targets. Burdock was leading the second team with Alex and Ellie. They were assigned to protect any hostages and secure any documents, computers or identifying information about who might be organizing these hunts.

The Lechuzas were the air support, assigned to watch the perimeter and eliminate any vamps that slipped past the ground team.

As Alayna and her team moved off to the east, Burdock signaled to Alex and Ellie that they were moving to the west, toward the buildings they had seen flying in. Chances were good the hostages were there.

As they moved over the rise, Ellie motioned for them to freeze, her eyes being the most sensitive in the dark. There were three vampires guarding one of the buildings, a low structure with no windows. Bingo.

Burdock motioned to each of them and pointed to a vamp, assigning one to each of them.

Burdock slipped forward silently. His gaze focused about fifty feet to his left and his body went tense and still. A loud pop of superheated air split the night.

The vamps all turned in that direction, turning their backs toward the team. They moved like liquid shadows; dark, silent and deadly.

Alex moved faster than he thought possible, closing the distance in what seemed like the blink of an eye. His Ka-bar made a wet sound as it cut the vamp's throat, followed by a crunch as he shoved it through the spinal column. The body slumped in his arms. Then Burdock was on his vamp. He closed his fists around the vamp's throat and channeled his fire into his palms, his mouth twisting in a feral snarl. The fire ate through the vamp's neck in a split second, the head falling and rolling away.

Alex turned to see Ellie rising from the motionless body of her vamp, a shapeless shadow under her cloak. They'd managed not to raise the alarm.

Burdock drew his finger in a small circle on the wall of the building, cutting through the metal like a blowtorch. He pushed the small circle of metal in and looked through. Alex peeked through when Burdock stepped back, careful to avoid the glowing metal edges. A dozen people ranging from children to young adults were crowded into the dark, windowless building. No vamps, though.

"No hostiles. Twelve hostages," Alex told them. "Let's move on."

They formed up and headed over a small rise. Ahead, there were two vamps dragging a teenaged girl between them. They were dressed in black; she was in torn jean shorts and tank top that had once been pink. Alex saw that one of the straps was ripped and dangling. His vision went a little red around the edges at the sight. Her long, dark hair hung in stringy clumps, hiding her face, but her posture said she was barely conscious.

Behind the trio was a male vamp. He was dressed for the outdoors, but it was expensive gear, and the vamp was just too polished. He looked like a rich boy on safari, white shirt tucked into khaki pants. Alex supposed that's what he was, in a way. A really twisted fucking way.

There was a sick gleam in the vampire's eyes. Anticipation, Alex realized, a sick feeling twisting in his stomach.

The two handlers shoved the girl to her knees. The hunter stepped forward and gripped the girl's dark hair in his fist. He sniffed deeply, taking her scent into his lungs and savoring it.

Alex saw his eyes go red and fangs descend. The predator was coming out to play. The girl screamed in horror when she saw the change. Her terror echoed off the trees, just a few yards away.

"I'll be seeing you soon, sweetheart," the hunter said softly, almost sweetly. "Now, run as fast and as far as you can."

The girl started crying through her screams. She scrambled to her feet, her sandals slipping in the wet grass.

The hunter smiled at the two handlers.

"She's going to taste so good," he told them.

Burdock turned to look at Alex and mouthed "mine." Alex nodded.

Burdock's face relaxed into concentration, as he pulled on his power from that place within him. He held up his hands toward the vampires, who were watching the tree line where the girl had disappeared.

Three balls of blue fire, as intense as an acetylene torch, flew toward them as fast as thought. They didn't so much burn as vaporize into hot embers.

What was left dropped to the wet grass, charred chunks with a few guttering blue flames licking over the surface and patches glowing like coals in the darkness.

Burdock swayed for a moment beside Alex, and he put a hand out to steady him.

"That one cost," Burdock said. "But it's worth it."

He gave the signal, and they started forward again. It was impossible to tell how many handlers and hunters were out here tonight. The Lechuzas said that it varied week to week.

Burdock read his mind when he said in a low voice, "Let's try to take one alive and see if we can get him to tell us their numbers and locations."

They all nodded as one.

* * *

Alayna, Dumeril, and Lu moved silently, just inside the tree line, toward the group of vampires and sapiens. There was a group of six handlers, three vampires that Alayna identified as hunters, and three sapiens.

The sapiens were all young-looking, probably less than twenty years old. One was female, the other two were male. Their clothing was torn and dirty and they only had flimsy sandals covering their feet.

The vampires standing around them were talking and laughing like they were at a fucking tailgate party, and Alayna felt the rage rising within her. She pushed it down and silently pointed at Lu and then the human captives. She pointed at Dumeril and then the handlers. She pointed at herself and indicated the hunters. Then, she held up a hand to wait.

Her whispered voice began to weave the spell she had chosen. It was a little flashy and would probably give away their presence, but she was tired of sneaking around. It was time these scumbags knew the pain and fear they caused their victims. And she was going to bring it to them tenfold.

As she finished her spell, she moved her hand in an arc and flames sprouted from the ground around the group of vampires and humans. Alayna relished the looks on their faces as their surprise turned to fear.

Lu, in her hulking, furred form, leapt the six-foot flames easily. She slung her overly long arms back and forth, knocking several handlers and hunters aside. She had one sapien over her shoulder and another slung under her arm in a matter of seconds. One of the handlers had managed to grab the third sapien, the girl, and had a gun to her head. Lu shook her head, and leapt the wall of flames, carrying the other two hostages to safety.

Alayna created a gap in the flames, and Dumeril rolled

through, a dazzling light spell flying from his fingers and blinding the handler holding the hostage. With blurring speed, he was on the guy in seconds, his kukris biting in the vampire's flesh as the hostage sagged to the ground.

Alayna walked slowly through the flames, feeling them lick her skin, but causing no damage. The fire was hers and obeyed only her command. She knew that she looked like an avenging demon walking through those flames, and she saw the fear in the eyes of the hunters.

The remaining handlers and hunters were frozen in place, weapons in their hands, as they stared at her. As she moved through the wall of flame, she bent and removed her whip from her boot, letting its length coil out and drag behind her in the grass.

Dumeril moved, and another handler fell to the ground under his assault. For just a moment, she wished she had Alex and his marksman's aim. But she couldn't risk having him with her. She was not entirely sure she could make objective decisions if she was worried about his safety. So she'd sent him with Burdock and Ellie, hoping they wouldn't run in to any trouble.

She turned to the four remaining vampires.

"Who the fuck are you?" one shouted.

She didn't answer him, but snapped out a spell and hit the group with a blast of electricity that bounced between the four vampires, bringing them to their knees as their screams filled the air.

"How many of you are there?" she asked them, trying to keep her voice under control, even as she wanted to scream and tear them all apart.

There was stunned silence from the group. The remaining handler spit a mouthful of blood that landed near her black leather boots.

"Wrong answer," she said through clenched teeth.

She hit them with the electricity again and tried not to enjoy seeing the pain they were in as they writhed on the ground. She refused to feel sympathy for these monsters. They had been about to hunt those people down. For fun.

"I'll ask one more time. How many?"

One of the hunters shot to his feet and lunged at her. She caught him with a bladed fan that took half his face off. His blood arced through the air and splattered against her leathers. He fell to the grass gurgling.

"Oh, god. We were just having a little fun. Please, don't hurt us," one of the hunters begged.

Jackpot.

Alayna strode forward and grabbed him by the throat, lifting his shoulders a little off the ground.

"How. Many?" she ground out through clenched teeth, her face inches from his.

She planted a booted foot on his balls, just for good measure. The vamp was blonde and good looking. Clearly had money, but he was young, maybe sixty or so. Probably a natural born from one of the old families. Maybe even a scion.

"Ten hunters and maybe twenty handlers," the vamp croaked out.

"What are you doing out here?" Alayna had her suspicions, but she wanted to hear it from his mouth.

"It was just supposed to be a little fun," he said again, fear making his voice high and tight.

"You think killing sapiens is fun?" she asked, anger edging into her voice and making it more of a growl.

"They don't always die," he said defensively. "Most of us just chase them down and feed on them. They just taste so good when they've been running for awhile."

She'd heard enough. She felt his neck snap in her hand. It would heal in a few hours, but he'd be unconscious until then. She flipped him over and zip tied his hands.

Alayna approached the handler.

"Was he telling the truth?"

"Fuck you," he spat.

With a snap of her whip, the length wrapped around his neck. With a jerk, it tightened, and his head rolled away through the grass, his lifeless body crumpling to the ground.

"Next!" she barked.

One of the two remaining vampires leapt to his feet and ran for the wall of flames. One of Dumeril's kukris caught him between the shoulder blades, but he barely slowed as the blade sunk deep. Before she could summon a spell, he was leaping through the flames, fire catching in a few places on his clothing as he continued to run.

With a screaming cry, a Lechuza that she was pretty sure was Rolando swooped out of the darkness and snatched the vamp up in his talons. The vamp's scream mixed with the Lechuza's screech as the talons tore the bloodsucker apart. The blood and flesh fell like rain against the grass.

"He was telling the truth! I swear it," the remaining conscious vampire said, holding his wrists in front of him in surrender.

Alayna stayed quiet and walked slowly toward him.

"I'll tell you anything you want to know, just please don't hurt me!"

She narrowed her eyes at him but stayed silent. Dumeril moved to her side, his blade dripping blood in the firelight as the loomed over the vampire, faces set in masks of stoic rage.

"We paid fifty grand each through a website. You only got the link when you were invited by someone who had been on the hunts. He was telling the truth when he said the sapes don't always die. We just have a little fun chasing them and then feeding. We leave them in the woods, and the handlers are supposed to pick them up. That's all I know, I swear it!"

Alayna squatted next to him and looked him in the eye.

"Who's in charge?"

"I never met him," the vamp said. "The handlers met us in town and drove us out here. I did hear them talking about someone called Culebra, but that's all I know."

Tears were starting to leak from his eyes. Ugh.

With a sound of disgust, she pulled his hands behind his back and restrained him.

"Don't fucking move from this spot or I will straight up decapitate you," she told him.

She dropped the wall of fire just as she heard one of the Lechuzas screech above her. Turning, Alayna saw that six handlers and a hunter were advancing on her and Dumeril in a rough semicircle. They hadn't been able to see the vamps beyond the flame wall.

Damn her for a fool.

Dumeril moved quickly to stand at her back.

"I've got a bad feeling about this, Commander," he said, flashing her what was meant to be a reassuring grin.

"We've been in tighter spots than this," she answered, matching his smile.

Alayna tallied the score quickly in her head. Seven pissed off vamps. Lu was unaccounted for, probably securing the sapien hostages. The Lechuza was several seconds overhead, and it was just one bird. And, yup, the vamps were starting to charge.

Great.

She and Dumeril couldn't outrun them. These fuckers were fast. She might be able to weave a spell for flight, but it was difficult to control and it would take longer to factor in carrying Dumeril.

The vamps were on them, and there was no more time for thought or planning. She reacted on instinct. Her whip sailed through the air, expanding its width until it was as thick as her forearm, and knocked one of the vamps off his feet. Fire flew from her fingertips and hit two of the vamps square in the face, setting their clothes and hair alight. They dropped to the ground, trying to put the flames out.

There was the distinctive pop of gunfire. Alayna's vision spun as a body slammed into her from the side, hands squeezed her throat, and bloody fangs filled her vision as the vamp lunged for a killing bite. She flipped her whip in her hand, hit a hidden button in the handle, and a silver blade sprang free.

She plunged the blade into the vamp's neck, hot blood flowing over her hands and splattering her face. His eyes went wide and he reared back away from her, his grip loosening as he tried to staunch the flow of blood. She freed the blade and swung, taking his head off. A momentary surge of relief poured through her.

She wiped the blood from her eyes and stood in time to see Lu rush past in a furry blur, her enormous form barreling through the remaining vamps. One of them had an automatic rifle and tried to fire as Lu's claws tore through the group, but the shots were all over the place, bullets zinging past Lu without so much as a scratch.

The enormous shifter picked up two of the vamps by an arm and began slamming them into each other, the ground and the remaining vampires. Screams and the sound of bones breaking filled the air. Lu's fangs and claws made short work, and soon every vampire was restrained, unconscious or dead.

"Commander, we have a problem!" Dumeril's voice reached her from several feet away. The flames she had called were dying embers now, smoldering in the grass and casting an orange light over everything.

Dumeril was crouched over the unconscious female hostage. Blood seeped from a chest wound. One of the stray bullets had found her. Damn it! She looked like she was sixteen, tops. The thought of losing her after they had come so close to saving her was more than Alayna could stomach.

"What can I do?"

"Keep the hostiles off my back. It's going to take everything I've got to heal this."

As he spoke, his hands covered the wound and a look of deep concentration creased his features.

As Alayna and Lu moved into position to cover the angles around Dumeril and the hostage, Ellie's voice crackled over the radio.

"We've got a situation here, Commander."

* * *

Alex's heart was pounding and blood coated his hands.

"Fuck! This is bad!" Burdock said through gritted teeth, fear and pain vibrating at the edges of his words.

He was not wrong.

As Alex, Burdock, and Ellie had been moving to take out two handlers who'd been moving hostages, the dirt bags had turned and fired at them with an automatic rifle. The high-powered rounds had missed Alex and Ellie, but Burdock hadn't been so lucky. He'd taken one in the upper arm, one in the thigh, and one just below his damn tac vest, just north of his groin.

Ellie had taken out the handlers, her daggers dropping their gurgling corpses to the ground, but the damage had been done.

Alex tried to control his racing pulse as he knelt over Burdock. His frantic heart rate was moving nowhere near as quickly as the thoughts spinning through his brain.

The arm injury looked bad, the flesh torn and oozing blood, but it didn't appear to have hit the bracheal artery, so it could wait. The thigh injury on its own would have been panic inducing. That was a severed artery for sure, judging by the blood flow. Luckily, it was far enough down that a tourniquet could slow the bleeding significantly.

Then there was the groin injury. The bullet hadn't hit the family jewels, but there were a lot of important blood vessels that ran through pelvic area, and depending on the angle of the bullet, they were almost certainly looking at intestinal involvement. That could spell all sorts of doom, starting with massive of internal bleeding. And he couldn't apply a tourniquet.

There were coagulating agents, hemostatic pressure bandages and ratcheting tourniquets in the pack on his back. He just needed to get to them. Just needed to move his hands. The hands that were coated in Burdock's blood.

In the back of his brain was a voice that was calling out the necessary steps to stabilize Burdock and begin treating those wounds. Get the vest off. Cut his pants and shirt away. Get the coag agent on that abdominal wound, then a pressure bandage. Get Ellie to apply pressure to the gut. Move on to the thigh wound…

But his body was refusing to obey his brain. Instead, his blood soaked hands filled his vision. The sounds of his own hammering heart and the air sawing in and out of his lungs drowned out Burdock's agonized groans. He was going to bleed out if they didn't do something. So much blood. Another abdominal wound. Just like Kelly. Why was it always abdominal wounds?

With the thought of Kelly, he didn't even see his frozen, bloody hands anymore. He only saw blood soaked sand and all he could hear was screaming and gunfire.

The sting of a small palm striking his face brought him part of the way back around. Ellie's face swam into view, her voice screeching at him.

"Do something or we're going to lose him! Dumeril can't get here. You're all he's got."

Why couldn't she understand that his body had disconnected from his brain?

This was exactly what had happened in the ambulance that night three years ago. The first bleeding gunshot victim and he'd been in a panic-induced stupor in the corner in the rig. This is why he wasn't a medic anymore. This is why he'd never be a doctor. Blood. Screams. Drilling into his brain, making him freeze. Couldn't take it.

His pack was ripped from his shoulders and Ellie screamed, "What do I do with this stuff? Tell me what to do!"

Alex opened his mouth and closed it, but the words wouldn't come. It was like in nightmares when you tried to scream, but nothing came out. Ellie dug through the pack, came up with a pair of shears and started cutting Burdock's clothes away. Smart little gnome.

Alex's gaze drifted to Burdock's face and was surprised to find his eyes open. Most people would be unconscious, but Burdock wasn't most people.

The mage's hand drifted up and pressed something into Alex's palm. A photo. Of a girl. Pretty. Young.

"If I don't make it," Burdock rasped, "find her. Tell her what happened to me."

Alex looked down at the photo and back at Burdock. He wanted to ask who she was but his tongue felt like lead in his mouth.

Even bleeding to death, Burdock saw the question in his eyes.

"Christi Clark. UT student. Sapien. No one knows about her. Keep her secret. You're the only one I can trust. If the Council finds out that she knows what I am, they'll kill her. And tell her I—" Burdock's eyes drooped shut for a moment before springing open again. "Love her."

Alex wanted to nod, but the swirling vortex of panic in his brain wouldn't let him. Burdock's features sagged again and he lost his battle with unconsciousness.

Suddenly, it made sense. Memories connected in his head. Burdock's opposition to Alex being on the team. His open hostility during the nutcracker that had seemed a little over the top. Burdock had been trying to put himself firmly in the Sapiens Suck camp so no one would suspect he was dating one. Not just dating one, but he had revealed what he was to her. All of Burdock's maneuvers had been to protect her. Alex tightened his hand around the photo.

Ellie was trying desperately to slow the flow of blood by pushing pressure bandages against Burdock's wounds. No tourniquets. No coag agent. She was maybe sixty pounds soaking wet, and because of her size, she could barely reach both wounds at once, much less put any weight on them. She was still doing more than he was.

Out of nowhere, one of the Lechuzas swooped in, dropping Alayna a few feet away. She raced forward, her platinum hair streaking back from her face. God, she was beautiful.

"What have we got?" she asked, skidding to a stop beside them.

"Burdock took three bullets. Losing a lot of blood. And Alex has decided doing his impression of a human statue is more important than chipping in."

There was venom in her voice, and he wanted to stumble away, run from here, far from here. He desperately wanted to squeeze his eyes shut and cover his ears. His hands shook violently and he couldn't get enough air in his lungs, like a Blackhawk had landed on his chest. It felt like dying.

Alayna held her hands over the gut wound and said a long, complicated series of words he didn't understand. When she finished, the blood flow stopped and she sagged, her breath leaving her in a rush.

"Whew, that took a lot of juice," she mumbled.

Her eyes scanned the other wounds and landed back on Alex, locking his gaze to hers.

"Eyes on me, soldier." Her voice was low, steady and commanding. "Dumeril is tied up healing a hostage. I don't have enough juice or skill to heal all these wounds. If I don't get your help, Burdock's going to bleed to death."

Her hands rose up, cradled his face and her eyes bored into his.

"I know you're in a bad place right now, and I'll never forgive myself for putting you there, but right this minute I need you to take a deep breath, open your mouth and tell me what to do to save him."

Something in those indigo eyes caused a circuit to snap back in place in his brain. Signals started flowing to his body again. Not to all parts and not in the right order, but his mouth started moving, his finger pointed to his bag.

"Tourniquet."

Deep breath, air moving in his lungs, oxygen to his brain.

Alayna jerked one of the tourniquets out of the bag. He touched his finger to the right spot on Burdock's thigh. She moved with blinding speed, clicking it into place.

"Tight as you can."

As she cranked the mechanism, Burdock groaned and shifted. Pain receptors still firing. That was a good sign.

"Now what?"

"Coag agent. Red pouch. Tear it open, pour it in the wound."

She obeyed. Next came the pressure bandages. With every word he said, he gained more control over his body. His pulse slowed. His breathing became more even and he wasn't in danger of passing out anymore.

But when he reached for a tourniquet to start to work on the arm wound, his hands were shaking too badly to pick it up. Luckily, Alayna was already moving, her fingers moving with surety through the steps of treatment. She would occasionally glance at him in silent communication to check that she was doing it right.

Alex wasn't sure if it was minutes or days that passed when running footsteps thundered out of the darkness toward them. Then, Dumeril was kneeling beside Burdock, a look of deep concentration on his dark face as he pressed his hands to the wounds. Lu stood off to the side with an unconscious hostage in her arms.

Alex gained enough control over his body to move back away

from the team gathered around Burdock. He didn't stop until he was several feet away, kneeling in the grass as shame tore him apart from the inside.

* * *

An hour later, Alayna stood with Ellie and Alex in the outbuilding they had discovered. Several of the Lechuzas in their human forms were outside acting as guards, automatic rifles taken from dead handlers in their hands. The effect was not at all ruined by the fact that they were naked.

Burdock, along with Lu and Dumeril, was back at HQ, having taken one of the vans the vamps used to transport the hostages. While Dumeril had said the big mage was out of the woods, she was still worried.

The cleanup crew would be here soon to collect the hostages, wipe their memories, and deal with the bodies of all the vamps they'd killed.

She tried her best to put thoughts of Alex out of her head. While they were out of danger, this op was far from over. But she was worried about him and kicking herself for putting him in the position she had.

She'd sent him with Burdock and Ellie, two of her deadliest fighters, and on the assignment she'd thought was less dangerous. She'd been worried that Alex would distract her at some critical moment. And she'd inadvertently put him in the middle of his worst nightmare.

But she was going to have to deal with the fallout later.

Before her, four of the surviving hunters and two of the handlers were arranged. All were restrained in vamp-proof cuffs. One of the handlers, who had been badly burned by her fire attack, was conscious. The others were out cold.

She stepped toward the handler, her face an icy mask, and grabbed the front of his burned T-shirt and lifted him up so she could look him in the eye. He didn't have any eyelids left, so it was little easier.

"Where's your boss?" she asked.

"He'll kill me," the vamp croaked out.

"I'll kill you first if you don't tell me!" she shouted. "Where is Culebra?"

"Culebra's been out of the picture for weeks. No one knows where he is. We just get texts telling us where and when to move the sapes and when to pick up the hunters."

Damn it. That wasn't good news.

"I'm pretty sure Culebra's not the boss," the vamp said quietly. "He handled shipping and the warehouses, maybe recruited a few hunters, but he was never the boss."

The vamp took a gurgling breath, and Alayna nodded for him to continue.

"He liked the hunt. Got a real kick out of it. Killed more than a few of the sapes. I heard he lost it and killed some girl at a club a few weeks ago. All of a sudden he stops showing up for the hunts and everyone stops hearing from him."

Her ears perked up. Behind her, Alex stiffened. He'd been silent and shut off since that debacle with Burdock.

Another gurgling breath brought her attention back.

"Please. I told you everything. Please help me. I don't think I can heal from this. It hurts so much."

She dropped him to the concrete. Fuck if she was going to use any of the scraps of her remaining energy to heal this sack of shit. If he died, good riddance.

She turned to Alex and Ellie, hiding her exhaustion, her

horror, her anger. Her posture was all authority. She was a general and this was her battlefield.

"Ellie, did your search turn up any files or hard drives?"

The gnome held up a thumb drive. Hell yeah.

"Scan it for anything you can find about this sick fucking operation. I want the names of every son of a bitch that touched this or knew about it."

"And after that?" Alex said.

"We let the Lechuzas tear this place apart and reclaim it for their hunting grounds," she said, a smile touching her lips for the first time since the attack began.

As she looked around the room, she took in empty cages like the ones these monsters liked to keep hostages in. The building was a prefabricated metal structure, one of the ones that could be put together in a day. A concrete floor had been poured and the metal building put up around it. At the back of the building, there was a large roll-up loading door, a pickup truck, cans of gasoline and tools. Along one wall was a table loaded with booze and several chairs. A break room of some kind, or where the hunters entertained themselves while their prey was unloaded?

There was something in the corner under a large brown plastic tarp.

Alex moved toward it. As he got closer, he covered his mouth and nose and turned a very pale shade of green beneath his tan. Concern for him twisted in her chest and she moved toward him. That's when the smell hit her.

Blood. And rotting meat.

He pulled the tarp down and what they saw turned her stomach. It was a large wood chipper, the kind with a trailer hitch that could be pulled behind a truck.

The thing was disgusting. The input and output chutes were covered in a thick coating of dried blood and there were bits of skin, hair and bone stuck in it.

"Oh, God," he breathed. It was half exclamation and half prayer.

Alayna moved up beside him, her teeth grinding with rage. She cursed loudly, her voice echoing off the metal walls.

"I'd hoped to find some bodies we might be able to identify. To tell their families what had happened."

Alex turned away from the blood soaked machine, thoughts churning behind his eyes. His features were thunderstorm dark when he met her gaze.

"I'm more worried about why you found bodies scattered all over town when they had this," Alex said.

20

Chapter 20

As he closed the door to one of the tiny crash rooms behind him, Alex let out the breath he'd been holding on a long sigh. It seemed like he'd been holding his breath since they'd all returned to HQ. Or maybe since Burdock had been hurt.

He'd had a chance to check on him, and the big guy was stable, awake, and well on his way to healing up. Dumeril had some powerful magic. Too bad his own brain had been too scrambled to so much as pull a Band-Aid out of his pack to help his teammate.

Shame ripped through him again at the thought. He'd let Burdock down. He'd let the team down. He'd let Alayna down. Because he was broken and messed up. He belonged behind a desk, tracking white collar criminals, not out on a battlefield. What had made him think that he could handle that?

Alayna had, he realized. She'd had so much confidence, so much faith in him. She couldn't see how fucked up he was.

Almost as if the thought had summoned her, there was a soft knock at the door and Alayna's voice.

"Alex?"

He put on his mask, the one he'd learned to paint on when drill instructors were screaming in his face, and opened the door, blocking the entrance with his body.

"Yeah, Commander?"

"I came to check on you."

Concern shone in her eyes and he hated the sight.

"As you can see, I don't have a scratch on me. Unlike some of us. You wanna check on someone, go see Burdock."

He hated the edge in his voice when he said it. The concern was replaced by something harder in her eyes.

"That was not your fault."

"He could have died. Because I had a fucking panic attack."

"But he didn't."

"Doesn't matter. My little episode tonight just proves one thing: I don't belong here."

She took a shocked step back, hurt coloring the beautiful features of her face. He nearly shut the door just to shut out the pain he'd put her in. But this needed to happen. He needed distance. Wait, more like she needed distance, from the epic failure standing in front of her.

"What are you talking about?" she asked.

"I'm not the man you need. I can't be the man you need. I'm not some fairytale hero. I don't have magick powers. Hell, I can't even make my body move when my teammate is dying. I'm broken. Useless!"

Anger darkened her indigo eyes into hurricane clouds, and she planted a palm on his shoulder, pushing him back and slamming the door behind her. There was barely enough room for both of them with the twin bed and nightstand in the tiny crash room.

"Don't say that! You are not useless. A panic attack does not make you useless. You are one of the smartest, bravest men I've known. I don't need a fairytale hero or someone with magick powers. I have that. I *am* that. What I need is your brain, your insights, your humor and your trigger finger."

"My brain is the part that's broken," he said, sinking to sit on the edge of the bed. "It almost cost Burdock his life."

She was silent for a moment, calculations churning behind her gaze. But nothing she could say could change what happened or change the fact that he didn't belong.

"Did you ever stop to think about what would have happened if you hadn't been there at all?" she asked, leaning against the wall in front of him, her arms crossed over her chest. "Burdock would have had even less of a shot, and Ellie might have died right along with him."

"What could have happened doesn't matter. What did happen is disgraceful."

"You—"

"No, Alayna! Listen to me. I'm a liability out there. I'm going to get someone hurt or killed. What if it's you next time? I need to step back."

The calculations ground to a halt and her eyes went wide, her muscles going still.

"What are you saying?"

"I'm going to see this through. Blanca's killer needs to be brought down, and anyone associated with this trafficking ring needs to pay. I'll support your operation in any way I can; I'll go back into combat if I need to. But when this is over, I have to go back to my old life."

Alayna looked like she'd been stabbed in the gut. He knew the feeling because that was exactly how he felt in that moment. As much as this hurt, it needed to be done, to protect her. He loved her, that much was true, but he wasn't sure anymore that it was enough.

"What?" Her voice was soft, trying to mask the pain he'd caused her.

"I thought I'd made it pretty clear from the beginning that I've worked too hard to rebuild my life to throw it away. I have a career that I need to get back to. I belong behind that desk where I can't get anyone hurt."

This was all for the best. Causing her a little pain by leaving would be better than the mountains of pain he'd hand her when he inevitably failed her.

"So, when this is over, you're leaving?"

"I've learned what I needed from you in order to protect myself. No one will know about my abilities. I'll be fine on my own."

She opened her mouth to speak, but closed it again, turning suddenly toward the door. He couldn't see her face, but he knew she was putting her own mask back on.

"I'll respect your wishes, Alex," she said, her voice steady and strong. "I don't have to like them, but I'll respect them."

With that, she was gone, leaving him alone, where he belonged.

* * *

As Alayna stormed out on to the training floor, Lu intercepted her. The look in those dark brown eyes that saw too much said that her best friend wanted to talk. Fucking peachy.

Ducking her head to hide the tears she was fighting, she grunted, "What's up?"

"Spill," was all Lu said as she matched her pace.

"Spill what?"

"Don't play coy with me, blondie. I could smell him all over you for days, even though you tried to cover it with perfume and some of that body wash Ellie gave you for your birthday," Lu said. "And now you look like you're about to cry. So, spill."

Her index finger was out and waving a little with her sassy tone. When the Sassy Finger came out, it was best not to argue with Lu.

"I'm not about to cry. I don't cry. Ever."

"You think I don't know what my-man-done-me-wrong tears smell like. I've cried buckets of those. Do I need to rip a motherfucker's head off? 'Cause I will."

With a deep sigh of frustration, Alayna ground to a halt and met Lu's hard gaze. Lu was her best friend, the one who brought over a bottle of tequila when bullshit overwhelmed her. She was also a little overprotective at times.

"I slept with Alex. Past tense. It's over as of five minutes ago. Don't do anything to him. And I'm not going to cry."

Turning away, she headed for the stairs to the office. Now that Burdock was settled in the med-bay and she'd gotten the all clear from the cleanup team, it was time to see what Ellie had pulled off of that drive. There were doubtless other locations that the trafficking ring had been using to hold victims. Battle plans started now.

"What happened?"

Alayna stopped with her boot on the first step, the look of concern on Lu's face softening her features. Damn it, she didn't need anyone's pity.

"I don't want to talk about it."

"You need to talk about it. It's your first breakup. Give yourself a minute before you go charging off to the next thing."

"I don't get a minute," Alayna growled. "Who knows how many

victims are in the hands of homicidal vampires right now? I've got work to do. I can't break down, especially over some guy."

She met Lu's gaze, begging her to drop this, asking her to let her run and hide in her work.

"Alex isn't just some guy," Lu said, stepping up next to her. A frown creased a line between her brows. "I know you care about him. I've been watching you two make eyes at each other for weeks. It's been kind of hard to watch, actually."

"It was that obvious, huh? Ugh. I can't believe I broke my own rule. This is why I don't date teammates."

"If it's any consolation, I don't think Burdock or Ellie have noticed anything. Burdock only stops cleaning his guns long enough to kill the things you point at, and Ellie is so absorbed in her computers, the world could stop turning and she'd only notice when the coffee ran out," Lu said. "So what happened?"

"He's convinced himself that because of that panic attack tonight that he's a liability. He said after this case is done, he's going to back to his old life. Says he doesn't belong in this world. He's pushing me away," she said, taking a deep breath. "And I'm going to let him."

"What? Honey, he's just being a man. He's just been through something traumatic. Give him a couple of days to start thinking clearly again. Why are you giving up without a fight? That's not the Alayna I know."

"You know why I need to let him go."

"Your fucking curse? Chica, none of us are long for this world. When happiness comes along, you have to grab it with both hands."

"This isn't happiness. This is fucking torture. He told me he loves me, and now he's willing to walk away without a backward glance."

"It's fucked up, but he's probably walking away because he loves you and he's trying to protect you," Lu said. "Well, that and he's probably scared."

After a long moment, Alayna began to climb the stairs in silence, her legs feeling like they had iron weights strapped around them.

Lu's voice froze her halfway up.

"Do you love him?"

How the fuck would she know what love is? She'd lost her father at eight. In her grief, her mother had disappeared into her work. She'd lost her brothers to their own torment. And her only sister had deliberately disappeared just a few weeks after she'd been told Alayna was a Whisperer, probably because she couldn't deal with the pain of losing another family member.

She didn't have words for what she felt for Alex. But if he knew what she was hiding in her heart, he might follow her to the gates of hell in some misguided attempt to save her. She didn't want her last thoughts in this world to be that she failed him.

"If something happens to me, if my time's up, please promise me you'll look out for Alex. Don't let him go down with me."

"Jeez, girl, where is this coming from?"

"I have a bad feeling, Lu, have for a few days. Something's coming. It's like…I can feel the book closing."

Without another word, she bounded up the stairs two at a time and slammed the office door behind her.

* * *

The bang of the door hitting the wall of the crash room brought Alex's head up so fast, something popped.

"What the fuck did you do?"

Dumeril's voice was as sharp as barbed wire. The Svarturan's violet eyes were snapping with accusation and anger, his lips pulled back in a snarl that revealed his long canines. Combined with the war braids in his long silver hair, he was a very menacing picture. And Alex didn't give a fuck.

"Look, I'm sorry for what happened out there—"

"I'm not talking about that. Nobody cares about that. I'm talking about why Alayna is sitting upstairs looking like someone ripped the heart out of her chest. I want you to explain that, shithead."

"That's between the two of us."

"Bullshit!" Dumeril snapped. He took a slow step forward, looming over Alex. "Try again."

Alex met that fiery gaze and assessed his angry teammate. He wasn't going to stop. Alex was going to have to play ball.

"How did you know about us?"

"Bitch, please. I'm the only son of the Svarturan Grand Matriarch. Growing up at court, you learn to read people and situations or you end up dead."

"Wait, you're a prince?"

"It doesn't mean the same thing in this realm. Males are considered property under the matriarchy. Royal males are somewhere between concubines and sex slaves. Rather than become the sexual plaything of one of my seven sisters before being married off in a political alliance, I ran. To the Earthly Realms. I knew my mother's minions would catch up to me eventually, at which point they were probably going to cut off my feet so I couldn't run again, but I was resigned to that. Then along came Alayna."

"As a member of the Mage Corps, my mother can't touch me

without risking the wrath of the Council. I don't have to run anymore. I tell you all this to illustrate that I owe that woman my life. So does everyone in this building, including you. So, it is my business and I ask again, what the fuck did you do?"

"We got involved. But after what happened tonight, I realized that I don't belong here. I'm a liability to her. So, I'm doing the responsible thing. After this case is over, I'm out," Alex said.

"You're a fucking idiot."

"I love her. I'm trying to protect her!"

"Then don't send her into battle with a broken heart. Look, I know she appears like she's made of steel, but she's not. Girl's got soft feelies just like the rest of us. And she's on unfamiliar ground right now. She may have fucked a lot of guys, but she's never really been with one."

"She seems more than willing to let me walk away when this is over."

"Yeah, well, she's got her own stupid reasons for that."

* * *

Several hours later, the team was assembled around the table in the conference room, Alayna at the head, a satellite image of a warehouse on a large screen behind her. She studied her team, noting they were exhausted and jittery.

"Thanks to Ellie's superior decryption algorithms, we managed to pull a likely location where more hostages are being held," she said, indicating the warehouse.

Lu spoke up. "I tried to do some recon on the place, but it's sealed up tight. Couldn't even slip in as a mouse."

The faces around the table were grim. Alayna met Alex's eyes. There were so many things she wanted to tell him, but hadn't had the chance. Yet.

"We need ideas for next steps. I'm opposed to going in blind, but we need to move quickly. The ringleaders have probably already heard about our raid on the hunting ground. If we're going to have a shot at saving those hostages, we need to move on this place tonight."

"I, for one, would like to avoid being murdered by human trafficking vampires that like to hunt people for sport, but maybe that's just me," Dumeril chimed in.

"You never want to do anything fun," Ellie grumped.

Alayna silenced them with a look.

"I could try to open a portal into the building," Dumeril said, "but it's risky. Without knowing the layout, I could spit us out inside a wall. Not to mention the fact that the glowing hole in reality tends to give one's position away. And then there's the whole leaving a weak spot in the dimensional fabric thing."

Dumeril was right. While his skill with portals was a handy one, it was rarely used. Portals were unpredictable. The one opening them generally had to be able to visualize exactly where they were opening the portal to, otherwise travelers could end up several feet off the ground or inside the duct work.

And you could never really seal a portal completely. Once opened and closed, they left a weak spot, like a scar, in the fabric of the dimension. Some of those really experienced with portals claimed they could see the old scars. Even more speculated that all sorts of things were drawn to the scars across dimensions. Because portals didn't just make a hole in this reality—they made holes in the all the multilayered dimensions they shared space with.

There were tales of spirits, creatures, and even demons that could seep through old portal scars and go crawling around this reality. Alayna had never seen it first hand, and she wasn't sure she believed in demons. Still, it didn't hurt to limit the portal use as much as possible, just as a precaution.

Everyone talked over everyone else for a few minutes. In a lull in the conversation, Alayna injected, "I think I might have to try projecting."

Dumeril and Burdock immediately began shouting objections to this plan.

"It's too risky!"

"Not a chance!"

She held a hand up.

"It's the only way I can think of to get in there undetected," she told them.

They couldn't risk tipping off anyone that they knew what was going on. The hunting grounds they had discovered indicated they were dealing with a ring, not just one killer. The destruction of that property likely had the bad guys scrambling, but it wouldn't be long before those hostages were moved around and they lost them, maybe for good.

Projection involved separating one's consciousness from one's body for a short period of time and sending the consciousness to a specific location. It was rumored that there were powerful mages who could project through time even, but Alayna had no desire to push the boundaries that far.

Just projecting a few miles across town would take a tremendous amount of energy and several hours of ritual preparation.

Alayna hated rituals. She rarely had the patience for them. Ritual magick used specific incantations, symbols, and items to focus and direct a mage's elemental energy to a specific purpose. While Alayna had to use incantation and movement to direct her energy all the time, most mages could manipulate their element with a thought. They only used ritual magick for things like communicating across long distances, scrying the future, or changing the nature of an object, such as making a blade stronger.

It was similar to drawing a ward, but on a much larger scale.

The risk with projection was that, occasionally, a mage's consciousness didn't make it back in their body. Without the consciousness, the body would die after a few hours, even with the protection of a ritual circle.

And she'd never attempted it before.

It was risky, dangerous, and there was no guarantee of success. Basically, her life in a nutshell.

"It's the only way, guys," she told the group.

Alex looked confused and more than a little concerned about the objections of the others. She ran down a list of components she would need and asked Lu to get them and meet her downstairs.

21

Chapter 21

As Alayna walked down to the training floor, she motioned Dumeril to follow her. Ellie returned to her desk and her machines.

Burdock, who had made it out of the med-bay, was sticking unusually close to her, and Alayna wasn't sure why. His big body was throwing off tension.

"What's got you jumpy?" she asked him.

"I don't like this plan, Commander."

"Duly noted, Sergeant."

"If ritual projection is the only way to obtain a look inside that warehouse, then let me do it. It's a bad idea to put you at risk at this point," he said.

"You suck at ritual," Alayna said. "More than I do. Besides, if this fails, the team is going to need some serious firepower to bust in there and a leader who can get them out of there. That's you."

Alayna regarded the big fire mage for a moment and reminded herself that he was just three years out of the Academy. He was rigid and a bit too linear in his thinking at times, but he was young. She'd been that young just four short years ago, but this job had aged her soul.

Burdock could be a little quick on the draw and a little too eager to put himself in harm's way to protect others. She desperately wanted to protect him long enough for him to grow a caution center in his brain. Almost losing him the night before had her gun shy.

Alayna met Alex's concerned gaze over Burdock's shoulder. She sent him down to the training floor and took Alex aside.

"Listen," she said. "It might be better if you stay up here for this. Ritual magick can get a little spooky for those that aren't used to it."

"I'm not leaving you," Alex said, crossing his arms over his chest and looking at the floor.

That was certainly a different tune than he'd been singing a few hours ago. She didn't want to press him about it. Maybe he just wanted to make sure this went smoothly so the case could be wrapped up that much faster and he could get away from her.

"I'm also a little worried about your magick sucking chi disrupting my ritual."

"I'll stay back, but I want to be there."

She nodded and headed for the office door, unwilling to argue with him. This hot and cold routine had her stomach in knots. Not what she needed before a potentially dangerous ritual.

"Just be careful," he murmured.

She wasn't sure if she'd been meant to hear that.

She headed downstairs while Alex stayed on the landing just outside the office door. She took up a piece of chalk and drew a large circle on the concrete floor. She began inscribing the intricate symbols needed to focus and direct her power. It took time and patience, but she let her mind get lost in the delicate work.

When she was finished, her back and knees were aching a little from having knelt on the floor and the squares of sunlight coming in the high windows had changed position.

Lu placed a box next to her while she worked with the other components she would need. Next, she took salt and poured it over the white chalk of the circle and poured a line of black charcoal over that. She wanted the circle as strong as it could be.

Alayna took a worn scrap of yellow cloth from the box, without disturbing her circle and held it up, calling the guardian spirits to watch over her.

"Spirits of the East, guardians of the air, watch over and protect me."

She placed the cloth, a scrap of Tibetan prayer flag that her brother had brought her from the Himalayas, just inside the circle. It had snapped in the mountain wind for countless years and the air element was bound in every thread.

Next, she took up a candle and called the flame with a whispered word and wave of her hand.

"Spirits of the South, guardians of fire, watch over and protect me."

She had poured the candle herself, and her blood was mixed into the wax.

She took a blue glass bottle of water from the box next and called, "Spirits of the West, guardians of water, watch over and protect me."

The bottle had been a gift from her brother Xander. It had arrived in the mail several years ago with a note from him that said he'd found it on the beach after a hurricane. If anything carried the spirit of water, this vessel did.

Lastly, she took a large pink quartz from the box. She ran her hand over it. The stone had been a gift from her sister, Kyla, before she disappeared. Kyla had been a powerful earth mage even as a teenager and had called the stone out of the ground.

"Spirits of the North, guardians of the earth, watch over and protect me."

Gifts held a special significance for mages, and they almost always wore something that had been given to them into battle as a kind of armor. There was magick in gifts. Knowing that someone she loved had thought of her when they held these objects held the kind of impact she was going to need to get through this.

She touched her fingers to the circle and closed it with a few words. The air in front of her took on a slight shimmer as the magickal field snapped into place.

Alayna lay down within the circle, careful not to disturb the intricate symbols she had drawn. Long minutes passed as she worked to clear her mind and focus her energy.

When she felt at peace, she began. The words of her spell poured from her throat and she began to feel her power drawing her consciousness out of her body.

At first it was just a feeling of floating, but gradually she became aware of looking down on her own body. She saw Dumeril, Lu, and Burdock gathered a few feet away. She floated by Alex, still standing on the stairs, arms crossed over his chest and a look of worry in his beautiful eyes.

Before she could think too hard about that, she was moving up and away, out of the building and over the city. In the March sunlight, it was shining.

The pink granite of the capitol building was sparkling in the sun. The light was dancing on the river, just visible to her left.

In just a matter of seconds she could see the target warehouse and felt herself descending through the roof. It was pitch black and it took a few moments for her spectral sight to adjust.

There were no windows, just thick metal walls. There were rollup doors on one wall, regular doors on another. Two beefy vampires, clearly guards, were walking through the cavernous space.

She moved toward the door they had just come out of and slid through it. That was the oddest feeling.

There were storage rooms here, smaller than the giant room she'd just left. There were racks of guns, wicked looking black blades, and explosives. Another room held refrigerators full of bagged blood. Another room had protective equipment, like vests and helmets. In the corner was a stack of about twenty-five adjustable rods with loops of steel cable at one end. They looked like the kind of equipment animal control officers used, but these loops had wicked looking steel barbs protruding from them. Most had dried blood.

The sight unsettled Alayna as she turned away and moved back through the cavernous main room. There were more guards here now, about a dozen or so. Some were gathered at a table to one side, others were grouped in twos and threes, talking. She didn't recognize anyone.

Along one wall, she saw cages like the ones the vamps had used to keep people in at the other warehouse. There were more than thirty, and they were filthy. There were about a dozen figures huddled back away from the hatches. They all appeared to be adult men.

She desperately wished she could do something for them, but in spectral form, they couldn't even see her.

She drifted toward the back of the warehouse. It was darker

here and harder to see. She had to find out what was back here. She pushed against the blackness, but it was getting thicker and harder to move and see.

She mentally frowned and pushed at the darkness again. She'd never seen anything like this.

Suddenly, she felt like she had come up against a solid wall. There was a green flash of light, and a sigil glowed in the air in front of her.

Shit! This area of the warehouse was warded. And against astral walkers too. She spun back around and saw that the guards had seen the ward become active and begin to glow. They might not be able to see her yet, and she needed to get out of here fast.

Slowly, a dozen pairs of gleaming eyes turned in her direction. If they couldn't see her, it was a good bet they could sense her.

Eyes started to bleed red, and fangs descended as the vamps went to predator mode. Several sniffed the air. They could smell the magick. Whether they could smell her under the power that ward was throwing off was a good question, but not one she wanted to stick around and find out the answer to.

Taking one last look around, she willed herself back to her body. It was a short fast trip and a few seconds later she found herself lying on the concrete floor of the headquarters building, gasping for air.

A worried looking Dumeril and Alex crowded the edges of her circle, but didn't dare cross it.

"What the hell happened?" Dumeril asked her. "You were fine, and suddenly you started breathing like you were running a marathon. Scared us half to death."

"The place is warded but good," she answered. "Couldn't see what was behind the wards, but I saw enough to know that we need to go in there. They have hostages."

Standing up slowly, she broke the circle with her foot and released the guardian energies. She described what she had seen, from the guns to the guards.

"I need everyone upstairs in five," she said.

As the others collected themselves, Alex took her shoulders in his hands and looked into her eyes, fear and concern making his eyes a little wide.

"Are you really okay?"

Not even close. She had screwed up, miscalculated, and now those hostages were in danger. She'd put them there. Guilt gnawed at her.

"The wards. They almost had me. Scared the shit out of me, but I'm fine now," she lied.

"Did they know you were there?"

"They know something triggered those wards."

He ran a hand through his hair in what she had come to recognize as his anxious/frustrated gesture.

"That was a close one, Commander," he said, looking around to make sure they weren't being watched, though he needn't have bothered. The whole team knew anyway.

* * *

A few minutes later, they were all upstairs and Alayna was sketching out the layout of the warehouse and what she had seen. She indicated the warded area and where the storage rooms were.

"As far as we know, the only entrances and exits are these two rolling doors in front," Alayna said, indicating the sketch.

"How many guards?" Dumeril asked.

"I saw a dozen, but you can bet there will be more there soon," she said.

"Is it possible to make a door?" Burdock asked.

"The walls were reinforced, so it would take an attention-grabbing level of firepower to open one."

Ellie chimed in. "Catwalks?"

"Around the perimeter of the main room and two running across," Alayna answered. "The main area of the warehouse is easily seventy-five yards by thirty. That's not counting the warded area I couldn't see."

Ellie spoke again. "I've been running some thermal imaging from that building and pretty sure the roof isn't reinforced. I think I have a good chance of making myself an entrance there and setting up on one of the catwalks with a sniper rifle."

Alayna nodded and drew an X on the catwalk to indicate where Ellie might have the best vantage point and most concealment.

"Burdock," she said, turning to the big fire mage. "You are on demolitions and heavy artillery. I want you to rig up some charges to take down the main doors."

They all knew Alayna could take the doors down with a wind blast, and Burdock could melt right through them, but the mages would need to conserve all their energy for the fight.

"Once we're in, you will have free reign to neutralize targets," she told Burdock. "Load up on grenades and high caliber ammunition. And when we're done, we may need to bring that building down in a way that looks like it was a gas leak and explosion."

"You ever wonder if the sapiens are going to catch wise to that tactic?" Burdock wondered to no one in particular.

"They haven't yet," Ellie answered. "And let's hope they never start to wonder why we have such leaky gas lines in this town."

Alayna turned their attention back to the board.

"Dumeril, I want you to concentrate on getting the hostages clear. Once they are secure, you are free to engage at will. Use your medic skills as needed and get anyone critically injured clear of the building."

Dumeril nodded.

"Lu and Alex, I want you working as a team. Lu, I want you in your hulkingest, flesh shredding form. We're going for maximum impact and damage here. Alex, you'll be providing cover fire for Lu. Stick close to her, and make sure nothing gets close unless it's on the end of her claws."

They both nodded.

"What will you be doing?" Dumeril asked.

"I'm going after that warded area," she said. "Whatever is behind those wards is something these folks took a lot of time and effort to conceal. Only a powerful mage could have crafted something like what I saw, and to call in a rogue mage is damned expensive."

Internally, it galled her that a rogue mage had come waltzing through her city and right back out again undetected while giving aid to some of the nastiest creatures she'd ever encountered. If she lived long enough, she'd file a report with the Wraiths, the highly specialized mages that hunted rogues. Her brother, Xander, was one.

It would take time, she explained, and she'd be out in the open, but with a little luck, she could unwind those wards and find out what was there.

"Any questions?" Alayna asked her team.

Dumeril put his index finger in the air.

"So, just to sum up, we're busting in the doors on a location with a warded area that could conceal anything, while taking on an unknown number of pissed off vampire guards, all while trying to rescue a dozen sapien hostages and hopefully keep ourselves alive in the process. Have I got the shape of that?"

Alayna nodded, a slight smile twisting her lips.

"Don't forget that we have to keep all of this from grabbing the attention of sapien authorities," she said.

"Honestly, Commander, I'm beginning to feel underutilized. I feel like you never challenge us," Dumeril replied.

She laughed, his attempt at humor breaking her tension. She was asking them to walk into a dangerous unknown and the fact that they could still joke about it told her that she had made all the right choices in choosing a team.

These were her dearest friends, and they were all closer than her own family. She hated to lead them into danger, but they had all known what they were signing up for.

"I need to make a report to the Corps brass and apprise them of the operation. We'll see if there are any additional resources they may be able to provide, but we all know not to hold our breath on that one. In the meantime, get your equipment together, get your affairs in order, and say your prayers, because come midnight, we're pulling the trigger on the biggest operation we've ever tackled."

The team should have looked somber, but instead they looked ready to cheer. They had been chasing these cases for too many months and they were finally ready to kick in the doors and knock some skulls together.

* * *

As Alex headed out of the office to start one last equipment check, Burdock caught his attention and motioned to follow him to the firing range.

"What's up?" Alex asked the fire mage.

"Couple things." Burdock was a tense as a coiled spring. "First up, I heard about what went down during the raid on the hunting grounds. I appreciate what you did."

Alex's mouth fell open in surprise.

"I froze. You could have died."

"That shit's not on you, man. You did what you could, and that was enough."

Alex nodded solemnly, not knowing what to say.

"Second thing. The stuff I told you about Christi—"

"That secret is safe, dude."

Burdock held out a folded slip of paper.

"This is her contact info. If you make it out and I don't, I trust you to get word to her."

Alex took the paper. He stared at it.

"You have my word," Alex said quietly.

Burdock's face remained expressionless. He turned and moved down the hall like a stalking big cat.

* * *

Three hours later, Alayna sat in one of the empty crash rooms at headquarters, trying to center her thoughts. Meditating had never come easily to her, but she felt it was important to review her spells and incantations before the coming fight.

She looked over to the small nightstand in the closet-like room. There was a stack of envelopes. She had written a letter to each one of her team members. There was one for each of her three siblings, though she had no idea where to send Kayla's letter.

There was one for her mother. She had wanted to write one for Alex, but every time she had put her pen to the paper she had drawn a blank.

What could she possibly say to him?

She wanted to tell him how much he meant to her. That in just a few weeks he had changed the way she saw the world and saw herself.

Alayna had always prided herself on seeing the best in the world and the people in it, even though she had seen all the horror it had to offer. Because of her curse, she knew her time was limited and she refused to let darkness cloud even one day.

Despite this, fatigue had begun to creep in around the edges of her life. She had grown tired of always being the strong one, of always being shut out by the Corps and the other mages. She had grown tired of finding a few moments of comfort in the arms of strangers. That fatigue had turned to quiet anger.

She would never let it show to her team, but it had been there.

Then Alex had come along.

He had accepted her and her world with little hesitation. He had offered his easy smile and lame jokes without asking for anything in return. Then he'd offered his body and his heart just as easily.

Her thoughts turned to his warm brown eyes, shining with lust. For her. To that gorgeous body, all rippling muscle, and the feel of his solid weight on her and the way he had used that body to take her places she had never been.

She loved him, for everything he was and for everything he made her feel, but she didn't know how to tell him that. There was every chance that she wouldn't walk away from this fight. Did she dare to tell him that she loved him just so he could lose her?

Was it kinder to leave him wondering?

And if he was the one who didn't make it? Could she let him go to the next world not knowing how she felt? Could she carry that in her heart for the rest of her, albeit numbered, days?

Her thoughts were interrupted by a knocking on the door. She called out, and Dumeril stuck his head in.

"Your brother is here," he said.

"My what?" Alayna sprang to her feet.

He gave her an eye roll and spoke slowly.

"Your brother, Theron, is here. He's the tall gorgeous blonde one that was born a couple of years before you," Dumeril said. "And he has a message from the Council."

Her stomach dropped at his words. This wasn't good.

"Tell him I'll be out in a minute. I'll speak with him in the conference room."

When she got upstairs, Alex was checking his equipment at one of the long tables. Theron was beside him.

"I'm a big fan of the Desert Eagle for stopping power, but I also carry the 1911 for ammo capacity," the big blonde mage was telling Alex.

Theron was nearly six and half feet tall, with broad shoulders, narrow hips and arms like a weight lifter. He was built like Captain America, and he had the All-American good looks to go with it. His hair, which had grown a little longer than his usual military short cut, was several shades of blonde, with strawberry low lights and platinum highlights. In the sun, it shown like a flame.

His eyes were indigo blue, like hers, but they were hard as he turned to look at her.

"Alayna," he said.

"Theron," she said, mimicking his flat tone.

"You didn't mention in your report that your new pet FBI agent was so handy with a gun."

She sighed. She really didn't want to discuss Alex with her brother. She would have preferred if the two had never met.

"Alex served with the Army and the FBI. He's formidable in a fight," she said, meeting Alex's warm, brown gaze. "And he's not my pet. He's not my anything."

She had turned her gaze back to Theron before she said the last part, unwilling to see Alex's face when she said that. Her voice had been harder than she'd meant it to be. He'd see it was for the best in time.

"You also didn't mention that he was a lithseach," Theron said.

At Alayna's alarmed look, he waved her down.

"Your secret's safe with me sis, but this has the potential to complicate shit."

Crossing her arms over her chest, Alayna remained silent and gave Theron a you-think-I-don't-know-that look.

"The Corps brass received your report," he started. "The Council also reviewed it."

She could tell from his tone of voice that she wasn't going to like what he said next.

"Let's do this in the conference room, Theron. Please."

He shook his head. "They're a part of this too and they need to know," he said, gesturing to the others.

There was pain in his voice as he said it. She looked around and realized that the team had gathered around them.

He handed her a roll of parchment sealed with a red wax.

"Commander Blackwell, as the oldest surviving Whisperer, you are hereby authorized to carry out the Reckoning in conjunction with this operation and at your discretion."

She took the roll of parchment from him and crushed it in

her hand, feeling the wax seal of the Council snap and crumble.

"And let me guess, they're not sending any additional resources?" she said.

Theron stepped toward her, his hand reaching for her shoulder. Stepping to the side, she evaded him and looked up at him.

"Alayna, I'm sorry," his voice was soft. "Even I can't stay. I have to catch a flight to Damascus tonight. Things are getting hot there."

"I know you're sorry, Theron," she said, rage bubbling in her voice. "But we all knew it was coming, right? This is what everyone has been waiting for, for fifteen years. When it's all over you can breathe a sigh of relief and move on with your lives, right?"

Her hands trembled and angry tears were starting to form in her eyes. Alex's brows were drawn together in confusion as he looked between them.

Theron's eyes narrowed. "He doesn't know."

"That is none of your business, Theron!"

"It's plain as day that you two are involved. I can see it when you look at each other," Theron said. "He has a right to know might happen tonight."

Alex stepped forward, reaching for her.

"Alayna, what is going on? What is this Reckoning thing?"

Without answering him, she looked at Theron.

"Go catch your plane, big brother," she said. "Tell the Council that I will do my duty. And when I'm dead, they can go fuck themselves."

Theron reached for her, but she moved back again.

"I don't want to leave it like this," he said. "You're my sister. I love you. This isn't how I want to say goodbye."

"You said goodbye years ago when they told you I was cursed. You said goodbye every day we walked the halls of the Academy together and you distanced yourself from me. You said goodbye every day that you lived a two hour drive away and never came to see me."

Her voice was rising steadily with each word and anger poured from her body.

"You've been saying goodbye for fifteen years!" she shouted. "Stop saying it and just go."

She turned her back on him and didn't watch as he left the office. She heard Dumeril speaking quietly to her brother as he showed him out.

22

Chapter 22

Her body shaking with anger, she barely felt Alex's hands come around her waist. He pulled her back against his front. Her head fell back against his shoulder.

Without knowing how she got there, she found herself in the conference room with Alex. Her anger was like a living, blazing thing inside her, twisting and angling for a way out. She wanted desperately to put her fist through the wall, but she took deep calming breaths instead.

"What was that all about?" he asked her.

"The Council—that's the group of self-righteous assholes that rules us from a distance—has given me permission to use a very dangerous and devastating spell to achieve success in this operation, but they won't send any other mages to help us."

Alex was silent for a moment.

"What did your brother mean when he said I had a right to know what might happen tonight?" Alex asked.

Alayna took a deep breath and sighed. "The spell is called the Reckoning. It's the darkest kind of blood magick and the ultimate in mage firepower. It can level entire city blocks. And it can only be performed by a Whisperer."

Alex nodded, taking the information in.

"Some say the Reckoning is the sole purpose for a Whisperer. That's why for centuries we were kept locked away, sequestered in libraries or healing centers. They called us too valuable to risk. We were like walking nuclear bombs kept in silos."

She saw the concern creasing Alex's face, but she pressed on. It was time he knew the whole truth of it.

"The spell itself isn't all that complicated to perform, although it requires opening a couple of veins," she said, her voice dropping to a whisper. "But it's always fatal to the Whisperer who weaves it."

Alex's brows slammed together and his body stiffened.

"No," he said simply. "No."

"It has always been and it will always be," she said, repeating the words that had been said to her so many times. "Do you understand now, Alex? Do you see why I'm the way I am? Do you see why I have so few attachments in this world? I have to be ready to leave it at any time."

He ran his hand through his hair and Alayna could see his considerable mind working at light speed. Shit, he really did love her. She was going to have to do her best to prepare him for what was coming.

"I've had to fight my whole life to be seen as anything other than a weapon, something to be used. But it's allowed me to take risks, too. Like building a team with non-mages on it. You don't know how uncommon that is." She paused. "And I've been able to protect a very special sapien with potentially dangerous powers."

He met her eyes and in a flash, she was in his arms, crushed against his chest. His arms were like steel and she welcomed the feel of him, the weight of him surrounding her.

"If the worst happens, Alex, look to the team. They'll make sure you're safe and that the Council can't get to you," she said.

"It's not me I'm worried about right now," he said, his voice harsh. "How can you be so accepting of this? They're basically giving you permission to kill yourself."

"Because I've had fifteen years to mentally prepare myself for this. And it's my duty to protect this city and I'll do whatever I have to in order to make that happen," she said against his chest. "And you'd do exactly the same thing."

He had spent years with his life on the line every day. He had to understand.

Alayna leaned back and looked into his beautiful eyes. Her hand touched his face, her thumb stroking his cheekbone. She could feel his clenched jaw.

"I'll say this, though," she told him softly. "For the first time since they told me what I was, I have doubts about my ability to walk away from this life easily. You really make me want to stay."

His eyes squeezed shut at that and he pressed his forehead to hers.

"Then don't leave," he said softly, his voice cracking slightly.

"I may not have a choice," she said.

"Then we'll run," he said. "We could go somewhere remote. Live off the grid, just the two of us. They'd never find us."

"They'd hunt us down in less than twenty-four hours," she said, her voice hard. "There is an entire group of mages called Wraiths. Their job is to hunt down and eliminate rogue mages. My older brother Xander is one, and they'd probably send him to execute me as a sort of retribution."

"There has got to be some other way. I won't accept you just walking into a suicide mission," Alex said vehemently.

"I may not have to use the spell. It's our ace in the hole," she said, trying to infuse her voice with a hope she didn't feel.

"All right then," Alex said. "We'll just have to make sure we don't need it."

"That's the spirit," she said, a sad smile tugging at the corners of her mouth.

As Alex turned toward the door, he stopped, his back to her.

"Don't think we're done talking about the fact that you kept something that important from me," he said quietly. "That hurts."

"I was trying to protect you," she said.

In reality, she had been afraid that he would push her away like every other male in her life when he found out, too afraid to lose her when the time came.

"Well, stop it," he said and pushed through the door.

* * *

As Alex left Alayna in the conference room, he was met with the somber looks of the other team members as they paused in the preparations for the coming fight. Rage and cold, hard determination boiled in his chest.

He met Dumeril's eyes and growled, "We need to talk. Now."

In a dark corner near the firing range, Alex rounded on the tall Svarturan.

"Tell me everything you know about the Reckoning," Alex demanded.

"So she finally told you," Dumeril sighed. "I'm sorry, my friend."

"Fuck your apologies and fuck your pity," Alex said. "I need details on the spell."

Dumeril was silent a moment, his gaze downcast.

"I've never seen one performed, but from what I understand, the Whisperer makes two deep cuts, usually the wrists, and performs a very specific incantation. Once the words are said, the spell is woven, and nothing can stop it until the Whisperer is dead."

Thoughts whirled through Alex's brain, chasing each other and colliding. There had to be something, some loophole. Some way to save her.

"It's an incredibly destructive spell. Supposed to be able to level a small village and kill anything in it."

"Is it the blood loss that kills the Whisperers?" Alex asked.

"Hard to say. It's most likely that the spell just drains all their energy. Stops their hearts. But the blood loss may be a factor," he said.

"That's what I needed to know," Alex said.

"What are you up to?" Dumeril asked, suspicion narrowing his gaze. There were less than twelve hours left before they were going to hit that warehouse.

"She's not the only one that can keep a secret. Don't tell anyone that we've spoken about this," he said, his hand on Dumeril's shoulder. "And I need one more thing from you."

23

Chapter 23

Alex pulled his truck into the garage at Alayna's house well after dark. He'd gone by headquarters, only to find her bike gone. Lu, who had been checking equipment in the training area, had informed him that Alayna had gone back for something at her place and if he hurried he might catch her.

He grabbed the cooler and headed inside, excited to tell her about his plan. After demanding that Dumeril hand over one of the vials of Alayna's blood he had stashed, Alex had taken it to an old Army buddy who worked as a nurse at University Medical Center. He'd helped Delia out a time or two back in Iraq and she owed him a favor.

Delia had typed the blood sample and managed to sneak eight units of whole blood out of the hospital in the cooler he was carrying under his arm like it was full of diamonds. That, combined with the portable defibrillator he had in his med kit, might be enough to pull Alayna through if she did perform this suicide spell.

Magickal healing couldn't help her if her heart stopped, Dumeril had explained. But Alex could. Fear gripped him at the idea. There would be a lot of blood. What if another panic attack froze him up? He shook the anxiety away. Failure wasn't an option. Losing Alayna might kill him, so it was his life on the line, too. They were going to come out the other side of this, one way or another and he was going to find a way for them to be together.

The sun had set and the dense woods around her house had taken on what seemed like a sinister cast to Alex. Everything felt off, ominous. Probably just nerves, he told himself.

It wasn't like he'd never been in a fight before, but it had never been one like this. He shivered slightly as the chill in the air touched the skin beneath his jacket.

He stepped inside and set the cooler in the kitchen, calling for Alayna.

"Up here," he heard her call from the dojo.

As he climbed the stairs, he heard a rhythmic scraping sound. When she came into view, he saw that she was sitting on the floor with a large war fan in her lap. She was using some kind of stone to sharpen the gleaming blades that extended from the top of the fan.

Her whip lay coiled on the floor in front of her. Beside her was a carefully stacked pile of shimmering black pieces. The things were so dark, they seemed to pull in light and swallow it.

Her long blonde hair was done in a severe French braid, and she was head to toe in fairy leather. The top was high-necked and long sleeved, with a zipper in front. Tight pants were tucked into the tops of knee-high boots. Her expression was grim as she ran the stone along the black blades of the fan. She looked ready for war.

Alex opened his mouth to tell her about what he'd been up to, when she rose quickly to her feet.

She put her arms around and him and said, "I'm sorry about earlier."

"Yeah, me too," he said. "I wish you felt like you could tell me about that part of yourself."

"It's just that…for once in my life, someone saw me for who I really was, beyond the command, beyond the power, and you wanted me anyway," she said softly. "You have no idea what that means to me. I was terrified that the curse would push you away. It's pushed everyone else away."

His hands came up, cradling her face.

"I never want you to feel fear with me, Alayna. I love you."

She kissed him then, wrapping her arms around his neck. It was a gentle kiss, at first. As he put his arms around her waist, something sparked between them. Her mouth opened for him and he slipped his tongue inside, desperate to taste her.

Her caresses became urgent, and his grip on her hips became hard. He lowered himself to the mat and pulled her after him until she was straddling his hips. Her breath was coming hot and fast as he reached for the zipper on her top. He slipped it from her shoulders and sat up slightly to take one of her perfect, hard nipples in his mouth. He sucked hard and scraped it lightly with his teeth, pulling a breathy moan from her throat.

Her fingers twined in his hair, holding him to her. She ground her hips against his and he could feel how hot she was for him through his pants and her leathers.

"I need you, Alex," she said, her eyes closed and head tossed back.

He practically tore off his jacket and shirt. His boots and pants disappeared, as did hers.

Alex lay back on the mat, as a gloriously naked Alayna rose above him. She touched her breast, caressing the nipple he'd had in his mouth just a few moments before. His erection was straining, and he was desperate to get inside her.

She took him in hand, stroked him solidly, and he thought he might come right there. She raised her hips and circled the head of his cock around the silky, hot folds of her sex. She was so ready for him.

He caught her hips in his hands and thrust upward. She moaned as the head of his cock entered her and took a ragged, halting breath as she slid the rest of the way down his length, taking him fully inside her.

He pulled her lips to his, taking her mouth as fully as he took the rest of her. He thrust his hips against her hard and felt the delicious friction between them. She threw back her head and moaned again with her ecstasy. The fingers of her right hand danced over her clit, and she was so close to climaxing he could feel it in the way her muscles gripped him.

Just as he felt her pleasure crest, he let his own orgasm take him. With several powerful thrusts he filled her with his release. He collapsed back against the mat and drew her down on top of his chest.

Completely spent, she draped bonelessly across him. She lazily kissed his neck and absently traced a swirling pattern across his chest with her index finger, whispering in a language he didn't understand. It was beautiful, though.

Gradually, his heart slowed and his breathing normalized. His thoughts floated somewhere out of reach and his limbs felt heavy. Too heavy.

With a sudden moment of panic, he tried to sit up and found that he couldn't move.

"Alayna?" His voice was slow, and his tongue felt thick in his mouth.

As she lifted her hand from his chest, there was a flash of green light and an intricately drawn ward sparked to life on his chest.

"What…is…"

She rose from his body and his softened erection slid from her.

"I'm sorry, Alex," she said, a deep sadness in her voice. "This is the only way I know to keep you safe."

He tried to speak, but found he couldn't move his jaw. He could only lie there and plead with his eyes for her to let him go. She had no idea about the blood, his plan to save her.

A strangled and frustrated noise escaped his throat as she began to put her gear back on. The whip went in her right boot.

She knelt down and stroked his face, like she was trying to memorize it.

"You'll be safe here. And in a few hours your powers will dissolve that ward. When they do, I'm begging you not to come after me."

From somewhere she pulled a blanket and settled it over him. Mentally, he strained against the ward holding him. His mind was working overtime trying to figure out a way around it.

She leaned over him and met his eyes.

"If I don't come back from this, please, just…take care of yourself," she said softly. "And remember me the way I was."

She kissed his mouth. He longed to return it, to pull her into his arms and tell her not to go, not to leave him.

"I love you, Alex," she said, her voice barely more than a whisper, touched by unshed tears.

No! He screamed internally, trying to transmit his thoughts with his eyes. It couldn't end like this. This could not be the last time he saw her.

She rose from the floor and gathered her weapons and the

dark material he had noticed earlier. As she began strapping it to her body, he realized it was armor. There was something like a chainmail shirt that went over her head and past her waist and elbows. It glittered like scales.

With a start, he realized they were scales—dragon scales. She was wearing armor made from Z's scales.

She strapped on forearm and shin guards. From a cabinet along the wall, she pulled out a heavy black leather belt with holsters and strapped two Desert Eagles to her thighs. The war fans went in holsters at the small of her back. She added grenades and two large hunting knives to her belt.

As she turned to head downstairs, she said, "Goodbye Alex. If I don't make it out of this, my last thoughts will be of you, knowing that you're safe."

And then she was gone, her stormwind scent the only thing marking that she had ever been there.

* * *

Alayna's eyes were swimming with unshed tears as she left Alex lying on the floor. She knew the ward wouldn't hold him for more than a couple of hours. She'd been careful to weave some serious protection into the ward as well. Nothing would be able to touch him while it was active. She'd built in a fail safe design that would cause the ward to dissolve at dawn, just in case.

By then, everything would be decided, one way or the other.

If his lithseach abilities caused it to fail before then, she just hoped he would stay away from the fight she was walking into. She had hurt him with that move, badly, and she hoped it was enough that he would write her off.

It was killing her to leave him behind, and she felt a sharp painful spot in her chest. Her eyes burned from unshed tears. But she wouldn't be able to do everything she needed to do tonight if he was with her.

Worry for his safety would occupy her thoughts and might get her or someone else killed. And if she needed to perform the Reckoning in order to destroy this ring of evil motherfuckers, she wasn't sure she'd be able to with Alex there.

He was everything she had ever longed for: love, connection, companionship…happiness. In the past couple of days, basking in the glow of his love, she'd let herself fantasize about the future, a future with him in it. How would she be able to cut herself and watch that future bleed away now?

She checked the straps on her armor again. The scales had been painstakingly collected from Z for more than ten years.

Together, they had created her whip, her battle fans, and her armor. The armor responded to her words and molded to her body, leaving no gaps. It could heal itself, given time. She just wished she had more of the stuff to make armor for her team, but Z shed scales so rarely.

Her thoughts turned to the big black dragon and tears almost overwhelmed her. If she didn't survive the night, she wasn't sure what would happen to him. They were connected on an emotional level. Would he feel it when she died? Or would he be left wondering what had happened to her?

There were tales of some mages' familiars who died when their mage died because it was so traumatic when the connection was severed. But no one else had ever had a dragon for a familiar.

She was sure Z would survive if she died, but she worried what he might do after that. She pushed thoughts of the dragon going on a revenge spree out of her mind and focused on what was in front of her.

Oh, Z, I'm sorry I didn't get the chance to say goodbye, she thought.

She moved quickly to the garage and fired up the Hyabusa. With a roar, she shot out into the night. If she hurried, she could rendezvous with the rest of the team at the rally point near the warehouse. Dumeril was scheduled to open the portal between headquarters and the rally point in fifteen minutes. She wanted to be waiting for them when he did.

The 'busa's engine revved beneath her as she turned on to Bee Cave Road, a vast winding thoroughfare that moved through the western part of the city. As she hit the freeway, she gunned it and let all of the motorcycle's considerable horses run.

This time of night, there wasn't much traffic, but there was more than she expected. The engine of the big bike roared as she wove between cars, pushing her speed over a hundred miles per hour.

As she pulled the bike onto the exit ramp, the traffic thickened again. It was nearly midnight; what were all these people doing out?

It dawned on her that tonight was the opening night of the city's largest music festival of the year. Every club downtown would be packed and streets would be shut down for outdoor stages and street parties.

She cursed as she rerouted the bike. And then her stomach sank as she thought about the proximity of the warehouse with the mysterious wards to the now-crowded downtown. It was just six or seven blocks away.

Alayna hoped to hell that it was just a coincidence, but she'd never been that lucky in her life. Something big was in the works and it had the potential to hurt a lot of people.

But not if she could help it.

She revved the engine again and shot through the underpass

of Interstate 35. Within a minute, she had pulled up at the empty lot where the team had agreed to rally. She was the first one there.

* * *

Burdock checked his weapons one last time as the team, minus Alayna and Alex, waited on the training floor for Dumeril to open the portal.

Dumeril's long, silver-white hair gleamed in the overhead lights. He'd plaited it in war braids at the temples and tied them at the nape of his neck to keep the rest out of his face.

Dumeril's back was to them as he concentrated on the space in front of him. He moved his right hand in a circular motion, muttering under his breath.

The air in front of Dumeril began to ripple, like heat distortion on one of Austin's hundred and ten degree summer days. Burdock took a deep breath and braced himself. He'd never liked portal travel. It always felt like he was falling and being turned inside out at the same time.

Burdock fingered the Desert Eagles on his hips. The guns were heavy, but necessary. He had speed loaders on his belt outfitted with various rounds, some silver, some incendiary, all deadly. He had a submachine gun with the grenade launcher attachment strapped to his chest over his body armor. The grenades were strapped to the small of his back. He had everything from flashbangs and smoke grenades to some really nasty frag grenades he'd put together himself.

Strapped to his back, he had two tactical shotguns with shortened barrels. They were loaded up with extended magazines and hand packed shells full of silver shot. The stocks stuck up above his shoulders and crossed behind his neck.

The phrase armed to the teeth didn't even begin to cover it. Burdock had always believed in preparation above all things, but he also knew that even the best laid plans went to hell upon first contact with the enemy.

In those cases, superior firepower usually won out.

He looked at Ellie to his right. The little gnome was draped in dark blue, the cloak pulled around her and the hood obscuring her face. He knew that cloak hid a hundred deadly things, including, somehow, the vicious sniper rifle she favored in cases like this.

She had a hand held computer clipped to her belt that would put anything the NSA had to shame. If they ran into anything electronic, she'd be able to hack it with that little machine. As they waited, she pulled a set of goggles from her belt pouch and fitted them over her large eyes. She could see perfectly in the dark, a common adaptation of subterranean dwellers like her. Bright lights and flashes, like the ones from gunfire or his grenades could blind her momentarily. Ellie was probably the only creature that had to wear shades to a night fight.

Beside him, Lu had already assumed her loosely lupine form. She stood on two legs for now, but he knew that hulking from could drop to all fours and run like the wind. Her wickedly sharp black claws clicked against the concrete floor and he could hear the rasping of her rough footpads as she shifted her weight. The knees on those legs were reversed, just like a wolf's.

The torso, which was covered in black fur the same color as Lu's hair, was huge and her shoulders and arms bulged and rippled with dense muscle that reminded him of a pit bull. Her hands still held a vaguely human shape, retaining the opposable thumbs. The fingers were impossibly long, with an extra knuckle joint thrown in the middle.

The claws at the end of those fingers were black, curving nightmare knives.

Burdock had worked with Lu for years, and the sight of those claws still made him slightly nervous.

He glanced at her face and looked away, his stomach twisting.

Her eyes had become large, round and bright yellow. The eyes of a predator.

Her face had elongated into a horrifying muzzle. It was long like a wolf's, but the jaw was bulky and square, like a pit bull's. And the teeth. They protruded over the thick black lips, various sizes and lengths, but all razor sharp.

Burdock turned back to Dumeril as he heard a series of pops. The swirling air had changed colors, taking on blue and purple tones, with white and yellow flashes. The portal began expanding and Dumeril motioned them through.

Budock went first, to secure the other side.

As he stepped through into the empty lot, he had a moment of disorientation and nausea, but it passed quickly after a few deep breaths. Even though they knew the layout of the warehouse, thanks to Alayna's astral walking, they had decided not to open a portal inside the warehouse. Too risky, since they had to come through one at a time and the portal gave away their position to easily.

Alayna was waiting for him.

She was a vision, a contrast of darkness and light. In the moonlight, her platinum hair, pulled back in a severe braid, looked almost white and glowed slightly. Her pale skin looked like porcelain against her dark clothes.

She was covered from neck to foot in fairy leather and dragon scale armor. From her shoulders hung the traditional black mage battle robes. The robes didn't cover her arms, instead looping under her arms and hanging from clips on the back of her armor.

The robes wouldn't impede movement in the slightest, but they helped conceal weapons and hide movement. They also obscured the outline of the body just enough that projectiles were more likely to miss. The material was also well spelled with protections.

She looks like a goddamn avenging angel, he thought.

"If I'd known we were dressing up, I would have dug my robes out, Commander."

"This is just a little bit of show," she said. "I don't expect it to get anyone to back down, but a little intimidation factor never hurts."

And it might be the last chance she ever got to wear them. The notion hit him like a punch to the solar plexus and he tried to shake it off. If she went out tonight, at least she'd do it looking every inch the mage battle commander she was.

After a moment she added, "Besides, yours are covered in scorch marks. That standard issue stuff doesn't stand up to your flame slinging."

He chuckled and smiled. She was right about that.

Lu came through the portal next, and Alayna helped her pull a large black cloak over her eight-foot frame. She hunched down close to the ground to hide her height, but she was still massive. Luckily, they didn't have far to go, and this side of town was almost deserted with the festivities in full swing a few blocks away.

Ellie was next through and Dumeril was right behind her. He shut down the portal in just a few seconds.

"Where's Alex?" Dumeril asked Alayna.

"I asked him to sit this one out. He's at my place. If I don't make it through this, I'd appreciate someone checking on him," she said.

"I'll just bet he took that real well," Dumeril said sarcastically. "And you can be the one to unchain him in the morning, because if anyone is coming out the other side of this, it's you, Commander."

He smiled at her, but she didn't return it.

She nodded and Ellie began throwing her best glamour around the group. They moved like silent shadows toward the warehouse a few hundred yards away.

* * *

Alex lay in the darkness, struggling against the ward that bound him. It was like the thing was blocking all the signals his brain was sending to his muscles. No matter how hard he told his hand to move, it remained stubbornly still.

He could still blink, swallow and breathe, but that was about it. Over the past hour or so, he'd gained more control over his breathing and could tighten the muscles around his vocal cords so that he could make strangled little noises in the back of his throat, but he couldn't open his mouth to scream.

Not that anyone would hear him all the way out here.

Alayna had left one of the sliding doors open, and he could feel a March breeze blowing across his skin. There was a hint of ozone in the air, the smell of a coming storm.

While outside he remained perfectly still, inside he was raging. Mentally, he was throwing things and breaking shit. How could she do this?

He knew why she had done it. To protect him. But it hurt so

much that she didn't want him with her. And she had no idea that he had the means to bring her back. Maybe. And that was a big maybe. But it was better than nothing, damn it.

He tried again to move some part of his body, any part. No luck.

Outside, a soft wooshing sound caught his attention. This wasn't the sound of the wind through the trees that had been the only thing he could hear for the last hour. This was new.

This was a rhythmic movement of air, but soft. Whoomp. Whoomp. Whoomp. He heard a soft thud and the sound of cracking twigs and leaves in back of the house.

Struggling to turn his head toward the open window, he was able to move his eyes in that direction. He could just see the outline of the window in the darkness, just inside his peripheral vision.

His head turned just the barest of millimeters, and internally he jumped for joy. *Now, we're getting somewhere.*

Outside, he heard something moving. Its heavy footfalls moved across the grass and leaves behind Alayna's house. Bushes rustled as it moved past. Whatever it was, it was big.

Alex was able to turn his head just the tiniest bit more and saw an inky black shape within the darkness outside. There was a massive form outside the window, blocking the moonlight and the stars peeking through the clouds.

Fear gripped Alex. If something came for him now, he'd never be able to defend himself like this. He was a sitting duck.

"Hello, Alex."

The sound was more rumble than voice, like a thundercloud trying to speak.

It was Z!

After he recovered from the momentary shock of hearing

the dragon's voice, he tried to focus his thoughts so the dragon might be able to hear him.

"What are you doing in there?" the dragon asked him.

Alex tried to think at the dragon about what Alayna had done and where she had gone.

"I can't understand your thoughts, human, they are very confusing. Perhaps if I remove that ward on your chest, you can tell me what is happening."

Alex thought one word, very clearly and very loudly. *YES.*

"All right, you don't have to shout," the dragon said.

Z's head poked through the open door, his graceful horns scraping lightly at the top of the jam. His large nostrils were less than a foot from Alex and the dragon breathed in deeply. Alex felt the blanket catch a bit in the air current. When the dragon breathed out, it smelled like the inside of a barbecue pit, all charred meat and smoke.

A deep rumble came from the dragon's elegant throat and the sound vibrated in Alex's chest.

Suddenly, he could move a little bit more. He wiggled his fingers against the exercise mat. The rumble deepened and Alex felt something give way. There was an almost inaudible pop, and he was finally able to sit up.

"Z, Alayna's in trouble!" Alex said, shouting because he wasn't used to having control over his voice.

"I felt something was wrong. She was in great emotional pain. She hasn't been that sad since her father died. It felt like my own heart was breaking. I felt it here, and I came to see what had caused it."

"She's going into battle, Z. She's going to perform the Reckoning and I have to stop her."

"Were you the one that caused her such pain? Is that why she had you warded so that you could not move? If you have hurt her, I will roast you alive and—"

"It wasn't me. Well, not exactly. She warded me to protect me until the fight is over. She didn't want me to get hurt."

The dragon said, "That is something my little sparrow would do."

Alex was on his feet, grabbing his clothes and pulling them on.

As he struggled with his shoes, it occurred to Alex to ask, "How did you get here without anyone seeing you?"

"It is cloudy and dark. I am dark," the dragon told him. "And humans never look up anymore. They seem to spend most of their time staring at small glowing things in their hands."

Alex nodded as he stood and prepared to grab his gear from downstairs.

"I've got to go, Z. If I can get to her, I might be able to help her."

24

Chapter 24

Burdock reveled in the surge of adrenaline as Alayna nodded, giving him the go signal. With a press of a button, the rolling doors on the warehouse disintegrated. Alayna held her hands in front of her and used her powers to direct any blastback from the explosion into the warehouse.

Not that there should be much. With the plastique he had used and the way he had shaped and placed the charges, the force and heat was only going where he wanted. The commander had also dampened the noise from the explosion, so anyone more than a block away would hear nothing more than a soft *whoomp*, likely to be mistaken for thunder or loud music from the festival going on a few blocks away.

The team was moving through the doors before the smoke and dust had even begun to clear. Burdock's Desert Eagles had cleared the holsters as the last pieces of the doors had hit the concrete. He took aim on the forms moving quickly through the smoke, which he assumed were the guards coming to meet them.

The commander's voice rang out, "I am Commander Blackwell of the Mage Corps! Everyone put your weapons down and your hands up, by order of the council!"

Unsurprisingly, the vamps kept coming, but it was important to observe protocols, he supposed.

With a wave of his hand he heated the air in front of him and cleared the smoke just enough to get a bead on one of the guards. The dark haired vampire's eyes went wide as the .50 caliber slug took him in the throat, nearly decapitating him. The body crumpled to the ground, blood pouring from the wound.

Burdock moved further into the warehouse, and his visibility was improving quickly. The other team members had disappeared, intent on their own objectives. That was certainly fine with Burdock. He preferred to work alone.

Another guard, this one large, with light colored hair, moved in from the side and Burdock got off a shot to the chest before the vamp was on him. It was only when the vampire hit him full force that Burdock realized he was wearing body armor. Hell, they probably all were. Damn it; that was going to slow things down.

He dropped the Eagle in his left hand and let the flames come out to play. The fire was always with him, just beneath the surface of his skin. Most fire mages didn't conjure the flames they used, like air mages conjured wind from nowhere. And they didn't control the element around them like water and earth mages did.

The fire was always with him. The trick wasn't calling it when he needed it—it was containing it when he didn't.

Fire was such a simple element. It only wanted to burn and consume. Occasionally, his priorities and that of his element aligned.

Flames licked up his left arm, and as it connected with the jaw of the vampire that was currently trying to tear his throat out with his fangs, flames poured over the vampire's face and head. The creature screamed as he fell back, slapping at his head, but his hair had already caught.

That one would be out of the fight for awhile if the burns didn't kill him. Burdock got to his feet and retrieved his gun from the floor, bringing his weapons up to find the next target.

* * *

Ellie watched through her scope as Burdock took the big vamp down. She loved watching the fire mage work. He was barely restrained violence in motion. His fighting style was not elegant, like Alayna's, or surgical, like Dumeril's. It was just strength and speed and efficiency of movement.

She turned her attention to a vampire moving up behind him as he rose from the tackle the now flaming vampire had thrown at him. She took down the new threat with a clean shot to the head, the body crumpling into a heap. Burdock didn't even seem to notice.

It was just as well. The big guy didn't like to think he needed anyone else in a fight, and Ellie wasn't going to be the one to bruise that ego. She'd lost count of the number of times she'd saved his ass from the shadows.

She looked away from her scope and down at her handheld computer. The thing was somewhere between the size of a smartphone and tablet, with a slide-out keyboard. She'd designed and built it herself, and the thing could dance circles around almost any piece of hardware out there.

She'd hacked the warehouse's security system using remote splicers that were transmitting signal wirelessly to her. Her little inventions were spliced right into the hard cables, so any loss of power or signal in that part of the warehouse would not leave her blind.

More guards were moving out of the storage rooms, she saw on the video feeds. There must be about two dozen by now. They must have upped their numbers after Alayna tripped the ward. A bubble of nervousness crept up Ellie's throat at the thought. Those were long odds for five people. And they still didn't know what was behind that ward.

Pushing back her doubts, Ellie took aim again with her rifle and started picking off targets as they emerged from the storage room.

* * *

Lu shook her hands and flung blood from her claws, watching it splatter against the concrete. She had subdued two of the vampire guards. She wasn't sure if they were dead or not, but they wouldn't be getting up any time in the next couple of weeks.

Lu didn't relish killing the guards. They were likely just there to do a job. Some of them may have been among the hunters that had roamed that killing ground up north. Others were probably there just because they were being paid to be.

If they were smart, they would have given up when Alayna had announced that this was a Council sanctioned raid by the Mage Corps.

However, muscle like this was rarely hired for their brains. Loyalty to the paycheck, yes. The ability to the put the hurt on anything that came through the door, definitely. Lu, knew the score. If it weren't for Alayna, she probably would have ended up just like these guys. That is, if the drugs or her abusive ex hadn't killed her first.

She shook away the sympathy for the guards that were currently circling her. There were three. She almost laughed.

With one swing of her arm, she caught the right-most vamp on her claws and slammed him into the middle one. As they tumbled to the floor in a tangle, she picked up the third vamp and smashed his body down on top of the other two. Repeatedly.

The three vamps were soon a bloody mess of broken bones. All three were solidly unconscious, if the skull fractures were anything to go by. She gave the pile one last contemptuous kick as she moved on to her next target.

She was trying to stay away from the cages so she wouldn't spook the hostages any more than they already were. She spotted Dumeril fighting off a couple of vamps as he tried to get the cages unlocked. As she moved to help him, she felt a sting in her hip. She looked down to see a little blood and a small hole in her flesh.

She'd been shot.

She kept moving so she wouldn't be an easy target but turned her concentration to pushing the bullet out. In under a minute, the bullet slid from her skin, and she had shifted the tissue around the injury so that it wasn't bleeding anymore.

Lu turned her hulking form back in the direction she thought the shot had come from and saw a vamp with a submachine gun pointing it right at Alayna. The commander had her back turned to the vamp as she engaged two others hand to hand.

With a running leap and an ear splitting roar, Lu launched herself at the vamp. She felt two bullets graze her, and then she was on top of the vamp, his throat between her teeth. The hot gush of vampire blood hit her throat as it washed over her tongue, tasting of copper.

She looked down at the dying vampire for a moment before moving on to the next target.

* * *

Dumeril cursed as he maneuvered the bolt cutters around the padlock on the cage. There was a man inside, screaming at him in Spanish. If he'd had more than a few seconds to think about the situation he was in, he'd probably be screaming too.

He heard running footsteps approaching and picked up the kukri he'd set on top of the cage. He turned just in time to catch the vamp, who was moving so fast even Dumeril's eyes had a hard time seeing him, right across the face.

The blade sliced and hung on something, as blood splattered across Dumeril and the floor. The blade's grip was wrenched from Dumeril's hand, and it clattered to the floor. As he went to draw the other kukri from the sheath at his back, the vampire, who was now sporting a nasty ragged gash that ran sideways across both cheeks, slammed Dumeril back against the cage, pinning his arm.

Fangs unsheathed from the ruined, bloody mouth. Dumeril's slash had opened the vampire's face almost from ear to ear. The blade must have hung on the jawbone. The guard opened wide, going for Dumeril's throat.

Ramming his remaining free arm against the vampire's throat, Dumeril pushed with everything he had to try to free himself. As he slipped the arm from behind him, he pressed that hand against the vamp's forehead and over his eyes and unleashed a dazzling light spell.

It wasn't something he typically trotted out during combat, but it was a simple spell that didn't cost him much. It was a small illusion that could be seen for a few hundred yards in the dark. And in this case, it was hilariously effective.

The vamp, which had vision adapted for low light, screamed as the bright multicolored lights were unleashed just millimeters from his sensitive eyes. As he reached up to cover his eyes, he overbalanced and fell back. Dumeril kicked the vamp squarely in the balls as he tumbled to the ground, screaming.

He brought both kukri blades to bear, crossed them, and decapitated the vampire in one swift movement, cutting off the scream as he did.

With a weary sigh, he turned back to working on the padlock. The sapien inside had stopped screaming and was just staring blankly at him. That was fine with Dumeril.

As he worked, a movement to his right caught his eye. As he turned slightly, he froze at what he saw. His stomach dropped. It couldn't be.

Striding in like he owned the place and like there wasn't a huge battle going on around him was Dominic Spino, his former teammate and a man he would have called a friend up until a few seconds ago.

Dominic was dressed in a custom tailored suit, his dark hair slicked back from his face. He looked just like his old friend. Except for the eyes. Something was off in those dark eyes. They were just a little too wide, a little too shiny.

Behind him was Camille, his trusty assistant. She was in black slacks and a white silk blouse. Carried casually over one shoulder was a wickedly sharp looking Japanese long sword.

Dominic pulled a black handgun from his jacket and pointed it. Dumeril turned to see where, and he almost screamed. Alayna had her back to Dominic, fighting three guards at once.

The shot rang out, and sparks fell from the shoulder of her

dragon scale armor. Still, the impact had clearly hurt as she put a hand to the shoulder and whirled.

Emotions flickered across her face as she saw Dominic. Surprise was followed by hope and then quickly by confusion and pain as she realized that he wasn't here to help them. He was here to kill them. Because he was a part of all of this.

Without turning to look at the three vamps she had been fighting, she flicked her war fan in a dismissive gesture. All three went flying into the wall of the warehouse with a loud clang as a hurricane gust of wind took them off their feet.

With a mixture of despair and murder in her eyes, she stepped toward Dominic.

* * *

Alayna looked at Dominic, still not believing it was him. It had to be some kind of trick or illusion.

"I was wondering when you'd figure it out," he said, his voice almost conversational. "Took you long enough."

Rage flowed through her, turning her vision red around the edges.

"How could you?" she asked him, her voice raw with pain.

"It was easy, actually," he said, a smile pulling at his thin lips. "There are so many desperate people that will do anything to come here. Did you know they actually paid us to bring them here? Paltry sums, certainly, but I do just love the irony that they paid to be turned into food."

"You're a sick son of a bitch, Dom," Alayna said.

"Only because you made me this way," he told her.

They stood a dozen feet apart now, and at the confused and angry look on her face, he spoke up again.

"I gave up everything for the Corps. Money, power, the love of my family. And then I had to give up the Corps because of you. You ruined everything. After I left, that's when the voices came to me and told me how I could get it all back."

"You're not getting anything except my boot on your neck, Dom. Call off the guards, bring down that ward, and you might live through the night. Keep up this fight and I'll personally see to it that you die slow and painful."

"Oh, it's not time for that yet," he said, a hint of mania in his voice.

She looked closely at him and realized there was something very wrong with her old friend. She didn't know why she hadn't seen it before. He was thin, almost gaunt. He had picked up little nervous habits, like fidgeting with his fingers. His eyes were just a little too wide, and there was a brightness to them, like burning embers.

He's lost his damn mind, she thought.

"I thought you would have figured it out long before now," he continued. "I left them, their bodies like little Easter eggs all over the city for you and you never figured it out."

She stayed silent, but took another slow step toward him, hoping to close the distance. Her body and stance were loose, but she was ready to spring if she needed to. She still had a war fan in one hand and wondered if she should go for her whip. Around her, the fighting had stopped. Her team was waiting on her orders, his guards were waiting on his.

"But then Medina killed that girl and everything went to hell," she said, taking a guess at what had actually happened.

"Exactly," he said. "I was too used to working with professionals. Medina turned into an addict. He wanted to hunt and kill every night. Then he goes and tears a girl's throat out right in the middle of my club. Well, you understand why I had to get rid of him."

"Totally," Alayna said, taking another slow step. Camille moved closer to her boss and glared at Alayna, fingering the hilt of that long sword. Alayna met her stare and stayed still.

"Except he was in charge of shipping the prey," Dominic said angrily. "My supplies started to dwindle, so I had to step up my game. I take it you figured out I set you up at Hellraisers?"

She nodded. She had suspected that, but hadn't known for sure and didn't want to tip him off.

"But then you surprised me, my smart girl," he said. "You destroyed my hunting grounds and freed so many of my prey. You ruined the surprise!"

His voice was full of so much anger that spittle was flying from the corners of his mouth. His eyes were starting to bleed to red.

"So I knew I had to bring you here, to show you my plan and everything I've done so that we can be together."

Her stomach rolled at the thought, but she kept her expression blank and her body still, hoping he would give something away.

"I know that you took that fucking sapien to bed, Alayna," he said, his voice harsh and grating, almost screaming. "I couldn't believe that you turned me down, but you chose him. Ugh. It's just sickening. But I forgive you because I'm better than that."

"How did you know?" she asked. The longer she could keep him talking, the longer she hoped she could give her team to get something in place.

"I've been watching you since I left the Corps," he said. "The voices said it was important. You were always so careful about outside threats, but you never thought about internal ones. You never suspected that I would hurt you."

Her stomach twisted at his words. He was right. While they hadn't parted on the best of terms, she'd thought they had repaired their relationship enough to at least call it neutral. She had no idea what had happened to his mind in the two years since then. She'd had no idea she could inspire so much madness in a man.

She was about to open her mouth when she heard something crash against the warehouse's metal roof. The whole building shook and reverberated with the impact. It sounded like a small plane had crashed up there.

A few seconds later, there was the sound of screaming; tearing metal and wind began to whistle and howl through a small opening. More tearing noises and a hole began to open in the roof as something peeled the heavy metal back.

Black claws and then a scaly black head appeared, peeking inside.

"Z!" she shouted, shock ripping through her.

The head disappeared, and she heard air rushing outside and the whoomp-whoomp of his huge black wings.

Suddenly, with a horrible crashing sound of wrenching metal mixing with a dragon's roar, Z dove through the opening.

Astride the dragon's shoulders was the most welcome and unwelcome sight she had ever seen in her life.

Alex's hair was blown back from his face, his combat boots braced on Z's front shoulders. Both 1911s were in his hands, and he let out a war whoop as the dragon descended.

"Yee-haw, motherfuckers!"

He opened fire on the vampire guards just as Z hit the concrete. The impact cracked the floor, raising jagged chunks. Alex rolled off Z's back and came up firing, taking out three guards.

Alex was furious grace and deadly precision given form as

he moved across the floor, diving behind a crate for cover and popping up again to take aim at a new target. Alayna's heart swelled to see him here. She didn't fool herself into thinking for a second that he had forgiven her for leaving him behind, but he was here.

They might just have a shot at surviving this fight.

Z whipped his spiked tail across the floor, sending another two guards into the wall. The dragon caught a third in his jaws and shook him back and forth like a dog with a rabbit. Alayna could hear the sickening pop of bones from where she stood.

That was the only cue the team needed.

Violence erupted around her.

The bark of Ellie's sniper rifle mixed with the boom of Burdock's shotguns and the ringing of steel from Dumeril's kukris.

She charged at Dominic, whip in one hand, war fan in the other.

* * *

Alex popped up over the top of the crate he'd taken cover behind and squeezed off a series of shots. One took a huge vampire in the shoulder, and the creature turned, lunging in Alex's direction. The guard moved with the speed and agility Alex had come to associate with vampires.

In the split second he had, Alex squeezed off another shot, but it went wide. Suddenly, the vampire was on him.

The first blow caught Alex darckross the face, and he felt his head and neck snap around. As his vision started to clear, Alex realized he was on his back, the vampire straddling him. Alex brought his left hand up and clamped it around the big guy's throat while he drove his right fist into his gut.

They traded blows for a few seconds. The vampire's hands came around Alex's throat, and he started to squeeze. With his air cut off, Alex started to panic, grabbing the guy's wrists. Red eyes and long fangs swam in Alex's failing vision.

As Alex's vision started to go black around the edges, he could see the red was fading from the vamp's eyes, and the fangs were retracting. The grip around his neck was loosening.

As Alex drew a tortured breath, he realized the vampire was weakening, his predator mode fading. He drew back his fist to strike the thing in the face. Every ounce of his survival instinct, fear, adrenaline, and desperate need to protect Alayna and his friends was behind that punch. As it connected, he felt something crack open inside himself, and the vampire disappeared.

As Alex scrambled to his feet, he saw the guy laying about fifteen feet away, unconscious. The lower half of his face was at an odd angle. Dislocated jaw, Alex realized.

He looked down at his fist. The knuckles weren't even split. With a surge of awareness, he realized that he had sent the vampire flying. Z had told him that his abilities were a well and that well would fill up. It appeared that he had just figured out how to unleash that power.

Movement caught his eye. Two vampire guards were moving toward him from the left. He turned, squared his shoulders, clenched his fists. And smiled.

* * *

As Alayna charged at Dominic, she swung the war fan in and arc toward his face, but she was blocked by Camille as she brought that long blade down on her armor, aiming for the weak point where it met her neck. Alayna turned at the last moment so the blade slide off her shoulder, drawing sparks.

She brought her war fan up as a distraction and kicked out at Camille's knee. The female vampire was fast, though, and the strike fell short as she danced back.

With that sword, Camille had the reach on her. She began to call the wind, but before she could complete the incantation, Camille charged, the sword held low and ready for an upward strike. Alayna brought the fan to meet it and caught the sword's blade between the blades of the fan. The impact as the sword met the bottom of the fan rang up Alayna's arm. With her other hand she snapped the fan closed around the sword, twisted and wrenched it away from Camille, sending it skittering across the floor.

Disarmed, Camille brought her hands up, the muscles in her legs coiling to pounce. She was not out of the fight yet. It was a fight Alayna was all too willing to give her. Suddenly, a shot rang out and crimson bloomed on Camille's perfect silk blouse. Her eyes rolled back and she crumpled to the ground.

Alayna turned in time to see a shadow move up on the catwalk. Ellie was watching her back.

Another bullet dinged off her armor and she turned to face Dominic. He wasn't trying to kill her, just wound her.

"Damn it, Dominic, stop this before someone else gets killed," she shouted. He spared a glance for Camille's bleeding body on the floor and met her gaze.

"You don't understand, Alayna. They all have to die for us to be together," he said.

Instead of aiming the gun at her, he pointed it over her shoulder. The gun barked and she turned in time to see Lu clutch her shoulder in pain.

That's it, she thought. She uncoiled her whip and sprang the blade. She was going to put him down like the monster he was and then mop up this mess.

Alayna charged and swung the whip. Dominic dodged it with lightning reflexes, but that put him off balance when she reached him with her blade.

The upward stroke caught him across the chest, slicing open his suit, shirt, and skin. Blood poured from the wound. He wasn't armored.

She watched as his eyes went full predator and his fangs descended. He launched himself at her, going for her throat, and knocked her back. Alayna stumbled as his full weight came down on her and only managed to keep his fangs from her flesh by pressing the hilt of the whip across his throat.

She was able to roll away from him, and he came at her with a flurry of blows to the face and throat, putting her on the defensive. They were getting closer to the outer wall of the warehouse, and she didn't want to be pinned between the ferocious threat before her and the metal wall behind her.

Glancing to her right, she saw Alex get buried under two vampire guards. Alarm rose within her as he disappeared beneath their huge bodies. Suddenly, the two were flying in opposite directions and Alex was standing, muscles coiled in a fighting stance.

What the hell?

She didn't have time to process what she had seen because Dominic was on her again. She saw an opening and pressed it, parrying his blows with her own and using the blade end of the whip to slice at his arms and hands.

He howled and came at her again with stunning viciousness,

spittle flying from his mouth, blood pouring from the wound on his chest.

Alayna stumbled on something unseen and felt herself falling backward. Dominic's snapping fangs were inches from her face as they fell together. In one last desperate move, she drove the blade upward toward his chest.

His body went completely still, his expression becoming one of confusion. She pushed him off of her and discovered that her silver blade was buried in his heart.

Over the course of seconds, the red bled from his eyes, and his fangs retracted. He seemed thinner, almost deflated. If she pulled the blade out, he would die in a matter of seconds. If she left the blade in, there was a chance to save him.

She settled him on his back, and he looked more like her old friend. His eyes no longer held that maniacal gleam.

She turned to look back. The fight was slowing down. Several of the guards had put their hands up or were running out of the building through the blasted doors.

"It's over Dom," she told him.

His breath was ragged, gurgling and he struggled to meet her eyes.

"The voices are gone," he whispered.

"What voices, Dom?"

He closed his eyes and winced in pain.

"They started after I left the Corps," he said, struggling to speak. "They told me to do things, hurt people, hurt you. I was weak. I listened. They said they were strong and they could make everything right again."

He coughed and bright red blood splattered across his lips.

"We don't have much time, Dom. What's behind that ward?"

"Don't touch it, Alayna. You can't fight them. Just run. That's all you can do."

She felt Alex kneeling behind her. He gripped her shoulder through her armor. She noticed the rest of the team was moving up around them.

"Dumeril, can you do anything for him?" Alayna asked.

"I can try," the Svarturan said, moving to kneel beside the vampire.

Dominic batted Dumeril's hands away.

Dominc's voice grew frantic. "They're coming, Alayna. They are coming for you, for all of you, and they are going to tear this world apart."

With that, he gripped the hilt of whip and pulled the blade out of his chest. He screamed, the sound mixing with Alayna's cry of alarm.

There was a small geyser of blood, and Dominic fell back against the concrete.

"I'm sorry," he hissed as black blood poured from his mouth. His eyes slid closed, and his features went slack as death took him.

Everything was silent for a moment.

Alayna turned her attention to the black wall that stood about twenty feet from where she knelt.

Whatever was behind it would have to be dealt with. She stood and turned to the team.

"Report," she said, her voice raw from the fight, from emotion.

"I'm a little banged up, but ready to go," Dumeril said, wiping Dominic's blood from his hands.

Burdock spoke next. "I took a bullet in the shoulder, but it's not bleeding too bad. I've got still got some juice left, but I'm running low."

"Same here," Lu said. The words came clipped and slow as

she worked to shape them with those fang filled jaws. "Don't have much fight left, but what is left is yours."

Alex just nodded and shot her a thumbs up.

"All good up here, Commander," Ellie said through her mic.

Z just gave a rumbling purr.

"Dumeril and Lu, secure the guards in one of those storage rooms. Burdock, melt those damn locks off the cages and get those people outside."

She looked at Alex. "And why don't you tell me what the hell was going on in that fight?"

He was silent for a moment as he looked down at his hands.

"I think we found the flip side to my abilities," he said.

"We're going to have to process this later, but in the meantime, keep the Superman moves to a minimum until we know more about how this might affect you," she said.

As the rest of the team moved to follow her commands, she moved to the warded area. As she drew closer, the ward sprang to life, glowing green and hovering in front of the wall of darkness about ten feet off the floor.

She studied the pattern. It was beyond intricate, clearly woven by a master. She really wished Dominic had stuck around long enough to tell her who he had hired to do this. She would love to take a rogue mage with this kind of power off the streets.

Concentrating, she began to sing softly, pulling at the threads of the ward with her voice, coaxing them apart. Z joined her, adding his rumbling voice to the mix, and they worked together to untangle it. After what seemed like an hour—but was probably closer to two minutes—the darkness began to dissipate. Sounds began to leak through first. Shuffling sounds, soft moans.

Figures became visible in the dark haze. They were human

shaped, but they didn't move like humans. The movements were too quick, too jerky. And the sounds weren't human. There were growls, howls, and groans.

As the ward finally died with a pop of sound and flash of green light, they could see what they were up against. And Alayna almost screamed in horror.

Her knees buckled, and she might have fallen, but Alex was there to support her.

There was a heavy chain link fence that ran from one wall to the other and from floor to ceiling. Beyond the fence were about a hundred figures moving around. Their skin was grey and hung from their frames. What used to be clothing hung in tatters. Their eyes were horrifyingly red, and large fangs protruded over lips that had pulled back from gaunt faces.

Some climbed the fence and pulled at it. Others shuffled aimlessly. Others darted faster than an eye could track, from one end of the enclosure to the other.

"Oh, gods," Alayna breathed.

Alex still supported her weight, and she wasn't sure she would ever be able to stand again. Her brain was not computing what was in front of her.

"Are those…zombies?" Alex asked.

"There is no such thing," Alayna answered, her voice sounding far away to her own ears. "These creatures are a thousand times worse."

She heard Dumeril curse as he caught sight of the things.

"What are they?" Alex asked anxiously.

"Revenants," she said.

One of the creatures began to frantically pull at the fence, sniffing the air and screaming at the top of its lungs. Almost as one, a hundred pairs of eyes turned to look at them.

"And now they know we're here," she said.

"What are they, and how do we kill them?" Alex said.

The rest of the team was starting to gather around them.

"Revenants are just a myth. It's supposedly what happens when a human is turned by a vampire but starves during the transition. The vampire virus keeps their body moving, but the brain and body are essentially dead. They have one instinct: to feed. And the only way to kill them is to decapitate them or incinerate them."

Dumeril turned to her, "What's the plan, Commander?"

She just stared at them for a moment. They were beginning to gather at the fence, tearing at the metal links with their bare hands. The flesh on their fingers began to shred, but they didn't bleed. Hard to bleed when you didn't have a heartbeat.

Z spoke, "Let me burn them for you, little sparrow."

She closed the distance with the dragon and put her hand on his scaly muzzle. Alex and Burdock moved with her, each one standing at her shoulder and eyeing the increasingly agitated revenants.

"You would take these lives?" Alayna asked.

The dragon abhorred killing intelligent things. She knew that the deaths of the vampires he had already killed would weigh on him. What would a hundred do to him?

"I am not the one to kill them. They died by others' hands. I will put them to rest," he said stepping toward the fence and taking a deep breath and preparing to incinerate the revenants with his fiery breath.

Suddenly, he reared back, roaring in pain. Thick orange mucus poured from a wound in the dragon's neck, splattering on the concrete at his feet. From the other side of Z's scaly body, Camille, covered in her own blood emerged, the long sword dripping in her hand.

Her face was bone white, her eyes burning red and her fangs hanging over her bottom lip. Her hair was matted with blood, and her formerly white blouse was now red and clinging to her. She was vengeance come to life and horror flashed through Alayna at what Camille had done.

Z's mighty body writhed in pain, his long neck whipping back and forth as he tried to put his clawed paws to the wound. Alex was knocked back by a flailing claw, and Burdock rushed forward, unable to see Camille.

Camille moved faster than Alayna could track. With a single stroke of the sword she cut through the flesh of Burdock's neck, and his head went tumbling from his shoulders. His big body sagged to the concrete as a scream tore from Alayna's throat.

No!

She wanted to drop to her knees and cradle that body, weep until her eyes were dry. But she also wanted to rip and tear and destroy the thing that had taken Burdock from this world.

She pushed the first instinct away and embraced the second.

Alayna turned on Camille. The female vampire advanced on her slowly. Slow enough that Alayna had time to weave the spell she needed. A vortex of wind lifted the vampire off the ground, her leather boots kicking at the air.

With a word, Alayna ripped the sword from her hand and sent it blade first into the metal wall of the warehouse.

"Just kill me, you fucking bitch!" Camille shouted.

Alayna just stared at her.

"Why?" Alayna's voice was raw.

She glanced over her shoulder to see Alex getting to his feet. He took a step toward Burdock's body, but realized that he couldn't do anything and froze. His eyes found her.

"You killed him!" Camille screamed, flailing uselessly in the vortex.

"Not that, you psychopathic wench," Alayna said. "Why all of this? The hunting and the revenants and the murders?"

"It was all for you," the vampire said. "Don't get me wrong, it was good fun hunting those sheep, draining them, turning them and then watching them writhe and starve and die."

A sick and twisted smile spread her painted red lips.

"But he was trying to draw you in. He wanted to kill your team, turn you and then unleash hell on this city. We could have run this town, turned the sapiens into cattle and told the Council to go fuck themselves."

Alayna almost laughed.

"You're fucked in the head, Camille, if you think that would have worked. The Council would perform the magickal equivalent of nuking this city from orbit rather than let it fall into the hands of a madman and outing us to every sapien in the world. You know that."

It was Camille that began to laugh.

"Speaking of nukes, Whisperer…" Camille nodded toward the revenants tearing at the fence. It was starting to bow outward in several places from the pressure of their bodies. That fence wouldn't hold for much longer.

"With that lizard out of commission, you don't have a choice. If you want to save your city, you better get to cutting."

Rage bubbled up in Alayna again, but the bitch was right.

Dragons needed two liquids, stored in glands in their throats, to produce their fire breath. Camille had wounded Z in such a way that he wouldn't be able to incinerate the ravenous horde that was trying to claw its way toward her friends and her city. If even a few of those things got loose, they would head right for the festival, killing and destroying as they went. It was likely that any sapiens they drained along the way would eventually rise as revenants themselves as clueless sapiens tried to deal with the aftermath.

The city would be overwhelmed in days.

Alayna pushed the vision out of her mind.

"You're right, of course," Alayna told Camille, her voice sounding eerily calm, even to her own ears. "But you'll get a front row seat for the show."

She turned to Z, who stood panting nearby, trying to focus through the pain of his wound. The wound was nasty, having opened up one of the soft areas below the dragon's jaw. Camille had known just where to strike. Must have planned it this way.

I'm sorry I cannot destroy these things for you, sparrow, he said in her mind.

"I know, Z. Don't worry about it."

Climb on my back and I will fly you far from here.

"Can't do that, old friend. I have a job to do here," she said, stroking his muzzle. A terrible lump was forming in her throat, and she fought to speak around it. "I need you to get clear of this. Go to the high places in the world, try to find more of your kind. I can't stand the thought of you being the last one."

He started to speak again and she cut him off with a gesture.

She leaned in and whispered, "Get Alex out of here for me. Just do that one thing, please."

The dragon nodded his black-scaled head. Tears in her eyes, she turned away and shouted at Dumeril, "You have thirty seconds to get everyone clear of this building. Go!"

Alex made a move toward her, shouting something she didn't hear. Z grabbed him in his claws and began to beat his massive wings, aiming for the hole in the roof. The last glimpse she had of Alex was his outstretched arms reaching for her, his eyes wide with panic.

She pushed the image from her mind. A glance behind her told her that Dumeril and the others were clear, along with the hostages. Some of the guards that littered the ground may have been unconscious and not dead, but she didn't care. They had stood by while this happened and they were going down with her.

Alayna pulled one of the long hunting knives from her belt and put it against her wrist. She hesitated only a moment before she let the razor edge slice the delicate pale flesh. The cold bite of the steel felt almost like relief. It was finally ending.

She had come to the place she had dreaded most of her life, and she was strangely okay with what was about to happen. Her friends would be safe. She glanced at the hole in the roof. Her love would be safe. He would be angry for a while, but he would go on.

She repeated the cut on the other wrist. The blood began to fall in fat drops on the concrete. *That should be enough*, she thought.

She began to sing the harsh words of the Reckoning. The words were ragged, discordant notes. This was not the song of creation or conjuring or manipulation. It was the song of unmaking, destruction, and death.

She felt the weaving take hold of her, the pull of energy leaving her body. A feeling of floating seeped through her. As she closed her eyes, she felt her feet leave the floor.

This was it.

* * *

Alex struggled against Z's hold, but the dragon's claws were wrapped firmly around his shoulders and upper arms.

They hovered several dozen feet above the roof of the warehouse. Through the hole in the roof, he saw Alayna make the cuts to her arms. He screamed at her to stop, but she couldn't hear him. Around them, the wind was beginning to pick up, and raindrops were beginning to pelt them. He wasn't sure if this was a part of the spell or if the weather was just finally coming in.

Inside the warehouse, air currents began to toss crates around. Alayna's arms extended to the sides and her feet floated off the floor. Her eyes were closed, but that horrible song continued to pour from her lips.

Blood flowed from the wounds on her wrists and the other small wounds she had taken in the fight, bright drops of crimson swept away on the air currents swirling around her. The drops began to merge into larger masses, elongating and hardening.

Alex could feel the cold pouring from the building and saw frost beginning to form around the edges of the hole in the roof.

The fence keeping the revenants at bay was beginning to buckle in places. The roof was starting to shake and buck beneath the force of that wind.

Bits of debris began to tear at crates, the fence and the bodies of the revenants. The hole in the roof was starting to open up, peeling back around the edges and offering Alex a bird's eye view of the entire grim spectacle.

The flying masses of Alayna's blood had frozen into long, impossibly sharp shards and were tearing into the bodies of the revenants. These were joined by the blood that spilled from Burdock's body. As the shards and debris tore through Camille's body, which Alex saw was being tossed in the whirlwind, her blood joined the storm.

Alayna was untouched by what she had created, her body floating in the center of the maelstrom. Her song fell silent, but the spell had already taken hold.

He was powerless to stop any of it. Rage and helplessness and grief clawed at his guts. He felt cold tears running down his face as he watched the woman he loved sacrifice herself in slow motion.

Alex continued to watch as the roof collapsed in and the revenants were chewed to tiny pieces in that blender of a storm. One of the walls partially tumbled with a soft boom.

At that moment, the sky opened up, and rain began to pour. Thunder rumbled in the distance. At least the rain would drive people inside, and the thunder might be able to cover for any strange noises.

The storm consumed the warehouse and began to suck at nearby buildings, toppling walls and sweeping up cars.

The spell was beginning to slow down, and Alex saw that Alayna's limp body was beginning to descend to what had been the floor of the warehouse.

"Bring me down," he shouted at Z.

The dragon decreased the speed at which he pumped his wings, and they began to drop through what was left of the roof.

The place was a horror show and smelled like a slaughter-house. There were bones with grey flesh clinging to them scattered about the warehouse. Blood and other substances spattered the walls. Alayna's body had come to rest on a pile of wood and metal.

As Z's back legs touched down, he released Alex, who scrambled to find his feet. For one impossibly long moment, he froze.

Alayna's battered and broken body lay twenty feet from him. Her skin was impossibly pale, the wounds in her arms like silent, red screams. Panic shouted at him that he couldn't do this. His feet were rooted to the concrete, and everything within him had gone as cold as a morgue.

He squeezed his eyes shut for a second and told himself that this was not the desert. She was not Kelly. He told his racing heart to slow down and took several deep breaths. He opened his eyes and grounded himself. His fingers found the little clay pendant she had hung around his neck what seemed like a lifetime ago, her magick pushing at his fingers.

His eyes snapped back to where Alayna lay, and calm purpose coursed through him.

He could do this.

He dropped to his knees beside her and put his fingers to her throat. No pulse. No breathing. He quickly checked her for other injuries. There were the cuts on the wrists, still bloody, no clotting but largely superficial.

Didn't appear to be any broken bones or other trauma.

He bent and picked her up, moving her to a clear space on the concrete.

As he did so, Dumeril and Lu—who had returned to her regular form—came running up.

"Get the black backpack tied to Z's back!" Alex shouted.

Alex tilted Alayna's head back to establish her airway, checked her pulse again, and started chest compressions. He fell into the old rhythms of his medic days, his hands going where they were needed, the next step of care popping up in his head without thinking about it.

She felt so impossibly fragile under his hands, but he kept pumping her chest, hoping to keep brain death from setting in.

One of her ribs broke and he kept going.

Dumeril slid to a stop on the opposite side of Alayna's body and handed him the pack. Dumeril touched her and then looked at Alex, his face grim.

"She's gone, man. Just stop," he said, his voice rough.

"Bullshit!" Alex said quietly, but with the force of everything he was holding back at the moment. "There is still a chance."

"Her heart has stopped. There is nothing I can do for her," Dumeril said.

"Yes, there is," Alex snapped. "Your magick may not work, but you can pull the defibrillator out of that bag. It's the bright orange box—yeah, that's the one. Now flip the switch on the side."

He turned to Lu.

"Take over chest compressions."

He grabbed her hands and put them in the appropriate place on Alayna's sternum. He showed her exactly how hard to press and how often.

His hands dove into the bag and came up with coagulant and hemostatic gauze. He ripped open the packet of powdered coagulant and poured it over Alayna's wounds. The powder would form a nice seal when it came into contact with her blood. He began wrapping the hemostatic gauze around her wrists.

Dumeril already had her armor off and had ripped her shirt open. She wore a black lace bra underneath, and the sight almost gave Alex pause. It was so incongruous with the armor, the weapons, the warrior who wore it. It was so totally out of place. And yet, Alex had watched her put it on as she had left him lying on the floor under her ward.

He pushed the thoughts away and placed the defibrillator pads on her chest. The machine was one of the fool-proof models available on the civilian market. It spoke in a woman's voice. It was a calm voice telling him, "Measuring pulse rate. No pulse detected. Please stand clear. Initiating shock."

Alayna's body jerked and arched off the concrete for a moment.

"No pulse detected."

Alex hit a pause button on the machine and motioned to Lu to resume compressions while he inserted two needles in Alayna's skin, one in the crook of each arm. He pulled a unit of blood and hooked the tubing quickly, handing it to Dumeril and telling him to gently squeeze the bag. He hooked a bag of saline to the other needle, wrapping his blood pressure cuff around the bag and pumping it up, hoping to speed the fluids into her system.

He waited a few seconds, told them to put the bags down, and hit the button on the defibrillator again.

"No pulse detected. Please stand clear. Initiating shock."

Her body arched again. Alex felt for a pulse but couldn't find one.

They all stayed silent. Alex took the bag of blood from Dumeril and squeezed gently, rhythmically, silently praying that the blood would do its job.

His eyes were focused like lasers on her face, watching for the faintest signs of life. He would not lose her. He had lost too many people to violence, and he was not about to lose the one and only woman he had ever loved to the same thing.

"Come on, baby. Come back to me," he said in a soft voice.

"Initiating shock," the machine said again.

This time, when Alex felt for a pulse there was a faint flutter beneath his fingers. He almost whooped with joy.

"Pulse detected. No shock advised," the machine said.

Alex handed the blood back to Dumeril and removed the

shock pads from her chest.

"I'll be damned," Dumeril whispered. Lu had started to cry, fat tears rolling down her face to hang on her chin.

The blood bag was almost empty, and Alex replaced it with a fresh one.

"We need to get out of here," Dumeril said. "I need to open a portal to the Citadel. She needs healers. And we need a cleanup crew."

Alex nodded, but didn't make any moves to leave her side.

"Lu and I will have to take her," Dumeril said softly. "She didn't want you anywhere near the Council, and for good reason."

Alex nodded again, unable to take his eyes off her. She was breathing, albeit a little shallowly for his taste. Color was returning slowly to her face. There was life in her body again, and he had never seen anything quite so beautiful.

Lu gently took the bag of blood from his hands and held it aloft along with the saline. Dumeril knelt and took Alayna in his arms.

A few seconds later a shimmering blue and purple oval appeared in the air in front of Dumeril, and they stepped through.

Alayna was gone. Every muscle in his body sagged for a moment. They'd pulled off a miracle. Successful resuscitation was rare, and he'd only seen it a handful of times. She wasn't out of the woods yet, but she wasn't dead. The only sound in the stunned silence was Z panting.

Ellie was beside him now and took his elbow, helping him to his feet.

"Gotta get you out of here, Alex," she said.

She led him back to the empty field and opened a portal back to headquarters.

"Just stay there until I get there," Ellie said. "I'm going to deal with the cleanup crew and then I'm right behind you, okay?"

He nodded, but didn't say anything as he stepped through. He found himself on the training floor back at headquarters. He let himself collapse on the floor, closed his eyes and let unconsciousness take him.

25

Chapter 25

Alex slammed his fist against the metal door for what felt like the hundredth time and shouted, "Let me out of here!"

He knew it was useless, that his captors wouldn't pay any attention, but it made him feel better than sitting and staring at the wall. The windowless room he was trapped in was painted a stark white, with white tile floors. It was cramped, maybe ten feet by ten feet, tops. A table with a chair on either side was the only furniture.

He'd been in the FBI long enough to know what an interrogation room looked like.

He wasn't sure how many hours had passed since he'd returned to consciousness back at HQ. When he had, two scary looking mages had been standing over him. They'd zip-tied his hands while he'd been out. The men had hauled him to his feet and shoved him through a portal without saying a word.

He'd been spit from the portal on the other side with enough force to bounce him off a wall. When his head had stopped spinning, he'd found himself in an institutional looking room, led down solid white corridors and stashed in this windowless hell.

From the descriptions Alayna had given, he could only be in one place.

The Citadel.

The stronghold of the Council and the Mage Corps was buried under a mountain in Colorado, and everything he'd seen had a distinctly underground feel.

He turned on his heel and paced to the opposite wall. They'd at least had the decency to cut the cuffs off him. Exhaustion pulled at him, but he wasn't going to rest until he saw with his own eyes that Alayna was all right. These Council fuckers had sent her to her death. He didn't trust them to care for her.

He wasn't sure how long he'd been pacing when the click of the lock turning made him freeze. Dumeril came through the door, his expression grim. Alex's gut twisted with dread. Had they lost her?

The Svarturan pulled Alex into a tight embrace and released him after a moment, scanning Alex up and down—for what he didn't know.

Almost afraid to ask, Alex said, "How is she?"

"Awake and asking for you."

Relief flooded through him so suddenly, his throat tightening. It had worked! She was alive. Talking meant she hadn't suffered catastrophic brain damage from lack of oxygen. He wanted to whoop with joy, but Dumeril's expression stopped him. Something else was up.

Pushing past his friend, Alex headed for the door.

"I need to see her."

He was brought up short by a gray haired man in black tactical gear who stood in the doorway. He was about to shove the guy out of the way when Dumeril's voice brought him up short.

"Agent Alex Martinez, meet General Silverthorn, High Commander of the Mage Corps."

Alex met the general's dark gaze.

"You're the one in charge around here?"

The older man nodded not saying a word, but his narrow look was assessing. Alex knew what being weighed and measured by a superior officer felt like, and it pissed him off.

"Then I strongly suggest you get the hell out of my way and remove the obstacles between myself and Commander Blackwell."

The general looked momentarily surprised and amused. He snorted and raised an eyebrow before stepping aside and indicating which way Alex should go.

Dumeril fell in beside him as Alex practically jogged down the hallway. The general's footsteps echoed behind them.

After a series of twists and turns down seemingly identical corridors that left Alex feeling lost, they arrived at the hospital wing. Alayna had been tucked in a private room, and when Alex entered, a striking woman with long dark hair rose to her feet beside the bed, blocking him and taking up a protective stance.

"It's alright, Mother. It's Alex," came Alayna's exasperated voice.

As Alayna's mother stepped aside, he caught sight of Alayna herself.

She was pale and looked thinner than when he'd last seen her. It had been maybe twenty-four hours by his math, but she looked like years had passed. Her long platinum hair was loose around her shoulders and had been brushed. The wounds on her wrists were gone, the skin now unmarred. A green robe covered her from neck to knees, and he couldn't see if her other more minor injuries had been healed.

He was by her side in two quick strides, his hands on either side of her face. Until he touched her, he hadn't been entirely sure it was real.

"You're here," he whispered.

She reached up and covered one of his hands with hers.

"Thanks to you," she answered.

Suddenly, emotions that he hadn't let himself feel in the hours since he'd held her last overwhelmed him. His eyes squeezed shut against the wetness that threated to spill out, and he touched his forehead to hers as relief, joy, fear, pain, guilt, anxiety, and anger washed through him.

"Hell of a thing you did," came the general's voice from behind him.

Alex's eyes snapped open, but they didn't leave Alayna's face. "Thanks."

"That was not a compliment, son."

"I'm not your son," Alex snapped, letting his irritation creep into his voice.

The general was silent a moment before continuing.

"You may not know it, but you just turned the mage world upside down. Whisperers are not supposed to survive a Reckoning."

Rage boiled within Alex's chest, and he rounded on the general.

"Maybe if you had bothered to update your medical protocols within the last fifty years, they would have. Magickal healing may not be able to save someone once their heart stops, but we have this little thing called science. Resuscitation is a thing now. Look into it."

The general snorted again.

"There are those who would say that magick, especially such

deadly magick, has a price. A price that has to be paid."

Alex gave the man a hard look, turning his body so that he was between him and Alayna.

"Are you one of those people?" Alex asked, mentally preparing for a fight if it came to it.

He'd only just gotten Alayna back; he wasn't about to lose her again because of some sort of misplaced fanaticism.

The corner of the general's mouth turned up. "No, I am not."

Leaning around Alex, the general said to Alayna, "It seems you've found yourself a rather formidable protector, Commander. I think he's worth keeping."

Turning back to Alayna, Alex saw a look of suppressed amusement on her face.

"I agree completely, General." A note of sadness touched Alayna's voice. "And I tragically find myself in need of a sergeant."

The general turned back to Alex, that narrow, assessing gaze having returned.

"I've been contemplating very carefully what to do with you since I learned of your existence a short time ago. We could try another memory wipe and send you back to your old life, but at this point and given your powers, it will probably destroy your mind." He continued. "We could release you on your own recognizance. Commander Blackwell assures me you can be trusted to keep our secret out of sapien hands, although I am not sure that I agree."

He was quiet a long moment. "Or you can take the commission that she's offered. You'll have the protection of the Corps and the Council. And you'll be with her."

A smile tugged at his mouth on the last part. Alex didn't even have to think about it and didn't hesitate.

"Where do I sign?"

"Love the attitude, Killer, but hold up. There's a bit more you need to know. And that goes for you too, Commander."

The general was silent for a moment before he continued.

"I've had a chance to review the reports filed by your team in the wake of what happened in Austin. I believe, and many of our analysts concur, Dominic Spino's crazed plan was likely part of a larger scheme."

Alayna looked skeptical.

"He was out of his mind," she said. "Hell bent on destruction, nothing more."

"He spoke of voices that compelled him to act," the general said. "Consider the level of destruction releasing that many revenants on a city would cause. When combined with some of the chatter we're hearing from other sources, we believe we may be looking at Demonic influence."

"Demons? Are you serious? No one has conclusively proved they exist." Alayna's voice dripped disbelief.

Dumeril chimed in. "Think about it. Dominic said he was in an emotionally weak place when the voices started telling him what to do. The few semi-credible accounts of Demonic influence claim those entities are non-corporeal in this realm. Those in a weak state would be more easily influenced. When you look at what kind of devastation those revenants could have caused, consider what that would have done to the dimensional walls."

Alayna's eyes went wide. "You mean we might be looking at an attempt to create an entry point for an extra-dimensional invasion?"

Dumeril nodded and Alex sat hard on the bed beside Alayna.

"Furthermore," the general said, causing Alex's stomach to

twist, "Given your miraculous survival, I believe you and your siblings may have a significant role to play in the coming days, Commander."

Alayna sighed. "Are we back on the stupid prophecy? I thought they decided that wasn't about us when it turned out I was a Whisperer."

"What prophecy?" Alex demanded, feeling like everyone in the room knew what they were talking about but him.

Alayna's mother spoke from the corner.

"Four and four and four
They will stand against the darkness
They will bar the door against the ravenous ones
A child of the golden air
A child of the burning sun
A child of the troubled water
And a child of the wild earth
Born of the same womb
Will unite the people of the sun and moon
In victory, there will be peace."

Silence hung in the room when she finished speaking.

The general spoke up. "The Blackwells were the first set of four siblings, each controlling a different element and born to the same mother, ever recorded. When Alayna manifested the Whisperer's curse, it was decided it couldn't be about them. But she just lived through the gods damned Reckoning. If anyone's destined to stop a Demonic invasion…"

Silence descended in the room like a thick fog, everyone's faces gone somber.

"Everyone out," Alayna said. When no one moved, she raised her voice. "Out!"

She pinned Alex with a look.

"Not you," she mouthed.

The others shuffled out. Alayna's mother gave Alex a worried look as she shut the door.

When they were alone, they were both silent, neither meeting the other's eyes, the only sound in the room the shush of air circulating through the vents.

She broke the silence first.

"So, you sure you want to stick around?"

Her tone was the same one she'd use to ask if he wanted pizza, and he burst out laughing.

"Yeah, fuck it, I'm in," he said when he'd finally caught his breath, sitting on the edge of the bed and taking her hand.

"You heard the general. We're staring down the barrel of a possible demonic invasion. The fight we just went through is the tip of the iceberg. Safety won't be a part of the picture anymore. We're talking about a possible war here. I can't ask you to be a part of that."

He flashed her a smile, placing his hands on either side of her face. He claimed her mouth in a deep kiss that left them both breathless and hot.

He pulled back and looked in her eyes.

"I'd go to war for you. I'd follow you through hell and back. As long as I'm with you, there's nowhere I'd rather be," he said, his voice strong, emphatic. "Where you go, I go. Understand?"

"Not gonna lie. A selfish part of me wants you with me."

"Someone's gotta patch your ass up when you do something crazy and heroic." A lopsided smile tugged at one side of his mouth.

"You're one to talk. You busted through a roof on the back of a dragon."

"Actually, can we do that again? That was fun," he said, teasing her. "How is the giant lizard, by the way?"

"Recovering," she said soberly.

Silence stretched between them again.

"I wanted so badly to give you your life back," Alayna said. "And that is never going to happen now."

He laughed.

"Before all this, that wasn't a life, Alayna. It was existing. This, this thing between us. This is a life."

He kissed her again, his mouth trying to tell her what his words couldn't.

Pulling back, she whispered, "I love you, crazy man."

"It's really good to hear those words when I'm not pinned under a ward," Alex said softly. "Because, now I get to say them back."

"Alex, I'm so sorry I did that! I was trying to protect –"

"I know why you did it and I forgive you. Just don't do that again, okay? It nearly killed me to watch you walk out that door." He gently cupped her face in both hands. "I love you, Alayna. Whatever comes, we got this," he said, his voice firm with an unshakable confidence.

With that, he stretched out beside her, pulled her gently against him, and reveled in the feeling of holding the love of his life in his arms again.

About the Author

Rose has been obsessed with ghost stories and the paranormal since she can remember, and she's been telling stories just about as long.

A Texas native, she loves horseback riding, knitting, practicing martial arts, and archery. She lives with her husband and offspring in Central Texas.

She has been known to drop everything to listen to a ghost story and if you have one to share, or just thoughts in general to share, send it all to her at roseobrienauthor@gmail.com.

Acknowledgements

There are so many people that made this book possible. I want to start off by thanking my mother for her never-ending support and cheerleading. Through so much self-doubt, she was the one that told me that my words mattered. I also need to acknowledge my long-suffering husband who put in more than his fair share of housework and childcare so that I could write these words.

To all the members of the Austin RWA chapter, thank you for your support, advice, wisdom, experience and all the chocolate you shared. I could not have done this without you.

Huge thanks to my editors Jami Nord and Emmie Mears for the invaluable work, advice and feedback. This book is what it is because of them. Check them out at www.chimeraediting.com.

Thank you to my amazing cover designer, Amala Benny. She can be contacted at mayflowerstudios.com. Original photography for the cover was provided by belphnaque@depositphotos.

And to my readers. Thank you so much for going on this adventure with me. Stay tuned, because there is plenty more to come!

Author's note

Dear readers,

Thank you so much for coming on this adventure with me. This book has been the work of more than 10 years, off and on, and I'm so glad you stayed with me to this point.

If you enjoyed "Air of Darkness," please head over to Amazon or your favorite online bookstore and leave a review so that others can know what you think.

If you'd like to keep up with future releases in the Elemental Mages series, sign up for my newsletter at roseobrien-author.com. I share exclusive giveaways. writing updates, cover reveals and occasional recipes. You can also follow me on social media on Facebook, Twitter (@RoseOWrites) and Instagram (RoseObrienAuthor). I also blog weekly at roseobrienauthor.com

Thank you again for buying this book and spending so much time with my characters.

Love,
  Rose